"What's wrong, MacLean? Afraid of a little competition?"

Alexander's body reacted immediately to Caitlyn's nearness. "It's an inordinate amount of trouble, but"—he allowed his gaze to travel across her in a suggestive manner, lingering on her breasts and hips—"I can think of nothing I'd enjoy more than to see you lose."

"We'll see who loses." She gave him one of those damned mysterious, feminine smiles that made his body flame to life, then she turned away, her fingers trailing along the small side table, absently brushing over a silver-filigreed candy dish.

He watched, wondering how that feather touch would feel. The sight of her, so elegant and so damnably tempting, raised his blood, and he was astonished at his impulse to just give her this and anything else she wanted. *Damn it, what's wrong with me? I'm no lapdog to be led around by a chit who looks too young to be out of the schoolroom.*

He slammed his hands onto the desk.

Caitlyn jumped, her color high, her lips parted.

He leaned forward. "I accept."

Turn the page for rave reviews of Karen Hawkins's romantic storytelling . . .

The Laird Who Loved Me is also available as an eBook

Also by Karen Hawkins

Available from Pocket Books

Look for the next sparkling Hurst Amulet novel

Scandal in Scotland

Coming soon from Pocket Books

The Laird Who Loved Me

KAREN HAWKINS

POCKET BOOKS

New York   London   Toronto   Sydney

Pocket Books
A Division of Simon & Schuster, Inc.
1230 Avenue of the Americas
New York, NY 10020

This book is a work of fiction. Names, characters, places, and incidents either are products of the author's imagination or are used fictitiously. Any resemblance to actual events or locales or persons, living or dead, is entirely coincidental.

Copyright © 2009 by Karen Hawkins

All rights reserved, including the right to reproduce this book or portions thereof in any form whatsoever. For information address Pocket Books Subsidiary Rights Department,
1230 Avenue of the Americas, New York, NY 10020

This Pocket Books paperback edition May 2011

POCKET and colophon are registered trademarks of Simon & Schuster, Inc.

For information about special discounts for bulk purchases, please contact Simon & Schuster Special Sales at 1-866-506-1949 or business@simonandschuster.com.

The Simon & Schuster Speakers Bureau can bring authors to your live event. For more information or to book an event contact the Simon & Schuster Speakers Bureau at 1-866-248-3049 or visit our website at www.simonspeakers.com.

Front cover and stepback illustration by Alan Ayers, hand lettering by Ron Zinn.

Manufactured in the United States of America

10   9   8   7   6   5   4   3   2   1

ISBN 978-1-4516-0771-0
ISBN 978-1-4391-6415-0 (ebook)

THE MACLEAN FAMILY TREE

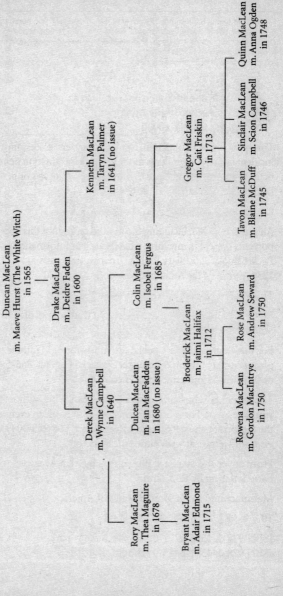

Duncan MacLean m. Maeve Hurst (The White Witch) in 1565

Drake MacLean m. Deidre Faden in 1600

Derek MacLean m. Wynne Campbell in 1640

Kenneth MacLean m. Taryn Palmer in 1641 (no issue)

Rory MacLean m. Thea Maguire in 1678

Dulcea MacLean m. Ian MacFadden in 1680 (no issue)

Colin MacLean m. Isobel Fergus in 1685

Bryant MacLean m. Adair Edmond in 1715

Broderick MacLean m. Jaimi Halifax in 1712

Gregor MacLean m. Cait Friskin in 1713

Rowena MacLean m. Gordon MacIntrye in 1750

Rose MacLean m. Andrew Seward in 1750

Tavon MacLean m. Blaine McDuff in 1745

Sinclair MacLean m. Scion Campbell in 1746

Quinn MacLean m. Anna Ogden in 1748

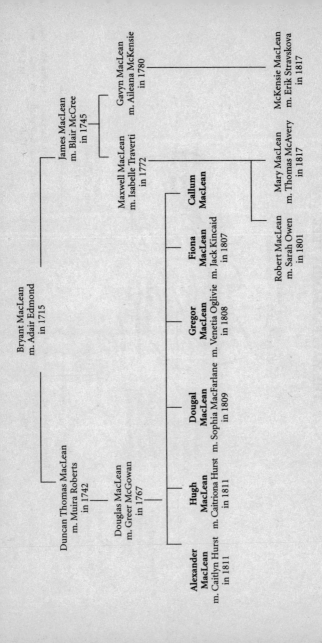

Bryant MacLean
m. Adair Edmond
in 1715

Duncan Thomas MacLean
m. Muira Roberts
in 1742

James MacLean
m. Blair McCree
in 1745

Douglas MacLean
m. Greer McGowan
in 1767

Maxwell MacLean
m. Isabelle Traverti
in 1772

Gavyn MacLean
m. Aileana McKensie
in 1780

Alexander
MacLean
m. Caitlyn Hurst
in 1811

Hugh
MacLean
m. Caitriona Hurst
in 1811

Dougal
MacLean
m. Sophia MacFarlane
in 1809

Gregor
MacLean
m. Venetia Oglivie
in 1808

Fiona
MacLean
m. Jack Kincaid
in 1807

Callum
MacLean

Robert MacLean
m. Sarah Owen
in 1801

Mary MacLean
m. Thomas McAvery
in 1817

McKensie MacLean
m. Erik Stravskova
in 1817

The
Laird
Who
Loved Me

Prologue

If e'er a mon needed a lass to show 'im how the world truly be, 'tis Alexander, Laird o' Clan MacLean.

OLD WOMAN NORA FROM LOCH LOMOND

TO HER THREE WEE GRANDDAUGHTERS ONE COLD EVENING

"hen it is set," he said, his deep voice rich with satisfaction. "Caitlyn Hurst will finally pay for the harm she's caused me and my family."

There was no denying the pleased expression on the man's strong, sensual face, and Georgiana, the Duchess of Roxburge, was glad she wasn't the recipient of such revenge. "It wasn't easy to get her here, especially with the company I had to keep." She curled her lip as she pulled a silver-handled brush through her long, red tresses. "I don't enjoy mingling among tradesmen."

"Really?" The hard mouth curved into a faint smile. "Even though there's always the pleasant possibility of meeting a relative . . ."

The brush hung in midair for a startled moment before she snapped, "I don't know what you're talking about!"

His brows rose, his gaze mocking.

She forced herself to continue brushing her hair with long, even strokes, though inside she quaked with anger and fear. She knew she shouldn't be surprised; Alexander, Laird of Clan MacLean, was known for his ability to ferret out the truth; she should have known he'd eventually discover hers. She might now be a duchess, but once—

Her stomach in knots, Georgiana watched from under her lashes. He'd turned toward the window, the fading afternoon light limning his face, lighting his green eyes, and tracing the bold line of his nose and the sensual harshness of his mouth. She shivered a little as she looked at his mouth and remembered—

"And so the game begins." He turned back toward her. "How did you convince Mrs. Hurst to accept your invitation for her daughter?"

Somewhat mollified by his attention, Georgiana pouted her full lips. "It took me two weeks to get that woman to even hear me out, and then I had to promise to watch over her precious daughter as if she were my own."

"She's held Caitlyn under lock and key for the last three months. I haven't been able to get near the blasted woman." Alexander sent her a look that actually held some warmth and her heart fluttered. "Thank you for your assistance, Georgiana. I shall repay you."

She shifted so that her dressing gown opened to reveal her new French-style negligee, made of lawn so fine that the nipples on her full breasts were revealed.

Any other man would have been panting to be at her, but not MacLean.

He remained reclined in the chair across the room, his long, muscular legs stretched before him, his starkly handsome face in deep reflection. His gaze was fixed on some unseeable, distant object, a considering smile tugging the chiseled hardness of his lips.

It had taken her almost two years of carefully art-less teasing to get him into her bed, and less than three months for him to tire of it. The thought burned her cheeks, and she gripped the silver handle of the brush until her fingers cramped. "What is your plan for the Hurst girl? You've never really said."

His gaze shuttered. "Caitlyn Hurst owes me dearly. She turned my name into a mockery."

Noting with satisfaction how MacLean's mouth thinned, Georgiana adopted a sympathetic tone that covered her triumph. "Everyone was talking about how the Hurst chit announced she would marry you, one way or the other. She made you both the talk of the ton."

His face tightened. "And now I will exact my pound of flesh from her soft, pampered hide. When does she arrive?"

"Within the week. I am sending my coach to fetch her."

"Excellent." He leaned his head against the tall back of the chair, shifting his broad shoulders as he crossed his shiny black boots at the ankles. "Caitlyn Hurst is as impulsive as they come. All I have to do is lead her into some sort of impropriety, and her reputation will be in tatters. Only this time, neither her sister nor my brother will be close by to save her."

"Just be careful *you* are not caught in the parson's trap, like Hugh." Georgiana had been with Alexander the night he'd discovered how Caitlyn had set a plan in motion to force him to offer for her hand. Her ill-conceived actions had forced Alexander's brother and Caitlyn's sister into marriage as they attempted to stop her heedless rush to ruin.

Fury didn't begin to describe Alexander's reaction when he'd learned of that. He had paced his library, white-faced with blazing anger, and the once-clear night sky boiled into a melee of wild, dangerous storms. Remembering them even now, months later, Georgiana shivered. She'd heard the rumors about the MacLean curse, but before that moment, she hadn't believed them.

His lip curled. "I'd marry a scullery maid before I'd marry that woman."

"You're much too smart to be caught unawares by her," Georgiana purred. "I hope I am not too embarrassed when this girl arrives. The other guests will wonder why I invited such a rustic creature."

"You need not worry; Caitlyn turned herself out in first style during her season in London. Even Brummell mentioned it."

Georgiana hid a flicker of worry. "How old is Caitlyn? Twenty, correct?"

"Twenty-three."

"How funny. There are the same number of years between you and her as between Humbolt and his young wife," Georgiana said idly, glancing under her thick lashes at MacLean.

Alexander's expression hardened and Georgiana hid a smile. Viscount Humbolt had been MacLean's best friend. To everyone's surprise, at the age of forty-two Humbolt fell wildly in love and married a woman almost twenty years his junior. His mother, who'd believed her son would never marry, had been blissful, but Alexander had had reservations about such an uneven match. Humbolt was in no mood to hear anything negative about his bride, however.

The viscount's newfound happiness was short-lived. The new viscountess was an insatiable woman who, over the next seven years, dragged her husband through countless public scenes and humiliations, and eventually, total financial ruin.

One day Humbolt's man of business found the viscount dead, a smoking pistol in his hand, a letter beneath a paperweight on his desk. The letter condemned his wife but brought little consolation to those who truly loved him.

MacLean had been devastated at his friend's death. Even now, four years later, just a mention of that time made his eyes darken and his lips turn white. "I have no interest in Caitlyn Hurst, if that is your meaning," he snapped.

"I'm sure you don't," Georgiana soothed. "You are far too sophisticated for a vicar's daughter. I always thought Clarisse was far too young and too beautiful for Humbolt; he should have realized how it would end. She wanted his money, and once she had it . . . She was mocking him all along."

Alexander's expression grew guarded, though his eyes sparkled with irritation. "Perhaps."

She took comfort that he didn't argue. He never flirted with very young women, yet it had worried her that perhaps Caitlyn Hurst was different. Whatever he might have once felt for the girl, he couldn't possibly feel it anymore, though. Not after her conduct made him the talk of London.

With an impatient gesture, he stood. "I should be on my way. I'm to ride with the Duke of Linville and try his new bay."

Georgiana's gaze flickered over his broad shoulders, the smooth fit of his coat that cut in at his narrow hips, the powerful thighs—

"Do my breeches meet with your approval?"

Her gaze jerked up to his, her cheeks burning, and she pasted what she hoped was a teasing smile on her face. "You can't blame me for having fond memories."

"So long as you know they *are* memories, and nothing more." His gaze narrowed and he added softly, "I hope you don't see my request for assistance as anything more than a favor between friends."

She managed a faint laugh. "Friends we are and, hopefully, always will be." *For now, anyway.*

He bowed, his eyes warmer than they'd been since he'd arrived two days ago. "Good day, Georgiana. Until dinner." His steady tread took him to the door, with an athletic grace that made her mouth go dry.

Then he was gone, leaving the room achingly empty.

Chapter 1

It takes a woman who dinna knows the word no *to conquer a MacLean, especially one wit' a heart o' stone.*

OLD WOMAN NORA FROM LOCH LOMOND
TO HER THREE WEE GRANDDAUGHTERS ONE COLD EVENING

"A real, live duchess?"

Caitlyn Hurst laughed at her younger sister's wail. "Yes, a real, live duchess, not a real, dead duchess."

"Oh, you know what I mean." Mary threw herself on the bed with her sister's worn portmanteau, three ball gowns, a stack of freshly folded unmentionables, and a pair of well-worn ball slippers. "I wish *I* could go to a real, live duchess's house for a three-week house party!"

Caitlyn placed a pair of only-mended-once stockings into a small trunk on the floor. "Surely you're not begrudging me the only fun I've had in months?"

"No, I just wish I might go *with* you." Mary threw her arms out to the side. "The letter from the duchess said there will be walks through the park, horseback rides, archery, card games—"

"Mother was not happy about that aspect."

"No, but Papa slipped you a guinea that you might play, so it can't be *too* bad. Besides, it wasn't the gaming that had Mother in a taking; it was the masquerade ball. I truly thought she'd refuse to allow you to go when the duchess wrote that you'd need a costume."

"I had to promise not to wear a mask and to behave as any gently raised young lady should."

Mary's brow rose. "Can you do that?"

"I *will* do it," Caitlyn said fervently, and meant it. She always did; the trouble was remembering she wished to behave herself when she lost her temper. She didn't have a burning desire to thwart society's rules; but when she was challenged or angry, her competitive spirit burned through all caution or thought.

Caitlyn stuffed a shawl into the portmanteau with more force than necessary. Blast it, if only she'd kept her temper three months ago and hadn't allowed Alexander MacLean to irk her into saying and doing things she shouldn't have. But there wasn't anything she could do about it now—except use this incredibly fortuitous invitation to reestablish herself and her family into society's good graces.

Mary reached out to touch one of the new gowns spread upon the bed, ready to be wrapped in tissue paper before being packed. "Certainly no one at the duchess's house will have as beautiful gowns as these. You sew better than most of the modistes on Bond Street."

Caitlin smiled. "Thank you! That's quite a compliment. I'm very proud of the silver one; it's for the masquerade."

"It looks wonderful on you, even though Mother made you sew the neckline so high." Mary grimaced. "If she had her way, you'd go to the masquerade sewn chin to toes into a large burlap potato sack. Mother worries far too much, even though you—" Mary's face pinkened.

Caitlyn's humor evaporated. "I will never allow my temper to get the best of me again. If I hadn't behaved so badly that Triona had felt compelled to come to London to rescue me, then she wouldn't have been forced to wed and—" Caitlyn's throat tightened painfully.

Mary grasped her sister's hand. "It all worked out well in the end. Triona is deeply in love with her new husband and said she had *you* to thank that she met him. And you made Mam a very happy woman. She's excited as a lamb with a wool sweater about the match."

"Grandmother thinks anything having to do with the MacLeans is wondrous—especially if it means she might get some great grandchildren out of it."

"Oh, that would be so—"

A noisy thumping came from the hallway, sounding like a herd of romping calves. A fast knock later, the door was thrown open to reveal William, their oldest brother, followed by a surprisingly elegantly dressed Robert and a much-too-thin Michael.

They were all so tall, especially William, who, at twenty-one, had reached the impressive height of six feet four inches, his shoulders a proportionate width.

Michael, only recently recovered from another chest complaint, threw his lanky, sixteen-year-old length into the chair by the fireplace. "Well?" he asked, looking at the gowns and slippers and gewgaws placed on every surface of the room. "I thought you'd be packed by now!"

Mary grinned. "Caitlyn's only had two weeks to pack; you know that's not enough."

Caitlyn gave Michael a flat stare. "Have you all come to bother us? I assure you that we have enough to do without entertaining you."

Robert eyed the contents of the bed through a quizzing glass he'd recently taken to wearing. "Good God, woman! How much stuff are you taking with you?"

Caitlyn narrowed her gaze on her brother. "Must you use that ridiculous eyepiece?"

"It's the fashion," he said stoutly, though he looked somewhat uncertain.

"For a nearsighted Cyclops, perhaps."

Mary giggled while Michael and William snorted loudly.

Robert slipped the eyepiece into a pocket and said in a lofty tone, "Just because you don't appreciate good fashion—"

"She does, too!" Mary interrupted. "You've seen the gowns she's made."

Caitlyn smoothed a blue morning gown on the

bed. "If the list of amusements offered by the duchess is to be believed, I have fewer gowns than I need, but these will have to do. I can always change my wrap and shoes and make minor alterations so that my outfits look different."

"Caitlyn even redid her old riding gown." Mary reached into the portmanteau to touch with a loving hand the brown velvet riding habit. "When you return, will you help me make one like it?"

Michael snorted. "And where would you wear it? All we have to ride is the squire's old, fat mare."

Mary sniffed. "It doesn't matter what the horse looks like, just the rider."

"You spent hours making a riding habit you might only wear once or twice a month?" Michael appeared to be amazed at the thought.

"If it looked good on me, I might."

"Vanity is a sin. Father's told us that a million times."

"It's not vanity to wish to appear good; it's vanity if you think you look so good that it won't matter how you dress."

That opened up a discussion between Mary and Michael that grew in volume as Robert and William egged them on.

Caitlyn ignored them and tucked away a spangled shawl she'd purchased during her brief stay in London three months ago. *Has it only been that long?* The entire episode seemed a faded nightmare.

She couldn't clearly remember the balls and gowns anymore, or the sumptuous foods or town attractions, but she remembered every second she'd spent dangerously flirting with Alexander MacLean. She clearly recalled how she allowed him to teach her to ride. Though she'd made certain one of the grooms stayed nearby for appearance' sake, MacLean had quickly and easily dispensed with the man, sending him to fetch various "fallen" gloves or to look for a scarf that was blown away, even on days when there was no wind.

Her cheeks heated when she thought of her own participation in duping the servants. At the time, all she'd been able to think about was how much she wanted to feel MacLean's strong arms about her, how she longed for his heated kiss and— She clamped the memories away. Those days were gone, and they'd meant less than the imaginary wind.

She forced herself to smile at Mary. "I'll make you a riding habit when I return. We can use the blue velvet from your old pelisse and that old gold opera cape Mother has in the trunk in the attic. The colors should be perfect, and if we place some silk flowers where the material is a bit worn, no one will notice. I did the same with one of my remade newer gowns."

Momentarily forgetting his jaded, man-about-town pose, Robert snorted. "You plan on hoaxing the crème of the ton with the clever placement of a few flowers? They'll be onto your hoax in a second."

Caitlyn folded a deep blue silk scarf and placed it into the portmanteau. "Oh, they'll never know. They didn't realize it before." She set a pair of satin slippers in the trunk beside the others. "Only three pairs of slippers. I wish I had two more."

William, who'd been lounging in the doorway, lifted his brows, a lazy twinkle in his eyes. "How many pairs of slippers are needed for a simple country house party?"

"It's not a simple house party at all," Mary protested. "It's at the castle of a real, live duchess!"

"I should have at least one pair of slippers for each color of gown. I shall just have to make do." Caitlyn placed the final gown into the trunk, carefully tucked it in, then closed the lid. "I keep expecting Mother to walk in and say she's changed her mind."

"She won't," Robert said, a superior tone in his voice.

Caitlyn eyed him. "How would you know?"

"I overheard her talking to Father. Mother thinks you will behave yourself for a few short weeks, and that you've made wonderful progress on your temper. You've hardly lost it at all in the last three months. Plus," he smirked, "she's hoping you'll meet someone eligible."

Caitlyn's cheeks burned. "I don't want to meet someone eligible." She just wanted the chance to reestablish the family name and prove to her parents that she'd learned from her horrible mistake.

Honestly, one thing that infuriated her about the incident was that no one seemed to place a bit of blame on MacLean, and he'd been just as much of a part of Triona's ruin as Caitlyn. If he hadn't been so intentionally *intriguing,* she'd never have paid him the least heed. But the second they'd met, he'd taunted and challenged her, and she'd discovered she didn't have the self-discipline to ignore him.

One thing was for certain, MacLean had been determined to kiss her: she knew because he'd told her so the third time they'd met. Of course, she'd then said something entirely inappropriate like "Just try it!" and that had been the beginning.

There'd been an unmistakable attraction between them, one that had flared hot and ready and left Caitlyn feeling things she'd never before felt. One kiss from Alexander MacLean reduced her to a quaking mass of heated passion. Worse, it was as addictive as chocolate, and she'd found herself seeking more and more of those kisses, taking more and more risks to secure his attention, challenging him even as he challenged her, until they were both dangerously close to stepping over the lines that might have protected them.

Oddly, it was the memory of those kisses that Caitlyn battled the most. Every night when she closed her eyes, she dreamed of them—hot, passionate, determined, and . . .

No. That's all in the past. She closed the portmanteau, then placed it beside the small leather trunk. "That's it! I'm packed."

Michael eyed the trunk. "You have clothes in that, too?"

Mary frowned. "You didn't think she could get all of her gowns and a riding habit into one portmanteau, did you? Now help carry Caitlyn's things to the foyer. The duchess is sending her own carriage for Caitlyn, and it should be here any moment."

Robert grabbed the portmanteau and headed out of the room, calling over his shoulder, "I bet the horses are a matched set of prime goers!"

William scooped up the leather trunk as if it were nothing, hoisting it to his shoulder. "I want to see the horses, too."

Grinning, Michael ambled toward the door. "Caitlyn, shall I tell Mother you'll be down soon?"

"Please do. I just want to make sure I haven't missed anything."

"Very well." He winked and left.

Mary hung by the door. "You'll write, won't you?"

"Every three days."

Mary sighed. "I suppose that will do. I *so* wish I were going with you." With a wistful look, she left as well.

Caitlyn gathered her faded wool pelisse and a thick scarf. She'd wear these with her sensible boots, and when they arrived in two days at Balloch Castle, she'd stop and change into her more fashionable, but far less warm, pelisse and boots.

She took a last look around her room. Then, satisfied she hadn't forgotten anything, she left, closing the door behind her.

Chapter 2

Och, lassies, ne'er trust a man who says he can keep a secret.

OLD WOMAN NORA FROM LOCH LOMOND
TO HER THREE WEE GRANDDAUGHTERS ONE COLD EVENING

*T*hree days later, Caitlyn unlatched the leather curtain that covered the carriage window. Cold air instantly blasted in and she shivered, huddling deeper into her heavy wool pelisse and tucking the carriage blankets more securely about her legs. Thanks to the thick wool blankets and the foot warmer at her feet, only her cheeks and nose felt the cold.

She'd never traveled in such luxury, but the trip was tediously long. The cost for such a well-fitted carriage came in the slowness of their travel.

For some, an extra day on the road would be offset by the pure luxury of the carriage, but Caitlyn found herself mentally urging the carriage on as it plodded along, picking its way over the bumpy, deeply rutted roads. They seemed to stop at every posting inn on the way, and while she couldn't help but be impressed by the offers of warmed lemonade, cheeses, and crusty breads, and the way the servants kept the foot warmers filled with hot coals at each stop, she was so *tired* of sitting still. She just wanted to get there!

She turned to her companion, a maid supplied by the duchess to attend Caitlyn and act as chaperone. "Muiren, how much longer before we reach Balloch Castle?"

Muiren, a thin, bony bit of a woman, dressed in the traditional black garb of a maid and wrapped in a thick pelisse, opened her eyes and blinked sleepily out the window. "We're almost there, miss. An hour, perhaps two."

"Oh, I hope so." Caitlyn rubbed her hip. "I'm tired of sitting."

"Ye may be tired, but ye'll be glad to have taken the extra time. If we hadn't, ye'd have arrived at Balloch Castle black-and-blue, hungry as a wolf, and cold as an icicle!"

Caitlyn managed a smile. "You're right, of course. I'm just restless."

Muiren settled into her corner. "Then take a bit o' a nap, miss. Ye'll feel the better fer it when we get there." She promptly closed her eyes and was snoring within minutes.

The maid's logic didn't calm Caitlyn's spirits one bit, and she continued to gaze longingly out the window. The road was now heading straight north, the air growing colder as they went, the landscape more wild and beautiful. She shivered and wished she hadn't changed into her more fashionable pelisse and half boots at the last inn in anticipation of their arrival.

After an hour, the road grew steeper as it wound around the greenish brown hills and spilled out by the shores of a beautiful lake, frosted on the sides with silvery gray stones. The water was a deep, glossy blue, the surrounding hills craggy and covered with heather-colored grasses. Framed between two hillocks was a worn mountain that cast a snow-tipped reflection across the lake.

Caitlyn smiled as a deep, abiding peace stole over her. The feeling surprised her; it was almost as if she were coming home. And why not, for her grandmother lived only a half day's ride from here, on the far side of the lake. As a child Caitlyn had spent many a day wandering hills like this, as she and Triona made up stories about the legendary MacLean family.

Mam had a fascination with the MacLeans, part of it stemming from the fact that her house was within view of the MacLean castle. The other part was curiosity about the MacLean curse. Caitlyn was curious, too—or had been, she reminded herself firmly. It was time to forget that foolishness; she'd never see wicked and wanton Alexander MacLean again, which was for the best.

Muiren stirred, then stretched, leaning forward to smother a yawn as she looked over Caitlyn's shoulder to the view beyond. "Aye, we're almost there."

"Excellent! I've never been in a real castle."

"'Tis no' a castle, really. Her grace says 'tis a 'castellated manor house,' which is a manor house *disguised* as a castle with stonework and such." Muiren shook her head. "What will the gentry think o' next?"

Caitlyn pointed toward the distant mountain. "My grandmother lives nearby, right across the valley from Castle MacLean. She tends the ill in the village below."

A hand gripped Caitlyn's arm and she blinked into Muiren's suddenly beaming face. "Miss, dinna say yer mam is Old Woman Nora!"

"That's my grandmother."

Muiren clapped her hands together. "Yer granny saved me sister's life when she had the ague! We thought she was goin' t' die, but yer mam came and made her drink a horrible potion." The maid's nose scrunched. "My sister said the potion smelled like death, it did, but it jolted her back to life, and she's ne'er been ill a day since."

Caitlyn nodded. "Mam has a gift."

"Indeed she do! They say yer mam makes her potions from the pure, frigid waters o' this loch and tha's what makes them so potent."

Caitlyn smiled at the beautiful blue loch that lay glass still, puffs of white clouds drifting overhead. "I must visit Mam while I'm here."

"If ye do, I'd be glad to travel wit' ye." The carriage swayed as they turned a sharp corner off the main road. "Och, we're on the castle drive!"

"Finally!" Caitlyn cast a glance at Muiren and said in a nonchalant voice, "I've heard the duchess is very fashionable."

Muiren blew out her cheeks. "Ye could say thet. She'll like yer gown, there's no doubt aboot that. I was noticin' it at breakfast this morning."

"Thank you. I fashioned it after a gown I saw in London."

Muiren blinked. "Ye *made* it? A lady o' quality like yerself?"

Caitlyn chuckled. "I'm a vicar's daughter, and I made almost everything I brought. Most of them are from patterns from *Ackermann's Ladies Journal.*"

Muiren eyed her. "If ye dinna mind me sayin' so, miss, ye're a mite different from her grace's other guests. 'Tis no' her grace's way to invite women who are both younger an' prettier than she is."

Caitlyn laughed. "I've never met her grace. She became acquainted with my mother at a dinner party, and they became quite friendly over the next few weeks. Her grace insisted that Mother send me to visit for a house party, and here I am."

Muiren's brows lowered. "Her grace upped and invited ye just like that? That dinna sound like something she'd—" The maid caught herself and forced an obviously false smile. "No matter what I think, o' course! I'm certain she'll be glad to have ye, miss."

Caitlyn's curiosity stirred. It was obvious from Muiren's demeanor that the duchess wasn't given to impulsively generous gestures. Then why *had* the duchess invited her? It had been such a wonderful surprise after being cooped up for months that Caitlyn hadn't bothered to ask many questions, but now she wondered. Mother might not understand how self-serving society's grand dames were, but Caitlyn, who'd spent two glorious months at her aunt's during the height of the London season, knew exactly how true that was. Perhaps the woman had a daughter her age or was desperate to create an even number of couples?

Traditionally, a hostess would invite the same number of men as women, so as to have an even number at dinner. This was how some lesser ladies in a community were able to develop an active social life despite certain social inequities. It was difficult to credit it, but perhaps no respectable lady was in the area to serve as an extra at dinner.

Well, whatever the reason, Caitlyn was going to make the best of this opportunity.

Muiren nodded toward the window. "This be the last turn to the house, miss, if ye've a mind to see it from a distance."

Caitlyn leaned forward. At first all she could see was a wall of thick trees, but then, like the sun breaking from clouds, the trees fell away and revealed Balloch Castle.

"She's beauteous, isna' she, miss?"

Caitlyn could only nod. A turreted, gray-stone house, built in the baronial style to look like a castle, sat upon a hill. The late-afternoon sun beamed warmly upon it, despite the frigid wind.

"She's new, fer all she looks old. Her grace had her built to order, she did. 'Tis a grand house and the kitchens are some o' the finest in Scotland. Why, there's even a water closet fer each guest room in the east wing which is where you'll be staying, miss."

"How modern! Still, it looks old-world and romantic." Caitlyn smiled. "I almost expect to see little elves to come dancing out of the doors to carry our bags!"

Muiren snorted. "Th' only elves ye'll be seein' are th' footmen, and a more lazy group ye'll be hard-pressed to find, though they look neat as a pin. Her grace won't have it no other way. She's determined we look as bang up t' th' mark as a Lunnon house, and she dinna brook no arguments."

"Very conscious of her station, is she? If I were a duchess, I'm sure I'd be the same."

Muiren looked surprised. "Would ye, miss?"

"Oh, yes. You wouldn't be able to stand me. I'd expect to be waited on hand and foot and demand the best of everything. Of course, that would only be fun if my brothers and sisters could see."

The maid grinned. "Ye'd just have to invite them to come and see ye queenin' it about the castle—"

The carriage rattled across cobblestones and pulled to a stop beneath the porte cochere.

"Och, we're here." Muiren collected their belongings.

Caitlyn smoothed her skirts and made certain her gloves were buttoned at the wrists, suddenly uneasy. She didn't know a soul, though she was sure she'd make some friends of some of the other ladies before the week was out. She lifted her chin. If she didn't, then she'd just enjoy the surroundings. It would be fun to explore the countryside with the gorgeous loch.

The coach door swung open and the steps lowered as a footman held out his gloved hand. Within moments, Caitlyn was in the most magnificent front hallway she'd ever seen. The gleaming parquet floor stretched out to a number of large double doors. The warm wood was accented by a long, white-and-gold table set beneath a huge gold-framed mirror and between two heavy, gilt chairs. Overhead, an ornate, gleaming gold-and-brass chandelier shone brightly, already lit though evening was still an hour away.

A door on the far side of the foyer opened, followed by a bustle of activity. Footmen scurried here and there carrying candelabra, linens folded over their arms. A maid hurried by with a basket of just-cut flowers, an empty vase tucked under one arm.

A distinguished-looking butler walked forward, pausing to bow before Caitlyn. "Miss . . . ?"

"Hurst." Caitlyn unbuttoned her gloves and pelisse and handed them to a waiting footman.

"Ah, Miss Hurst. We have been expecting you."

A groom entered carrying Caitlyn's portmanteau and trunk, Muiren following closely.

The butler flicked a glance at Muiren. "Her grace and some of her guests are in the pink sitting room. I will take Miss Hurst there before escorting her to her bedchamber."

"Thank ye, Mr. Hay." Muiren turned to Caitlyn and bobbed a curtsy. "Miss, would ye like a bath afore supper? It'll make ye a mite less stiff from all o' the travel."

"Oh, yes, please."

"I'll have one drawn fer ye. And I'll see tha' yer bags are unpacked and have a spot o' tea brought up, as well."

Caitlyn's stomach was already growling, and she knew from her time in London that it would be hours before dinner. "Thank you, Muiren. That sounds lovely."

The maid bobbed a curtsy and left, ordering one of the footmen to carry Caitlyn's portmanteau and trunk up the stairs.

The butler cleared his throat. "Miss Hurst, if you'll follow me, I'll take you to her grace. She and some of the guests just returned from a ride and are in the sitting room, discussing plans for their amusement tomorrow."

"Of course."

The butler took her to a set of wide double doors, threw them open, and announced in a monotone, "Your Grace, Miss Hurst has arrived." With a bow, he stepped out of Caitlyn's way.

The room gleamed with glass and mirrors, fully three times as long as it was wide and decorated with furniture of the ancien-régime style. Down two walls, magnificent windows, framed by heavily swagged and tasseled bronze silk curtains, poured light into the room. The walls across from these were covered in intricate wallpaper with a delicate pink, brown, and white pattern, interspersed with floor-to-ceiling mirrors. Large, salmon pink settees flanked two of the three roaring fireplaces that warmed the room, while a deep-pile, fitted carpet of salmon, red, and brown covered the floor. Added to this luxury were three ormolu chandeliers, one as large as a settee.

Caitlyn forced herself not to gape and focused on a small group clustered on two settees near the door. A striking red-haired woman measured her with a curious but cold gaze. She was dressed in a sapphire blue habit that made the most of her statuesque form, and her auburn hair was piled on her head, a rakish blue hat tossed to one side. Beside this magnificent creature sat a tall, handsome man with startlingly blue eyes, which traveled across Caitlyn in a bold manner. Across from them sat two ladies, one younger with brown hair and soft blue eyes, the other older with a sharp face and a significant nose.

The lady with the red hair looked Caitlyn up and down. "Well, well," she drawled in a low voice, as if speaking to herself. "I should have known."

Caitlyn, who'd been walking forward, paused. "I beg your pardon?"

The woman's expression closed and a tight smile touched her lips. "Miss Hurst, I am so glad you accepted my invitation."

So this is the duchess. She is lovely. Caitlyn stopped at the foot of the couch and curtsied. "Your Grace, it was very kind of you to invite me."

The man at the duchess's side had risen to his feet as Caitlyn approached. He bowed now, his eyes devouring her. "Georgiana, I believe introductions are due."

The duchess's lips thinned, but she smiled. "Of course. Miss Hurst, this is Lord Dervishton. I must warn you that he is a very bad man."

"Georgiana, really!" Dervishton's blue eyes gleamed with amusement as he took Caitlyn's hand in his own and placed a warm kiss to her fingers. "Miss Hurst, it is a pleasure. Don't listen to Georgiana. She's just angry that I beat her while racing back to the house."

"You cheated," the duchess said in her languid tone.

Caitlyn removed her hand from the man's grasp and dipped a brief curtsy. "Lord Dervishton, it's a pleasure to meet you, as well."

The duchess flicked a hand toward the other two women, who'd both risen. "This is Viscountess Kinloss, a very dear friend of mine."

The sharp-faced women tittered. "Oh, Georgiana! The things you say!" She stood and ducked a too brief curtsy. As she did so, a small, thin dog darted from her skirts, a large, pink bow fastened to a tuff of hair between its large, pointy ears.

"A dog! May I—" Caitlyn reached out a friendly hand but the dog growled and leaped at her, snapping and baring its teeth. Had it not been for Lord Dervishton's quick thinking in stepping between Caitlyn and the dog, she'd have been bitten.

Lady Kinloss scooped the dog into her arms.

"There, there, Muffin!" The dog quivered with rage, its bulging eyes fastened on Caitlyn.

"I'm sorry if I startled her."

Lady Kinloss sniffed. "He doesn't like strangers." She kissed her dog on its bony head and crooned, "Do we, Muffin?"

The duchess chuckled, the sound low and rich. "Miss Hurst, as you can see, we are ruled by a wild dog here at Balloch Castle. I hope you're not made uncomfortable by that."

Caitlyn felt more comfortable with the bad-tempered little dog than she did with the faintly critical air the duchess exuded. Looking at the duchess's perfectly fitted riding habit, Caitlyn suddenly felt crumpled and travel-worn and wished she'd thought to change into a fresh gown before introducing herself. She knew it wouldn't do to look uncertain, though. If she had learned one thing in London, it was that any show of weakness made one a target for the cruel.

Caitlyn turned an inquiring glance at the younger woman who stood quietly by.

The duchess frowned. "Oh, yes. And this is Miss . . . Oddwell."

The young woman smiled. "Miss Hurst, I am Miss *Ogilvie*."

The duchess shrugged. "Ogilvie, then."

Caitlyn smiled warmly at the younger woman and received a genuine smile in return. Caitlyn relaxed; here was one potential ally, at least. She moved a little closer to Miss Ogilvie.

Lady Kinloss kissed Muffin and placed him on the floor, where he retreated to her skirts, his head poking out as he growled at Caitlyn. "There, little Muffin. Be polite." The viscountess glanced at the door. "I wonder where the others are. They were just going to walk the path down to the original castle ruins; I'd think they'd have returned before us."

The duchess shrugged, an elegant gesture that showed off her delicate neck and shoulders. "I daresay they stopped to view the gardens. The Marchioness of Treymont has developed a propensity to go on and on about roses."

Caitlyn frowned. How had Mother, usually the best judge of character, been so trusting of such a *hard* woman? Caitlyn wondered if perhaps she was being hasty, though; she'd barely met the woman.

The duchess sank onto the settee cushions once more, gesturing for the others to do the same.

"If you'll pardon me," Caitlyn said, "I would like to rest a bit before dinner."

The duchess nodded. "It will be served at nine. That must seem dreadfully late for you." Her full lips twisted into a smirk, she looked at Lady Kinloss. "Miss Hurst comes from a horridly provincial part of the country. I was there not a month ago and I thought I should die from ennui."

How *dare* the woman! A sharp retort rose to Caitlyn's lips, but she forced herself to swallow it. *I promised Mother I wouldn't make a scene—but ohhhh!*

Lady Kinloss tittered behind her hand. "Perhaps Miss Hurst would rather have some bread and cheese at six than mutton and lobster at nine!"

That does it. Caitlyn pasted a smile on her face. "Oh, I don't care when you serve dinner; I just don't wish to miss it. I never miss the chance to experience a good meal, exchange pleasantries with my fellowmen, or witness a fool speaking."

As Lady Kinloss's smile faded, Lord Dervishton laughed. "Brava, Miss Hurst! A good retort! Now Lady Kinloss is left to wonder which of the three you meant."

The duchess's gaze narrowed. "Really, Dervishton, don't encourage the girl. She's known to be impulsive. Her mother warned me about that."

Caitlyn had to bite the inside of her lip to keep from slaying the entire lot of them with the sharp side of her tongue. "Your Grace, I'm not being at all impulsive."

Lord Dervishton chuckled. "Those of us who spent all afternoon in the saddle or"—he bowed his head at Caitlyn—"traveling the dusty roads will be exceedingly hungry come nine."

"Indeed," Miss Ogilvie said in her soft voice. "Nothing makes me hungrier than traveling." She smiled at Caitlyn. "It took me eight hours to reach Balloch, and if it hadn't been teatime when I arrived, I might have eaten one of the carriage straps!"

Caitlyn smiled gratefully at the young woman. "I'm glad you weren't forced to such lengths."

"Me, too!" Miss Ogilvie's soft blue eyes twinkled. "I thought I—"

The door opened and two more couples entered, accompanied by Muffin's snarling and growling. Lord Dervishton introduced Lady Elizabeth, daughter of the Duke of Argyll, and her companion, Lord Dalfour of Burleigh. Both were dressed extremely fashionably and greeted Caitlyn pleasantly. Following close behind were the Marquis and Marchioness of Treymont, a handsome couple who graciously said hello, but were soon engrossed in a conversation with each other over the layout of a new garden planned for one of their estates.

The duchess and Lady Kinloss greeted the new arrivals with far more enthusiasm than they'd shown Caitlyn, which was fine with her. All she really wanted was her bedchamber and the waiting bath. She glanced longingly at the doors.

"I'll go with you, if you'd like."

Caitlyn turned to find Miss Ogilvie standing beside her, a shy smile on the young woman's face. Caitlyn smiled. "If you don't mind, that would be lovely."

Miss Ogilvie linked her arm with Caitlyn's. "I'm sleepy and would like to rest before dinner, too."

Caitlyn sighed in relief and walked with the young woman toward the huge doors. "Thank you so much. I'm not quite sure where to go; the house is so large."

"And beautiful. Just wait until you see the bedchambers! They're appointed in such lovely colors. Mine is emerald green with tan curtain tassels and bed hangings—well, you'll just have to see it yourself. Lord Dervishton told me that every room has its own water closet, which is astonishing."

They'd almost reached the door when it opened and a tall, dark-haired man entered. His face was hard and sensual, his mouth carved, his eyes as green as mossy stone beneath an ice-cold river.

Caitlyn knew that face—it had haunted her dreams and her regrets for three months now. *"Alexander MacLean,"* she whispered, her voice lost in the greetings from the duchess and her companions.

MacLean smiled at the group, but as he walked toward them, his gaze flickered in Caitlyn's direction and locked with hers. Heat, sizzling and jagged, ripped through her, and in that second she remembered every stolen kiss, every sensual touch, every forbidden moment they'd spent together for three glorious weeks before his arrogance and her impetuous pride had nearly caused the downfall of her family.

Her body was instantly alive with a deep, pleasurable excitement. *Blast it, I should be over this!*

His gaze narrowed, but only for a moment, then—as if she didn't matter—he moved on, toward the group farther in the room.

"That was rude!" Miss Ogilvie sniffed. "He didn't say a word to either of us."

But he had. With one cool, composed look, he'd let Caitlyn know that though she might still be affected by his presence, he felt absolutely nothing at hers.

She couldn't seem to look away as he walked across

the thick carpet. He was dressed in tailored riding gear, his black boots gleaming while his perfectly tailored coat outlined his powerful muscles.

Miss Ogilvie bent closer to Caitlyn. "As rude as he is, I must say Laird MacLean is a disturbingly handsome man."

She doesn't know the half of it.

Miss Ogilvie regarded MacLean's profile as he spoke to the duchess. "The only reason my father wanted me to come to the duchess's house party was because he hoped I might attract Lord MacLean's notice."

"Have you?"

"Lud, no. He's too busy looking at—" Miss Ogilvie blushed, and shot an apologetic look at Caitlyn. "I shouldn't gossip."

No, please! Please gossip more! But Miss Ogilvie's expressive mouth pressed into a determined line, and when she spoke next, it was about the wonderful dinners and how she'd never had turtle soup before and hoped it would be served again.

Caitlyn listened with half an ear, her gaze drawn back to MacLean, who was now talking to Lord Dervishton. Oddly, MacLean hadn't seemed a bit surprised to see her. Perhaps the duchess had mentioned her invitation. Or maybe . . .

"Don't you think," Miss Ogilvie said softly, "that Laird MacLean looks like Lord Byron?"

"I take it you haven't meet Lord Byron."

"No, but I've seen a painting, and he seemed dark and dangerous and—" Miss Ogilvie shivered.

Caitlyn forced a smile. "Byron is a bloated, white worm that's fallen in love with his own slime."

Miss Ogilvie's eyes widened, then she giggled. "Really?"

"I met him several times during my brief stay in London, and to be honest, he is rather fat and pale and talks with a lisp."

"A *lisp*?" Miss Ogilvie said in an outraged tone. "That's not at all the way I imagined him! Caro Lamb must be quite mad to go on about him in such a fashion."

"They are *both* mad. And rude. And vulgar. A match made in mud, so to speak."

Miss Ogilvie's lips quivered. "You are very frank."

"Oh, I'm sorry, I—"

"No, no! I find it very refreshing. Please do not guard your tongue on my behalf. I've been here for a week and that's the most honestly spoken statement I've heard yet."

"That's both my gift and my curse." Caitlyn smiled. "It will be a relief to be able to speak my mind with at least one person." Over Miss Ogilvie's shoulder, Caitlyn noted that MacLean had left Lord Dervishton and was once again speaking with the duchess.

The red-haired beauty held out a languid hand for MacLean to kiss. He bowed over it, his dark hair falling over his forehead as he smiled at his hostess.

The sight made Caitlyn's stomach clench. The man was a walking threat to a woman's well-being.

Miss Ogilvie had followed Caitlyn's gaze and tsked. "You'd never know her grace was married, the way she flirts. She spent all afternoon encouraging Dervishton to make the *most* inappropriate comments. I hope Lord MacLean takes care."

"Don't worry about MacLean; he can be quite devious on his own." *And can make a woman believe— even if just for three short, amazing weeks—that she is the only woman in the world.* "Shall we retire? I really am quite tired."

"Oh, of course! After your travels, you will wish to rest before dinner." Miss Ogilvie took Caitlyn's arm and they continued to the door.

Caitlyn felt MacLean turn to watch, his dark green gaze fastened on her as she left the room. The urge to look back was almost overpowering, and she was relieved when they reached the foyer.

A footman led them to their bedchambers, which were just three doors apart. The younger woman offered to meet Caitlyn on the landing at eight thirty so they could walk to dinner together. "It will take every bit of thirty minutes to find the dining room."

Caitlyn agreed and said good-bye, then entered her bedchamber, where Muiren was unpacking the small trunk and portmanteau. The maid cheerily bustled Caitlyn to the fireplace, where tea and cakes lay waiting, promising that the bath would be arriving shortly.

Seated before the crackling fire, tea and cakes at hand to assuage her hunger, the maid chatting cozily in the background, Caitlyn fretted about MacLean's presence, an unwelcome addition to the duchess's house party. If there was one person who knew how to goad her into doing and saying things no lady should, it was *that* man.

She bit down on a cake with more force than was necessary. Blast it, she refused to allow his presence to spoil either her peace of mind or her fun. Let him do what he would and say what he could; this time she'd resist his taunting and teasing. This time *she'd* be in charge, not her traitorous heart. And no darkly handsome, caustic-witted Scottish laird would change that.

Chapter 3

Och, me lassies! 'Tis a sad fact tha' many times a mon dinna ken the power a lassie has till he's raised her ire an' faced her fire!

OLD WOMAN NORA FROM LOCH LOMOND

TO HER THREE WEE GRANDDAUGHTERS ONE COLD EVENING

"Will that be all, my lord?"

Alexander flicked a glance toward his valet. MacCready was a proper gentleman's gentleman in every way, except one—he had an annoying tendency to consider himself his master's conscience.

"No. That is not all." Alexander had no use for a conscience; he'd hushed his long ago. "There is that other matter I asked you to see to."

The valet opened the wardrobe door and pretended to study the contents. "Ah. I shall have your riding boots cleaned and will see to the pressing of your good burgundy waistcoat for dinner tomorrow."

"That's not what I'm talking about, and you know it."

MacCready shut the wardrobe with a snap. "I must suppose you are referencing the errand you wished me to complete?"

Alexander crossed his arms over his chest.

The valet sighed. "Very well. I shall discover which room belongs to Miss Hurst."

"Tonight."

"Yes, yes. Tonight. It shouldn't be a difficult task, as *both* Lord Dervishton's and Viscount Falkland's valets were making the same inquiry when I was fetching starch for your cravats. I shall just ask one of them."

"When did Falkland meet Miss Hurst? She only arrived a few hours ago and he just returned from his ride."

"He hasn't met her. Lord Dervishton mentioned how beautiful the lady was, and as Falkand's man said, his lordship is now planning 'his strategy.'"

Alexander turned to the mirror and made a minute adjustment to his cravat. So, both Dervishton and Falkland were already sniffing around the prize, were they? They were doomed for disappointment. Caitlyn Hurst might move with the sensuous grace of an exotic courtesan, but she was nothing more than a tease. For weeks, she'd held him on a tether, seeming to always promise more, urging him on but then holding back with the perfect amount of hesitation. Like a greenhorn, he'd fallen for her seemingly wanton innocence—but he knew her now, knew what she was, and that would keep him from making the same mistakes.

Still, she was by far the most beautiful woman he'd ever met. Small and shapely, with full breasts, she also had a narrow waist and curved hips that begged a man's hands. Her silken blond hair and thick brown lashes made her brown eyes seem dark and mysterious. Something about that odd combination—the pale hair and creamy skin, accented by the dark, rich color of her eyes—made a man burn for her.

Yet more than her physical beauty was the way she moved. Even this afternoon, when she'd left the room, every masculine eye had been on her. Something in the way she moved was challengingly erotic, so innately graceful, so . . . *feminine*. She'd used that femininity to lure him down a path that had almost led to his ruin, but had instead caught his brother.

His gaze narrowed. Of all his brothers, Hugh was the one Alexander counted on the most. Gregor, Dougal, and Fiona were younger and less involved in the family holdings. Since the death of their parents, when the weight of the clan business and the responsibility of four brothers and a sister had come to rest upon Alexander's shoulders, Hugh had always been there offering his quiet support, even during the dark times after Callum's death. Hugh was steadfast and competent, though given to doing far more than asked. He often crossed the line from "helpful" directly into "meddling," which was how he'd been caught in the web of Caitlyn Hurst's spinning.

Alexander scowled. How dare she try to her tricks on *him*? She'd pay for that impudence, b'God, and he'd enjoy every second. He'd show her how a *real* seduction was played—and once he'd had her in his bed, he'd walk away and leave her wanting . . . just as he was sure she had planned to leave him.

Revenge would be sweet. Very sweet, indeed. While it would be simple to plan one large fait accompli, it wouldn't be nearly as satisfying. No, he would first toy with this little mouse, savoring the chase. What happened to her after he'd taken his pleasure wasn't his concern. He'd have made his point.

He turned from the mirror and pinned his valet with a hard look. "From now on, I want to know any speck of information, any tidbit of gossip that you hear regarding Miss Hurst."

"What if it's nothing of significance?"

"That's for me to decide."

The valet pursed his lips. "Let us say, just for the sake of argument—"

"Of course," Alexander said grimly.

"—that I heard one of the lower maids mention that Miss Hurst prefers her towels dried by the fire and not on a line near a window, which can cause the material to be less soft. Surely you don't wish me to report things as insignificant as that?"

"I don't care if you hear that she sneezed twice or prefers her toast plain and not buttered—I want to know."

MacCready sighed. "Very well, my lord."

"From what you've said, she is already a topic of conversation in the kitchen. What else did you hear?"

"Just that Dervishton's valet said his master thought Miss Hurst an angel on earth."

An angel on earth.

Alexander slipped a hand into his pocket and withdrew a heavy silver watch. He flipped it over and traced the engraving on the back. *To Alexander. From Eton to beyond! Charles.*

Alexander's heart hardened. "I've heard such language before, and it was applied to just such a woman—young, beautiful, and given to flirting with any man who'd have her. It led to naught but ruin."

"I take it you are referring to Viscount Humbolt," the valet said quietly. "We all miss him, my lord."

Alexander tucked the watch back into his pocket, wishing he could do the same with the sadness that weighted his heart. "Anything else?"

MacCready cleared his throat. "Dervishton has taken to calling her The Incomparable. Furthermore, his lordship seemed to think the lady would be easily won over."

"Oh? Why would he think that?"

"I believe it stemmed from something the lady did or said earlier today." The valet sniffed. "Should I take it that the lady in question is a bit . . . common?"

"No, she's not. Impetuous, yes. Foolish, absolutely. But not at all common; she's too complex for that. Just the way she moves is—" Alexander shook his head. "It doesn't matter. She's trouble."

"That's good to hear," MacCready said primly.

Alexander quirked a brow. "Worried I might lose my innocence?"

"As far as I'm aware, my lord, you've never had any."

Alexander grinned.

"It just seems a troublesome situation . . . so many cocks and just one hen."

Alexander choked on a laugh. "It could be. Fortunately, I have no interest in this woman other than securing retribution for what she's done to my family."

MacCready stiffened. "She's harmed the MacLeans?"

"Yes. It is *her* fault that my brother was forced to marry."

MacCready frowned. "But . . . my lord, your brother seems happy in his new marriage."

"Hugh's merely making the best of the situation, as he always does. Besides, that isn't the point." The point was that Caitlyn had tried to make a fool of *him*. "Miss Hurst must pay for her impertinence," he snapped.

"Absolutely, my lord. If what you say is true, then I shall of course do whatever you require."

"Miss Hurst is not your average opponent. To those who just meet her, she is quite sweet and projects an air of sensuality and innocence."

MacCready's thin brows rose. "Sensuality *and* innocence?"

"It's a heady combination, and I daresay *that* is what draws Dervishton and the others down the path." Dervishton, for all his man-about-town ways, was in for a surprise. Caitlyn Hurst would look at the fool through her wide, brown eyes, blink her long, thick lashes, and then—just as he thought he'd won her over—slay him with a cutting remark.

Alexander allowed MacCready to help him into his evening coat. "Visit the servants' quarters during dinner and see what you can discover about Miss Hurst."

"With pleasure, my lord."

His mind focused on the task ahead, Alexander left his bedchamber. At the landing, he was surprised to find Dervishton leaning against the rail, idly swinging his eyeglass. The younger lord smiled and nodded a greeting, but his gaze went down the hall.

Ah. So that's how it is. A flash of irritation ripped through Alexander. "Dervishton, are you waiting for someone?"

The lord flashed a wolfish grin. "Aren't we all? In fact, I believe our lovely hostess is breathlessly awaiting *your* arrival in the sitting room right now."

"I doubt it. Georgiana and I ended our tryst months ago."

"Really? I was under the impression she—" Dervishton's gaze went past Alexander, his mouth freezing half-open.

Alexander could tell from the glazed look on the man's face exactly what had occurred.

Alexander turned as a faint rustling noise approached, and just as he'd expected, Caitlyn Hurst walked toward them moving with that damnably mesmerizing grace. Dressed in a gown of the softest blue trimmed with tiny white flowers and a wide, white sash beneath her breasts, her blond hair piled upon

her head, small pearls shimmering on her creamy ear-
lobes, she looked innocent and ethereal.

She paused and curtsied, a smile curving her soft
lips. "Good evening."

Dervishton—usually the most calm and urbane
of men—stepped forward and said in an eager tone,
"Miss Hurst, may I say how lovely you look this evening! You quite outshine all of the other beauties here
at Balloch Castle."

For the love of God, must the man gush like a fool?

Caitlyn sent a sly glance at Alexander before she
bestowed a soft smile on Dervishton. "Thank you, my
lord."

Encouraged in his foolishness, Dervishton lifted
one of her hands and pressed a fervent kiss to it. "I'd
be honored if you'd allow me to escort you to the dining room. This house is confusing and I doubt you
were furnished with either a map or compass upon
your arrival."

"Unfortunately, no. I'd appreciate your assistance."

"Nothing would give me greater pleasure." Dervishton beamed as if someone had handed him a trunk of
newly minted guineas. "I am doing myself as much
of a favor as you. Walking into the sitting room with
such a beautiful woman on my arm can only increase
my own worth in the eyes of our company."

Alexander crossed his arms over his chest and
leaned against the railing. "Dervishton, you don't
need to assure Miss Hurst of her beauty. She carries
that knowledge with her like a thief carries a pick."

Caitlyn stiffened and locked gazes with him, fury sparkling in her fine eyes.

For a long second, they looked at one another. In that short time, Alexander remembered other, more private moments—moments when he'd foolishly allowed himself to be lured into tasting those sweet lips and had captured her moans in his mouth, moments when he'd slid his hands over those lush curves and felt her shiver with need, moments when the world had been lost because of the exquisite taste and the feel of her moving restlessly against him, separated by nothing but silks and satins.

He clenched his teeth. That was the past, and now the tables were turned. He'd never again trust her.

Alexander forced a wolfish grin and remained blocking the stairs as he boldly regarded her up and down. He allowed his gaze to dwell in places it shouldn't and was immediately rewarded when her cheeks pinkened and she started as if to snap out a sharp retort, but then visibly swallowed it.

Satisfaction warmed him. *Oh, yes, Hurst. I know exactly how to push you into doing something rash.*

Dervishton, looking uncertainly from one to the other, stepped forward. "I can see that you two have met before."

Caitlyn sniffed. "Lord MacLean's brother is wed to my sister."

"What?" Dervishton frowned. "Ah yes. Didn't I hear rumors that—" He sent a glance at Alexander before he smiled uncertainly at Caitlyn. "I'm—I'm sure that's all in the past."

"More than you know," she replied coolly, and placed her hand on Dervishton's arm, smiling up at him in a way that made Alexander's jaw tighten painfully. "Lord Dervishton, would you please escort me to where we're to gather for dinner? I was to walk with Miss Ogilvie, but she ripped her lace on her heel and she had to return to her room. She asked me to let the duchess know she would be down as soon as she could."

"Poor Miss Ogilvie! We'll let Georgiana know right away; I'm sure she will hold dinner." Dervishton placed his hand over hers. "Allow me. The stairs are a bit steep."

Alexander regarded the wide, sweeping staircase with a raised brow. It was definitely grand, but had little in the way of steepness. "Miss Hurst, pray cling to Dervishton's arm, for I know how unstable you get once you've had too many glasses of sherry."

Dervishton blinked. "Sherry? Miss Hurst, I didn't realize you'd been—"

"I haven't." Caitlyn snapped a glare at Alexander. "I haven't had any sherry this evening *at all*."

Alexander drawled, "I recall an evening when you'd had far, far too much and you told me you'd always wanted to—"

"Lord Dervishton, may we continue?" Caitlyn broke in hastily. "Miss Ogilvie is counting on me to deliver her message."

Dervishton looked disappointed to be cheated of Alexander's story. "Of course."

Caitlyn sent Alexander a fulminating glare and swept past him, as regal as a queen.

Alexander grinned. They'd been at the Lingefelts' supper ball and it had been inordinately stifling and airless, and the lemonade—the only beverage available for the younger ladies—had run out. Thirsty from dancing, Caitlyn had sipped her way through several tiny glasses of sherry. Before the night was over, she'd stumbled at the top of the long flight of stairs that led from the ballroom to the dining room, and Alexander had caught her just in time to stop her fall.

Holding her to him, her breasts pressed against his chest, he'd been inflamed with the desire to taste her. She'd been similarly affected, and in an unsteady voice she'd confided that she wanted nothing more than to be kissed—hard.

Over the years, Alexander had been with many experienced courtesans who'd requested sexual favors, and he'd given them willingly. He'd also been with other women—most of them married—who'd wished to experience raw passion, and he'd obliged. But he'd never had a woman request something as simple as a kiss in such a husky, passionate voice, one that inflamed him as none of the other requests had.

He'd immediately led her to an alcove hidden by long silk curtains, and he'd kissed her mercilessly. She had kissed him back with a fervor that had set his blood aflame. It was the first time he'd realized how his friend Charles had succumbed to the winsome, coldhearted woman he'd wed. It had been madness of the worst kind—heated by passion, fed by excitement and blinding desire, and foolish because of the belief that it was controllable—no wonder Charles had succumbed.

That kiss was the first of many risky encounters between Alexander and Caitlyn, each one taking them a bit farther down a path she'd planned with perfection. He hadn't even realized he was being led until much, much later.

Damn it, I knew better; I'm not a green youth just out on the town! But somehow she wormed her way into my life, and . . . I just let her.

A slow, simmering anger rippled through him, and he was vaguely aware that in the distance a rumble of thunder answered his anger. "Miss Hurst," he called down the stairs, "a word of warning. The Roxburge cellars are famous for their variety. Perhaps you should request lemonade with dinner, as anything stronger might send you tumbling into someone's arms."

Caitlyn's brown eyes sparkled with anger, her expression tight. "Thank you for your *concern* for my safety, Lord MacLean, but I will not imbibe more than is prudent. I never do."

"Never?" he asked softly.

He and Caitlyn locked gazes, and to his utter consternation, a slow, simmering heat began to thrum through him, building every time her breasts rose and fell, pressing against the fine silk ball gown. Many women did not look so beautiful when they were angered. Somehow he'd forgotten exactly how sensually gorgeous she was and it was a bit disconcerting to face her again. His body was anything but immune to the sight of her.

Dervishton cleared his throat. "Miss Hurst, should I—"

She yanked her gaze from Alexander and smiled blindingly at Dervishton. "Let's continue down to where the duchess and other guests are waiting, please."

"Of course," Dervishton murmured, sending Alexander a bright, curious look.

Alexander watched them go, his hand so tightly clasped on the railing that his fingers grew numb. As she reached the bottom of the stairs, Caitlyn glanced back, her eyes sparkling with fury. Alexander had the impression that with very little more goading, she would pummel him with her clenched fists.

Which was exactly what he wanted. The thought made him relax. He simply needed to remain more removed and keep his passions at bay. He already knew her weakness: vanity. All he had to do was keep pressing, keep taunting, and she would do the rest. God, he would enjoy this battle! Enjoy waging it and savor winning it.

Still, he had a momentary feeling that something had changed since the last time he'd seen her three months ago. Had she been so obviously goaded before, she would have responded in kind. Her quick passion was what had attracted him to begin with. So many London misses were mild lemonade and stale cake; Caitlyn Hurst was spicy mulled wine and rich, delicate pastry.

He watched her walk toward the drawing room holding Dervishton's arm, her hips swaying beneath her flowing gown. To the casual observer she appeared unaffected by their conversation, but he knew better. He could tell she was upset, for as Dervishton escorted her into the drawing room, her shoulders were lifted and her movements had lost some of their innate grace.

As they disappeared, Alexander pushed himself from the railing and followed his quarry down the stairs. For Caitlyn Hurst, dinner would be a long, long affair.

"Heavens, I'm exhausted! I can barely lift my feet."

Miss Ogilvie tucked Caitlyn's hand into the crook of her arm as they reached the stair landing. "It's no wonder you're tired; it's after midnight and you were traveling most of the day."

"We were on the road before dawn, too. Then, dinner went on forever."

"There must have been ten courses."

"There were twelve! I counted." And each had been delicious. The food Cook prepared at the vicarage was good country fare and none went hungry, but oh, the delights offered at the duchess's table tonight were beyond extraordinary. Caitlyn would write Mary first thing in the morning and share the details of her first night at Balloch Castle. Between the sumptuous meal, the luxurious setting, and the exalted company, there was plenty to entertain her family as they gathered to read in the evening.

Naturally she'd eschew any mention of Alexander MacLean or the duchess. Some things didn't fit on mere paper. Pushing her thoughts aside, Caitlyn smiled tiredly at Miss Ogilvie. "I don't believe I've ever had such a delightful dinner. The food—ah!" There weren't adequate words for the roasted salmon, delicate poached fish, stuffed quail breast, or the other amazing treasures that had arrived on the dinner table.

Miss Ogilvie grinned, her lovely pale skin just touched with a scattering of freckles. "The lobster was divine. It is my favorite dish."

"I wished for more, but it was gone."

Miss Ogilvie sent Caitlyn a sly smile. "Lord MacLean noticed when you took a second helping."

"Yes, he did, didn't he?" *The arse.* He'd mocked how full her plate was, then remarked again when it was empty. To the rest of the company, his words had seemed like gentle teasing, but Caitlyn had felt the sting behind the words, had seen the dark, humorless look that had accompanied them.

She sniffed. She wouldn't allow MacLean to ruin her evening. "However I might have felt about the lobster, Lady Elizabeth was quite enamored of the crème cakes."

"She must have eaten five! She's quite a hearty specimen, isn't she?"

"They say Lord Dalfour would have married her but that her father disapproved, so she refuses to have anything to do with another man."

Miss Ogilvie sighed. "It's so sad. They have stayed together despite her father's feelings by attending house parties like this. It's very romantic, but for me, the true romance at the table tonight belonged to the Treymonts."

"The marquis and his marchioness certainly seemed absorbed in one another. They reminded me of my own parents." One day Caitlyn would have a relationship just like that, too.

Miss Ogilvie glanced at the footman who walked several paces before them and leaned over and whispered, "Miss Hurst . . . don't you think the duke is a bit odd?"

Caitlyn nodded and whispered back, "He hardly spoke a word throughout dinner. And what was that object he kept fiddling with?"

"His snuffbox. He loves that thing more than life, I think."

"I suppose if I had a wife who flirted the way his does, I'd feel the same."

"She was *horrid* during dinner, was she not?"

"I couldn't tell which she preferred more—Lord MacLean, Lord Dervishton, or the footman serving the soup!"

Miss Ogilvie grinned, but it faded quickly. "And the things she said about your hair, saying it couldn't be a true shade and suggesting you had— Why, I was never so angry in all of my life!"

"Me, neither. Fortunately I had my revenge." Caitlyn smiled. "I ate *two* pieces of the fondant and there was none left for her."

Miss Ogilvie giggled. "I'm glad you're not angry with me!"

The footman stopped at Caitlyn's door and Miss Ogilvie waved him on. "Thank you very much but we can find our way from here."

He bowed and left. Miss Ogilvie waited until he'd disappeared down the stairs before she said, "Miss Hurst, I hope you don't find me forward, since I just met you today, but I do feel as if I've known you for much longer and—"

"Call me Caitlyn, please."

Miss Ogilvie beamed. "And you shall call me Sally."

"I'd be delighted."

"Excellent! I have to say that at dinner tonight, I couldn't help but wonder if Lord MacLean might have a bit of a tendre for you!"

Caitlyn could only stare. "Why on earth would you think *that*?"

"He couldn't keep his eyes off you all evening."

"Only because he was trying to find ways to make me angry."

Sally blinked. "And did he?"

"Yes. Several times, in fact. Some of the things he says seem innocuous, but—" Caitlyn folded her lips in a straight line.

"Why would he wish to do such a thing?" Sally shook her head. "Men are so perplexing."

"Not all of them." *Some* of them were clear in what they were trying to accomplish. Alexander was obviously trying to goad her into some sort of impropriety. But why? What did he hope to accomplish? Tomorrow she'd find out. If there was one thing she knew, it was that Alexander MacLean was a—

"Caitlyn, may I ask you a question?"

With difficulty, Caitlyn pulled herself into the present. "Of course."

"What did you think of the Earl of Caithness?"

"Who?"

Sally's cheeks pinkened. "You may not have noticed him, for he is very quiet and sat beside Countess Dumfries at the other end of the table."

"Ah yes. He seems like a very nice man."

Sally looked pleased. "I thought so, too." The talk turned back to dinner and the gowns the other women had been wearing, but soon Sally was unable to hide her yawns and they said their good nights.

Muiren met Caitlyn inside the door. "Och, miss, how was yer evenin'?"

"Lovely." Caitlyn loosened her ties and allowed Muiren to assist her in shedding her gown and petticoats and climbing into her night rail.

Muiren slipped a shawl around Caitlyn's shoulders. "Have a seat at the vanity, miss, and I'll brush out yer hair."

Caitlyn did as Muiren suggested, watching the maid in the mirror as she unpinned Caitlyn's hair and then gently began to brush it out.

Muiren smiled. "Did ye enjoy yer dinner?"

Soothed by the rhythm of the brush, Caitlyn replied sleepily, "The food was superb, and almost everyone was very nice."

"Almost?"

"Everyone except Lord MacLean and the duchess, who—" Caitlyn caught Muiren's gaze in the mirror. "I mean—"

"Och, that's no' a surprise," Muiren said as she pulled the brush through Caitlyn's hair. "I daresay MacLean took a likin' to ye, seein' as ye're so bonny and all, and if there's one thing her grace dinna like, it's when her beau pays attention to another."

Caitlyn frowned. "Her 'beau'?"

"Well, not now. They were close last year, but then he stopped visitin'. I dinna think the duchess liked that, fer she was a shrew till he came back, several months ago. Now he's here, but"—Muiren glanced at the door before leaning forward to say in a loud whisper—"he doesna stay overnight in her bedchamber as he did before."

"I'd imagine the duke would have something to say about that!"

"I dinna think he cares. So long as the duchess graces

his table and makes sure his house runs smoothly, he canna be bothered with her involvements. I think that's the way 'tis with a lot o' the gentry—and a sad thing 'tis, if ye ask me."

Caitlyn recalled how the duchess had watched MacLean when she thought no one was looking, and how the older woman's expression had turned more and more sour as the meal wore on. "So he is the one who ended the relationship?"

"Aye, although her grace's maid told me this morning tha' her grace is hopin' t' win him back."

Caitlyn realized she was gripping her hands in her lap, and she uncurled them and forced herself to relax. It didn't matter who MacLean was sleeping with. He was an irritant to her, nothing more. "I find it difficult to believe that the duke doesn't have issues with the duchess's . . . proclivities."

"La, miss! Did ye see 'im at supper this evenin'?"

"Yes, but—"

"Was he e'en awake?"

"He was for part of the evening."

"An' did ye note that he's a good thirty years older than her grace? She was practically a child when he first seen her and took her to wife." Muiren's voice dropped back to a whisper. "Her grace's maid got tipsy on strawberry wine last summer, and she once told me that the duchess was no' born a lady."

"She certainly seems to be one now."

"Aye, and mighty conscious she is of it, too. She was a weaver girl in one o' the duke's mills. Once't he seen her, the duke had to have her. But even as a lass she was a smart one, and she held out fer a ring. Once't he married her, he brought in all sorts of tutors, dressmakers, and dancing masters—an army o' people to teach her how to behave and talk."

"Goodness! Does . . . does everyone know about that?"

"Only a very few. I know 'tis a fact, though, because the day after I heard it, her grace's maid tried every way she could to convince me tha' she dinna mean a word she'd spoken."

Caitlyn couldn't imagine the elegantly disdainful woman who'd presided over the supper table as anything other than a duchess.

Muiren placed the silver-backed brush on the dressing table. "Miss, are ye ready fer bed? 'Tis late and I know ye must be weary."

Caitlyn climbed into bed, snuggling into the warmed sheets, listening as Muiren extinguished the lights and stirred the fire. "Good night, Muiren."

"G'night, miss. Sleep well." The maid left the room, softly closing the door behind her.

Caitlyn yawned, scooting farther under the covers as her tired mind whirled with the knowledge that the duchess had once been a mill worker and Alexander MacLean had once been the duchess's lover. The idea of the beautiful red-haired woman with MacLean made Caitlyn's stomach clench. She fluffed her pillow and tried to think of something else . . . and failed miserably. It wasn't that she'd expected MacLean to be a monk of some sort—heaven knew he'd never presented himself as anything other than a sensual libertine. It was more that her imagination was unable to leave the thought be. Every time she closed her eyes, she imagined MacLean's dark head bending toward the duchess's pale, beautiful face and—

"Oh, blast it!" She sat upright and thumped her pillows with a balled fist. The bed was obviously too lumpy for a good sleep. She dropped back on the pillows and stared into the darkness overhead, wishing she could erase the pictures from her mind. She didn't have the slightest claim on MacLean—and didn't want one, either! She was simply overtired. Yes, that's what was wrong with her; she was overtired and the surprise of finding MacLean here, of all places, had been an additional strain on her nerves.

She sighed. It was too bad she hadn't thought to bring a book from her father's library. As tired as she was, it was going to be a long, long time before she fell asleep.

Chapter 4

※❧◎❧※

Watch yer tempers, me dears. Fer if ye dinna, it'll watch ye.

OLD WOMAN NORA FROM LOCH LOMOND
TO HER THREE WEE GRANDDAUGHTERS ONE COLD EVENING

Caitlyn opened her eyes to a darkened room, a streak of bright sunlight breaking through a crack between the heavy curtains. She looked at the clock and immediately sat up, her sleepiness disappearing. Almost ten o'clock! Goodness, she'd slept late!

She started to rise, then realized that no sounds permeated the house. With a smile, she dropped back onto her pillows and snuggled beneath the covers. Muiren had already been here, since the fire crackled merrily in the grate. She'd been so exhausted when she'd finally fallen asleep that she'd slept right through the maid's morning visit.

It was all so different from the vicarage, where thinner curtains let the morning light stream in and stirred the inhabitants to action at the break of dawn. It was luxurious to lie in bed in a blissfully warm room in the middle of a cool fall morning, the heavy sheets soft on her skin. She smiled and tugged the heavy feather counterpane up to her chin. She could easily grow accustomed to this. Probably too easily.

She yawned, then rolled to her side, tucking an arm under her cheek as she watched golden dust motes float in the single beam of sunlight that streamed between the curtains. Three months ago, she'd been in a similarly luxurious bed at her aunt's London house. She'd also been in the midst of her relationship with MacLean and had been consumed with thoughts of him. Then she'd feared that she was falling in love and had even wondered if he felt the same. He'd aggressively sought her out, and she couldn't forget how his eyes had gleamed whenever she'd walked into a room.

Now she realized she'd been a momentary distraction to him and nothing more. Thank goodness she hadn't made a fool of herself by telling him of her feelings; he would have burst into incredulous laughter.

She winced. It was painfully obvious that he was angry with her. Surely he wasn't holding her completely to blame for what had happened in London and the near scandal that had ensued? Caitlyn was more than willing to take her part in the blame; she'd been foolishly thoughtless—but so had MacLean. They'd *both* allowed their urgent passions to interfere with their obligations to their families, and they deserved equal blame.

It was a pity they hadn't had time to sort this through when it had happened, but Caitlyn's parents had whisked her back to the country so fast that she'd never had the chance to speak to him. After that she was confined to the vicarage for three long, dreadfully dull months, left with nothing but her memories and an odd sense of loss.

Away from MacLean's intoxicating presence, she'd convinced herself that the hot tug of attraction she'd felt whenever he was near hadn't existed, that it was nothing but a figment of her too fertile imagination.

But the second she'd seen him walk into the duchess's sitting room, Caitlyn knew she'd been lying to herself. She was just as affected by him now as she'd been in London.

Memories flooded her, her mind lingering on the feel of MacLean's hot mouth over hers, his large hands sliding over her breasts and hips, his warm breath brushing her neck . . . She took a steadying breath and forced the memories away.

Before, when the attraction between MacLean and her had flared, she'd allowed it, going with the fiery flow, and repercussions be damned. She couldn't afford that luxury now. Perhaps it was a good thing MacLean was over their mad flirtation, for she wasn't certain she could say the same of herself.

Caitlyn groaned and sat up. "*Forget* about him! What I need is food."

She pushed back the blanket and swung her feet over the edge of the bed, her gaze falling on a delicate tray holding a teapot on the table before the fireplace. Unfortunately, no cakes were with the tea; she'd have to take her rumbling stomach downstairs to breakfast.

She rose and tugged the fringed pull by the fireplace that would ring a bell in the kitchen, then sat and poured herself a cup of tea.

Holding her bare feet toward the fire, her fingers wrapped around the warm porcelain teacup, she thought about home. There, everyone would have risen hours ago. Father would be teaching Robert and Michael their Greek lessons, while Mary, once she'd been dragged away from whatever book she was burying her nose in, would be helping Mother with the mending.

Caitlyn sighed. She missed the noise, the creak of the stairs and the slamming of doors, the sound of laughter. Even from her room on the third floor, she could easily hear the murmur of voices from the sitting room on the bottom floor where Mother gathered her chicks to her like a mother hen. Or so Mother liked to think of it, although Father always suggested that as soon as she'd gathered her "chicks," she would then disperse them more like a general issuing orders than a fluffy chicken. That always made Mother protest laughingly that she wouldn't have to be a general if she had less unruly chicks.

Caitlyn smiled wistfully. One day, she wanted a relationship like theirs, based on respect and love. She hoped her sister Triona had found that with her new husband, Hugh. From Triona's letters, it seemed she might have. A twinge of envy made Caitlyn feel even

lower. Would she ever meet a man she could respect
and love enough to marry? The only man she'd ever
felt a true attraction for had spent most of last evening doing his best to show her how little he thought
of her.

The door opened as Muiren arrived, and Caitlyn
was soon dressed for breakfast.

As she waited for Muiren to find her blue shawl,
Caitlyn found herself wondering yet again how
MacLean's onetime lover had come to invite Caitlyn
to visit. The more she thought of the circumstances
of her visit, the odder it seemed. *It doesn't just seem
odd—it is odd.* Caitlyn would pay close attention to
the both of them; that she and MacLean were invited
to the same house party was too much of a coincidence. Something was going on—and whatever it
was, she'd find out and put a stop to it.

Muiren brought Caitlyn the shawl and she went
down to breakfast.

"Are you going to eat that?" Roxburge asked.

Alexander was sitting at the breakfast table, idly
swinging his eyeglass on a ribbon as he waited for
Caitlyn to appear.

"*I said,*" the voice came again, querulous and even
closer, "are you going to *eat* that?"

Alexander reluctantly turned to face the aging
duke, who stood not two feet away, his ever-present
snuffbox clenched in one hand. Alexander lifted his

quizzing glass and eyed him. "I beg your pardon, but am I going to eat what?"

The duke pointed at Alexander's plate. "That pear. It's poached in cinnamon, you know. One of the few we managed to get off the trees from the garden."

Alexander looked at the pear. Delicately white, the flesh was sprinkled with cinnamon and sugar. "Yes, I'm going to eat it."

The duke looked disappointed, but after a moment he brightened. "Perhaps we can cut it in half and—"

"Roxburge!" Georgiana appeared beside her husband, her lips pressed into a thin line. "What do you think you're doing?"

The duke, his gray hair thinned to nothing on the top of his noggin, pointed a shaking finger at Alexander's plate and said in a querulous voice, "MacLean took the last pear from the buffet, so I asked him if he would share it."

Flags of high color marred Georgiana's cheeks. "You did *not* ask him such a thing!"

Roxburge rubbed his snuffbox with one thumb. "I . . . it's my house and my pear."

"Once it was placed on MacLean's plate, it became *his* pear." Georgiana clasped the duke's arm and literally began to drag him away, her mouth tight with anger. "Sit in your seat at the head of the table and leave our guests alone."

Roxburge allowed himself to be led off, though he complained loudly, "I just wanted the pear! It's the last one and—"

She shushed him as if he were a child of two. Lips thrust out, he plopped into his seat, smacked his snuffbox on the table beside his plate, and demanded that one of the footmen go to the kitchen and search for more pears.

Down the table, Dervishton chuckled. "It's Beauty and the Beast. I wonder what Georgiana sees in him."

"His bank accounts, I would think," Alexander answered.

"She's a beautiful woman; she could have anyone."

She can now. But in the beginning, Roxburge was the one who was doing the favor. Alexander had discovered that little tidbit quite by accident. He'd been in the stables and had overheard the butler—who'd been angry at Georgiana's peremptory manner toward his nephew, the new footman—discussing his employer's origins in a vigorous tone of voice.

It was amazing what one could learn if one merely listened. And after thinking about it, Alexander easily recognized signs that Georgiana wasn't born to the role she played. She was far more dismissive of the servants than most ladies of breeding were, as if she had something to prove. She reminded him of a person speaking a foreign language, overcorrect and stiff.

Viscount Falkland wandered into the breakfast room and came to stand beside Dervishton's chair. "G'morning! What's for breakfast?"

Dervishton grinned. "Don't ask for pears. MacLean here got the last one, much to our host's dismay."

Falkland looked to the head seat and watched as Georgiana placed strawberries on the duke's plate, then took her place at the other end of the table. "It's almost criminal, all of that beauty in bed with that shriveled-up shell of a man."

"Oh, I'm sure it's been years since Georgiana visited that bed," Dervishton said drily.

The viscount's plump, childish face cleared. "Thank goodness for that. I think he prizes that gold snuffbox more than his wife, anyway. It never leaves his hand, and they say he sleeps with it under his pillow."

"Poor Georgiana," Dervishton murmured.

"Don't waste your sympathy," Alexander said. "She isn't suffering overmuch; you're sitting in one of her many consolation prizes. Roxburge paid over eighty thousand pounds for this house."

Dervishton whistled silently while Falkland winced.

"At least she got something out of it." Falkland glanced at the buffet. "I'd better get something to eat before the ladies arrive. I came down late to breakfast yesterday because I had trouble getting my cravat to look just so, and by the time I arrived, there wasn't a single egg to be had."

Dervishton eyed the viscount's neckwear. "Yes, we can see that you decided to give up your cravat for eggs today."

"What's wrong with my crav—" Falkland gaped at the doorway, then frantically adjusted his cuffs and smoothed his waistcoat.

Alexander followed the plump young lord's gaze and found Caitlyn entering the room arm in arm with Miss Ogilvie. They made a pretty picture, and Alexander would wager the family castle they knew it.

"Good God, she's—" croaked Falkland, turning bright red. "She's an *angel*! A true angel!" He subsided into wide-eyed bliss.

"Easy, fool," Dervishton muttered. "You'll embarrass us all." He stood and flourished a bow. "Good morning! I trust you both slept well."

"I certainly did," Miss Ogilvie said.

"As did I. I slept until almost ten," Miss Hurst added in her rich, melodious voice.

Falkland visibly shivered, and it was all Alexander could do not to chide the fool. The youth was smitten, and judging from the way Dervishton was watching Caitlyn, he was in no better shape.

Good God, did every man except him fall madly in love with the chit? It was damnably annoying.

Falkland leaned forward eagerly. "Miss Hurst, can I carry your plate at the buffet and—"

"Don't even try it." Dervishton slipped his arm through Caitlyn's. "Miss Hurst needs someone with steadier hands to hold her plate."

Falkland stiffened. "I have steady hands, and I can also—"

"For the love of God!" Alexander snapped, unable to take another moment. "Leave the chit alone! She can get her own damned breakfast."

Falkland turned bright red. "I was just—"

"Sausage!" Caitlyn looked past him to the buffet. "There's only one left and I intend to have it. If you will pardon me a moment, please." She slipped her arm from Dervishton's, whisked around him, and began to fill a plate while exclaiming at the sight of kippers.

"Excuse me!" Falkland scurried off to pester Caitlyn. Chuckling, Miss Ogilvie followed him to the buffet.

Dervishton returned to his seat. "Well! I've never been dismissed for a plate of sausage before."

Alexander had to hide a reluctant smile. He should have been irritated, but his sense of humor was too strong to allow it. He watched Caitlyn chat animatedly to Falkland about the variety of fruit on the buffet as she filled the plate he dutifully held. Last night she'd been equally enthusiastic about their dinner, her reaction immediate and genuine. Their previous relationship had happened so quickly, so fiercely, that he hadn't learned her everyday likes and dislikes. Not that it mattered, he told himself, dispelling a flicker of unease. He knew her character, and that was all he needed to know.

"Falkland is a fool," Dervishton said into the silence. "He is escorting the charming Miss Hurst this way. I'd have taken her to the other end of the table, away from the competition."

Alexander watched as the weak-chinned viscount assisted Caitlyn to a chair down a little and across from Alexander. Caitlyn was chuckling at something the viscount said while he watched her with an adoring air that nauseated Alexander.

When Alexander turned to say as much to Dervishton, he realized that the young lord's gaze was locked on Caitlyn, too. "Watch," he murmured to Alexander. "You'll be glad you did."

"Watch what?"

A mesmerized look in his eyes, Dervishton didn't answer.

Muttering an oath, Alexander turned and regarded Caitlyn. The morning sunlight slanted across her, smoothing over her creamy skin and lighting her golden hair. Her long lashes, thick and dark, shadowed her brown eyes and made them appear darker. She looked fresh and lovely, no different from what he expected.

Irritated, Alexander shrugged. "So?"

"You're an impatient sort, aren't you?" Dervishton flicked a glance at Alexander, then turned back to Caitlyn. "Wait a moment and you'll see."

Alexander scowled, but as he did so, Caitlyn leaned over her plate and closed her eyes, an expression of deep pleasure on her face. Her expression was like that of a lover, a sensual yearning.

Instantly Alexander's throat tightened and his heart thundered an extra beat. "What in hell is she doing?"

"Smelling the ham, I believe." Dervishton's voice was oddly deep.

Alexander was fairly certain his own voice wouldn't be normal either as he watched Caitlyn savor the scent of her breakfast.

She smiled and lifted her fork and knife . . . and licked her lips.

"Good God," Dervishton whispered hoarsely.

Alexander's body flash heated, and for one wild, crazed moment he *wanted* that look—wanted to own it, to possess it, for it to be directed at him and no one else.

Caitlyn slipped her fork beneath a small bit of ham and brought it to her lips.

If he had thought her expression rapturous before, he'd been wrong. Her blatantly sensual expression now was beyond description. "Has she never had food before?"

Dervishton answered quietly, "I think it's the sophistication of the dishes that she savors."

"Ham and eggs?"

"Seasoned with chives, butter, and a touch of thyme—Roxburge keeps an excellent table. I have seldom—" Caitlyn slipped a forkful of eggs between her lips. "Damn," Dervishton breathed as Caitlyn closed her eyes and slowly chewed, her lips moist.

Damn indeed. The woman was talented at garnering attention, but this was beyond enough! Alexander saw that every man in the room was watching her eat—even Roxburge had a greedy expression on his faded face.

Alexander's jaw tightened. Then he leaned forward and said in a clear voice, "Miss Hurst, I've never seen a woman eat with such relish."

She lowered her fork. "I doubt I enjoy my food any more than anyone else." She turned to Miss Ogilvie, who'd just taken a seat. "Don't you think that's true, Miss Ogilvie?"

"Oh, we all have our weaknesses," Miss Ogilvie said promptly. "For example, no one loves chocolate cake as much as I."

Beside her, the Earl of Caithness grinned. "I've been known to hoard truffles."

"Don't let MacLean fool you," Dervishton added with wicked twinkle. "He almost fought our host over the last pear."

Caitlyn blinked. "There were *pears*?" She leaned forward and, with a look of deep longing, regarded his plate.

Alexander's jaw tightened as an unfamiliar stab of envy pierced him. *Good God, I'm jealous of a damn pear!* The ridiculous thought irked him yet more. With grim determination, he announced, "Yes, I have the last pear." Alexander cut a piece and made a show of tasting it. "Mmm! Cinnamon. Excellent."

Her gaze narrowed and her lips pressed firmly together, which made the pear taste all the better to Alexander.

Georgiana's sharp voice cut through the moment. "Lord Dervishton, you mentioned last night that you'd enjoy a ride this afternoon."

Dervishton nodded, his gaze drifting back to Caitlyn.

"It's brisk today, but I shall have the horses readied." Georgiana looked at Alexander and her expression softened. "You don't normally ride for pleasure, I recall."

He shrugged. "I ride while attending my lands. I don't normally find it a relaxing pastime."

Lady Kinloss, seated at Georgiana's left, clapped her hands. "A ride would be delightful! Though her grace and some others"—she sent a quick glance at Alexander—"are not much for riding, I'm sure the *rest* of us would enjoy it. Perhaps we could even visit the Snaid."

Miss Ogilvie looked up from a low conversation she was having with Caithness. "The Snaid? Is that a castle?"

Lady Kinloss tittered. "Lud, no! The Snaid is what the locals call Inversnaid. It's a very small village, but there's an inn there with exceptionally good fare and some astounding views of the Ben, which is quite a lovely mountain. We could ride to the Snaid this afternoon, have tea, and return in plenty of time to get ready for dinner."

"Miss Hurst, do you ride?" Dervishton asked.

"Somewhat. I was learning in London when—" Her gaze slipped to Alexander, and then, catching his sudden gaze, she colored. "Of course I can ride."

He lifted his brows, amused at her pink-stained cheeks. Though he knew that while she was *talking* about their rides in the park, she was *thinking* about the kisses that followed. As was he.

Glad to know that those moments still flustered her, he allowed his gaze to flicker over her mouth. "Miss Hurst is an excellent . . . *rider.*"

She flushed a deeper pink, her gaze flying to meet his. "Thank you, Lord MacLean, but I wouldn't classify myself as excellent."

"Oh, come now. Don't be so shy about your talents."

All eyes turned toward Caitlyn. She flicked Alexander a cold glance. "While I can ride, I don't know the horses in her grace's stables and—"

Alexander drawled, "You are worried they wouldn't be up to your standards, of course. Having seen you ride, I can certainly understand your concern."

Dervishton raised his brows. "You have ridden together before?"

"I had the privilege of teaching Miss Hurst when she was in London last season."

A distinct pause in the conversation followed.

Caitlyn's cheeks couldn't be brighter. "Fortunately, I've had more instruction since."

Alexander's humor disappeared. What in hell did she mean by *that*? Was she talking about riding, or kissing? Dammit, she'd been ensconced in the countryside for the last three months! Had some country bumpkin dared touch her?

Alexander's blood boiled at the thought of Caitlyn's pink-and-white perfection in the hands of a rough farmer.

"Your Grace," Miss Ogilvie interjected, "I'm afraid my riding skills are quite negligible. I will need a gentle mount."

Georgiana seemed amused by this artless confession. "Don't worry, Miss Ogilvie. I have quite a number of smaller, gentler mounts in the stables for just such a reason."

Miss Ogilvie sighed in relief. "Thank you, Your Grace!"

"Of course." Georgiana sent a look at Alexander from under her lashes and said in a lazy voice, "While most of you are enjoying a ride, I will stay here and attend to some correspondence. That should be a lovely way to spend the afternoon."

Alexander wished she'd try for a little subtlety, but he supposed it was beyond her. To show his disinterest, he turned back to his plate to enjoy his pear. But as he raised his fork, he realized the pear was gone.

Across from him, Caitlyn lifted the last piece of pear with her fork. She'd stolen *his* pear from *his* plate, the wench!

She smiled at him as she slid the pear between her lips and chewed it with obvious relish. Her eyes twinkled mischievously, and an answering spark of amusement lifted one corner of his mouth, but he staunched it immediately.

For a dangerous moment, he'd almost forgotten why she was here. Dammit, he had to be on guard that she didn't beguile him the way she'd already enslaved the majority of men here.

He turned toward Dervishton. "The wind is blowing from the north. It'll be a cold ride this afternoon."

Dervishton looked down the table at Caitlyn. "I don't care if it snows; I wouldn't miss this ride for the world."

Irritation flared and Alexander regarded the younger lord with a jaundiced eye. He knew exactly what would happen: Dervishton and Falkland would spend the entire ride to the Snaid trying to outjockey one another, which would gratify Caitlyn Hurst's vanity to no end. It was a pity he wasn't going. If anyone could keep the two lunkhead lords at bay, it was he.

Hmm . . . perhaps he *should* go. He thought of all the ways he could tease her while riding, when private conversation was more easily obtained. Not to mention he knew her true riding skills, and they weren't the best. It was one thing to ride the smooth, flat paths in Hyde Park and another to ride a narrow, uneven country lane.

Alexander smiled. "I believe I will go for that ride after all."

Georgiana's head snapped in his direction, her hard blue gaze sharp, and for an instant he thought she would blurt out something indiscreet. After a moment, she collected herself and gave an uncertain laugh. "Alexander, really! I've never known you to join in such mundane sport."

He shrugged. "I've decided I'd enjoy the fresh air."

A flash of displeasure marred Georgiana's face. "Since you won't be here ... Lord Dervishton, perhaps *you* will be so good as to stay. I shall be glad to have the company."

Lord Dervishton looked disappointed, but he quickly hid it. "Of course, Your Grace. It would be my pleasure."

Caitlyn felt a faint sense of satisfaction as the duchess glared at Alexander. Muiren's information about the duchess and MacLean must be true. Caitlyn shot a glance at the duke, who was happily polishing his snuffbox. Since he didn't seem bothered, perhaps she shouldn't be, either. After all, she had no claim to MacLean.

Of course, if he'd been her husband, she wouldn't have stood for such nonsense. When she married, she'd make sure her husband respected their relationship *and* her, just as her parents respected each other.

The thought of her mother gave Caitlyn pause. Already, she'd allowed MacLean's goading to push her down the same path that had caused the trouble from before—the oh-yes-I-can-and-you-can't-stop-me that had led her into such indiscretions. She'd let his teasing keep her silent on her limitations as a rider, even claiming that she knew more now, which was a blatant falsehood. She simply could not allow him to lure her into altercations.

There was something insulting in the way MacLean looked at her, as if he found her wanting in some fundamental way. That look had the power to push her into rash behavior, which was why she'd stolen his pear. The pompous ass had been so patronizing that she'd longed to take him down a notch. Fortunately, only the Earl of Caithness had witnessed her theft, and he'd merely grinned and returned to his own breakfast.

Caitlyn could see why Miss Ogilvie thought Caithness an interesting man. He had a steadfast, calm quality. It was a pity Caitlyn didn't find such men attractive, but she was invariably drawn to the more volatile, less predictable sort.

She regarded MacLean from under her lashes and wished he weren't quite so handsome. He looked far too much like a hero from a novel, though his actions were anything but. She wondered what his intentions were. He was certainly out to embarrass her, but why? What did he hope to gain?

Perhaps she could discover that when they were riding. She'd find a way to speak privately with him and—

The duchess leaned forward to say something in a low voice to MacLean. He listened, then shrugged and turned away. The duchess looked furious, while MacLean merely looked bored.

A faint flicker warmed Caitlyn's heart.

Sally leaned across the table. "Caitlyn, instead of riding, perhaps I should stay here and look at the grand portraits." She glanced down the table at the duke, before saying in a low whisper, "I'll count how many have the unfortunate Roxburge chin."

Caitlyn had to laugh. "No, no! You must ride!"

"Oh, yes," Lord Falkland interjected. "You can't miss the views. Nothing like them for miles around."

Sally looked uncertain. "If you think I should go . . ."

Caitlyn nodded. "We two will ask for the slowest, fattest mounts from the stables, and we'll both be fine. If they have ponies, we'll request those."

Sally laughed. "A pony would be perfect for me, but not for you, although it *is* kind of you to offer."

Caitlyn pshawed the notion and was glad when the duchess rose from her chair. Since everyone had finished breakfast, Lady Kinloss suggested they meet in the foyer in an hour for their ride. The other guests agreed and left to change into their riding habits. Caitlyn was escorted to the foyer by Dervishton and Falkland as Alexander remained in his seat, his dark gaze following her.

Georgiana watched as Miss Hurst dominated the masculine attention, leaving with an eligible bachelor on each arm. *How pathetic. Men are such weak creatures, far too easily led by a youthful beauty.*

Knowing they were fools didn't reduce the sting; Georgiana wasn't used to sharing every bit of the masculine attention. It was quite acceptable for the Earl of Caithness to pay attention to Miss Ogilvie, for everyone knew he was on the lookout for a well-set wife. But it irked her to see a handsome, polished gentleman such as Lord Dervishton playing up to a pasty-faced ingenue such as Miss Hurst. What disturbed her even more was the way MacLean followed the girl's every movement, his green eyes considering . . . measuring . . . *interested.*

Lady Kinloss picked up a napkin and wrapped up a small slice of ham. "Muffin loves ham. I can't give him too much, though, for it makes him gassy. Muffin's stomach is so delicate! He never complains, but I can tell when he's—"

"Diane, would you mind leaving Lord MacLean and me alone for a few moments? I must ask his opinion about that set of matched grays I just purchased. One has drawn up lame, and I don't know whether to keep him or have him put down."

Diane hopped up from the table with a nervous twitter. "Oh! Of course."

Georgiana waited for Diane to disappear out the door before she moved down the table to where Alexander sat, his gaze still on the open doorway as if he was lost in thought.

Taking the chair beside his, Georgiana followed his gaze to the hallway, where Miss Hurst was talking earnestly with Lord Dervishton. Georgiana's lip curled. The silly chit had no notion of Dervishton's fickle nature, which was most useful to Georgiana in making MacLean jealous. The younger man was attractive enough, but he had nothing on the sheer masculine power and sensuality of the man now sitting beside her.

She watched MacLean through lowered lashes, an unfamiliar pang of longing twisting her heart. To most people in society, she was the Duchess of Roxburge, the most beautiful and wealthiest woman in all of Scotland and perhaps even England. Only she and her doddering husband knew that he'd first seen her at the tender age of fourteen, working in a cotton mill dressed in near rags, dirty and barefoot, the illegitimate child of the town whore.

Roxburge had been a jaded peer, tired of life and the vagaries of the ton, labeled an imbecile by the wits of the time because of a faint lisp and a tendency to turn bright red anytime someone looked his way. But Roxburge was no fool, and he had a deep appreciation for beauty in all forms—even in a girl dressed in rags with no shoes on her feet.

He'd taken Georgiana home that day and, as soon as he'd been able to procure a fake birth record, had married her. Thus, the Duchess of Roxburge had been "born." For the first two years, he'd sequestered her away in his northernmost estates, where she was scrubbed, tutored, and polished until even he sometimes forgot where she came from. The marriage was not one of great passion; she had no love for him nor he for her. Theirs was a simple marriage of convenience. Roxburge gained a young and beautiful wife who excited envy among his peers. In return, Georgiana received a title and a generous monthly allowance. The birth of a healthy, handsome son with the family birthmark on his left elbow sealed the deal.

When the time came, the duke presented his lovely duchess to London society, which, as he'd expected, she took by storm. When anyone asked about Georgiana's heritage—as a few did—he let it be known that his wife was from an ancient family in the northernmost reaches of Scotland, hinting at a lineage linked to that delicate and tragic beauty Mary, Queen of Scots.

Georgiana navigated the murky waters of the ton with a sure step, welcomed for both her beauty and that faint air of superiority that she'd developed to keep the more curious at bay. This intriguing combination opened more doors for her than her husband's lineage and money ever could. She was quick to see that to truly advance, she'd have to choose her lovers wisely, develop a reputation for discretion, and select only the most discriminating of friends. She did just that and was soon one of the leaders of the ton.

She had everything she wanted and more, and she'd enjoyed it. But lately, something didn't feel quite right. Her beauty was beginning to fade, and her husband was now a doddering old fool who leered at the upstairs maid and fell asleep at the dinner table with his mouth wide open.

Georgiana found herself restless for something more, for the one thing she'd never had—true love. She wasn't certain, but she thought she'd found it in Alexander MacLean, that mysterious, maddeningly handsome, and damned elusive Scottish laird; a man with black hair and a blacker soul and dark green eyes that hinted at both deep passion and the ability for cold cruelty.

As if sensing her thoughts, he finally dragged his attention from the hallway and turned her way. "Yes?"

His voice held only boredom. Already frayed by his inattentiveness, Georgiana's temper sparked to life. "Watching Miss Hurst and her conquests? Or wishing you were one yourself?"

His gaze narrowed, his eyes shimmering like green ice.

She snapped, "How unlike you, MacLean. I'd never saw you as the sort to chase schoolgirls. I'd have thought Humbolt's demise might have been a lesson."

A cold smile touched his lips. "What's wrong, Georgiana? Jealous that Dervishton has forgotten to worship at your altar?"

Chilled by the icy gleam of his eyes, Georgiana swallowed a sharp retort.

Alexander's gaze had already returned to the open door. Outside, Georgiana watched Caitlyn Hurst, who looked positively ravishing as she laughed up at Dervishton. The chit's gowns had a deceptive simplicity that was instantly recognizable as having come from a modiste of the first water. Where had she gotten such a wardrobe?

Georgiana tapped her fingers on the table. "MacLean, you told me you'd decided to teach Caitlyn Hurst a lesson."

He shot her a bored look. "What I do or don't do is really none of your concern."

"It's my concern when I work to get the chit invited to *my* house, and then have to sit and watch you fawn over her like all of the other men here. You're infatuated with her! Admit it!"

His eyes blazed hot green, his mouth white with anger. Outside, a roaring wind slammed against the house; the sunshine blotted by the sudden appearance of a roiling bank of clouds.

Georgiana shivered, frightened and aroused. To own a man like this . . . How had she let him escape? He was gorgeous and overwhelmingly masculine, but his power was what made her bones melt. She touched his arm and leaned forward, her blue silk morning gown cut provocatively low. "Alexander, please . . . I didn't mean to make you angry. I'm just curious about your plan. And I *am* a part of it, since I'm the one who invited her here."

He regarded her for a long moment. Outside, the wind slowly died down; the clouds calmed, though they didn't disappear. "I am merely toying with her. She didn't ruin my brother in one single moment; he had to face the knowledge of his fate for a while. I want her to do the same. She knows I have plans, but she doesn't know what they are. She's curious and concerned; I see it in her face." His hard mouth curved in a faint smile. "When the time comes, she'll know what's in store for her. Until then, I want her to worry."

Relief swept through Georgiana. "You're torturing her! I was worried that you were succumbing to her like that fool Falkland and the others. But how do you plan on punishing the girl while she's constantly surrounded by admirers? It's going to take some deviousness on your part."

"So it will." He stood, forcing her to drop her hand from his arm. "For now, I want her to stew in uncertainty. I'm coming for her, and she's beginning to realize it. That's all you need to know."

Georgiana opened her mouth to protest, but he forestalled her with a sharp frown. "I must change for the ride."

That was all she was going to get. Georgiana stood as well. "Of course. I'll let the footmen know how many of you will need mounts. And, Alexander?"

"Yes?"

"When you return, I'd like to hear how things went." She held her breath. She was taking a risk, asking for such a thing, especially in a tone of voice that suggested she knew his answer would be yes.

To her relief, he merely shrugged. "I'll stop by your apartments when I return."

Her heart leaped. When he returned, she would entice him into more than conversation. She managed to keep her triumph from showing. "I will speak with you then."

He bowed and left, walking with that animal grace that made her shiver. She watched him until he disappeared up the stairs, then turned to look out the window. The storm clouds were still hanging low on the horizon, and the taste of rain still lingered.

Shivering, she rubbed her arms. Alexander MacLean was a challenge; a delicious, delectable, and difficult challenge. But she was not the average society miss; she was much, much more. And she, more than anyone else, didn't know the meaning of the word *quit*. She'd find a way to capture him. One way or another, he would be hers.

Chin high, she left the breakfast room.

Chapter 5

❧

When ye've a problem, lassies, 'twill do ye no good to pretend 'tis no' there. Fer when ye turn t' walk away, it'll rear up and bite ye in the arse.

OLD WOMAN NORA FROM LOCH LOMOND
TO HER THREE WEE GRANDDAUGHTERS ONE COLD EVENING

An hour later, Caitlyn sat clinging to her horse with both hands, wondering how she'd found herself in this predicament.

Actually, she knew *exactly* how and it had to do with the six foot three inches of smirking masculinity who sat on a bold black gelding five feet behind her, laughing every time her mount—a prancing bay mare with a stubborn streak as wide as Caitlyn's—decided to shy at some imaginary danger.

So far, Caitlyn had retained her seat, but only through sheer force of will. Clutching the reins, she jealously watched Sally, who sat prettily on a small, fat mare that had no inclination to do more than amble. As a consequence, Sally could make casual conversation with Lord Caithness anytime she wished, while Caitlyn could only smile tightly

at Lord Falkland, who'd planted himself at her side
the second she'd stepped into the foyer. She barely
dared to make a sound, for it took every ounce of her
attention to keep her horse from bolting every time
a leaf trembled.

"I say, is that a rabbit?" Falkland exclaimed, pointing with his whip toward a distant field.

Caitlyn's horse—whom she'd begun to call Devil—
shied at the sudden movement. Caitlyn convulsively
clenched her knees, hunching down and yanking on
the reins.

It was an amateurish move, but effective nonetheless. The horse fought her tooth and hoof, but the
ploy had the desired effect of taking Devil's attention
off Falkland's whip.

*Damn it, why didn't I tell the groom I needed an easy
horse like Sally's?* she asked herself for the umpteenth
time. But she knew why; she'd refused to bow before
the challenge she'd seen in MacLean's eyes. He'd stood
within earshot of the groom, looking as if he *expected*
her to ask for an easier mount, so of course that was
the last thing she'd do. *My pride will be the death of me
someday. Perhaps even today.*

She shot a resentful glare at MacLean. As usual, he
seemed oblivious of her as he leaned over to catch
something Lady Kinloss was saying. His face was in
profile, and Caitlyn admired the firm line of his jaw,
the sensual turn of his mouth, his black hair over his
brow, his skin far darker than was normal for a gentleman of fashion. Compared to the pale and fashion-

able Lord Dervishton, MacLean looked uncivilized, even a bit wild, as if his Scottish ancestors came from the battlefields and smithies, not a castle.

Yet a patrician fineness was in the straight cut of his chin, in his bold and well-defined nose. This was no common man, but a man of history and strength. A man who was fully at home at a long, burnished mahogany dining table in the largest, most ornate house Caitlyn had ever seen, yet who now, sitting astride a barely broken black gelding, seemed more like a highland marauder.

Even while dealing with a mount so difficult that it made hers seem merely impolite, he carried himself with an elegant grace that no other man could emulate.

Caitlyn stole a glance at Viscount Falkland, who was rambling on about the many horses he'd fallen from. His clothes were more fashionable with his high shirt points and exaggerated coat collar, frilled cuffs, and polished boots that positively shouted a desperate need for approbation. It was a bit of a pity, she decided, turning her gaze back to MacLean just as he looked her way, his deep green gaze burning into hers.

The second their eyes met, a jolt of pure longing raced through her, heating her from head to toe. Reflected in his face were the same reactions—desire and pure, hot lust.

Caitlyn had never wanted something more. He was so close, yet he couldn't have been more distant. Their time was over, and all that was left was his anger, and her deep, painful longing.

She forced herself to look away, though she was achingly aware of him. When she could speak, she announced, "I'm hungry."

Falkland blinked, but recovered quickly. "Me, too. It has been"—he consulted his pocket watch—"two hours since breakfast."

"I want tea," Caitlyn said. If she ate her body weight in tea cakes, then perhaps one part of her would be satisfied.

"I could use some tea," Sally agreed. She looked at Caithness. "Are you—"

"Parched beyond belief," he answered stoutly.

As Sally smiled at the young earl, a pang riffled through Caitlyn. Suddenly restless, and wishing for the ride to be over, she turned to Lady Kinloss. "Are we near the Snaid?"

Lady Kinloss didn't look pleased to be interrupted in her tête-à-tête with MacLean. "We've five more miles."

Good God, I'll starve before then. "I don't suppose there's a shortcut?"

Lady Kinloss's mouth pressed into a flat line, but her gaze flicked to the rocky field off to their right. "I suppose you could go through the field—"

"Excellent!" Caitlyn gathered her horse.

"Wait, you fool," MacLean snapped, his dark green gaze assessing the field. "That field is filled with rocks, uneven patches, and rabbit holes, and at least two fences that I can see."

Caitlyn's grasp tightened convulsively on the reins. The rocky field didn't worry her, and she was sure she could pick through any rabbit holes. But fences?

Lord Falkland turned his eager gaze her way. "If you wish to take the shorter way, I'll go with you!"

Alexander watched as Caitlyn eyed the field with a considering gaze even as she fought to keep her horse under control.

Surely she wasn't thinking of—

She gave Falkland a blinding smile that left him gaping in red-faced delight. "If you don't mind, I think I'd like to take the shortcut. It's not so very long and—"

"No." Alexander edged his horse up. "You won't."

Caitlyn's eyes sparked, her mouth thinned. "Why not?"

"Riding across such rough ground and trying to take fences on a horse you can barely control is fool-hardy beyond belief! You'll fall off and break your neck."

Falkland frowned. "If Miss Hurst wishes to ride through the field, she should be allowed."

Alexander eyed her grimly. "Have you ever taken a fence in your life?"

Her chin lifted and he could tell he'd managed to thoroughly goad her. "Of course I have," she said.

Alexander scowled. *You fool! Of all the things to lie about—*

"See? She knows what she's doing." Falkland looked at Caitlyn eagerly. "If you wish to take the fences, then

I will go with you. I can perhaps show you my technique, which is quite superior, if I say so myself."

Alexander gave a short bark of laughter. "In order to teach Miss Hurst your technique, you'd have to have one yourself."

Falkland stiffened. "Miss Hurst, I *personally* guarantee your safety!"

Alexander snapped, "Don't be a fool. If she falls, there isn't a damned thing you can do about it."

Lady Kinloss tittered. "Falkland could throw his body beneath Miss Hurst's to soften her landing." She sent a sly look at Falkland. "Of course, that could be what he's hoping for."

The viscount's face turned bright red. "You underestimate Miss Hurst's skills." He looked at Caitlyn and smiled, his expression softening. "But I appreciate them."

Lady Kinloss smirked. "Miss Hurst, I have complete trust in your horsemanship as well. It's your spirit I wonder at."

Alexander saw the exact moment Caitlyn decided to abandon common sense. She stiffened, her eyes flashed, and her hands tightened on the reins, which caused her mount to edge forward nervously.

Good God, the woman was a danger to herself. One cross word and she instantly became determined to follow whatever course lay before her, regardless of the cost.

Her chin went up and she said in a cool voice, "Lady Kinloss, I appreciate your concern, but I believe I can take the fences. They don't appear that high from here."

"Oh?" Lady Kinloss said politely, her disbelief plain upon her thin face.

Alexander could have throttled the woman. Caitlyn immediately turned her mount toward the field. The mare, seeing the wide-open spaces, gathered herself to bolt.

Before Alexander could grab her bridle, they were gone.

Lord Falkland blinked. "Goodness! I thought she'd—"

Alexander thundered after Caitlyn, who was bent low and gripped the reins and mane as if her life depended on it. And looking at the cruel outcropping of rocks that dotted the field, it probably did.

Good God, she'll be killed if she lets go.

Teeth clenched, Alexander leaned closer, urging his horse abreast of hers. It's eyes wild, Caitlyn's mount veered away, turning from the wide field and plunging toward the thick woods that lined the clearing. Alexander had to drop back and follow, the trees too close to allow him to pull up beside her. "Hang on, damn you!" he muttered through clenched teeth.

Just ahead, Caitlyn clung desperately to the horse. Her hat was long gone, her blond hair falling from the pins. Alexander locked his gaze on her bright golden hair. "Just hold on!" he shouted hoarsely, unsure if she even heard his words.

The trees thinned and a low rock wall appeared out of nowhere, covered in moss and dead limbs. On the other side, a small creek rushed, the sound filling the silence between the thudding of the hooves and Alexander's desperate breath.

If the horse took the wall, Caitlyn would fall. And it would be no soft landing, but a brutal throw into broken tree limbs and cold, slick rocks.

Alexander bent low, urging his horse to hurry. *Please,* he pleaded silently with the fates. *Please.*

Slowly, his horse gained. Just within a few strides of the wall, he reached out and grabbed the reins of her runaway mount.

Alexander turned the animal at the last possible moment, the horse neighing loudly. For a few heart-rending seconds he wasn't sure if the horse would keep its footing, but after one huge slip when its head was dangerously lowered, it straightened and cantered beside him.

Caitlyn clung to the mane, her body hugged against the horse's arched neck.

The second Alexander realized she was fine, a deep anger flared to life. The little fool could have been killed! What in *hell* was she doing on a horse like this? Yet even as he asked it, he knew the answer: it was because of his taunting. He'd pushed her, a woman who refused to be pushed, and this was the result.

Damn it all, I refuse to feel guilt for her poor judgment!

Alexander turned the horses down a short hill. The

bay yanked on the reins and pulled away, threatening to rear, but he held it steady. Finally he found a narrow clearing between some trees and he stopped, turning his horse around to face Caitlyn and her bay.

She had straightened, but her face was still pale. The afternoon light filtering through the trees was gray and uncertain, thanks to his barely contained temper, but it gleamed dimly on her golden hair. Her large eyes were even darker than usual. All around them, the woods grew misty and damp as the first drops of rain filtered between the few remaining leaves and sprinkled across them. The beads of water clung to Caitlyn's hair like diamonds in a web of gold, and his throat tightened inexplicably. The image of her delicate body broken at the foot of a stone wall . . .

She slowly released her death grip on her horse's mane and said in an unsteady voice, "Thank you for—" She closed her eyes and caught her breath before adding, "You may let go of my horse now."

"If I do, it will just bolt again."

"I won't let it."

"Damn it, must you argue with everything I say?" He was as furious with himself as with her, though he wouldn't allow her to see that. "Your horse was headed right for that wall! Do you know how fortunate you are that I was here to stop it?"

Her chin shot up, her eyes blazed, as color once again warmed her cheeks. "Perhaps I could have taken the wall!"

"And broken your damn neck!" He was shouting

and he didn't care. The wind whipped the trees over-head, rustling the branches as huge drops of water sprayed down upon them.

He'd had enough. He dismounted, looped the reins for his and Caitlyn's mounts over a low branch, then pulled her down, slipped an arm about her waist, and set her hard upon her feet.

"*Oh!* I didn't wish to get off my horse!"

"Too bad. This way, if it bolts, no one is in danger."

Her hands fisted at her sides, her chin lifting another notch. "Look, MacLean, I—"

He scooped her up and kissed her. He'd had enough with useless words and meaningless gestures. He wanted to *show* her what he meant, let her *feel* his anger. But the second his lips touched hers, something changed. The anger left and in its place was a flood of passion so hot it threatened to consume them both.

She didn't fight his embrace. The moment his mouth touched hers, she threw her arms about his neck and plastered herself to him. She was slight, and as he wrapped his arms about her and lifted, her feet cleared the ground and she was all his.

Their kiss consumed and burned, lengthening into an embrace that begged for more. Her soft mouth was intoxicating, and when her tongue brushed his lips, he moaned deeply, his passion roaring to life.

The hotter the kiss became, the more his inner voice told him to stop, to let her go, to walk away. *This is what took Charles down. This is how he began.* The thoughts cooled his ardor, but it still took every ounce of his inner discipline to finally set her down and step away.

She loosened her hold on his neck, but didn't drop her arms. She stared up at him, brown eyes wide, lips swollen and parted, a dazed expression on her face. He knew exactly how she felt.

What was it about this woman that ignited his passion in such a way? It wasn't just her beauty—he'd had plenty of beautiful women before, though none so stunning. But it was more than that. It was as if an invisible fire simmered between them that ignited at the mere brush of her skin against his.

She seemed to suddenly realize that he'd released her, and she hastily stepped away, hugging herself like a forlorn child.

Alexander's first instinct was to pull her back to him, but he fought it. *Was this how Charles had felt when he'd first met that witch who would become his wife? Had he been in the grip of just such an attraction?*

Large raindrops filtered down through the leaves, the water cooling his passion, allowing his thoughts to return to normal. *This was exactly how Charles felt, and it's why you won't allow it to affect you.* He set his jaw. "That shouldn't have happened."

"No." Her voice quivered a bit, as if she was uncertain.

"You made me angry and I—" He shrugged. "I reacted."

She took a deep breath. "You . . . you were right. Not about the kiss, but . . . you were right about the horse.

I should have told the groom I didn't have enough experience for such a mount."

The rain, plopping from the branches overhead and dripping to the dead leaves and moss of the forest floor, filled the silence. Alexander didn't know what to say. For the first time in his life, he was at a complete loss for words.

"I wasn't thinking, and I let my temper interfere with my judgment. I shouldn't have allowed that to happen."

He recognized the sincerity in her voice and knew it should have been enough; he was partly to blame for this debacle, and he knew it. Yet he wanted more from her. She *owed* him more. "You think you can do whatever you damn well want and just toss out an apology and it's over."

Her cheeks flushed and she shoved a strand of wet hair from her cheek. "No, but it's a start. Don't you apologize when you've done something wrong?"

He wished she didn't look so adorably mussed, as if she'd just been thoroughly loved, which she'd almost been. Even now, his manhood throbbed at the memory of her in his arms, of her lush breasts pressed against him, her soft mouth opening beneath his kiss— He fought a groan as a hot spear of longing ripped through him, the heat fanning his anger. "When I make a decision, it's because I've thought things out. That way I never have to apologize for a decision I've made."

"Oh! You are insufferable! And I thought *I* had too much pride! Beware, MacLean: statements like that might entice fate to teach you a lesson you well deserve."

He had to smile, though he shrugged. "I am merely speaking the truth, Hurst. If you'd stop and think before you acted, you might not have to apologize so much. You haven't ridden since you left London, have you?"

"Yes, I have. I rode the squire's extra horse."

"Oh? And is that a lively mount? As lively as Milk?"

"Milk?"

"That's your horse's name, which you would know if you'd listened to the groom."

She glanced over to where the bay was munching grass. "The squire's horse may not be *quite* as lively as Milk."

Alexander lifted a brow.

"Oh, fine, then!" She glared at him. "It was a perfect slug and wouldn't even trot, must less canter. There. Are you happy now?"

"I am if that's the truth."

She stiffened. "I'm not a liar, MacLean."

"No. You're a person who is willing to do and say whatever it takes to get what you want."

Her cheeks pinkened yet more. "I'm not like that at all!"

"I've never seen you act on anything but self-interest. You could have been hurt!"

She scowled. "I know, and so could the horse, as well, which is why I will never do such a foolish thing again. Will you *please* stop lecturing me? You sound just like my father!"

Alexander blinked. "Your father? The *vicar*?"

She nodded, her eyes suddenly gleaming with humor. "You sound *exactly* like him. 'Caitlyn, don't lean so far out your window or you'll fall!'" she mimicked. "'Caitlyn, don't run in the house or you'll trip over something.' My father's a dear, but a bit fusty."

Fusty! Alexander didn't know what to say. *No one* compared him to his or her father or to an old vicar. People called him dangerous! "You have a damn large amount of impudence."

She pushed her hair from her face. "That's exactly what Father would say—except for the *damn*. He's not one to use such language."

"Damn or no damn, it's what anyone with any common sense would say," Alexander said sharply. The wind whipped harder, rustling the trees and sending a shower of wet leaves to the ground.

Caitlyn plucked a large, wet leaf from her shoulder. "MacLean, you aren't really angry with me for accepting a horse that was more than I could handle. This is all about what happened three months ago in London."

He stiffened. "It's about your behavior and the fact that you put both yourself and your mount at risk."

Her gaze darkened. "I didn't mean to put anyone at risk—not now, and especially not three months ago. MacLean, I—"

"We are not going to discuss that now. In case you haven't noticed, it's going to rain. These sprinkles are just the beginning."

She glanced up at the sky through the break in the trees. "You made this storm."

He didn't answer but met her gaze evenly, waiting for the usual flicker of fear or a flash of envy, but all he found was a calm certainty. *She's brave, I'll give her that.* "As storms go, it's a small one, but it's still going to be wet."

"I'm not afraid of a little water," she returned smartly. "MacLean, whatever mistakes were made in London are long over. That was three months ago!"

His gaze narrowed. "Yes, but Hugh and your sister are paying for it now."

She sighed. "They're in *love*. While my thoughtless actions put them in the unfortunate position where they were forced to marry, they are happy now, and that's all that matters."

Alexander scowled. "No, that's *not* all that matters. You set a trap to force me to marry you."

Her lips thinned. "MacLean, I never wished to marry you. I was only going to hide in your carriage as you left town, showing myself after it was too late to return."

"Which would force me to offer for you."

She shrugged. "Yes, but I wasn't going to accept."

The rain began to fall in earnest, but Alexander was too stunned to notice. "You . . . you were going to *refuse* me?"

She nodded.

"Why in hell would you want me to propose if you weren't going to accept?"

"Because you said you'd never do it," she said with a touch of uncertainty. "You *do* remember saying that, don't you?"

He frowned. Had he ever . . . Oh, God. He didn't know. He'd kissed her senseless, which had the unfortunate effect of making him just as witless. Surely, he'd remember making such an arrogant statement.

She pushed her loose hair from her face, a raindrop glistening on her cheek. "I planned on refusing you and relishing every moment. I thought you'd find it humorous, too, after you realized I had no intention of going through with it." She bit her lip. "I suppose that was a bit naive."

She was telling the truth; he could read it as clearly as if it were printed across her forehead. Her plan had almost succeeded, too. His jaw tensed as the heat of the curse rippled through his veins, a hot surging that was both exhilarating and, because he knew the damage it could do, frightening. When he'd been a youth, he'd loved that feeling, had craved it. But as he grew older and saw the destruction the curse caused, he'd learned to fight it. Only one other feeling matched that pure exhilaration—the touch of a woman's hot mouth. And in his life, no woman had excited him more than Caitlyn.

The wind ruffled her skirts and tossed her golden

hair about her face. Damn it, what *was* it about this woman? Just looking at her in the leaf-covered forest, her hair damp and curling about her face, dressed in a severe, overly proper riding habit of deep brown, heated his blood. She glanced up at the rain-filled sky that peeked between the treetops, the light tracing her soft, full lips.

And once again, he understood the temptation Charles had felt when faced with his ultimate ruin, the pull of a totally sensual and inappropriate woman. Gritting his teeth, Alexander turned and strode to the horses. This was the woman who'd caused his brother harm, yet here he was, lusting after her like a slavering youth.

Disgusted with himself, he gathered the horses' reins and led them over. "We're leaving."

"But I—"

He picked her up and tossed her into the saddle, holding fast to the reins. She flashed him a hot, angry look, then hooked her knee over the pommel and arranged her skirts so that they weren't flapping down the horse's side. Her movements lacked her usual fluid grace, and he took grim satisfaction in knowing that she was as upset as he.

He leaped onto his mount and turned toward where they'd entered the woods, urging his horse forward at a hard trot and pulled her horse after him.

Caitlyn was left to hang on. Since he'd started without her foot being properly inserted in the stirrup, she had nothing to give her the leverage necessary to keep her seat. As a result, she was bounced all over the hard leather saddle. "M-M-MacLean, st-stop!" Her teeth were practically rattling in her head.

MacLean rode on, unaware or uncaring as she struggled to hang on. The wild bumping was painful and the rough pace sent her hair flying even worse. She didn't dare loosen her hold on the saddle to push her hair back until a stubborn tendril worked its way across her face, tickled her nose, and obscured her vision. Frustrated, she released one hand from the pommel.

But as she lifted her hand, her other slipped from its tenuous grasp and she fell to one side. Instantly, two large hands yanked her to safety.

Alexander had been lost in his own black thoughts when he felt rather than saw Caitlyn slip. He instinctively stopped his horse, leaned back, grasped her by one arm, and yanked her across his lap.

The skirt of her riding habit fluttered wildly as she struggled to sit upright. Cursing, he slipped an arm beneath her waist, lifted her, and settled her on his lap, her ass pressed into his groin. His body immediately responded, and he cursed again as the rain began to pour in earnest, drenching them.

She clung to him and buried her face in his shoulder, her breath warm on his neck. His body ached with awareness, and a short rumble of thunder reminded him that rain wasn't their only danger.

He quickly leaned back and tied Caitlyn's horse to the back of his saddle, then guided the horses through the small copse of trees, the rain pouring across them. With each step the horse took, Caitlyn's warm bottom rocked across his lap. The rose scent of her wet hair tickled his nose and mixed with the fresh-rain scent, and he found himself fighting the most absurd urge to settle her even more firmly against him until her full breasts pressed against his chest. A flash of desire, hot and raw, roared through him, and his arms tightened about her.

A faint tremor racked her body, and he immediately relaxed his hold. He tried to force his body to follow suit. Yet even the cold, drenching rain did nothing to quench his arousal.

She was a damnably sensual armful, and it was becoming an agony holding her in such a way. As soon as he reached the other side of the trees, the rain eased to a drizzle. He pulled his big bay to a halt and allowed Caitlyn to slide to the ground, his throat tightening as her full breasts pressed against his thigh.

"We should get you back on your mount." He climbed down and untied her horse from his saddle. "The pathway is narrow and slick, and it will be safer on separate horses."

She gathered the long train of her riding habit, blinking up at him through the rain, her lashes spiked about her large, brown eyes. "I hope we reach the inn soon; I'm cold."

"We're not going to the inn."

"But . . . that's where the group went and—"

"We're closer to the house, and I've no wish to catch

the ague." He grasped her by the waist and lifted her up on her horse. She hooked her knee over the pommel and he settled her boot into the stirrup, waiting until he saw her hook her heel firmly over the metal band.

Alexander swung up onto his own horse, then took her horse's reins and guided his horse on, careful not to go too fast now because the rain made every leaf-covered rock a potential hazard. For the next twenty minutes, they silently picked their way through a narrow stretch of woods before emerging above the house. Once they reached the drive, footmen rushed to assist them, Hay coming out with a large umbrella that he held over Caitlyn's soaked head.

Before entering the house, Caitlyn paused, grasped her hair, and twisted it, wringing water from its long length, and then followed Hay indoors. Alexander followed, trying not to watch Caitlyn and failing. Her hair was straight back from her face, and the severe style highlighted the delicate shape, her full, lush lips, and the pink-and-white cream of her skin. Her soaked brown velvet riding habit clung to her body and left nothing to the imagination. The delicate slope of her shoulders, the curve of her breasts, the flat plane of her stomach, were lovingly encased in clinging wet velvet. No woman had ever looked so good wet.

She shivered, crossing her arms and blocking his view of her breasts, which was a good thing since Alexander was certain he, and every footman in the

place, had seen her peaked nipples through that clinging velvet.

"Miss, you are freezing," Mr. Hay stated. "We must
get you into some dry clothing at once."

Or out of her wet ones and into a large, warm bed—
preferably mine.

Mr. Hay ordered footmen about and one of them
soon returned with a red-haired maid bearing a thick
wool blanket. Talking nonstop, she wrapped Caitlyn
in the blanket and led her away, a trail of water following her up the stairs.

"Good God!"

Alexander turned to find Dervishton coming from
the sitting room. He was staring up the steps at Caitlyn's retreating figure as well, pure admiration on his
face.

Irritation rifled through Alexander. He stripped off
his wet coat and handed it to a waiting footman. "I'll
need a hot bath in my room."

Mr. Hay bowed. "Of course, my lord."

Dervishton turned toward Alexander. "Her hair is
unbound. Did you see how glorious—"

"Yes." Alexander strode past Dervishton and took
the stairs two at a time, his boots squishing uncom-
fortably with each stride.

The sound of footsteps followed as Dervishton
caught up, dropping into step beside him. "Lord
MacLean, how was your ride? Or should I ask?"

Alexander stopped outside his bedchamber. "As
you can see, it was wet."

"And where is the rest of the party?"

"Miss Hurst's mount proved unruly and I had to assist her."

Dark humor lit Dervishton's eyes. "Playing nursemaid, eh, MacLean? That's not like you."

"I don't like to see a good horse get injured by his rider's incompetence," Alexander said sharply, wishing the fool would leave. Cold water was trickling down Alexander's neck and it was damnably annoying.

"I've never seen a woman look so good in rainwater as Miss Hurst." Dervishton glanced down the hallway toward the ladies' bedchambers, a hungry look in his eyes. "I'm glad you don't have an interest in the lady, for I intend on giving her a chase."

Alexander wiped water from his face. "I thought you were interested in the duchess."

"I was, but this afternoon she made herself available and . . ." Dervishton shrugged. "The charm was lost. What I really like is a good challenge. I think Miss Hurst will supply that."

"Oh, she's a challenge, all right. If I had a penny for every time I thought of strangling that woman . . ." Such as right now, for putting him through this painful conversation with Dervishton. Until these last few days, Alexander had thought Dervishton was an easygoing, rather intelligent man. Now the man's weaknesses were becoming glaringly obvious.

Dervishton lifted a brow. "You really should just go ahead and admit you have an interest in Miss Hurst."

"If I did, would you stop pursuing her?" Alexander asked bluntly.

Dervishton's eyes darkened and a smooth smile curved his mouth. "No."

Alexander shrugged. "Then why should I bother?"

"It would just mark the playing field more clearly." He waved a hand. "But you'll do what you want; you always do. As do I." Dervishton bowed and turned to leave.

"Dervishton?"

The man paused and looked back. "Yes?"

"I wouldn't get too wrapped up in a pursuit of Miss Hurst."

Dervishton's expression closed.

"While I agree she is beautiful—"

"Exceptionally so."

Alexander nodded. "She has no funds, nor is she likely to ever possess any."

Dervishton chuckled. "I don't plan on marrying the chit, any more than you did when you had your little flirtation with her in London last season."

Alexander's jaw tightened. "I see you didn't waste your time this afternoon."

"Yes, Georgiana explained how Miss Hurst served your family a bad turn. I shall be careful not to get caught in the same trap." Dervishton smiled. "I must say that I find her intriguing. She's a vicar's daughter, all purity and irksome notions of propriety. But somehow, between her prudery and the way she walks, there is a spark of something wild and naughty." A hungry expression arose in Dervishton's eyes. "So you see, she *is* my usual pursuit."

Alexander shoved his hands into his pockets to keep from planting a fist in the man's mouth. Caitlyn *was* impulsive and naturally sensual, and in the hands of an unscrupulous man, such a combination could be dangerous.

As if reading Alexander's thoughts, Dervishton added, "Whoever captures her when she finds vent for that wild flare will benefit beyond his wildest dreams."

Alexander scowled. "She will expect marriage."

"She may well be worth it." Dervishton met Alexander's gaze. "Don't you think?"

A swell of pressure grew behind Alexander's eyes, and his temper simmered to the level to tease the curse. A sudden wind swept across the roof, rattling the shingles, and the steady rain became a furious, voracious torrent.

Dervishton's smile faded as he sent Alexander a hard glance. "Careful, MacLean. You don't want to send water down Georgiana's brand-new fireplaces. She may think her house impervious to the MacLean curse, but she's wrong."

"You have no idea what the curse can do."

"But I do; I saw what happened when Callum died."

The words chilled Alexander to the bottom of his heart. Callum had been his youngest brother, the baby of their large family. A stupid taproom brawl, started under suspicious circumstances, had stolen Callum from them. Devastated and furious, Alexander and his siblings had allowed the curse free reign. The results had been deadly. The valley below the castle had flooded, lightning had caught barns and houses on fire, and hail as big as a fist had devastated fields and crops. For once started, the curse couldn't be stopped. Or so they'd believed at the time.

"Good," Alexander growled. "Then you know you'd do well not to provoke me."

"By not telling you how beautiful and exciting I find Miss Hurst?"

The shingles rattled more wildly, and somewhere in the distance, a door slammed shut.

Dervishton's gaze never wavered. "So you *are* staking a claim." He threw his hands up, though his faint smile was mocking. "If you're going to make the lady yours, I'll step back"—he dropped his hands—"for now."

Alexander frowned. "For now?"

"Once you've grown bored, I shall begin my pursuit again. I am willing to wait my turn. As I said, she's worth it." Dervishton smiled and turned away. "Just let me know when the chase has palled. I shall be waiting."

Alexander stalked inside his room, as outside, the wind swirled and slammed, rattled and banged. Rain was pounding hard and fast upon the roof.

He closed his eyes and fisted his hands at his sides, pushing his anger down . . . down . . . making it smaller, forcing it away. Slowly, his breathing returned to normal. The rain didn't change, for the storm had been stirred to life and would have to beat itself out upon the hills and mountains. But at least his temper wouldn't feed it more.

Sighing, he crossed the room to the crackling fire. Staring into the flames, he knew one thing only: he might not want Caitlyn Hurst for himself, but he damn well didn't want Dervishton or any other man to have her, either.

Chapter 6

❦

'Tis said that the MacLean curse can rattle the very center o' th' earth if they're angry enough. 'Tis a power ye dinna wish t' see and shouldna' wish t' know.

OLD WOMAN NORA FROM LOCH LOMOND
TO HER THREE WEE GRANDDAUGHTERS ONE COLD EVENING

Caitlyn bent to adjust the overskirt of her gown and winced.

"Yer arse achin' from yer ride, miss?" Muiren stooped down to move the tangled skirt.

Caitlyn straightened thankfully. "My entire backside must be bruised top to bottom. Not even the hot bath set things completely to rights."

"I'm sorry about that, miss. When ye return from dinner, I'll see if I can't find some liniment fer ye." Muiren straightened, then stood back to regard Caitlyn's gown. "Och, ye look as pretty as an angel! I've never seen such a beautiful gown."

"Thank you! I am rather proud of how it turned out." The gown was made of light brown lace over a rich cream silk underskirt that shimmered. Trimmed with cream silk bows at each shoulder and decorated with a wide cream silk sash that tied just beneath her breasts, it was modest and elegant. Most women with blond hair thought their coloring limited them to pastels, but Caitlyn found the warmer colors darkened her eyes and made her hair appear brighter.

She smoothed her hands over the skirt and admired her creation in the mirror. The back of the gown was slightly longer than the front, so that it would pull the split front panel open as she walked to reveal the silk cream undergown. "It drapes well, doesn't it?"

Muiren clasped her hands. "Och, miss, 'tis the prettiest gown I've ever seen, and I've seen me fair share. The duchess will be green wit' envy when ye go down to dinner, see if she's not!"

"Thank you. That will be most gratifying." Caitlyn picked up a small, cream-colored fan and looped it over her gloved hand. Her legs were as sore as her bottom, and she knew just who was to blame. "Sometime tonight, I hope to discuss a small matter with Lord MacLean."

Muiren quirked a brow. "Och, now, ye look serious, ye do."

"I've thought about this all afternoon, ever since I returned from our ride. It cannot be simple coincidence that the duchess, MacLean's past lover, befriended my mother and convinced her to allow me to attend the same party he was attending. Since I arrived, he's glared at me with an air of . . . it's almost a threat, but . . . I can't quite describe it."

It seemed to change from one moment to the next. One minute he was glaring at her as if he'd like to tear her limb from limb, and the next he was kissing her as if— Her cheeks heated. *As if he cared in some way and didn't like the fact.*

"Why would his lordship glare at ye?"

"He believes that something I did harmed his brother." At Muiren's considering gaze, Caitlyn hurried to add, "It *could* have, but it didn't. In fact, his brother, Lord Hugh, is quite happily married to my twin sister."

"Ye dinna say!"

"Yes. Yet MacLean still bears a grudge, and I have begun to believe he arranged that I come here for a reason."

To Caitlyn's surprise, Muiren said, "I've wondered about that meself, miss. It isn't like her grace to invite a younger, more beautiful woman to the house, not unless she can help it."

"Now that I've met her, I think the same."

"Aye, and she went out o' her way, too, which is odd, fer 'tis rare her grace will bestir herself for anyone." Muiren frowned. "If MacLean believes ye harmed his brother and wished ye nearby to cause ye harm, he could well have talked her grace into bringing ye here. MacLean's a one fer family, he is. All of them are."

"I know—but it was an honest error and no true harm was done. While I'm willing to apologize, I refuse to sit by meekly while he tries to goad me into doing something stupid." Caitlyn frowned. "I think he hopes I'll make a misstep and ruin myself."

"Ye'd never let him do tha' to ye!"

"I almost did it once already. I'd have never gotten on that horse if he hadn't egged me on." Caitlyn scowled. "Tonight I'm going to tell him that I won't accept his needling any longer."

"I've heard his man say tha' his lordship likes a glass o' port before his meals instead o' after. Perhaps if ye went down to dinner a wee bit early, ye'd find him in the library."

"That would be perfect. We could talk without any interruption."

"Just be careful, miss. The MacLeans are cursed, they are. If ye make his lordship angry—"

"I know, I know. The clouds will gather, the skies will crash and flail, and the rains will flood the earth. I know the MacLean curse backwards and forwards, thanks to my grandmother."

"Old Woman Nora knows everythin' there is to know aboot the MacLeans."

Caitlyn grinned. "That's because she has a telescope, and her house is on the opposite side of the valley from their famed castle."

"No! She's been peekin' in their windows?"

"All of the time." Caitlyn chuckled. "I'm surprised she doesn't have a permanent circle around one eye from staring into her telescope for so long."

Muiren giggled. "Och, I daresay she even knows the laird's birthmarks."

"Oh, he doesn't have any." At Muiren's surprised look, Caitlyn's face heated. "I'm sure if he had, Mam would have mentioned it." She handed the maid some hairpins. "If you'll help me with my hair, I'll try to catch MacLean before the others come down for dinner."

Though Muiren looked as if she might say more, she went to work with the pins, twisting Caitlyn's hair into an elegant mass of curls. In a remarkably short time, she stepped back and said with a note of satisfaction, "There ye go, miss."

"Thank you, Muiren. It's perfect!" The deceptively simple style had a cascade of curls framing Caitlyn's face, making her eyes appear larger than usual. "I never could have done that."

"Most women don't have such lovely curls."

"Most women don't have you for a maid, and that's the real difference." Caitlyn stood and gave Muiren a swift hug.

Muiren turned bright pink. "Thank ye, miss!"

Caitlyn grinned and said a quick good-bye before hurrying downstairs, her mind already racing ahead to MacLean. *Just speak plainly and keep your temper.* If she didn't, the overbearing laird would fluster her and she'd never pin him down about his intentions. And if he kissed her again the way he did this afternoon—

She abruptly halted outside the library and pressed her hand to her chest, where her heart thudded hotly. She hadn't allowed herself to even think about that punishing embrace all evening, afraid that her sharp-eyed maid would notice how that kiss had affected her. And, oh, had it ever. Even now, the mere thought of it, of the way he'd swept her up off her feet and held her body flush against his, of his hard mouth capturing hers, of the way his hands—

She took a shaky breath. *I must keep some distance between myself and MacLean this time!* Yet her more impulsive side whispered into her other ear, *Ah, but imagine what it would be like to be kissed again in such a way!*

But she was determined not to listen to that side ever again, especially not where Alexander MacLean was concerned. She glanced at herself in one of the long mirrors, tweaked one of the cream-colored bows, then walked through the open library doors.

The room was empty. Disappointed, she walked across the thick rug, keeping an ear open for the sound of someone coming down the stairs. As she passed a large oak desk, she paused to pick up a small book that lay open. It contained translations of stories about King Arthur, and his cousin, Culhwch, and she knew her father would have enjoyed it. In many ways, he was as much of a romantic as his mother, Mam.

She returned the book to the desk, then walked toward the tall terrace doors that lined one end of the room, the moon illuminating the last lingering storm clouds scattered across the dark sky.

The more she was around MacLean, the more she realized how little she knew about him. Their shared time in London didn't begin to encompass the complex man he was. Just when she thought she had him figured out, he surprised her. Such as today, when he'd saved her from her foolish pride by catching her runaway horse.

That moment could have ended badly, had he not been so quick to act. Though she hadn't allowed him to see it, she'd been seriously frightened. She crossed her arms over her chest and leaned against one of the terrace doors, the smooth glass cool against her shoulder.

If she wasn't careful, her pride would be the death of her. It almost physically pained her to admit that she couldn't do something, especially when someone looked as if that was exactly what he or she had suspected all along. Somehow MacLean had figured that out and used it against her, looking at her as if he thought every word she uttered was a lie.

He'd taunted her into taking the unruly horse from the groom, and she'd let him do it. She'd almost paid the ultimate price for that bit of nonsense. She sighed and rubbed her rump—

"Bruised your ass, did you?" asked a low, satisfied voice.

She hurriedly dropped her hand and whirled to face MacLean.

He stood just within the doorway, dressed in evening clothes of unrelenting black, broken only by a severely tied snowy white cravat held in place with a blindingly beautiful emerald pin. The emerald had surprised her when she'd first seen it, for she hadn't thought him the sort to wear such an obvious vanity. But it became him well and paled in color when contrasted with his frosty green eyes.

He grinned wolfishly. "Perhaps a sore bottom will teach you not to be so foolhardy in the future." His hard gaze flickered across her, lingering on her gown before lifting to her face.

She refused to allow the shiver that danced up her spine to show, gripping her hands into fists at her sides. "My lord, I'm glad to see you. I was hoping you might come here."

"To tell me of your aching ass?"

"I didn't come to discuss my injuries."

His smile disappeared. "Injuries? Did you—"

"No, no! I should have said I hadn't come to discuss my aching ass, but that seemed a bit vulgar."

He gave a burst of surprised laughter, and the warm sound bolstered her confidence. "MacLean, I came to ask a question."

Still chuckling, he said, "If you want me to give you more riding lessons, the answer is no. I daresay Dervishton would agree to do it, for the man's nothing but a fawning pup."

"I wasn't going to ask any such thing. I just want to know why you brought me here."

All traces of humor fled. "The duchess invited you, not me."

She lifted her brows in polite disbelief.

He returned her look for a minute, then went to the sideboard and poured himself a drink. He came back to the desk and leaned against it, crossing his legs at the ankles as he took a sip from the heavy cut-crystal glass.

"Well?" She crossed the room to stand beside the settee, watching him through her lashes. He was so distant, it was as if he'd surrounded himself with a wall of ice. Well, she knew how to shatter ice. "You're angry."

He merely sipped his port, but his eyes glittered with suppressed anger.

"That's what I thought," she said. "I hope this isn't about what happened between Lord Hugh and my sister. For if it is, then you, my lord, are being *silly*."

His mouth went white, his eyes flashing furiously. Outside, lightning flashed, sending a stark white flicker into the room. A deep-throated rumble of thunder followed, the floor quaking at the sound. She glanced outside and saw that in the twinkling of an eye, the storm had rebuilt and large, boiling black clouds loomed ominously overhead.

Caitlyn shivered, not just at the force of the storm brewing, but at the quickness of it. *Such power. Such power, and carried with such careless grace. How that must burden him.*

She turned back to MacLean and noted the lines beside his mouth, the way his skin had paled and how his eyes gleamed hard and bright. She'd thought those were signs of his fury, but now she wondered if they were signs of the weight of the curse—a silent acknowledgment that he didn't have the luxury to completely free his tempestuous temper—ever.

The thought staggered her. *What a horrid curse!* Caitlyn's heart ached in a new, different way. She didn't feel pity—for God knew, the man didn't inspire such an insipid emotion—but she did feel a sudden and unusually strong flash of empathy. All of her life, her grandmother had repeated larger-than-life stories of the MacLean curse. Now, facing it, Caitlyn had caught a glimpse beyond the surface.

It made her conduct in London all the more reprehensible, for she'd been curious and had tried to force MacLean into losing his temper and exhibiting the power of the curse. She'd done so without any thought of how it might affect the man, and that was inexcusable. "MacLean, this has gone on long enough. We can't keep hurting one another. We *must* talk. There are so many things I wish to explain and—"

He placed his glass of port on the desk, the heavy glass clunking on the wood as he turned on his heel and walked toward the doors.

He was *leaving*? She'd asked for a chance to explain herself, and he was going to just walk away and—

He closed the doors to the hallway and locked them, the click of the tumblers loud in her shocked silence.

Caitlyn couldn't breathe. They were alone now. The only other entrance was through the terrace doors, and with such horrid weather, no one would enter from there.

She wondered if she should ask for the doors to be left opened, but as she caught MacLean's gaze, she recognized the sardonic glint in his eyes and realized that was exactly what he expected her to do.

"Thank you. I'm glad you closed the doors; now we won't be interrupted." A surprised look crossed his face, and she had to grin.

A reluctant answering smile touched his hard mouth. "You're a bold one, I'll give you that." He returned to the desk to retrieve his glass of port. "Speak, Hurst. Now's your chance, and it's the only one I'll give you."

Ha! We'll see about that. "You've done nothing but torment me since I arrived."

He smiled at her over the edge of his glass, his eyes so dark that they appeared black. "I have not yet begun to torment you."

"MacLean, if this is about our behavior in London—"

"*Our* behavior? *Your* behavior, you mean."

"We were *both* pushing societal rules, you as much as I. We *both* had a hand in the events that forced your brother to wed my sister."

"That's not true." He swirled the port in his glass, warming it even as his gaze grew chillier. "All I did was embark on a harmless flirtation, which you apparently took for something much more."

"I did no such thing! If we'd been caught—"

"We wouldn't have been, except for your behavior," he said impatiently. "We're both adults. You've been out of the schoolroom for a long time, and you knew better than to publicly announce—"

"What do you mean, I've been out of the schoolroom for a long time? I am not an antidote."

His gaze flickered over her insultingly. "Some might say you're long of tooth."

"Oh! *You*—" She gathered her skirt and marched to where he sat on the edge of the desk. "You are just trying to distract me from the real issue. We are *evenly* at fault for what happened in London, and you know it!"

The line of his jaw tightened. "My brother went through hell when he realized he had to marry a woman he didn't even know."

"Your brother wasn't the only one to suffer! How do you think my sister felt?" Caitlyn said hotly.

"We've all suffered at your thoughtlessness. You boasted to the entire world that you would force me to offer for your hand, which set the entire ton on its ear."

Her face heated. She *had* boasted that, and it was that impulsive indiscretion that had brought her sister racing to London to halt the whispers. "MacLean, I don't—"

"Had our siblings not married, it would have been a huge scandal. It was weeks before the ton could speak of anything else, and my name was tossed about like chaff on the wind." The wind rattled against every window in the house as if trying to beat its way inside.

"Ah!" Her gaze narrowed. "You're not angry about your brother at all. You're angry because you were made a fool in front of the *bon ton*!"

A flash of white illuminated the room, followed by a deafening crack of thunder that made the decanter tremble on its silver tray. MacLean came off the desk, moving with a deadly intent that froze her in place.

He grasped her by the shoulders and yanked her close, his face only inches from hers as he snarled, "I will not be made a fool of by a chit like you! *Not now. Not ever.*"

The nerve of this man! "Ha! If that's all it takes to make a fool of you, then you'd best expect it to happen again—and *soon*!"

Hot white lightning blinded her as his warm hands slipped from her shoulders to encircle her throat. She gasped as his thumbs came to rest on the delicate skin where her pulse beat.

Caitlyn found herself staring directly in his green, green eyes. Had any other man held her so, she'd have been frightened. Instead, she felt oddly excited and had to fight an urge to lean forward, to move even closer. He was not a man to harm women; he would scorn those who did. The danger came from her reaction to his touch.

She was agonizingly aware of him, of his height, of the breadth of his shoulders, of the bold line of his nose and the gleam of his unusual eyes, of the fall of his hair over his forehead. Every aspect of him was magnified and distinct, even the faint scent of sandal-wood soap on his hands.

Caitlyn grasped his wrists and moved forward, into his arms. His brows lowered, and as if against his will, his hands slid to the back of her neck, his fingers deliciously warm as they traced across her nape.

A shiver danced through her, raising goose bumps, tightening her nipples and making her breath ragged. She struggled to think. She had to close her eyes and take a breath before she could say, "MacLean, why did you have the duchess invite me to her house party?"

He leaned close until his lips were by her ear, his port-flavored breath warm. "I had Georgiana bring you here so that I could punish you for what you did to me and my family."

Caitlyn opened her eyes. "Punish me?"

"I will ruin you, the way you would have been had your sister not rescued you from your folly."

She pulled back and stared up at him. He was deadly serious. He meant what he said—and he could do it, too. She glanced at the closed door, and he chuckled softly. "Exactly."

Why, oh why, had she allowed him to close the door? She'd been so wrapped up in trying to appear in command of the situation that she'd even thanked him. *Blast my rebellious nature.*

One could cross society's rules only if one had enough clout, and never publicly. Not that he needed the aid of a closed door. The sad truth was that, for a woman, a hasty word or an embrace—even unwanted—could be enough to tarnish her name and banish her and her family from society. And unless the lady was from one of the leading families, there would be no second chances. "Blast it, MacLean, you must let go of this misguided notion of revenge."

"Misguided?"

His voice was soft and threatening, yet deep and warm, like his hands. The goose bumps renewed and she shivered, finding her gaze locked on his firm, sensual mouth. What she wouldn't give to feel those lips again. Perhaps she'd imagined the feel of them and had exaggerated her reaction in her mind. Suddenly, she needed to find out . . . *now.*

"What are you doing?"

She leaned against him, slipping her hands about his waist, pressing against him. "I was thinking . . ." Only she wasn't thinking at all; she was already in action. She pressed herself to him and kissed him, unable to resist the lure of that finely chiseled, hot mouth that was too close, too tempting.

He gathered her hard against him, his strong hands molding her to him.

She moaned, opening her mouth to him, her entire body aflame. God, how she loved his hands on her, the warmth of his touch even through her clothing. He slid a hand to her breast and traced his thumb over her nipple, which was hard through the thin silk of her gown and chemise. Caitlyn gripped his coat and yanked him closer, desperate to close the small distance between them, wanting to—

"*No.*" His hands closed around her wrists and he yanked her hands from his coat and stood glaring down at her, his breathing as harsh as hers.

She struggled to think, to pull her gaze from his mouth, now pressed into a firm, straight line. "No, *what*?" How could he want to stop something that felt so good?

With a muffled curse, he turned and strode to the desk, where he grabbed his glass of port and took an angry swallow.

She rubbed her arms, chilled. "MacLean, I—"

He slammed the glass onto the desk, port sloshing onto its surface as he sent her a furious look. "What happened in London was a mistake I won't repeat, no matter how you try and tempt me. Had you not been such a flirt—"

She stiffened. "*Flirt?*"

"Why else do you think Falkland and Dervishton are so hot on your trail? Of course, such flirtations rarely last. You're not mature enough to hold the interest of a *real* man."

Caitlyn gripped her elbows tightly, fighting an answering flare of anger. "I enjoyed our flirtation in London. But if that makes me a flirt, then it makes *you* one, too, my lord. Because for every sin I committed, you did the same."

"I never attempted to trick you into a fraudulent offer of marriage."

"No, but you challenged me to do it, which makes you just as responsible!"

"Like hell I did!"

She plopped her hands on her hips. "Did you or did you not say you'd never ask me to marry you in a million years?"

He frowned. "I didn't—"

"*Oh!*" Caitlyn couldn't believe her ears. "Your exact words were, 'Hurst, there's no way in hell I'd ever ask you to marry me, *and there's nothing you could do to make me.*'"

"I—" He froze in place, his brows contracting, realization plain on his face.

She nodded, smugly pleased. "At the Manderleys' soiree, on the terrace."

"That wasn't meant as a challenge."

"And how would you have viewed it, if someone had said that same thing to you?"

He glowered and opened his mouth to respond, but she held up a hand. "*Honestly*—what would you have done?"

He made an impatient gesture. "Whatever I did, it would have been discreet, not have been performed in the full glare of public censure—which is what made your actions untenable."

"Discreet? Like the time you kissed me in the antechamber at Devonshire House, and the prince walked in?"

He looked thunderous. "That was an error of judgment, but one instance doesn't—"

"And the time at the Treveshams' dinner party, when you pulled me into an empty sitting room and the butler came in to collect something, and we had to hide under the settee until he left and Lady Trevesham walked—"

"*Enough!*" He clamped his mouth firmly shut, the wind furiously beating against the windows, the panes clattering in their frames. "You can't count those. You teased me mercilessly and—"

"*I* teased *you*? You, you, you—" She fisted her hands and advanced on him until they were toe-to-toe. "I wish my original plan had worked! I wish you had been forced to offer for me, just so I could have had the pleasure of *refusing* you!"

His jaw tightened and rain slashed across the terrace doors.

"Oh, keep your blasted rain and wind; it doesn't scare me one bit! You'd be *lucky* if I married you, and you know it!"

His mouth turned white, his eyes a brilliant, hard green, his wounded pride emblazoned across his furious face. He towered over her, angry and threatening. "They don't make enough port to get me inebriated enough to ask you to marry me, regardless of whether you were 'ruined' or not."

"That's— Why, you— Oh!" She stomped her foot. "MacLean, if I wished to, I could *make* you want to marry me!"

"Like hell." A cold smile that was no smile turned up one corner of his mouth, and he bent down until his eyes were level with hers. "But I *know* I could make you come to my bed willingly—without the sanctity and disaster of a marriage."

"Not in a million years! There's no way in ... in ... in *hell*!" The word curdled on her tongue, but she said it anyway.

MacLean's brows flew up and he burst into a deep, rich laugh that surprised them both.

Outside, the wind abated a bit, and Caitlyn let out a frustrated sigh. "I'm glad you find this funny, for I don't."

He grinned now, dark and wicked. "Hurst, sometimes you are so very much a vicar's daughter." His smile turned wolfish. "What do you say to a little wager? If I win, you come to my bed."

She fought an instant picture of herself in his bed, his large hands moving over her bared skin. Instantly her stomach tightened and her nipples tingled as if his hands were even now cupping her breasts.

If she closed her eyes, she could see him— warm-skinned and deliciously masculine. For the briefest moment, she wondered if losing would be so bad . . . Then she met his gaze and there was no mistaking the superior air that he regarded her with.

He doesn't think I have a chance! Why, that fiend! "And when *I* win," she snapped indignantly, "then you will go down on bended knee before the entire party here and ask for my hand in marriage. In front of *everyone*, MacLean."

MacLean shrugged. "Fine. It doesn't matter what you wager, for I'll be damned if I let you win anything."

"As if you could stop me." *I can picture him on his knee before me, asking for my hand while the duchess glowers in the background.* It was too delicious! "But I should give you fair warning: I may decide to say yes to your offer of marriage just to irk you. Then where will you be?"

"Then you will have one very angry husband."

She grinned. "If you're angry, then you'll have a very *happy* wife."

His hands curled into fists and she thought for an excited moment that he would reach out and grab her again, but instead he said in an icy voice, "We've set the stakes. Name the conditions."

Conditions? Good God—how did one set conditions for such a wager? A wager of his freedom against her virtue. She swallowed, the enormity of what they were doing settling about her like a cold mist. Blast it, what was it about him that always made her forget her vow to remain calm and unflustered?

Whatever it was, she was going to put an end to it once and for all. She had to construct the conditions in a way that benefited her, and not this great lummox who could outride her, outrace her, and outdo her in every physical way. But what? She glanced around the room, seeking inspiration and not finding it . . . until her gaze fell on the open book on the desk she'd seen on entering the library. With startling clarity, an idea instantly formed.

She whirled around MacLean and reached for the book. "I know exactly what we'll do."

"What's that?" His voice was softer now, edged with suspicion.

She flipped through the pages eagerly. "We will set this wager to follow the tale of Olwen and Culhwch."

"Who?"

She almost chuckled. He didn't know the legend and she did, which could be an excellent advantage. She flipped through the pages quickly, excited at the idea of having this proud and arrogant man at her feet. "My father loves this tale and used to read it to us when we were children."

"How fortunate for you," MacLean said in a dry tone.

Caitlyn ignored him. "Olwen and Culhwch are of Arthurian legend. Culhwch, King Arthur's cousin, was cursed by an evil stepmother to fall in love with only one woman—Olwen. The trouble was, Olwen's father was a very large, very angry giant. In order to win Olwen's hand, Culhwch was sent to perform a series of deeds to prove himself." She tapped her finger on the text. "We'll use this old myth as the basis of our wager."

"That's preposterous."

She lifted her brows and said coolly, "You said I could set the conditions, did you not?"

He glowered. "I suppose I did."

"Culhwch's tasks were fairly basic: find the sweetest honey of the season; fetch a razor, scissors, and comb, and mirror from between the ears of a wild boar; and such."

"Fetching a mirror from between the ears of a wild boar is *basic*?" He took the book and frowned down at it. "This is a ridiculous idea."

"No, it's not. The quest for honey can be just that, for it needs no translation. The items from the boar's head could be . . ." She bit her lip, then brightened. "I know! It could be the bow from Lady Kinloss's dog."

MacLean shook his head, although he gave a faint smile. "Lady Kinloss's dog is indeed a bore."

Caitlyn fought an urge to grin in return. "That's a very poor pun."

"Most of them are." MacLean paged through the book. "So how do you propose to do this, Hurst?"

"We must each complete three tasks based on the myth."

"Sounds fair. Who sets them?"

"We set them for each other. Furthermore, I don't want the other guests involved, and I don't think you do, either."

"Definitely not."

She nodded toward the book. "Do you see any tasks that look intriguing to you?"

Looking skeptical, he nonetheless turned a few pages. "Perhaps."

"Then do you agree to follow the tasks set in the myth, so we can settle this issue between us once and for all?"

Alexander closed the book and tapped it against the palm of one hand as he considered her. He had to admit she was making it tempting, for it would add sweetness to not only best her, but to do it at her own game.

Still, it wouldn't do to accept too quickly, so he shrugged. "I don't know, Hurst. When I suggested that you set the conditions, I assumed you'd fix upon something more common, like the turn of a card or a race of some sort."

Her chin lifted and she walked right up to him, her dark brown eyes sparkling with mischief. "What's wrong, MacLean? Afraid of a little competition?"

Alexander's body reacted immediately to her nearness. "It's an inordinate amount of trouble, but"—he allowed his gaze to travel across her in a suggestive manner, lingering on her breasts and hips—"I can think of nothing I'd enjoy more than to see you lose, and watching you struggle through your tasks will only make it the sweeter."

"We'll see who loses." She gave him one of those damned mysterious, feminine smiles that made his body flame to life, then she turned away, her fingers trailing along the small side table, absently brushing over a silver-filigreed candy dish.

Alexander watched, wondering how that feather touch would feel on his cock, which was even now straining to get to her. *Damn it, but she ignites me.*

She turned her head, and for an instant her pure profile was in stark relief against the darkened terrace door windows. "It'll be good for you to engage in a competition against someone who isn't afraid of your temper."

"People aren't afraid of me."

"Oh?" She looked back over her shoulder at him in a flirtatious move as old as Eve. "You believe that? You crash and thunder your way over everyone, then pretend that no one cares about your curse." She gestured toward the gardens where he knew limbs would be strewn across the hedges. "How could someone not be?"

"You're not."

She sent him an impatient look. "Because I grew up listening to tales about you and your clan. I knew of the curse from the time I was old enough to climb on my granny's knee."

"Ah yes. Old Woman Nora is your grandmother. Hugh mentioned that when I saw him last." Alexander knew Old Woman Nora well, and he had no love for the village healer. She was a capable witch, he'd give her that, and he'd trust her with his life if he ever needed a healer. But he also knew that she was a busybody and gossip who spent far too much time analyzing his business.

Caitlyn turned to face him, one other hand resting on her hip as she regarded him with a taunting smile. "Well, MacLean? Are we decided? The myth sets our tasks. Three each, decided by the other. And no inclusion of the other guests allowed."

The sight of her, so elegant and so damnably tempting, raised his blood, and he was astonished at his impulse to just give her this and anything else she wanted. *Damn it, what's wrong with me? I'm no lapdog to be led about by a chit who looks too young to be out of the schoolroom!*

He set the book on the desk. "I'm not a man to play such silly games; we'll find another, more usual avenue."

She looked at him pityingly. "Perhaps you're right. You're far too mature to engage in anything truly enjoyable and fun. I suppose a man your age must be cautious of his dignity at all times."

A man your age? She thought he was too *old*? Too old to partake in such a silly game; too old to perform her tasks. *Too old for her.* He didn't move a muscle, but his blood roared in protest and the storm outside echoed it.

The most irritating part was that she was merely throwing his own words back at him, when he'd told her she wasn't mature enough to be of interest to a real man. She'd deftly turned the tables.

Alexander slammed his hands onto the desk.

She jumped, her color high, her lips parted.

He leaned forward. "I accept."

For a long second, she just looked at him, then a pleased expression entered her eyes. She walked to the desk, so gracefully that it was painful to watch, placed her hands on the opposite side, and leaned forward until she was within tantalizing reach. "Then we're agreed, MacLean. Shall we say the best out of three?"

They were face-to-face over the smooth oak surface, their poses militant. His first impulse was to reach across the desk, grasp her by the waist, and pull her to his side. There, he'd plunder her sweetness, brand her with his kiss, and *show* her what he was capable of, regardless of his age.

But that was how things had gone so awry last time. She'd tempted, and he, like the most callow of youths, had succumbed. This time, it wouldn't be *him* left panting with desire. This time it would be her.

He leaned forward until his lips were within an inch of hers. Her warm brown eyes seemed almost liquid, her flawless skin silky. "I'm up to any challenge you dare to name."

"*Any?*"

His gaze roamed boldly over her. They were so close to one another that he could feel the heat of her creamy skin. "I'll accept your conditions, but realize this: if I lose, I'm risking my freedom, which you've admitted you might well take should the mood suit you. So if I win, I want more from you than a tumble in my bed."

Her gaze grew wary. "What more is there?"

He grinned, relishing the worry in her voice. "If I win, then not only will you come to my bed, but you'll become my mistress for two entire weeks—and you'll do it in front of the entire world."

He could see the pulse beating wildly in her delicate throat. She attempted to swallow, but could not. Finally she managed to say huskily, "Done."

"When *I'm* done, you'll be sorry you ever set eyes on me."

Her chin lifted, and she whispered with such sincere regret that all humor fled, "It's too late for that, my lord. Far too late." She turned on her heel and walked away, her hips beckoning as she left.

She opened the door, then looked back. "We'll discuss the particulars tomorrow, after breakfast. That should give us time to decide the first tasks."

He nodded once, his body so aflame that he didn't dare risk speaking. With a sense of profound relief, mixed with a staggering sense of disappointment, he watched her slip out of the room and disappear from view.

Alexander turned and leaned against the desk, his hand closing around his glass. He took a hard gulp, then another. It was a sacrilege to drink good port in such a way, but he didn't give a damn. In a short week or two, he'd have Caitlyn Hurst at his mercy. She'd be his in bed.

He smiled, already savoring his victory. He'd dress her in scandalous clothing that showed her delectable figure to one and all. He'd escort her all over London, place her in his high-perch phaeton, and drive her down St. James's Street past the bow window at White's, something a genteel lady would never do. Then he'd escort her to Vauxhall Gardens and have her sit with the other ladybirds on display there. He'd humiliate her so thoroughly that there would be no last-minute saving by a sister or brother or anyone else.

For two weeks, she'd be his to do with as he wished, in bed and out. And, oh, how he'd take pleasure in that.

From out in the hallway, he heard Dervishton's voice raised in greeting as Caitlyn joined the others waiting for dinner.

Alexander tossed back the rest of his port and left the library. Soon he'd have his revenge, and Caitlyn Hurst would learn a lesson in humility she'd never forget.

Chapter 7

❦

Always fight fair. Those as fight dirty will find tha' the mud on their hands lets their enemies slip awa' every time.

OLD WOMAN NORA FROM LOCH LOMOND
TO HER THREE WEE GRANDDAUGHTERS ONE COLD EVENING

lexander reached blindly for a towel. "Did you discover anything new about Miss Hurst?"

"Oh, yes." MacCready placed a fresh towel into Alexander's hand and waited until he'd dried his face. "In fact, I discovered several things about the young lady. Lord Falkland is planning on surprising her with a picnic after breakfast. He heard from the young lady's maid that Miss Hurst is especially partial to roasted beef and strawberries, and he's had Cook in a tizzy trying to procure the berries."

Alexander handed the damp towel to the valet. "The fool. Anything else?"

"Miss Hurst is apparently a rather indifferent correspondent. She's begun no fewer than four missives home, but hasn't finished a one."

Alexander wasn't one for letter writing, either. Reading, though, was a different matter altogether. He rarely left home without the company of a good book. He thought of the way Caitlyn had paged through the small leatherbound book last night, with a comfort and familiarity that indicated someone used to being around books. She was obviously a reader.

He caught his reflection in the mirror and was startled to see a satisfied smile curving his lips. Shocked, he scowled. *Damn it, what does that matter if she reads or not?* Since Hugh's marriage, Alexander had thought so much about Caitlyn Hurst that he felt as if he knew her, and his assessment had been of the darkest, most insulting kind.

Now that he was face-to-face with her and not just stewing over her selfish manipulations, he was forced to recognize all of the seductive and alluring things about her that had made him pursue her to begin with.

Of course, that didn't make his previous assessment less accurate; her true nature was obviously impulsive and self-centered. But now a part of him whispered that perhaps . . . just perhaps . . . his faults were just as much to blame as hers had been.

He shook off the disturbing thoughts. "What else have you found out?"

"Lord Dervishton has been making inquiries as to the location of her ladyship's bedchambers—" At

Alexander's sharp look, MacCready added in a sonorous tone, "As you were doing just two days ago."

He had been, though he doubted it was for the same reason. He'd just wanted to know the location of his enemy. Dervishton's motives were less pure.

Damn Dervishton. "I don't trust that man. Tell the footmen to keep an eye on him."

"My lord, this isn't our house. I can't—"

"Fine. I'll tell Georgiana to see to it. Anything else?"

MacCready's mouth thinned in annoyance, but all he said was "The maids are in a tizzy over the quality of Miss Hurst's wardrobe, and there are rumors she sewed it all herself. The footmen are half in love with her, which has caused some strife among some of the staff, as you can imagine. One individual has even gone so far as to stock her fireplace with twice the wood necessary, and as a result a large log hit the floor at two this morning, startling Miss Hurst and scaring Lord Caithness."

Alexander whirled on MacCready. "They were together?" His voice was dark and dangerous.

MacCready's brows lifted. "No, my lord. Lord Caithness's room is directly below Miss Hurst's."

Alexander realized he was glowering at his valet. *Bloody hell, I need to calm down. The sooner Caitlyn and I get this business settled, the better.*

The valet held out a freshly laundered shirt. "Lord Caithness's man informed me this morning that his lordship actually leapt from bed and hit his head on the bedpost, which caused quite a commotion, as you can imagine."

"So long as he was in his own room, I don't give a damn if he split his head open."

"Pardon me, my lord, but do I detect a hint of jealousy? I thought we *disliked* Miss Hurst."

"We do." *But she's mine, and I'll be damned if I allow every buck at Georgiana's house party to land hands on her before I do.* Alexander pulled the shirt over his head. "Did you discover anything else about Miss Hurst?"

"Yes. In addition to roast beef and strawberries, Miss Hurst is also fond of walnuts and marmalade."

"She likes pears, too," Alexander muttered.

"Pardon me, my lord?"

"Just thinking aloud."

"Hmm. Am I still to collect useless information or have I given you enough to satisfy your curiosity?"

"Keep collecting."

"But I don't know what I'm looking for."

"I'm sure you'll eventually hear something." Something Alexander could use when planning these "tasks" they were to complete.

He couldn't believe he'd allowed Caitlyn to talk him into such a silly game, but God knew he'd enjoy taking her to his bed, and having her as his mistress would be particularly sweet. His body warmed at the thought.

Perhaps this was for the best. Had she a mind to, she could easily keep herself surrounded with the sycophantic idiots who seemed to have taken over Georgiana's house party. She was usually more intelligent about whom she included on her guest list.

Alexander finished dressing and made his way toward the breakfast room, where the quiet told him that he was unfashionably early.

He turned on his heel and strode into the library and went to stand before the terrace doors. The storms had passed and left the grass and leaves a pale orange and tan against the winter brown. Here and there a tree was down, and the lawn was scattered with broken branches and dead leaves, but other than that there was little damage. He rubbed his chin as he surveyed the mess, glad he hadn't allowed himself to get too furious. In his youth, he hadn't been able to control his temper. And when he'd been older and Callum had died . . . He closed his eyes against that memory. His youngest brother had been full of life and laughter. His smile could light any room, his temperament mercurial and swift. He'd been the center of the family until he'd been killed at the age of nineteen.

At the time they'd blamed the Kincaid family, and Alexander and the rest of his brothers had been set on vengeance. Fortunately, their sister, Fiona, had stepped in. Her solution had been to marry that wastrel Jack Kincaid to stop the erupting feud, but Alexander supposed it had worked out for the best. For all of his failings, Jack seemed to be a good husband and a devoted father. Of course, that could be because he knew if he ever stepped a foot out of line, Fiona's four brothers would take it out of his hide. Surely the man knew better th—

"MacLean?"

He turned and found Caitlyn walking toward him. She was dressed in a cream-colored gown that had bows and gewgaws at the rather high neckline. But the bows accentuated her curves nonetheless.

She came to stand beside him, her hands clasped before her. "I'm glad to have found you alone. Have you been thinking of the tasks?"

He regarded her sourly, irritated that she managed to look so damnably *tempting*. Worse, when other women's eyes looked puffy or red in the morning, hers sparkled, her emotions plain within. It was a pity such beauty hid such a questionable character. "You're excited about this."

"More than you know. I love winning."

The minx. "I thought of a task or two."

"So have I." Her eyes bright, her cheeks flushed, she leaned forward, gesturing earnestly. "I have your first task and it's simple."

"I'm to find a pig with a hair comb between its ears?"

"I'm saving that for later. There is a beehive along the drive to the house. Bring me a piece of it."

"That's it?"

She smiled smugly. "I should think that would be enough. It's *very* high in the tree."

This would be astonishingly easy. "Fine." His gaze lingered on her golden hair, on the thick sweep of her ridiculously long lashes, on the rich chocolate of her eyes— He stirred restlessly, his jaw tightening. All of his life, Alexander had surrounded himself with beauty—in his castle, his fashionable town house in London, in the fine clothes he wore and the excellent horses he rode. He didn't always find beauty where others found it, so there was rarely competition for what he wanted.

But now he wanted *this* particular beauty. He wanted Caitlyn's lush, sensual beauty in his hands, against his naked body, in his bed. He wanted to taste her, to enjoy her, to *own* her. And he wanted her now, this very second.

Just seeing her standing by the tall terrace doors, the morning sun warming her skin, sent primal lust thundering through his veins. She had but to look at him from beneath her lashes and his cock sprang to attention as if she were a general and it a lowly soldier.

She looked at him now and smiled. "Have you thought of a task for me?"

He had, but his irritation made him shrug and turn away. "I don't remember the myth well enough to—"

"Then we'll look at the story." She swept to the desk and perched on the edge as she picked up the book. "My father is quite a literary scholar, and he's particularly fond of Welsh fairy tales so I know this one frontward and back."

"Oh?" More to amuse himself than because he particularly cared about Arthurian legends, he followed her to the desk and settled himself into a chair where he had full view of his fair opponent.

"Father's convinced that Arthur was of Welsh decent. He . . ." She rattled on, but Alexander didn't follow a word. His entire attention was on the rounded ass perched just feet away from him at eye level. A rounded ass barely covered by thin muslin that was caught tightly beneath one luscious cheek.

He curved his hand, imagining cupping her to him. As he watched, she shifted as if the desk was too hard for such a firm ass. That ass deserved a softer seat. Perhaps his lap, although right now it was anything but soft. In fact, his cock was so hard he—

". . . do you think?"

Alexander blinked, forcing his gaze to her face and away from that tempting ass. "Pardon me?"

She frowned impatiently. "I was giving you suggestions for a task."

He wondered how warm those rounded cheeks would be beneath that thin muslin gown. He could almost reach over and—

"MacLean!" Her gaze narrowed and followed his gaze to— "Blast it!" She dropped the book and hopped off the desk, a delicious pink flushing her skin. "You were looking at my behind!"

He smiled and leaned back in his chair, lacing his hands behind his head. "Yes."

She plopped her hands on her hips. "What do you mean, 'yes'?"

"What else should I say?"

"You should apologize for being so improper."

"As I recall, you were no proponent of proper behavior when you were in London. In fact, I remember one time when you dragged me behind a curtain at a ball and gave me a very improper kiss."

She flushed but met his gaze steadily. "Our relationship just kept escalating, and I should have resisted more." She shook her head. "But I didn't."

"You never once said no to anything I suggested. I had the impression that no matter what I said, you'd agree."

"You kept challenging me, and that's my weakness, as you know. But, that was before, and this is now. We will be careful not to engage in anything improper."

Alexander lifted a brow, amused and oddly uneasy with her admissions. "We will?"

A definite tone of regret was in her voice when she said, "I must, for I promised my mother."

Alexander blinked. "I beg your pardon?"

"I promised her I would set things right and not engage in impulsive behavior."

"Impulsive? Like our wager?"

"That isn't impulsive," Caitlyn said just a touch too swiftly. "I know exactly what I am doing."

Alexander rubbed his mouth to hide a surprised grin. He didn't know what to make of this woman.

One moment she was beguiling him and every other male within a five-mile range with her seductive grace and fine eyes, and the next she was as disarming as a child, challenging him to do something totally foolish such as fetch a piece of an abandoned beehive.

As disarming as a child . . . That said it all. His smile faded. Georgiana had been right; Caitlyn Hurst was too young for him. Society was filled with examples of uneven and poorly thought-out unions, just like Charles's. Such uneven matches invariably began with the men in control, but ended with the women leading their older, smitten men around by the nose until they had no pride left.

"What's your task for me?" Caitlyn asked.

She picked up the small leather book and opened it.

He rose and took the book from her. "I'll find one myself, thank you. I want to find something suitably wretched for your first task. Now be quiet while I look."

She was able to sit quietly for less than twenty seconds, sighing loudly and crossing and then uncrossing her arms. Alexander knew the exact time because he watched the clock. She really couldn't sit still, could she?

Finally, he lowered the book. "Hmm."

"What?"

He shrugged and lifted the book again.

She managed to keep silent for less than ten seconds this time. "MacLean! Surely you've already decided what to—"

He closed the book. "Fetch me the magic cauldron: Roxburge's golden snuffbox."

She tried to hide a wince but failed miserably.

He chuckled. "It will be difficult, to say the least. The duke keeps that snuffbox beside him day and night. You'd have the devil of a time getting it from him, especially without any of the other guests knowing." He placed the book on the desk. "So all I must do is bring you a piece of a particular bee-hive?"

Caitlyn fought a smug smile. According to one of the footmen, the hive was in a tall tree, high off the ground. "You'll find the hive where the drive turns in from the main road."

"Done."

"It won't be that easy. It's well up the tree." She eyed his clothes. "I daresay you'll get dirty before the day's out."

"We'll see, won't we?" He crossed his arms over his chest. "It shouldn't be too difficult; unless they're honeybees, the hive will be empty."

Caitlyn felt her smile freeze in place. "What?"

He looked amused. "The queen sleeps for the winter, along with a few drones, but the majority of the hive dies off."

She scowled. "Oh."

"You didn't know that?"

"No, I thought they— Oh, blast. It doesn't matter." She hadn't wished him hurt, of course, but she'd hoped to make it more difficult. Now she'd given him a ridiculously easy task, while he'd given her an extremely difficult one.

Lord Roxburge was notoriously attached to his snuffbox, and she had to procure it, show it to MacLean, then return it before his lordship even knew it was gone. Well, she simply needed to be careful and clever. "I hope to get the snuffbox by tomorrow."

"I'll definitely have your piece of beehive by tomorrow. I'd do it today, but I promised her grace I'd assist her in choosing a mount for the ride tomorrow." His lips twitched. "I'd say her skill on horseback is just a hair over yours."

Caitlyn wanted to smack the smirk off his face. Instead, she managed an unaffected shrug. "I'll have to make your next task more difficult."

MacLean grinned and headed for the door. "Feel free, Hurst. Just know that I'll do the same. Now, if you'll excuse me, I must have my breakfast."

She watched him walk out the door and cross the hallway to the breakfast room. Once he was out of sight, she threw herself into a nearby chair and wondered how on earth she was going to sneak off with the duke's snuffbox without raising a hue and cry.

What she needed to do was think like MacLean, who knew how to flirt with a woman right under society's easily-out-of-joint nose. He knew when to sweep someone away, when to yank the curtains closed, when to sneak off so no one noticed—and when not to.

She nodded to herself. She'd borrow from *his* all-too-familiar book, which would add to her pleasure when she won. He might have been the master of their battle in London, but she would win the war when she won their wager.

Immensely cheered by the thought, she arose and went in search of Muiren to see what she could find out about the duke and his snuffbox.

Chapter 8

Lassies, if ye hold back yer curiosity, yer fears, an' yer desires, then ye'll ne'er truly live.

Old Woman Nora from Loch Lomond
to her three wee granddaughters one cold evening

"Och, miss! I'm sure ye'll find a way to fetch the duke's snuffbox."

"I have to." Caitlyn hadn't intended to tell her plight to Muiren, but the tale had slipped out when she'd asked the maid about the duke's fascination with that blasted snuffbox. According to the conditions set for the wager, only the other *guests* should be kept in the dark about their efforts, not the servants. That suited Caitlyn well; Muiren's information was useful, if daunting.

According to Muiren, Roxburge had had a bizarre attachment to his snuffbox since he'd first purchased it twelve years ago; it was almost always in his hand or placed in plain sight. It was maddening. Last night, the box had sat at the side of Roxburge's plate all during dinner. Though he removed his hand from it while he ate, the second he finished, he would nervously grasp it and flip the lid open and shut, over and over. She didn't know how the duchess stood it.

The rest of the time, the box stayed in his pocket unless he was shining it with his sleeve. Her only hope was that he'd drop it or look away from it long enough so that she could slip it into her pocket. Waiting and hoping for her chance, Caitlyn had determinedly stayed in the duke's presence all day. When the rest of the guests had taken carriages out for a picnic at a gazebo built on a picturesque bluff overlooking Loch Lomond, she'd pleaded a headache and the desire to sit quietly and read. MacLean had been amused, but he'd left with the rest of the group, the duchess clinging annoyingly to his arm.

While the party was out having fun, she'd sat in the library, watching the duke snore in a chair across from her, his snuffbox safely secured in a pocket. Thank goodness Lord Falkland had remained behind and kept her company, or she'd have gone mad with boredom.

All she needed was one chance—a few seconds would do it—to grab the box. Luckily, Muiren was a constant source of ideas. While most of them were wildly improbable, they at least kept Caitlyn's spirits up.

The maid now handed a mirror to Caitlyn so she could see the red rose placed in the curls over her ear. "What if ye tripped his grace an' got the snuffbox then?"

Caitlyn placed the mirror back on the dressing table and tightened the sash on her robe. "I can't trip the duke! He's old and feeble."

Muiren looked regretful. "Och, I suppose ye're right. Ye canna hurt him." The maid was silent a moment, adjusting a hairpin. "It's too bad ye canno' just snatch it from the dinner table tonight."

"But then I'd have to explain myself to the other guests, and they can't know what MacLean and I are doing."

The maid sighed. "It's no' the quest as is so difficult. 'Tis all of the rules."

Caitlyn frowned. "There has to be a way to get that dratted snuffbox! Yesterday I couldn't even get close to the blasted thing, and today was no better. MacLean is going to hand me that piece of beehive any minute now, and I won't have a thing to show for my own task!"

"Aye, the duke even sleeps with the box under his pillow. I asked his man jus' this morning. Ye'll have to get it from him at dinner this evenin'. That's all there is to it."

Caitlyn leaned her elbow on her dressing table and plopped her chin in her hand. "There must be a way—"

There was a knock on the door, and the housekeeper stepped inside carrying Caitlyn's green evening gown. Mrs. Pruitt was short and round, with two chins and a stern, sour expression that made her look as if she could easily be a termagant.

Muiren hurried to curtsy. "Och, Mrs. Pruitt!"

"Sorry to bother ye, miss," Mrs. Pruitt said to Caitlyn. "I brought yer gown. Muiren here had the laundress iron the flounces."

"Oh, thank you!" Caitlyn was particularly proud of the gown. It was a round gown of green Urling's net over a white satin slip, the bottom trimmed with lace flounces festooned with bouquets of roses and bluebells. It had taken her almost two weeks to get the flounces to lie just right, and after much thought, she'd added an extra row of lace to the bottom of the overskirt, which made it softly drag the floor as she walked and added a little drama. It had turned out perfectly, and she smiled every time she saw it.

Mrs. Pruitt carefully placed the gown on the bed and adjusted the skirt. "Pardon me, miss, but is this Parisian?"

"Oh, no," Muiren said before Caitlyn could answer. "Miss Hurst made it herself!"

"Noooo!" Mrs. Pruitt bent to inspect the stitching. "'Tis a nice, even hand ye have, miss, if ye dinna mind me saying so. And the lace is very fine."

"It's Belgium point lace, and it took me quite a while to gather the funds since it's quite dear." Almost a year, and if she hadn't been able to tutor the squire's rather slow son in Latin, she wouldn't have been able to afford it.

Mrs. Pruitt appeared impressed. "Her grace has more clothes than ye can shake a stick at, but I've never seen anything in her wardrobe to match tha' dress."

"Thank you."

The housekeeper came to eye Caitlyn's pinned-up hair. "Och, 'tis lovely, Muiren."

Muiren beamed.

"She is very talented," Caitlyn said.

"So she is." Mrs. Pruitt nodded encouragingly. "Miss, ye look fine as can be. Ye'll charm tha' snuffbox fra' Lord Roxburge before ye know it."

Caitlyn blinked.

Muiren cast her an apologetic glance. "I'm afraid I tol' Mrs. Pruitt aboot yer wager."

"Aye, an' I wish ye well. Lord MacLean could use a takin' down a peg or two, if'n ye ask me," the housekeeper said with a dark look. "He's a mite too handsome fer his own good, in my opinion."

"I promise to do my best."

The housekeeper curtsied. "I'd best be gettin' to her grace's dressing chambers. She's havin' trouble gettin' her gown t' fit. Seems she's gained weight since she last wore it, but o' course, she'll blame the laundress fer shrinking it."

Muiren tsked. "The duchess can be a piece of work."

"Her grace has a redhead's temperament, that's a fact. Best of luck to ye on gettin' the snuffbox, miss." Mrs. Pruitt went to the door. "I'll keep me eyes peeled fer a way to help ye. Ye ne'er know when an opportunity may present itself." With a bow, the housekeeper left.

Muiren eyed Caitlyn hopefully. "If anyone can find a way to snatch that snuffbox, it'll be Mrs. Pruitt. Ye canno' pass wind in this house without her knowin' aboot it."

Caitlyn laughed. "I can tell. Now help me into that gown. I can't get my hands on that snuffbox while I'm in this room."

Grinning, Muiren fetched the gown. Caitlyn rose from the dressing table, her determination rising. All she needed was one small opportunity. And when it came, she'd be ready.

"Alexander, you really must stop that!" Georgiana crossed the room to his side, her gown fluttering about her. It was after dinner and the men had returned from enjoying their port. Now the party had settled in, some to play cards, some to talk.

Alexander turned to Georgiana. "I need to stop what?"

"Glaring across the room at Miss Hurst as if she were an ill-behaved child and you her father."

By Georgiana's smile, he knew she was sure she'd hit her mark. For the last two days, she'd managed to mention the disparity between his and Caitlyn's ages more than once. It was wearing, to say the least.

He glanced past her to where Caitlyn stood beside Roxburge. "If I were you, I'd be more worried about your husband. He seems quite taken."

Georgiana shrugged. "If she wants him, she can have him. I have his name, and that was the best part." She watched her husband flirt with Caitlyn. "At one time, it might have bothered me to see Roxburge flirting so. Now I just find it—and him—pathetic."

Alexander ignored her. It had been an interesting two days, and he'd come to respect Caitlyn's determination. It'd had been amusing to watch her try to manipulate Roxburge into giving up his precious snuffbox. It would take quick thinking to get the box if she ever got near it. Alexander smiled at the thought and found a good vantage point by the fireplace to watch.

She was seated by Roxburge's side, attempting to cajole the old duke into showing her his prize.

She sent the old man a sideways glance from beneath her long lashes, smiling at the old roué as if he were a veritable Adonis. She listened to his muddled stories with rapt attention, laughed when he smiled, and in general flirted with him outrageously. Because of Roxburge's advanced age, no one would think aught of it, and she was taking full advantage of that. So far, all she'd managed to get for her pains was one look at his snuffbox. When she held out her hand and asked prettily to hold the box, she'd been jovially but firmly rejected. Alexander had to grin.

As if she could read his thoughts, Caitlyn sent him a resentful glance. He merely bowed, letting her know he was enjoying the show.

Her cheeks red, Caitlyn renewed her efforts on the

duke. Alexander wondered if Roxburge's eyesight was good enough to appreciate the cream of her skin and the way her disappointed lips curved downward.

The old duke said something to Caitlyn that made her blush and look away—right at Alexander. Her lips firmed into a thin line and she sent him a don't-say-a-word glare before turning back to the duke. Though Alexander had no view of her except for one pert, challenging shoulder, he was sure she was now smiling for all she was worth. He chuckled softly.

"What's so amusing?" Georgiana asked.

"I vow but I think Roxburge's eyes have grown worse over the last few years."

She glanced indifferently at her husband. "They've never been good, even when we first met."

"That explains a good deal," Alexander said smoothly.

Georgiana gave him a sharp look.

Across the room Miss Ogilvie played a light piece on the pianoforte, much to Lady Elizabeth's delight. Unfortunately, that austere woman had no musical tone, and she marred the performance with her off-key hum.

Georgiana curled her lip. "I must invite more talented people for my next house party. I was just telling Dervishton how much I love a good play, and he suggested we do a reading one afternoon." She continued on, but Alexander ignored her. She'd lately taken to throwing Dervishton's name about, but if she thought to make Alexander jealous, she was wasting her time.

He could care less, and though she might not yet realize it, she wasn't the younger lord's primary target.

Dervishton was now standing by Lady Kinloss, though he gazed at Caitlyn with a hungry look in his eyes. His expression was so obvious that Lady Kinloss couldn't help but glance between him and Caitlyn, obviously dying to know more.

Scowling, Alexander turned his attention back to Caitlyn, who now sat with her hands fisted on her knees. He had to stifle a grin. While Caitlyn might know her Arthurian history, he knew the people at the house party and had used that knowledge to his benefit. She hadn't known how fanatical the duke was about his snuffbox and, since he could barely see his own hand when it was directly in front of his face, how he kept his treasure all the closer. The old man was a formidable guard for the small gold trinket.

Georgiana sniffed. "Miss Hurst would do well to watch herself. There are times when Roxburge can be quite out of line."

Alexander gave a short laugh. "I would hardly call Roxburge dangerous."

"Oh, but he can be," Georgiana murmured, watching her husband squint at Caitlyn. "He is a lecherous old man."

"He can barely see," Alexander scoffed.

"Which is why none of the maids are safe, be they old or young, pretty or homely."

Suddenly the old duke's expression seemed a bit more leering and less pitiful.

As Alexander watched, the duke leaned forward and— "Damn it, he is looking down her gown!"

Georgiana nodded. "He is fascinated with breasts."

"He can barely see!"

"Which is why he has to lean so very, very close." Georgiana gave a witchy smile. "I've warned him time and again that if he doesn't have a care, he'll fall in."

Alexander took a step forward, but Georgiana grasped his arm, all humor gone from her face. "What are you going to do? He does it to every woman. Besides"—Georgiana sent a hard glance at Caitlyn— "as out of line as Roxburge can be, I daresay our little princess can handle herself."

Indeed, Caitlyn had just said something to Roxburge that had the old man turning red and blustering noisily. From the way Caitlyn's arms were crossed over her chest, she was evidently far from pleased.

"See?" Georgiana said smoothly. "I knew the girl could handle the old baggage. Considering her position in life, I daresay she's had to deal with worse."

Alexander frowned. He'd never considered that before, but Georgiana was right—Caitlyn wasn't as well protected as a young lady whose father commanded a title and a fortune, which was why he'd had such access to her in London. He hated to think that a more unscrupulous man had such an opportunity.

Although, according to her, he'd been unscrupulous enough. He scowled, not liking the thought. He'd never taken advantage of any woman and it was irritating that Caitlyn seemed to think he'd done just that. She'd welcomed his advances, had encouraged their improprieties just as much as he had.

But—had she simply been more of an innocent than he'd thought? Perhaps, as he was older and more knowledgeable, more of the responsibility for their relationship should have rested with him?

An odd weight sat upon his chest. Damn it, that was *not* how their flirtation had gone. Georgiana's comments were clouding his memory.

He watched as Caitlyn put some distance between herself and her host. The duke looked positively sulky as she curtsied and left, obviously in high dudgeon.

Before Alexander could make his excuses to Georgiana, Dervishton swiftly attached himself to Caitlyn's side.

Georgiana chuckled. "Out of the frying pan and into the fire. The poor girl isn't left alone for even a moment. I predict this will cause some problems with your plan for revenge."

It damn well could have, as Caitlyn herself had pointed out. But now he and Caitlyn were playing a much more enjoyable game. The thought made him grin once again.

Dervishton took Caitlyn's arm and strolled with her to a large portrait of Roxburge that hung on the wall down from the fireplace.

Watching, Alexander was struck anew by her grace. Every movement was an unconscious glide of sensuality. He wasn't sure what it was, but he couldn't help but watch her, and neither could any other men in the room.

Georgiana curled her lip. "She is making quite a production of herself, isn't she?"

Alexander shrugged. "She's just walking across the room."

"Shall we join Treymont and his wife?" Georgiana said coolly. "They recently returned from an auction of antiquities, where they acquired an Egyptian sarcophagus."

"Certainly." Treymont and his wife were just a few feet from Dervishton and Caitlyn. Perhaps Alexander could overhear their conversation and make sure she wasn't enlisting the young lord's help.

Georgiana slipped her hand through Alexander's arm and they walked toward the fireplace, where the marquis and his wife sat talking before a crackling fire. Alexander found out that Treymont and his wife possessed a surprisingly vast knowledge of antiquities, and not until a good five minutes had passed did Alexander realize Caitlyn and Dervishton were no longer nearby.

He looked around the room. By the pianoforte, Falkland and the Earl of Caithness were arguing over the merits of a certain hunter while Lady Elizabeth and Miss Ogilvie looked on, laughing at the exaggerations the gentlemen were shamelessly employing. Dervishton was pouring himself a drink from a sideboard, looking put-upon, while apparently the duke had already retired. He rarely lasted more than an hour after they had port.

A movement caught Alexander's eye, and he finally saw Caitlyn, partially hidden beside two large palm plants beside the double doors. He could tell from her gestures that she was speaking with someone.

How odd. Alexander shifted to one side and saw a starched black skirt peeking from the other side of the plant. He shifted back another step and caught sight of reddish curls and a freckled face and recognized Caitlyn's assigned maid.

The woman was whispering excitedly through the plant while Caitlyn listened intently, nodding. Soon the maid slipped away. Caitlyn glanced around, and Alexander barely managed to turn back to the marquis in time. Apparently satisfied no one had noticed, Caitlyn slipped from the room.

Alexander made his excuses from the group, ignoring Georgiana's frown. He would wager his best riding boots that whatever drew Caitlyn from the room had to do with her task.

He was almost to the door when Lady Elizabeth appeared before him. "MacLean, just the man to settle a wager between Falkland and myself. You know something of the displays at the British Museum, do you not?"

"I've been on their board of directors for two years now, but—"

"Precisely! I explained to Lord Falkland here that

I've read numerous articles on the antiquities now being brought from Egypt—"

"As have I!" Falkland snapped.

"Yes, but apparently not the *correct* articles," Lady Elizabeth said with all the confidence of a duke's daughter. "MacLean, explain to Falkland that the Egyptian collection is—"

"I'd love to stay and help, but I'm afraid I must—"

"Come, MacLean!" Falkland blustered. "It will only take a moment. I cannot believe Lady Elizabeth believes such drivel!"

It was a full five minutes before Alexander managed to escape their rambunctious disagreement, and by the time he reached the hall, Caitlyn had disappeared from view. He stared up the stairs, wondering if she'd gone to her room. Unfortunately there wasn't a single footman in sight to ask, so Alexander reluctantly returned to the assembled party. One way or another, he'd find out what she was doing. Of that, he had no doubt.

Chapter 9

※

If ye canna compromise, then ye canna win. Oft in life, one depends upon t'other.

OLD WOMAN NORA FROM LOCH LOMOND
TO HER THREE WEE GRANDDAUGHTERS ONE COLD EVENING

Caitlyn met Muiren in the hallway, where she stood with Mrs. Pruitt. The housekeeper was clad in her usual black, a white mobcap upon her stern white curls.

Muiren said in an excited voice, "Mrs. Pruitt discovered the duke asleep in the library! It looks as if he went there fer a glass o' port afore retiring to bed."

The housekeeper smiled slyly. "His grace fell asleep his snuffbox on 'is knee."

A wave of relief swept through Caitlyn. "Mrs. Pruitt, that's the best news I've had all week!"

"I wouldna help ye so much, except Lord MacLean needs some adversity in his life," Mrs. Pruitt said firmly. "It'll be good fer him, it will. Handsome men all need takin' down a peg now an' again."

Caitlyn blinked, surprised at the vehemence in the housekeeper's voice.

Mrs. Pruitt lifted her chin and said stoutly, "I've put up wit' enou' grief at the hands o' scoundrels just like him."

Muiren said in a low voice, "Mrs. Pruitt says all men from the upper classes are reprobates an' scoundrels."

"All men?" Caitlyn asked, wondering what incidents had caused Mrs. Pruitt's bitterness.

"Aye." Mrs. Pruitt turned and marched toward the library. Before she reached the doors, she paused. "Jus' one thing."

"Yes?"

"Ye'll return the snuffbox to his lor'ship quickly? I dinna want any trouble for the staff."

"I'm just going to show it to Lord MacLean, then immediately return it to the duke. He won't even know it's gone."

"Very well, then." Mrs. Pruitt peeked around the open doors, then gestured for Caitlyn to join her.

Caitlyn carefully tiptoed to the door. She could just make out the duke's bald pate over the back of a large, ornate chair by the fireplace.

"Ye canno' see it from here," Mrs. Pruitt whispered, "but his hand is restin' on his knee and he's holdin' his snuffbox."

Caitlyn almost hopped with victory. "That's perfect!"

"No' so much as ye might think," Mrs. Pruitt warned. "He's almost deaf, but he doesn't sleep very sound, sometimes wakin' up an' yellin' at the charwoman to be quiet when she's no' even in the room."

She gestured Caitlyn inside. "Go ahead," the housekeeper whispered. "Muiren and I'll keep watch in th' hallway."

Caitlyn nodded and slipped inside the library, her slippered feet making no sound on the thick rugs. Lord Roxburge was snoozing deeply, his head dropped forward on his chest. He was dressed in proper dinner clothes from a past era: knee breeches, a long coat, and a waistcoat, his black shoes pointed pigeon-toed. One liver-spotted, heavily veined hand rested on his knee, and the edge of his gold snuffbox glittered between his fingers.

There it was! And soooo close. All she'd have to do was move his hand . . .

Holding her breath, she slipped one finger into his ruffled sleeve and lifted. His hand raised slowly . . . so slowly . . . his fingers tightened instinctively over the snuffbox and he lifted it with him.

Blast it! She carefully lowered his hand back to his knee. The clock ticked loudly into the silence as the seconds passed. Finally, to her vast relief, his grip slowly loosened once again.

Perhaps, instead of lifting his whole hand, she could just lift one of his fingers and slip the box out.

She glanced at his face, and satisfied that he was still sleeping, she carefully attempted to lift one of his fingers.

He stopped snoring. Caitlyn froze in place as a frown settled over his face and he muttered something. Her heart pounded and she held completely still. Finally, he subsided, snoring even louder.

She let her breath out, her heart beating wildly as she carefully released his wrist and stepped away. She looked around, assessing bric-a-brac that decorated the marble-topped tables, and found what she was looking for: a small box of ivory that was almost the size of the snuffbox.

She carried it quietly to Roxburge's side and compared it for a moment. *Close enough.*

She readied herself, flexing her hands as she prepared to perform a magician's trick. She'd once seen a street performer who'd whipped a tablecloth from under an entire table setting of plates, glasses, silverware, and even a candelabra. Her goal was to remove the snuffbox and replace it so quickly that the duke wouldn't notice the difference.

She reached for his arm and was just about to lift it when a movement by the doorway caught her eye, and her heart began thudding in an odd way.

Caitlyn turned her head and saw MacLean standing inside the doorway, Mrs. Pruitt's apologetic figuring hovering just outside.

Damn the blackguard! He stood with his feet planted apart like a sea captain's, his arms crossed over his powerful chest, his sensual mouth curved in a smile.

She scowled. This caper was difficult enough without a critical audience.

As if he could read her thoughts, he uncrossed his arms and made an elaborate bow, gesturing for her to continue.

There was both challenge and condescension in his gestures.

Caitlyn sent him a black look and turned back to Roxburge. She wiggled her fingers to loosen them up and imagined exactly what she'd do. If she lifted just two fingers and slipped the ivory box into his palm, it might dislodge the snuffbox . . .

Her heart beating unsteadily, she gingerly lifted his fingers. Ever so carefully, she pushed the ivory box into his hand, pushing the snuffbox out the other side. He stirred, his snoring interrupted as his fingers fumbled with the ivory box a moment before closing over it. His restless movements dislodged the snuffbox from his broad knee, and it silently tumbled to the thick rug.

Caitlyn snatched it up, her arm brushing his leg. Roxburge muttered in his sleep, his hand closing tightly over the ivory box.

For a long second she remained frozen in place, waiting for the comforting sound of his snore. Finally, after an eternity, the old man's lips parted and a roiling snore filled the room.

Caitlyn sighed in relief and turned to show the box to MacLean . . . but he was no longer by the doorway. Frowning, she looked around and saw him standing beside the large desk that fronted the windows overlooking the garden. He was leaning against the desk, negligently tossing and catching a paperweight, his gaze twinkling with dark amusement.

A warning trill shot through Caitlyn. What was he up to?

He slowly lifted the paperweight over the desk and held it there.

Oh, no! If he dropped it . . .

She opened her mouth to whisper "No!"—then— *THUNK!*—the paperweight fell onto the wood desk.

Roxburge bolted upright, his eyes fixed on Caitlyn. "*Damned charwoman!*" he yelled.

Caitlyn froze. *What am I going to do now?*

Roxburge's eyes flickered once.

Please, *go back to sleep.*

He slowly settled back in his chair.

Please, please, *go back to sleep.*

The third time, his lids slid closed and a snore slipped from his lips.

Caitlyn pressed a hand to her thudding heart. That'd been a close one. She glared at MacLean, who was looking at her with a mixture of frustration and reluctant admiration.

Holding up the snuffbox in victory, she turned to go—but couldn't. Frowning, she looked back and saw the lace trim of her gown was caught under Roxburge's shoe. Worse, it seemed to be hooked under his heel. Bending down, she saw no way to slide it free without lifting his foot or tearing her costly flounce.

She frowned and stood—only to discover that MacLean now stood beside her, so close that her breasts brushed his thigh as she stood. So close that if her skirt weren't caught, she could easily rise up on her toes, wrap her arms about him, and pull him into a kiss.

The thought made her heart pound, and the very air seemed charged with heat. When she shivered, he smiled. God, she loved his mouth. It was firm yet sensual, warm and questing and—

He whispered in her ear, "If you don't stop looking at me like that, I won't be responsible for what happens."

Desire swirled through her so hard, her knees began to shake.

He bent down again, his lips by her ear. "Shall I release your gown from Roxburge's shoe?"

His warm breath sent chills through her. What *was* it about him that affected her like no other man? It was as if some inner fire heated the very air about him, seeping into her and melting her control.

She managed to find her voice. "I-I can handle this without any help, thank you."

"Afraid I won't credit your possession of the treasure since you didn't get away?"

She nodded.

His smile was wicked. "You'd be right."

She looked down at her caught gown and tried to focus on her predicament, but all she could think about was the way MacLean's hip was pressed against hers and the wonderful feeling of being touched.

Stop that! Think of a way to get free.

No ideas came. In an effort not to look into MacLean's eyes, she looked everywhere else and was captured by the powerful muscles under his coat, the way his forearms strained against his sleeves as if fighting the confining fabric.

She shivered and hazarded a glance up at him and couldn't move, couldn't breathe, as his gaze slowly traveled over her face, lingering on her lips and chin, then moved lower to her throat, and the neckline of her gown.

She burned both hot and cold, and her breath fought to be free of her throat. He had the most beautiful mouth—firm and yet unrelentingly sensual.

That mouth curved now into a self-satisfied smile. "What's wrong, Hurst?"

His low voice curled around her thudding heart and tightened, and he leaned closer so that his thigh brushed her hip.

She caught her breath, trying desperately to hold on to any calm. Finally, she whispered, "Nothing's wrong. I'm just trying to think of a way out of this mess."

"Hmmm. Perhaps you can't and should just admit defeat."

"You'd like that," she sniffed. "But I *won't* quit!"

"No?" His fingers grazed the bare skin at the neckline of her gown.

She jerked as if burned, and he smiled wickedly. "Afraid, Hurst?"

"Should I be?"

"Oh, yes." He slowly traced the line of her gown from the crest of her breast to her shoulder, then back.

She tried to contain a wave of shivers that danced through her, but couldn't.

His fingertips continued to slide across her skin. Then he paused at the lowest point of her gown's neckline . . . and stayed there.

She couldn't breathe. Her hands clenched at her sides as she tried desperately to focus on something else . . .

Then she gave in, threw her arms about MacLean, and kissed him for all that she was worth.

Chapter 10

If ye e'er have the chance to bend the ear o' a great mon, dinna break it off wit' the weight o' yer words. Just bend it gently an' speak yer piece an' ye'll do well enou'.

OLD WOMAN NORA FROM LOCH LOMOND
TO HER THREE WEE GRANDDAUGHTERS ONE COLD EVENING

Alexander expected Caitlyn to get angry, to berate him for teasing her. What he didn't expect was a hot, passionate assault.

Her mouth opened beneath his and her tongue traced across his lip, hot and seeking. His groin tightened and he moved closer, running his hands over her back, her narrow waist, her rounded hips.

Caitlyn's arms tightened about his neck as she pressed herself to him. Her soft, full breasts rubbed against his chest, then he felt her hand slide down to his neck. In her excitement she tugged on his cravat, her other arm bent around his neck, holding him to her as if she couldn't bear to let him go.

God, but she was lush, her mouth hot, her body warm and pliant. *This* was why they'd taken such chances; *this* was why he'd flirted with a woman so different from his usual type.

The passion between them was hot and instantaneous, flaring brighter. None of the women he'd made love to had sent his senses reeling in such a way. Perhaps that was why he'd been so angry when he'd discovered her trickery.

That memory chilled his passion. He had to stop this, this very second—if he didn't, he wasn't certain he'd ever be able to stop. It took all of his self-control, but he broke the kiss and took two unsteady steps back. His entire body ached, protesting the delights he was missing.

Her hand, still tangled in his cravat, caught him. "What . . . why are you—"

He forced himself to lift a brow and say as coolly as he could manage, "We are done with this."

Had she known him better, she might have detected the faint quaver in his words or noticed that his hands were fisted at his sides. A hot flush flooded her face as she released him. "I see," she said stiffly. She lifted her chin and said in a firm tone, "Fine, then. Just go."

Roxburge stirred as if to awaken.

Caitlyn stiffened, but she didn't look the duke's way.

Alexander knew he should leave, but somehow he couldn't shake the feeling that he'd left something undone. "Caitlyn, I—"

She grabbed one of Alexander's hands, then shoved

something in it. Swiftly she bent, grabbed her gown by the train, and yanked it from beneath Roxburge's foot.

The duke awoke with a startled cry, which she ignored as she marched from the room, her head held high. She swept out of the room and slammed the door behind her.

"Demme!" The duke rubbed his eyes with a shaking hand. "Can't a man sleep in his own house?"

Alexander started to answer, but his attention was caught by the realization that Caitlyn had shoved the snuffbox into his hand before she'd left.

"MacLean?" Roxburge blinked up at him and yawned. "What in hell was that all about? Miss Hurst seemed quite put out."

"What gave it away? The fact that she nearly toppled you from your chair, or the way she slammed the door?"

"Did she do that? By Jove, whatever for?"

"I believe her anger was directed at me, and you just got in the way."

"While I was sleeping?"

"Apparently so. Before you resume your slumbers, I should return this."

Alexander handed the snuffbox to the bemused duke, who took it, then opened his other hand and regarded the small ivory box with a confused air. "I thought this was— How did that get there? And how did you come to have my—"

"I'd love to stay and explain, but I have a climbing date with a tree." Alexander gave Roxburge a short bow and then stalked to the doorway.

"Damn it, MacLean, you're not making sense! Why on earth would you wish to climb a tree?"

Alexander gave a sardonic laugh. "For the honey, of course."

Next time he'd find a task that was *truly* difficult—something where she couldn't be helped by the servants she'd beguiled to give her a hand.

It had surprised him to find the housekeeper and the maid standing watch outside the library. Caitlyn Hurst had a way of collecting admirers, both male and female.

Well, no more. From now on, she'd only get tasks that she could complete by herself. And when she failed the next task, he would enjoy every moment she spent in his bed. Two weeks didn't seem long enough to enjoy such hard-won pleasures, and he wished he'd asked for two months—perhaps even more. Well, if she enjoyed it enough—and he would make certain she did—she might consider lengthening the time. He'd take her to Italy perhaps, where there weren't so many prying eyes. He'd enjoy showing her the treasures there, the art and the architecture. Venice was one of his favorite places. Perhaps he'd rent a palazzo for her, one that would suit her golden beauty, and enjoy the warmth of an Italian winter.

The thought lightened his mood. He would make her his, brand her with his passion, very, very thoroughly.

His body, never quiet after an encounter with the lush Caitlyn, leaped to full readiness. He ached for her, imagining her beneath him, crying his name as he— Alexander halted his wayward thoughts. First, he had to complete his own task.

Despite Alexander's words to the duke, it would be tomorrow before the beehive could be fetched. It was a pity, but it was too dark now.

In the meantime, he'd retrieve that damned Celtic book from the library, and the next task he gave Caitlyn would be damned near impossible.

Chapter 11

There's an old sayin': "If'n ye must fight, then do it wit' yer honor on yer shield and no' under it."

OLD WOMAN NORA FROM LOCH LOMOND
TO HER THREE WEE GRANDDAUGHTERS ONE COLD EVENING

"Let me help ye, miss." Muiren grasped the edges of the long glove and held it out.

Caitlyn slipped her hand into one, then the other. "Thank you, Muiren."

"Ye're welcome, miss." Muiren glanced at the clock. "Ye've eight minutes to reach the blue sitting room."

"I know, I know. Where did I put my— Oh, there's my shawl. I can't seem to think clearly today. I wonder if Lord MacLean has already gone down to dinner and—"

Muiren looked at her oddly.

Caitlyn frowned. "Yes?"

Muiren cocked a brow. "'Tis interestin' ye said those two sentences together—that ye were disoriented and askin' about Laird MacLean. Ye aren't weakenin' to the enemy, are ye?"

Caitlyn's cheeks heated. "Of course not! I'm just distracted. It's probably because of the weather or something." She refrained from looking out the window, where the night sky was just as clear as the day's had been.

Her problems had begun last night. When she'd retired to bed, she'd been euphoric at having completed her task. But the more she rested in her soft bed, the more she thought about MacLean's face when she'd left the library after placing the snuffbox in his hand. Once he was over his surprise, she'd known he'd appreciated her efforts. He enjoyed a good challenge, just as she did. She wished she could catch a glimpse of the real Alexander MacLean, the man behind the cynical shell.

When she'd met him in London, they'd been so caught up in the madness that had engulfed them, there hadn't been room or time to connect in any other way. They'd been so engrossed in teasing the flame between them to new heights, in pushing the boundaries of acceptable behavior just a little further, that they hadn't ever stopped and just . . . talked. So at the end of that mad time, neither knew the other at all. She didn't know what made him sad or if he liked orange marmalade or what sort of things made him laugh, how he felt about his brothers and sister, if he preferred the quadrille over a Scottish reel. She didn't know if he liked to dance at all because they'd been so busy doing other, less . . . socially acceptable things.

She sighed, doubting they'd ever have a normal, casual conversation. Right now, she had her hands full trying to win their wager. And when she won, he would be too angry, his pride too wounded, for them to ever share a simple conversation. For some reason, that saddened her.

"Och, look at the time!" Muiren adjusted Caitlyn's shawl, then went to open the door. "Ye'd best hurry, or ye'll be late fer yer dinner. Ye know how her grace can be when it comes to time."

Caitlyn left her bedchamber. Where *was* MacLean, anyway? Why hadn't she seen him even once today?

This morning she'd looked forward to seeing him at breakfast. She wasn't going to gloat over her accomplishment, but she did plan on *enjoying* it. But MacLean hadn't given her the chance. He hadn't even come to breakfast. In fact, he'd avoided her all day.

She hadn't been the only one to miss him, either. The duchess had made several comments at breakfast and had snapped at a surprised Lady Kinloss, who'd made the error of asking his whereabouts at luncheon. Caitlyn had spent most of the afternoon taking a long walk down to the original castle site with Lord Dervishton, Sally, and the Earl of Caithness. She'd tried not to think of MacLean on the walk, but it had been impossible. Where was he?

The whole thing was a bit odd. Maybe he had—

"Caitlyn!"

She turned as Sally Ogilvie came down the hall. The young woman was dressed in a lovely gown of white crepe spotted with white satin over a sarcenet slip, trimmed at the neck and sleeves with wreaths of black silk flowers. Her brown locks were curled about her face, and a lovely China shawl was draped about her shoulders.

Sally regarded Caitlyn with an admiring look. "My, but that's a simply gorgeous gown!"

Caitlyn smiled. "Thank you." It was one of her favorites, made of white British net over a blue satin slip, ornamented with a row of blond lace at the bottom and decorated with knots of blue ribbon at the neck and sleeves.

Sally shook her head in wonder. "Honestly, if you'd had that gown smuggled in from France and had to meet a mysterious woman in a black cloak under dark of night to receive it, I wouldn't have been a bit surprised."

Caitlyn laughed and hugged Sally. "That is the nicest thing anyone has said to me since I arrived."

"That really doesn't say much. The duchess has barely spoken to me, and she's yet to remember my name."

"I find a few of the ladies a bit intimidating, too."

"They can say very cutting things in a nice voice, and I don't know how I'm supposed to take that," Sally said.

"It's a quandary. Do you ignore the words and accept the tone? Protest the words and ignore the tone? Are we even allowed to do so, considering we are so outranked?"

"Lady Kinloss isn't too bad; she only speaks to me when she wants the salt. The rest of the time she looks at me like this." Sally reared back, tilted up her chin, and looked down her nose, her eyes crossing slightly.

Caitlyn burst out laughing at such a creditable imitation. "Promise that you will be on my side if we play charades."

Sally grinned. "With pleasure."

"Excellent, for I've never been very good at it. My sister Mary is quite accomplished and has often said she'd like to work upon the boards, which horrifies my mother."

"I can't imagine mine would have much patience with such a suggestion, either."

They reached the lower landing and heard voices in the front room, where the guests had gathered.

Sally adjusted her shawl at her elbows and said idly, "I wonder if Laird MacLean will be at dinner after his accident."

Caitlyn halted in her tracks. "Accident?"

"Didn't you hear? No, I can tell you didn't from your expression."

"Was he badly injured?"

"Lud, no! I know, for I saw him enter the house about an hour after we returned from our walk."

Caitlyn pressed a hand to her chest, where her heart thumped so hard she could feel it beneath her fingertips. "Thank God for that," she said weakly. Had he been injured while attempting to collect the beehive? Surely not. "Do you know what happened?"

"Yes, and it's most odd. For some reason, he attempted to climb a tree."

Oh, no! "And?" Caitlyn asked breathlessly.

"I asked him why he was climbing a tree, but he was quite vague, and even his limp—"

"He was *limping*?"

"Lud, yes. It was obvious he'd been through quite an experience, for he was thoroughly wet and covered in mud and leaves, his face was swollen, and—"

"Oh dear!"

"He said it all began when he was chased by bees."

"But . . . at this time of the year, aren't the bees gone or asleep? That's what he—" Caitlyn caught herself. "That's what I've heard, anyway."

"Yes, but it's been unseasonably warm. I daresay the bees were quite angry at being bothered."

Caitlyn pressed a hand to her forehead.

Sally's grin faded. "I thought you'd find it humorous."

"Oh, I do! I just have a headache." A big headache—a six-foot-three-inch, black-haired, green-eyed headache, which was the worst headache of all. "Did Lord MacLean seem very upset when he returned?"

"He was positively black with irritation." Sally broke into a huge smile, her eyes twinkling. "You haven't heard the best part of the story yet. When MacLean returned from his misadventure, he was on Dervishton's horse."

"How did *that* happen?"

"After our walk, Dervishton went to exercise his new horse. Lord MacLean's horse bolted when the bees swarmed, and he was forced to walk back to the house. But somewhere between there and here, MacLean 'borrowed' Dervishton's mount."

"You think MacLean *took* Dervishton's horse?"

Sally's eyes twinkled. "Dervishton didn't return until much later, and he was on foot. He was furious, too."

Who cared about Dervishton? "How injured was Lord MacLean?"

"He had several stings and they were beginning to swell. On seeing his condition, naturally Lord Caithness and I offered to fetch some remedies from the kitchen, but MacLean rudely refused our offer of help, sent for his valet, and retired to his bedchamber."

"I don't suppose you know how badly he was stung?"

"Oh, he'd sustained a dozen stings, and several bruises and scrapes, too. He took the brunt of the injury from falling onto his rump, for that was the part he kept rubbing."

"He fell out of the tree?"

"I have no idea. When I saw him, he was in no mood to talk." Sally frowned. "I do wonder how he came to be so wet, though. He looked as if he'd been caught in the rain, but the sky was perfectly clear today."

Caitlyn wished Sally knew more details. "You're certain he wasn't seriously injured?"

"I'd venture to say that his pride was hurt much worse than the rest of him."

Caitlyn could believe it. "As irritated as he must have been, I'm surprised the weather didn't turn."

As soon as the words left her mouth, Caitlyn wished she could unsay them. Sally's eyes widened, her brows shot up, and she grasped Caitlyn's hand between her own. "You know of the MacLean curse?"

"I've heard a few stories, but who knows if they're real?"

"It's probably all exaggeration and gossip, but sometimes I wonder." Sally slipped an arm through Caitlyn's. "We'd better hurry or we'll be late for dinner."

The duchess was already frowning when they entered, and her expression darkened when Dervishton, who'd been at her side, broke away as soon as he saw Caitlyn.

"Oh, dear," Sally said under her breath. "Her grace seems angry about something."

Dervishton reached them just as Lord Falkland did. They both bowed, and Falkland hurried to say, "Miss Hurst! I am so sorry I missed the walk today."

"Miss it? Lord Dervishton said you'd decided not to come."

"I *knew* it!" Falkland sent a hard glare at Dervishton.

The older lord shrugged gracefully. "All is fair, Falkland. All is fair."

"With you, all is *un*fair. I should—" Falkland's attention was caught by a movement at the door, and there it stayed. Every eye followed.

Though MacLean was dressed in his usual elegant evening attire, his bottom lip was swollen on one side while a large red welt rested on the crest of his cheek. As he walked into the room, his limp became obvious, as was the wince that crossed his face with each step.

Caitlyn had moved toward him before she even realized it, but the duchess was quicker. She swept forward, calling for a footman to bring a chair, which MacLean curtly refused. Lady Kinloss and Lady Elizabeth followed, both offering advice and asking a clamor of questions.

Over their heads, MacLean's gaze locked with Caitlyn's, his cold eyes hard.

There was nothing to be done. Caitlyn pasted a smile on her lips. As she turned to take her place beside Sally, she found Lord Dervishton's gaze on her.

He looked past her to MacLean, then back, his gaze considering.

Caitlyn's cheeks heated and she hurried to say, "I've heard that a poultice of salt and water can help a bee sting."

Dervishton shrugged. "MacLean's valet produced just such a cure, but his real injuries came from the thistles."

"Thistles?"

The viscount quirked a brow, sudden amusement in his gaze. "You haven't heard the story?"

Sally broke in, "I told her what I knew, but it was very little."

"Indeed?" Dervishton sent a darkly amused glance at MacLean before he said with mock concern, "You should all be informed of what occurred, then. For some unknown reason, MacLean was in a tree attempting to remove a hive when the bees swarmed out and chased him. He leapt to the ground—"

"From a tree? Is that how he—"

"No, no, he wasn't injured then. It's not that simple. He raced to his horse, but that noble animal bolted at the sight of so many bees, which left our hero with no choice but to make a run for the lake."

"Good God!"

"Exactly. He plunged into the icy depths and stayed submerged for a good half an hour before they left him alone. When he finally came out, he had to remove his wet boots since they were filled with water. When he did so, he realized that he couldn't walk with his boots sopping wet and rubbing his skin, so he tossed them into the lake."

"How wasteful!" Sally said.

"My dear Miss Ogilvie, one does not submerge the sort of boot Lord MacLean wears only to dry it out and wear it again. They were ruined, and I completely understand his irritation. However, he failed to take into account what the leather soles had been protecting him from." Dervishton smiled, an almost sweet expression on his handsome face. "Thistles."

Caitlyn winced. In Scotland, thistles were particularly virulent, with cruel needles. "No wonder he's limping."

Falkland chuckled. "I wish I could have seen him."

Caitlyn cast the young lord a scathing glare. Just as she started to say something, the Earl of Caithness joined their small group, his gaze also on MacLean.

At least now they'd hear a man of sense speak.

"MacLean!" the Earl of Caithness called. "Hail the conquering hero! Take off your boots and show the ladies your feet!" He turned to Sally and said with a chuckle, "They are torn to bits."

MacLean turned to them, his dark green gaze sweeping the group and coming to rest on Caitlyn.

Her face grew hot but she defiantly lifted her chin.

The old duke, who'd been asleep in a chair by the fire until Caithness had yelled his greeting, sat up and chuckled. "Ah, MacLean! I hear you fought and lost a battle with a furious hive of bees."

Good God, was *every* man going to celebrate because one of their own had fallen? Her brothers would have— Caitlyn frowned. Actually, they would have done the exact same thing. *Men!*

Caithness chuckled. "I hear you took a refreshing swim, as well."

MacLean's mouth thinned and he looked directly at Dervishton. "I can't imagine where you heard that."

Dervishton smiled graciously. "I couldn't resist sharing the tale. You were such a tragic figure when you entered the house, completely beaten and—"

"Cut and bruised, but not beaten." MacLean's gaze turned back to Caitlyn and a gleam entered his eyes as he reached into his pocket and pulled out a small, gray object. "In fact, I was absolutely victorious."

With those simple words, Caitlyn found herself smiling as well, and for an instant it was as if only the two of them were in the room.

Her heart warmed, and she decided that although she didn't wish him to succeed in his next task, she would make sure it wasn't dangerous.

Dervishton's smile turned sly. "Victorious in what, MacLean? I get the distinct impression that Miss Hurst knows."

Caitlyn managed a brief shrug. "I can assure you that I never asked MacLean to walk barefoot through a thistle patch or swim a lake."

MacLean's gaze gleamed with reluctant appreciation at her misdirection.

Dervishton looked unconvinced, but before he could comment, the duchess went over and placed a possessive hand on MacLean's arm. "It's time for dinner. Shall we go?"

Soon, they were seated for dinner. Over the past few days, Caitlyn had noticed that her place had progressively moved farther from the duchess and toward the duke. She was now directly on the duke's left, and as he tended to sleep throughout dinner, he made a far from ideal dinner companion.

Thank goodness Sally was nearby. She carried the conversation through dinner as it drifted to various topics, including the beauty and unexpected warmth of the day and the hope that it might continue. When she proposed playing lawn billiards tomorrow if the warmer weather held, the other ladies and Lord Falkland immediately took up the idea.

When dinner was over, the men followed the duke into the library for their port. The ladies made themselves at home in the blue sitting room to talk, sip ratafia, and await the arrival of the gentlemen. Lady Kinloss brought her ill-tempered dog, explaining that "the poor thing" had been ill and was just now "up to having company."

Caitlyn eyed the little dog with distaste. Between its large ears the tiny thing had a tuft of hair decorated with a large bow. Its eyes were cloudy and crossed, and many of its teeth were gone, with the remaining few sticking out at odd angles. It growled viciously at everyone except Lady Kinloss.

It was the least cuddly dog Caitlyn had ever seen, yet Lady Kinloss acted as if it were the most adorable creature on earth, calling it "Sweetums" and kissing its doggy lips, which was quite a feat since the dog tended to sneeze violently without warning.

Lady Elizabeth asked Sally to play the pianoforte, which she did reluctantly. Caitlyn rather thought Sally wished to stay with the group about the fireplace to secure Lord Caithness's attention when he returned with the gentlemen, but she could do nothing but graciously take her seat and begin playing a light aria. As Lady Kinloss regaled the duchess with stories of Muffin's prowess in catching spiders, Caitlyn wandered to the fireplace to warm her toes.

Lady Treymont soon joined her. A tall woman with a beautiful complexion and a rather pronounced nose, she had always seemed a little intimidating, but her warm smile made Caitlyn smile, as well.

"I do hope that dog doesn't give us its cold. I'm not usually susceptible to illness, but I rather think *that* dog's cold is especially virulent."

"I'm more concerned with getting bitten."

"It does have a horrible disposition."

"As does its owner." The words were out before Caitlyn realized it, and she clapped a hand over her mouth.

Lady Treymont chuckled. "I couldn't agree more. Poor Lady Kinloss is so attached to that creature. I'm not sure he deserves such lavish devotion, but she seems happy with him—so she may have him!"

"Lady Treymont—"

"Please, call me Honoria."

"And I'm Caitlyn."

"Thank you. You remind me of one of my younger sisters." Honoria gave a rueful grin. "Although your manners are not quite so hoydenish. One of them longs to become a sailor."

Caitlyn chuckled. "I have sisters myself, although none have yet run off to sea."

"Do you come from a large family?"

"Two sisters and three brothers."

"I have my fair share of brothers and sisters, too." Honoria tilted her head to one side. "We seem to have a lot in common. I should have made an effort to speak to you sooner."

"It's sometimes difficult to get to know every person at a house party."

"This isn't a large one, and there's no excuse for my lack of attention. My only excuse is that my husband and I were apart for an entire month before we came here. I was so glad to have him back that I've neglected everyone else."

Caitlyn smiled. "Pardon me for being forward, but you sound very much in love."

"Quite unfashionable, aren't we?" A faraway look entered her eyes, and her expression softened.

Caitlyn recognized that look; her parents had it when they spoke of each other. Her heart lurched, and she suddenly felt very alone. That was the kind of relationship she wanted; one where she could share life evenly with her partner. Where just spending time together held a sweetness and contentment that lit one from within.

It was such a simple desire, yet it seemed so very, very distant.

The butler opened the door and the men entered. Honoria brightened at the sight of her husband, made her excuses, and went to join him. Lord Falkland headed straight for the buffet, where more port waited, while Dervishton and Caithness greeted the duchess. The duke wandered to Lady Elizabeth's side, making a wide berth around Lady Kinloss's dog.

MacLean, looking rather dashing with his bruises, looked about the room and made his way toward

Caitlyn, his faint limp giving him the rakish air of a pirate.

Her hand tightened about her glass of ratafia as their gazes locked. A curious sense of expectation settled over her as he approached and—

"Alexander!" The duchess almost purred as she placed her hand on MacLean's sleeve. "Do come and tell Lord Caithness about the new Egyptian finds. He believes they are all fakes designed to sell tickets to the British Museum."

MacLean could do nothing short of making a scene. Caitlyn forced herself to act as if she didn't care, which was hard enough even without Lord Dervishton's appearance. The man was attaching himself to her side more and more, and she was beginning to get irked. It wasn't that she didn't like him, but with him and Falkland always lurking about, it was difficult to have a moment's conversation with MacLean.

Right now, Dervishton and Falkland were gallantly arguing over who should fetch her a new glass of ratafia.

Despite their noise, she listened with half an ear as MacLean related his opinion on Egyptian antiquities and, when questioned, on the day's events as well. Somewhere along the way he'd found his sense of humor and added embellishments that kept his audience alternately laughing and wincing.

Caitlyn had to bite her lip to hide a chuckle when she heard MacLean tell her grace that he'd climbed the

tree on "a mad impulse, as if led by some wild nymph."
He really had a wicked sense of humor and—

"—so I rode the elephant all the way through Vauxhall."

"Pardon me?" She blinked at Dervishton and realized he'd sent Falkland to procure the ratafia.

Dervishton's eyes crinkled with amusement. "Ah, you're back."

"I didn't go anywhere."

He looked over at MacLean with meaning. "No? I could have sworn you had."

She stiffened and would have left, but Dervishton caught her wrist. "I'm sorry," he said, surprisingly contrite.

She looked at her wrist and he released it. "Miss Hurst—Caitlyn—please. I'm truly sorry. I didn't mean anything by it."

She lifted a brow. "I rather think you did."

"Perhaps I meant a *little* something. I take it that his lordship used his time sitting silently at dinner to dress up his little escapade and will now use it as entertainment."

Despite herself, Caitlyn smiled. "I just wish we had as interesting of a story to tell. All we did was take a walk."

"It was quite vigorous," Dervishton protested. "And it would have been even *more* so if Caithness and Miss Ogilvie hadn't meandered so."

Caitlyn had to laugh. Dervishton took that as encouragement and spent the next half hour entertaining her with some funny and slightly naughty stories about various members of the ton, some of whose names Caitlyn recognized from her stay in London.

Though she was pleasantly amused, Caitlyn still wished she could have a few words with MacLean. But between Dervishton's attentions and the duchess's clinging to MacLean's arm, the opportunity never arose.

Eventually MacLean made his excuses to the duchess and her friends, pleading fatigue because of his adventure. On his way out, he stopped by Caitlyn.

"Dervishton, Miss Hurst." MacLean inclined his head in greeting.

Up close, she could see no bee stings on his face, but rather bruises. The sight made her wince.

Dervishton chuckled. "Miss Hurst is greatly affected by your injuries, MacLean. Perhaps you should bandage them the next time you appear in mixed company."

MacLean smiled coolly. "I've been meaning to thank you for the loan of your horse, slug that he was. I trust you didn't have too tiring a walk back to the house? I recently heard that you'd just returned from a walk when I borrowed your mount. If I'd only known!"

Dervishton turned red. "I was just riding my horse out the drive and back a few times to keep her in good form. She's newly broken to the bit, and as I'm sure you noticed, she's still a handful."

"She was perfectly docile for me," MacLean said smoothly. "But slow. I do hope you didn't pay too much for her."

Dervishton's jaw tightened, and Caitlyn hurried to say, "Lord MacLean, I was sorry to hear of your misfortune."

He lifted a brow in patent disbelief but bowed. "Thank you. It's not much; a cut here and there, and a bruise or two. I've gotten worse injuries from wrestling my brothers."

That diverted her attention. "You wrestle your brothers? Even now?"

His green eyes sparkled with amusement. "Only to remind them who is the oldest."

She would love to see that little display. "Miss Ogilvie said you were chased by bees. I don't know how that could be since it's fall. Someone told me they hibernated."

Dervishton shrugged. "It's been a warm fall. I daresay the bees hadn't all left their hive."

"Apparently not," MacLean agreed drily. "I was fortunate they were sluggish, or I'd have been in worse trouble."

Dervishton shook his head. "Why did you wish to see this beehive, anyway?"

MacLean's gaze met Caitlyn's for a moment. "I love a good challenge."

"In all my years, I have never climbed a tree out of idle curiosity."

"Afraid you might scuff your boots?" MacLean scoffed.

Dervishton's gaze narrowed. "I'm not as talented in the performance arts as you are. I wish we could have seen you running from the bees; that must have been quite funny."

"I'm sure it was," MacLean said smoothly. "But the ride home on your horse made up for it." He slapped Dervishton on the shoulder so hard that the younger man gasped. "Good God, Dervishton, you sound as if you've an inflammation of the lungs. I suggest you give tree climbing a try; it's very healthy."

Caitlyn fought a smile as Dervishton tried to pretend he hadn't just had the wind knocked out of him.

MacLean turned, captured her hand, and kissed her fingers, his lips warm. "Good night, Miss Hurst. I will see you tomorrow."

Caitlyn shivered at the promise in the deep voice.

Dervishton watched suspiciously as MacLean bowed and left.

As he walked out the door, Caitlyn realized that he'd placed something in her palm. Her fingers immediately closed over the small, uneven object, knowing what it was: a piece of beehive.

Smiling, she tucked it into her pocket, distracting Lord Dervishton by asking him about his new horse. Tomorrow she and MacLean would start round two, and this time it wouldn't be a tie.

She'd make sure of that.

Chapter 12

Och, 'tis but an old wives' tale that women will change their minds when the mood strikes. Women change their minds when they need to, and that's that.

OLD WOMAN NORA FROM LOCH LOMOND
TO HER THREE WEE GRANDDAUGHTERS ONE COLD EVENING

MacCready stood at attention by the wardrobe. "My lord, which shall it be today? Morning attire, riding attire, or tree-climbing attire?"

"Don't be impertinent."

"My lord, I would never dare. I have no desire that you should open the heavens and splatter me with rain."

Alexander cocked a brow. "I could have you replaced, you know. Find a younger, less witty fellow to buff my boots, iron my cravats, and whatnot."

MacCready looked pained. "It is the whatnot that is such a burden."

Alexander grinned, feeling quite energetic this morning. The more time he spent with Caitlyn, the more determined he was to beat her at her own game.

Last night he'd felt a great deal of satisfaction in handing Caitlyn that damned piece of beehive, regardless of the cost.

MacCready sniffed. "I have it on good authority that Miss Hurst has enlisted the assistance of both her maid and Mrs. Pruitt, the housekeeper."

"I know. They were keeping watch in the hallway when Miss Hurst was collecting his grace's snuffbox."

"You *did* return it?"

"Of course, and he hasn't mentioned it since."

"That's excellent news, my lord. Dare I hope that any future tasks you name for Miss Hurst will stay on the sunny side of the law, just for something different in tone?"

"The next task for the troublesome Miss Hurst is a mission of courtesy, rather than larceny."

"Excellent, my lord! And I hope your task is less physical. Your breeches have been consigned to the fire. I am a miracle worker, but even I cannot mend a tear of such raggedness."

"I don't give a damn about the breeches; I'm fortunate I didn't break my neck."

"In future endeavors, I hope you will take someone more"—MacCready pursed his lips—"shall we say, agile—to help?"

"I'm agile enough," Alexander growled. Damn it, why did everyone seem intent on suggesting he was getting old? "I was barely six feet aboveground. I was merely startled when bees came out of the hive."

"Of course, my lord. So very surprising, to find bees in a beehive. Makes one think that perhaps there are birds in birds' nests, horses in stables, foxes in dens . . ."

Alexander gave him a flat stare.

The valet sighed. "Just promise that in the future, when faced with some object higher than your head, that you'll get some assistance."

"I don't need help."

"Your nemesis, Miss Hurst, seems to think nothing of getting help. In fact, she has almost *every* female staff member swearing allegiance to her side."

"Her *side*? What is this, a war?"

"So it would seem. Mrs. Pruitt and the upstairs maid have been recruiting, and in a manner that was very unflattering to your reputation. It is an uprising of sorts. Mr. Hay and I did what we could to quell it, only to be told in no uncertain terms that we were 'for the enemy.'"

Alexander frowned. "I refuse to get embroiled in affairs belowstairs."

"Most unwise, my lord, for they are essential to your basic comforts." MacCready crossed to the tray that sat before the fire. "Normally for breakfast in your chambers you would receive poached eggs, ham, toast, fresh fruit, and coffee." He lifted a server from the tray. "Two pieces of black toast, a piece of ham fat, and a cup of tepid tea."

"Bloody hell! I should have gone down to breakfast

this morning. If I hadn't wanted a bath to soak the soreness from my back, I would have done so."

"My lord, there's more. Though I black your top boots myself, using my special champagne mixture, I don't usually polish your other shoes. Have you noticed the condition of your footwear this morning?"

"I hadn't looked."

MacCready shuddered. "Pray do not. *Do*, however, look at your newly starched cravats—a service performed by the laundress and her daughter."

"They left them wrinkled?"

"Oh, no, my lord. These are well-trained servants." MacCready crossed to the dresser, where a stack of fresh cravats lay. He removed the top one and held it out.

"Good God, it's as stiff as a plank of wood!"

"Exactly so. In order to bend it about your neck, you might need a hammer."

"Blasted hell! I'm going to rue the day I allowed that woman to talk me into a modified course of action."

"Oh, no, my lord. However difficult the current situation, this is a much better plan than ruining the young lady without a fair trial."

"She didn't need a fair trial; I already know what she did."

"My lord, a young girl—"

"She's not a schoolroom miss. She's three and twenty."

MacCready smiled tolerantly. "To me, she is a young girl."

"To me, she is a pain in the ass," Alexander muttered.

"I understand from Mrs. Pruitt that the young miss is the daughter of a vicar."

"Yes."

"And has been sequestered in the country most of her life."

"You'd never think it if you saw her in the drawing room, fending off suitors."

"*Fending* them off: exactly, my lord." MacCready collected the overstarched neckcloths and placed them on a small table by the door. "My lord, men our age know that actions speak louder than words." He paused. "I wonder if that's the message the young miss is attempting to deliver?"

"The only message Caitlyn Hurst is trying to deliver is that she needs her good reputation in order to return to London, where she'll dupe some fool into offering for her."

"Marriage is not a disreputable goal, my lord."

"It is when it's procured by guile."

"From what I've heard, I don't believe Miss Hurst is that sort of woman. However, you know her best."

"Damned right, I do." Alexander had told MacCready of his agreement with his fair enemy, but he hadn't mentioned the full price Caitlyn would pay if she lost. Some information was not meant for servants' ears. "MacCready, how am I to quell this ser-

vant uprising? I've no wish to find my unmentionables starched."

"Fortunately we have Hay firmly on our side, due to
Mrs. Pruitt's calling him a 'creaky old bag of musty bones'
during an especially tense moment this morning."

"That *is* fortunate for us. What will you do?"

"Recruit for our side, my lord. Since I cannot quell
the rebels, I can at least fortify the bastion."

"Fine. A footman or two to assist in the next battle
would be an excellent boon." *Let them climb the trees.*

"Very good, my lord. I require only one thing. I
must have your assurance that your behavior toward
the young miss is honorable."

Alexander eyed him coldly. "My behavior is my
own concern."

MacCready folded his hands behind his back and
stared at the ceiling.

A flicker of something that in another man might
have been guilt made Alexander's jaw clench. It was
merely irritation at having to explain himself, but it
left a sour taste in his mouth. "I'll be just as honorable
as the lady herself. How is that?"

MacCready beamed. "That will do quite well, my
lord. Quite well, indeed."

"Good. Now, I must dress. I've a meeting with the
'young miss' and I don't want to be late."

Downstairs, Caitlyn declined to go riding with the
others. Normally a picnic on the far edge of the lake

would be the exact sort of activity she enjoyed, but MacLean had sent a note requesting a brief meeting. She'd gladly give up a dozen picnics to settle the next round of their contest.

It had been the first thing she'd thought of this morning upon arising. She'd looked forward to breakfast with special excitement expecting to see MacLean, but he hadn't shown.

Caitlyn had hidden her disappointment, but her grace was another matter. As the minutes passed and MacLean still did not appear, the duchess's laugh had become brittle, her air tense. As if suspecting that MacLean might be watching from some hidden vantage point, the older woman had made a production of going on the ride, flirting heavily with a politely bored-looking Dervishton.

Caitlyn thought she knew why MacLean hadn't come to breakfast. If she'd fallen out of a tree, she'd have spent the entire next morning soaking in a deep copper tub. But he wasn't the sort of man to admit feeling anything other than perfectly well, even if his entire body was a mass of bruises.

She yawned as she leaned against the library window, her eyes heavy. She'd barely slept a wink last night. Every time she'd closed her eyes, the events of the day before would barrel through her mind— of her thudding heart when MacLean had kissed her, of his bruised face and lip after his fall, of the burning look he'd given her as he'd left the sitting room.

Caitlyn turned from the window and meandered about the room, admiring the opulent furnishings, running a hand over some ancient books set on a low wooden display table. Some were old texts, drawn in ink and so painstakingly painted that the letters themselves became the art. One book consisted of thin sheets of beaten metal that held intricate maps of the world as it had been charted in the late 1400s. "Fascinating," she murmured, running her fingers over the .carved maps. The workmanship simply astounded her.

She left the display table and sat at the huge oak desk, smoothing her hands over the polished wood and admiring the warm sheen caused by the application of multiple coats of furniture wax.

It would be odd to go home after being here. She smiled thinking of Papa's cozy and cluttered library. It was so small that any one of the dozen or so rugs in this library would cover the floor of the entire room. His desk was small and plain, the drawers often stuck, and the surface had a crack that he covered with a large felt blotter.

Her smile trembled, and she was suddenly acutely homesick. Right now, Papa would be teaching Robert and Mary their daily Greek lessons. He taught the more high-spirited William and Michael separately, saying they needed "more repetition." The thought made her chuckle, even as her heart ached.

To stave off tears, she picked up the small book of Arthurian stories, carried it to the settee, and settled among the cushions. She already knew what MacLean's task would be, and she flipped through the book looking for inspiration for the final task. One couldn't prepare too much for a big challenge. She smiled, thinking how funny MacLean had looked last night, dressed in his elegant evening clothes while sporting bruises and scrapes. Yet nothing could diminish his astonishing good looks or that dark, brooding presence. If anything, his wounds had only enhanced them.

Blast all men. Women aren't blessed with the ability to look good and *disheveled. Life is most unfair.*

His rendition of his adventures and his commandeering of Dervishton's mount had been humorous, although she hadn't laughed when she'd first heard he'd been injured. For one paralyzing moment, she'd been struck with raw fear. As if, in losing MacLean, she'd have lost something precious. Even now, if she thought about his being seriously injured or worse, her heart swelled as if to reject the thought. *That is ridiculous! I have no claim on the man at all.* But his next task—retrieving the bow from Lady Kinloss's nasty-tempered dog—wasn't dangerous in any way. Oh, he may get his fingers nipped, but no more.

She adjusted a pillow behind her and settled in for a nice read. The leather cover was soft beneath her fingers, the musty scent of leather and old paper tickling her nose. She carefully paged through the delicate leaves and found an interesting chapter. She was immediately drawn into the story of brave Culhwch and his passion for the beautiful Olwen, reading how he worked so tirelessly, performing task after task to prove his love.

It was a romantic story, filled with hope and promise. As she read, Caitlyn absently kicked off her slippers and tucked her stockinged feet to one side beneath her skirts, leaning on her elbow so that the sunlight spilled across the pages.

That was how Alexander found her when he walked into the library half an hour later. Caitlyn was curled on the settee, nose deep in a familiar, small leather book. The sunlight spilled over her shoulder and across the page, reflecting light on her face, her expression completely engrossed.

He couldn't help but think of his library at MacLean Castle, which occupied two floors of one turret; it was his favorite place in the castle. Seeing Caitlyn so engrossed in her book, her stocking-covered toes peeping out from beneath her skirts, made him wonder what she'd think of *his* library. She could curl up on its wonderful cushioned window seat, the sunlight warming her on winter days, and read to her heart's content.

He frowned. *Good God, next I'll be wondering how she'd like the gardens!*

She turned a page, her lips moving slightly as she read. Alexander instantly wanted to capture them with his own, to steal her attention from the book with bold, greedy kisses and a passionate touch. Yet even with the opportunity before him, he hesitated.

He wasn't the sort of man who had to prove his virility by conquering every bit of muslin who danced by. He preferred women who held their own, sophisticated women who knew the rules of the game and expected nothing but mutual pleasure in return. Women like Georgiana.

Yet he was reluctantly beginning to appreciate Caitlyn's fiery independence and spirit. She simply enjoyed life, living the challenges thrown her way with unflinching enthusiasm, just as she enjoyed the delicious dishes prepared by Georgiana's chef. In so many ways, Caitlyn's unfettered joy in even the simplest of things was damned appealing.

Unfortunately, it was equally obvious that she wasn't the sort of woman to accept a halfway anything—neither a friendship nor a relationship. From their flirtation in London, he knew she was all-or-nothing. Once she began something, she didn't stop until she reached the conclusion, good or bad.

As much as he hated to admit it, he was a hairbreadth from developing a case of pure, hot lust for the demure Miss Caitlyn. He rather wondered if perhaps it hadn't already happened.

She shifted on the sofa, and her trim foot and ankle slipped from under her skirt. He'd seen plenty of women's ankles, but this was the most of Caitlyn Hurst he'd ever seen. Her gowns, while fashionable, were tantalizingly conservative. Where other women might lower their neckline to expose the curve of their breasts, Caitlyn's were always neatly covered with rows of lace and ribbons. Seeing just an ankle made his body heat as if she were naked.

Damn it, why couldn't he feel this flicker of heat for an older, wiser, less . . . less *virginal* woman?

Before, he'd been certain her innocent air was false and that he'd fallen for it like the biggest lunk. Now, having spent some time with Caitlyn, he had to admit he'd been wrong. Innocence filled every movement she made; every guileless statement, every unguarded pout of her full lips. It was genuine—which wouldn't have been an issue if it didn't also drive him mad with desire.

So where did that leave him when he won the wager? Could he really take an innocent woman as a mistress? Looking at the slender, graceful foot encased in a silk stocking, he was afraid that he could.

She turned a page, one slender finger following the text down the page. The sunlight warmed her cheek and traced the delicate line of her throat. His throat tightened when he thought of tracing that line with his lips, of tasting her sweet skin and—

Hell, why was he standing here, just thinking about it? She was here, and they were alone. For both their sakes, he needed to convince little Miss Perfect Hurst how dangerous he truly was. The sooner she realized that and took more care *not* to be caught alone, the better it would be for both of them.

He moved forward until he stood at the very end of the settee. Her head remained down, her gaze moving across the page, and he waited for her to feel his presence the way he felt hers. It was an almost physical tug, as if a thousand heated strands tied them together, tightening more the longer they remained in the room together.

She lifted her head a bit. She blinked once, slowly. Then, her cheeks pink, she turned her head and lifted her gaze to his.

He'd had a quip ready, but on meeting her gaze, his words vanished. Everything melted away except her. Her soft, soft lips and big brown eyes, so beautiful that a man could easily drown in them.

She flushed, a soft blush of pink that crept through her skin and made him curl his fingers into his palms to keep from reaching for her. His body hummed, so aware of her that it hurt. She felt something as well, for her full breasts were rising and falling with her quick breaths under her modest blue gown.

He opened his hands and realized they would just span her waist. Once he had her against him, he would slide his hands to her rounded hips. His fingers curled when he thought of cupping her full bottom through her gown.

His body reacted swiftly, his cock swelling to a full erection.

Her lips parted as she, too, seemed to fight for breath. Her gaze flickered over him, touching his mouth, his shoulders, then down to his riding breeches. He knew she could see his reaction, and he waited for her to look away or express dismay of some sort, which would keep them both safe from the lust that surged between them.

But she didn't. Her gaze widened in sensual fascination.

Alexander could stand no more; he dropped onto the settee.

Eager, Caitlyn's brown eyes sparkled, her lips parted, and she dropped the book, letting it tumble to the floor as she reached for him.

Chapter 13

❧

Dinna be thinkin' that the way to a man's heart is through his stomach. That's no' the organ men think with.

OLD WOMAN NORA FROM LOCH LOMOND
TO HER THREE WEE GRANDDAUGHTERS ONE COLD EVENING

With one smooth movement, she grasped his lapels, pulled herself to her knees, and pressed her mouth against his.

He'd thought they'd talk, but there was no talking with Caitlyn Hurst. Not today. Stunned, he simply accepted her embrace as her hot mouth urged him on. He wrapped his arms about her and kissed her back with all of the passion built up inside him.

Her mouth opened beneath his and her tongue hesitantly brushed his lip. He moaned and deepened the kiss, pulling her more firmly into his lap. Her arms tightened about his neck, and his hands roamed over her, feeling the smooth line of her back, the gentle swell of her hips, the way the curve of her ass fit his hand.

He was afire, his body so racked with passion that he ached even as he held her.

The damn pillows on the settee were getting in the way. He stood, lifting her with him, kissing her madly, passionately, until neither of them could breathe. These were the kisses they'd once shared so clandestinely; kisses as forbidden as they were unexpected.

She rubbed against him, unconsciously rocking her hips and sending ripples of heat across his body. He nipped at her lush bottom lip before plundering her mouth anew. He couldn't get enough of those sweet kisses, so artlessly passionate, so generously given.

Damn, but she was a hot piece, eager and playful, and delightfully urgent. He slid his hands up her sides, allowing his thumbs to graze her nipples. She gasped against his mouth and arched fiercely, hotly passionate.

He cupped her breast, savoring the fullness, his thumb circling a nipple. She shivered in his arms, her breath catching as he increased the pressure. Her eyes closed and a moan escaped as she pressed against him with obvious delight. She grasped his shoulders and rocked her hips against his, tormenting even as she pleasured.

Unable to stand another moment, he lifted her up and carried her the few steps to the heavy display table. He set her upon the open books to keep her from rubbing against him and causing him to lose control. Heedless of anything but the need to keep her here, within his arms, he cupped her face between his hands and worshipped her warm mouth.

She slipped her hands about his waist and pulled herself forward, locking a heel around one of his legs.

Alexander stood stock-still and found himself staring directly into Caitlyn's wide brown eyes. Slowly, deliberately, she lifted her other leg and hooked her heel about his other leg until they were in the most intimate position imaginable, her legs splayed about his hips, her skirts rucked about her waist.

He'd never envisioned himself as the type to lust after an innocent, virginal, too-stubborn-for-her-own-good slip of a woman. And woman she was, for all that she looked like a schoolroom miss. A girl would simper and flutter every time a man looked at her. Caitlyn Hurst didn't flutter—ever.

She didn't even flutter when a prudent woman *should*. She calmly accepted heated glances from Dervishton, puerile flattery from Falkland, and definitive threats on her virtue. Those last were Alexander's forte, and if she had any common sense, she'd be afraid. *Very* afraid. She definitely wouldn't be perched on the edge of the display table in the library, her legs wrapped about his hips.

He wasn't used to walking away from such temptation, and she had little control over her impulses. She didn't seem to realize that the more time they spent together, the more danger she and her damned virtue were in.

But did it matter? Did anything matter, other than the feel of her against him?

Done with trying to understand her, he lifted her skirts by the handful, pulling them up, up, so that he could touch her warmed skin through her thin chemise and—

Outside, the sound of a group of horses approaching the house penetrated his fog of passion. The other guests were returning.

Alexander dropped his forehead to hers and held her tight, his mind slowly clearing. Damn it, what were they thinking? They had to stop this, had to fight it. But looking into Caitlyn's passion-drugged eyes, Alexander knew it was up to him. Though it was physically painful, he released her and stepped back.

"MacLean, wha—"

"No." It was all he could manage. His heart thundered, his skin burned as if her touch had scalded him, his cock ached with unreleased passion.

Caitlyn blinked rapidly, as if waking from a deep sleep, then slipped off the table, her skirts tumbling back into place. "MacLean, what—"

"The others are arriving. I heard their horses as they rode past to the stables."

She pressed her hands to her cheeks. "I didn't even hear them. I— Good God, I don't know what I was thinking—"

"We weren't." He couldn't stand the wounded look in her eyes. "This passion is what caused us such problems to begin with. It will sink us again, unless we control it."

Her face pale, she nodded. Then, her gaze averted, she walked to a mirror on the wall and began putting her hair to rights, her hands shaking.

The silence grew long. Alexander rubbed his face. He'd come so close to losing control, and he *never* lost control. It was a luxury he couldn't afford as a MacLean. Since Callum's death, Alexander had never, not once, allowed his passions to get the better of him.

Until today.

For a few glorious, blindingly exquisite moments, he hadn't been in control of anything. He ran a hand over his face. *Good God, what did I almost allow to happen?*

Caitlyn returned to the settee and retrieved the fallen book. "Well, that was a very pleasant interlude."

He frowned. *"Pleasant?"*

"More than pleasant." Her cheeks were still flushed. "We had planned to talk, and now is a good time, before the riding party reaches the house. Have you decided on my next challenge? I have decided on yours."

Alexander didn't know what to say. He'd been certain she would berate him for attempting to seduce her; instead, she'd calmly accepted part of the responsibility and moved on.

He realized she was still looking at him, a question

in her eyes, and he forced himself to find his voice. "One task Culhwch performed was to convince a reluctant visitor to come to a dinner party. Do you remember that part?"

She tapped the book with a slender finger. "Yes . . . there was something about a guest who'd declared he'd never set foot within the castle, and Culhwch had to convince him?"

"Which Culhwch did by completing errands for the guest, although I'm not convinced that ruse will work in this instance."

Caitlyn shot MacLean a glance from beneath her lashes. "So I'm to convince—"

"Lord Dingwall." He smiled, and it wasn't a nice smile, either.

"Who is that?"

"His estate borders this one."

"So I am to invite Lord Dingwall to attend a dinner here at Balloch Castle?"

Alexander nodded.

She frowned. "And I assume that he dislikes the duchess?"

"Why not the duke?"

"The duke is too self-absorbed to get into an argument. The duchess seems to relish that sort of encounter."

MacLean's lips twitched. "Point conceded."

"If I convince this Lord Dingwall to come to dinner, how do I know the duchess will allow him in?"

Alexander shrugged, arrogantly self-confident. "She'll do it if I ask her. She knows him well; his property is attached to hers in the west, his house almost visible from the largest curve in the drive."

"And they dislike one another."

"I'd use the word *detest*. According to Georgiana, Dingwall once called her an 'empty-headed piece of decorated fluff,' and she returned the favor by calling him a 'pompous relic.'"

Lovely, Caitlyn thought. She was to play nursemaid to a pair of squabbling adults. "What started their argument?"

His green eyes alight with amusement, he replied, "I'm sure Georgiana told me at some point, but I didn't listen."

She sniffed. "I'll have to find out what happened between them. Perhaps I can patch things up."

"And my task?"

Caitlyn smiled. "It's easier than falling from a tree."

"Excellent. My back has yet to recover."

"I promise that your back will be safe for this task. Your fingers, however—"

Noise arose out in the hallway. The first of the guests had returned from the stables, and Caitlyn heard her name mentioned by Lord Dervishton. It wouldn't be long now before they were interrupted.

Caitlyn said swiftly, "In the story, Culhwch is sent to fetch a comb and mirror from between the ears of a wild boar. MacLean, *you* are to fetch the bow from Lady Kinloss's dog."

Alexander straightened. "That monster?"

"That old, near-toothless monster. The one that snarls every time you come near." She set the book on the desk and smiled.

"It's a deal." He stood by the display table where they'd just embraced, looking elegant and menacing.

That was a particular talent of his. While she suspected that many men wished they could do the same, few were capable of it. For MacLean, it was as natural as breathing.

The commotion in the hallway grew louder as another group joined the first, and the duchess's voice could be heard over the clamor.

MacLean grimaced and moved toward the terrace windows, as far away from the hallway as he could get.

Dervishton appeared at the library door, his sharp gaze taking in the entire scene. "Ah, Miss Hurst, there you are!" He entered the room, nodding coolly to MacLean. "My dear Miss Hurst, you made the right decision not to ride. According to her grace, the trail was too steep, the sun too cold, the wind too brutal, and the company not merry enough."

"It sounds lovely." Caitlyn sent a glance at MacLean from under her lashes, but he was staring out the terrace windows, his attention obviously somewhere else. "Lord Dervishton, you once mentioned that you know this countryside rather well."

He looked pleased, stripping off his riding gloves and tossing them onto the display table without a glance. "My mother's family is from this area. I spent most summers of my youth in a house not far from here."

"So you know all of the people who live around here."

MacLean's attention swung in her direction.

Dervishton nodded. "Of course. Some of them very well. Why?"

She smiled sweetly. "I have a great favor to ask."

He could not have appeared more eager. "Yes?"

"If you're not too tired and will give me a few moments, I'll change into my riding habit and we can take an easy canter up and down the drive while you tell me about the history of the castle . . . *and* the surrounding properties." She cast a demure glance at MacLean, who now faced the room, his gaze considering as he watched her.

"It would be my pleasure!" Dervishton reached for his gloves. "We can ride down through the—" His eyes widened as he looked at the display table.

His expression was so shocked that Caitlyn, who was standing only a few feet away, moved to see what he was looking at. There, imprinted on the thin metal sheets of the ancient map, was a perfect impression of a woman's posterior. *Her* posterior.

Good God, no! Her face flushed and she instinctively turned to MacLean.

He crossed the room at her silent entreaty.

Dervishton frowned. "That looks like—" He sent an embarrassed glance at Caitlyn.

She pasted a smile on her lips. "I see some dents. I don't know what else there is to see."

"They look like—" His expression froze and he looked from Caitlyn to MacLean, then back to the map upon the table.

Caitlyn stared blindly at the cheek dents pressed into the old map. Not only was it painfully obvious what they were, but MacLean's having caused her to writhe, the imprints were well hollowed out and wider than they should be.

At least she *hoped* her behind wasn't that wide. She fought the desire to peer over her shoulder and see.

"Pardon me," a rich, silky masculine voice murmured in her ear. MacLean bent over her shoulder and examined the dents through his eyeglass. "Ah," he said after a moment. "Fascinating."

Dervishton's expression had darkened. "You could call it that."

MacLean straightened. "I'm certain Georgiana— I mean, *her grace*—would wish us to remove this map."

"Yes, but—"

"Dervishton," MacLean said in a voice heavy with meaning, "*her grace* would wish it."

"Yes, I heard—" Dervishton's eyes widened. "*Oh!*" He looked at the imprint again. "You mean—"

MacLean leveled his eyepiece at the indentions. "I'm positive." He placed his hand along the indentions as if to measure them. "Yes. Her grace would be most glad to see this map removed."

Dervishton nodded. "Of course. I see. *Her grace*—" He carefully closed the map, then slid it under another book.

"Thank you," Alexander said somberly, tucking his eyepiece back into his pocket.

Caitlyn had to hold her breath to keep from choking on a hearty laugh. She met MacLean's gaze, and for a moment both of them regarded one another, their eyes warm with laughter.

Caitlyn cleared her throat. "I should change into my riding habit."

Dervishton bowed to Caitlyn. "I shall await you in the foyer."

"I'll be swift." As Caitlyn curtsied good-bye to MacLean, she mouthed a sincere *Thank you*. His gaze softened and his mouth curved as he bowed in return.

The look warmed her from head to toe, and with a light heart she hurried upstairs to change into her riding habit, to discover all that she could about the mysterious Lord Dingwall.

Chapter 14

❧

One day ye might find yerself wantin' something so badly that ye think ye might do anything to get it. When that happens, be very wary, fer that's th' moment th' devil will dance in through yer door.

OLD WOMAN NORA FROM LOCH LOMOND
TO HER THREE WEE GRANDDAUGHTERS ONE COLD EVENING

"*Y*e have to do *what*?" Muiren, who was fetching Caitlyn's bronze walking dress from the wardrobe, turned an incredulous look on her mistress.

Mrs. Pruitt, who'd just brought in neatly pressed unmentionables, looked up from the dresser drawer and gaped. "Ye canno' be serious!"

The late-afternoon light bathed the bedchambers with a golden glow. Caitlyn was getting ready for a game of lawn billiards with the other guests to enjoy the mild weather. "I'm perfectly serious: my next task is to fetch Lord Dingwall to visit her grace."

Muiren and Mrs. Pruitt exchanged glances.

"Miss, I'm sorry, but I dinna think that'll happen," Muiren said.

"Why not?"

Mrs. Pruitt let out a long breath. "Lord Dingwall isna a nice man."

"He's a horrid ol' troll, is what he is!" Muiren said.

Mrs. Pruitt nodded, both chins wagging. "He is. And he hates her grace fer many things, but especially fer havin' house parties like this, with all manner o' people traipsing up an' down the paths. He dinna care fer that at all."

"But the real reason he's mad at her grace is because her drive runs near his own property. He liked to have had a fit when she had the lane cut," Muiren said.

"Aye, he came stormin' to the house, yellin' tha' she was on his property."

"Tha' was only one argument, though. They've had many."

"Aye," Mrs. Pruitt confirmed. "Her grace demanded that he repair the road in front o' his house, which becomes a lake whenever it rains. She doesna like how it splashes mud on her new carriage."

Muiren nodded vigorously. "Dingwall would have none o' it, though, and he near had a fit. Ye'd have thought she'd asked him to pay fer a brand-new road an' a house or two, as well."

Mrs. Pruitt sniffed. "While I can understand tha' her grace is no' always a reasonable sort o' woman, there was no need fer him to call her a"—the housekeeper looked around before whispering loudly—"hussy!"

"He didn't!" Caitlyn could see why Georgiana had been angry; the duchess was very conscious of her dignity. "Lord Dervishton's mother lives near here, and he told me some things about Dingwall yesterday. I'm hoping to quiz his lordship more during our game of lawn billiards. Did Dingwall really steal her grace's favorite dog?"

"Aye, he did," Mrs. Pruitt said. "But only after she had the men move the markers."

"What markers?"

"On his property. That's what started the *real* fight. Afore that 'twas naught but hard words. After tha', the war began in earnest."

"What did she do to the markers?"

"Her grace wished the drive t' the new house t' curve on the other side o' the park, and there was no arguin' with her, not e'en when she was tol' the drive would cross Lord Dingwall's land. Not by much, but 'twas enou.'"

"I can't believe she just moved the markers! No wonder Lord Dingwall is so angry. He could have taken her to court."

Muiren shook her head. "When the duke is the one who appoints the seat? I dinna think so."

"Aye, Lord Dingwall would be bangin' his head against a brick wall wit' that one. He was angry as could be when he found out the judge wasna goin' to give him a fair hearin'. He showed up during one of her grace's house parties, yellin' aboot how the duke and she had cheated him, and how he wasna going to stand fer it. Her grace ordered the footmen to keep 'im out and he's ne'er been allowed to enter since."

Muiren chimed in, "Which is when he took her grace's prize poodle. Stole it when the footman took it fer a walk and refuses to give it back. Now, just to make her mad, he walks th' dog right along the fence, he does. And if he sees her grace, he'll wave right big and point to the dog and dance up an' down like a troll."

"Does it work?"

"Och," Mrs. Pruitt said, "ye should have seen her grace! It happened once just before ye arrived, miss, and she was fit t' be tied, she was. Leaned out th' window of her carriage and screamed like a fishwife."

"Aye." Muiren's eyes grew wide. "I ne'er knew she could speak so! She'd have had 'im shot if she'd thought she could get away wit' it."

Caitlyn didn't doubt it a moment. The duchess had a hardness that couldn't be ignored, a brittleness that permeated her speech and, when she was upset, made her laugh as harsh as a mule's bray. Caitlyn couldn't possibly get upset with someone who succeeded so brilliantly in annoying the duchess. At times Caitlyn wished to do the same thing, especially after last night.

Yesterday's ride with Dervishton had provided her with excellent information on Lord Dingwall. Up until ten years ago, when Dingwall's daughter had died from an infection of the lungs, the old man had been fairly friendly to his neighbors. After that, he'd become a hermit and rarely had a good word for anyone.

Caitlyn felt quite sorry for the man. Added to his miseries, shortly thereafter the duke and duchess began to build the new house. From what she'd come to understand, they'd been insensitive about almost every issue possible. No wonder Dingwall had adamantly refused to take care of his portion of the roadway or do anything else the duchess asked. It would be a daunting task to get him to voluntarily visit the duchess's house.

"Are ye sure ye wish t' do this?" Mrs. Pruitt asked in a doubtful voice.

"Of course! I'm not the sort of person who wavers just because a strong wind comes by." A strong kiss . . . she might waver a bit for that. But not for mere adversity.

"If ye're decided, miss, then so are we," Muiren said stoutly. "I dinna know how we'll help, but we will."

"There is one way," Mrs. Pruitt said, looking meaningfully at Muiren.

"Och, now, Mrs. Pruitt, I couldna!"

"Aye, ye could. This is war, lassie! Of the old sort— we women must stand together!"

Caitlyn frowned. "What are you two talking about?"

Muiren sighed. "'Tis about me man, Sean."

"Why, Muiren, you never said a word!"

Muiren smiled shyly while Mrs. Pruitt sniffed. "That's because he's a footman, and Muiren's no' supposed to mingle wit' the help in such a manner."

"Mrs. Pruitt, I told ye I dinna *mean* to fall in love! But it slipped up behind me and knocked me in th' head." Muiren turned to Caitlyn and said, "T'were true love, miss. One minute we were fetchin' the linens to count the sheets, an' the next—" Muiren's cheeks couldn't be pinker.

Caitlyn blew out her breath. "I know exactly what you mean."

Muiren and Mrs. Pruitt sent her a surprised glance and she added hastily, "I've read in many books about how love can hit one unexpectedly."

"I daresay there's been tomes on the subject," Mrs. Pruitt agreed. "Muiren, tell Miss Hurst what ye and Sean can do fer her quest."

"Sean's cousin's wife's sister works for Lord Dingwall. I dinna know till I speak to her, but mayhap she can get ye into the house. 'Tis fer certain he willna let ye in if ye walk up to the front door. He willna even see the vicar when he comes callin.'"

"Oh, Muiren, that would be a great help! Now, if I can only convince him to visit her grace."

Mrs. Pruitt nodded. "That'll be th' trick, fer certain."

What a troublesome task! It made the snuffbox challenge look appallingly easy, blast MacLean and his fiendish imagination.

Lost in thought, Caitlyn prepared to join the other guests for an invigorating game of lawn billiards. It would be invigorating for her because she would not only attempt to garner more information from Lord Dervishton, but would also attempt to get a better look at Lord Dingwall's house from the lawn.

One step at a time, she told herself. *One step at a time will win this race.* She took her bronze bonnet and placed it over her curls, tying a saucy bow to one side. Feeling much cheered, she marched out of her room for the field of battle.

In the comfort of the back terrace, Georgiana sat in one of the wide, padded chairs that the footmen had placed outdoors, a light blanket across her lap, the canopy of trees protecting her from the unflattering light of day. Across the lawn Miss Hurst, radiantly lovely in a bronze gown trimmed with blue ribbons, dealt with the twin menaces of Lords Falkland and Dervishton.

As Georgiana watched, Caitlyn laughed at something one of the men had said, the merry sound rolling across the lawn.

Alexander had been speaking to Diane, acting politely interested in her rather vicious dog, but at the sound of Caitlyn's laughter he looked up. The sun slanted across his face, turning his skin a golden shade as he watched Caitlyn walk in the sunshine flanked by the two fashionably dressed lords.

Georgiana narrowly watched Alexander. His expression never changed, and while she couldn't detect the slightest tendency toward admiration, she couldn't help but notice the intensity of that guarded stare.

She clamped her teeth together, fighting off the most unladylike desire to claw Miss Hurst's too pert face. In the past week Alexander had grown more and more distant from Georgiana, while he seemed to be spending an inordinate amount of time with Caitlyn Hurst. And when he wasn't with Caitlyn, he was watching her.

Georgiana waited for Diane to finish explaining how her little dog could only eat finely ground liver and eggs before she interjected smoothly, "Lady Kinloss, I don't believe Alexander is interested in poor Muffin's diet woes."

"Oh, but I am." To Georgiana's surprise, Alexander sank to his haunches as if to examine the small dog more closely.

Muffin bared his crooked, jagged teeth, his hair bristling on his rounded back, his eyes bulging.

Alexander's gaze narrowed. "He looks as if he's about to have a fit."

"Oh, no! He's just *very* protective," Lady Kinloss said proudly.

"Of what?"

"Of me!"

"Nonsense." Georgiana wished they'd stop talking about the damned dog. "He growls just as much when someone tries to take his ball or if someone has on a scarf or something that scares him or—"

"Really, Georgiana!" Diane's smile appeared glued in place. "Muffin doesn't growl nearly as loudly when protecting his ball as he does when he's protecting *me*."

Georgiana lifted her brows and shrugged.

Alexander stared at the dog a few more moments,

but the dog continued its nervous growl. Slowly, Alexander straightened back up. "Does your dog bite?"

"Oh, no!" Diane said. "Well, except the stableboy and Lady Charley's nephew."

"And Lord Burgdorf," Georgina added, so bored she could scream, "and Mr. Melton and Sir Roland—don't forget them. Especially Sir Roland, who had to have stitches."

Alexander winced. "Good God!"

"Sir Roland deserved it," Diane sniffed, an air of pride in her voice. "Muffin is a *very* good judge of character."

Alexander crossed his arms, almost glaring down at the dog with its ridiculous tufts of hair and an equally ridiculous bow between his ears. "I'm surprised no one's yet shot him."

As if aware that his name was being taken in vain, Muffin bared his teeth.

Georgiana laughed. "You may be interested in Muffin, but he is not interested in you."

Alexander didn't look amused. "Lady Kinloss, are there any people he likes besides you?"

"No." She shrugged, her gaze drifting to the lawn billiards game. "He sleeps upon my bed at night and refuses to let any of my maids touch him."

"Lord Kinloss must love him, then," Alexander said under his breath.

"Pardon?"

He waved his hand. "Nothing. I was just thinking aloud."

Another peal of laughter arose from the lawn billiards game, this time by Miss Ogilvie, who'd just knocked the Earl of Caithness's ball into Lord Dervishton's. The two men were mock-sword-fighting with their sticks and generally making fools of themselves.

Georgiana shifted restlessly. "Poor Miss Hurst will freckle if she continues to stay outside in the sun as she's done today."

Diane sniffed. "Miss Hurst's manners are deplorable." With a glance at Georgiana, Diane turned to Alexander. "MacLean, don't you agree that Miss Hurst has a sad tendency toward hoydenish behavior?"

"Without question," he replied with gratifying quickness.

Georgiana couldn't hide a small smile. That was promising. Several times in the last few days she'd thought she'd detected the faintest hint of genuine interest in MacLean's demeanor. It was so difficult to tell; MacLean was as closed as an oyster. She would have to watch him very, very closely.

She caught Diane's questioning gaze and nodded.

Diane's sharp face seemed to grow even more pointed. "My dear Georgiana, I don't know why you invited such a *common* girl to join our house party. She doesn't fit in at all."

Alexander shrugged. "She seems to have found her place. Just ask Dervishton or Falkland."

Diane tittered. "I doubt their intentions are all they should be, though I do wish Miss Hurst would stop encouraging them. She is making a fool of herself."

Alexander's brows lowered. "She's not encouraging anyone. On the contrary, she is being pursued relentlessly, and Dervishton should count himself fortunate that Miss Hurst doesn't have a male relative on hand who might teach him a lesson in civility."

Good God, he felt protective of the chit! Georgiana's hands bit into the soft-cushioned arms of her chair. What'd happened to the deadly hate he'd once professed?

Her instincts had been correct; he *was* interested in the Hurst girl. Georgiana wanted to screech and yell, but one did not bring a hammer to a fight with a fencer; if she did so, MacLean would simply leave. She had to find a way to disengage him from the girl's side, to show him the obvious flaws in her character, while letting him think *he* was the one making the decision.

Georgiana took a calming breath and managed to say in a fairly languid tone, "It's good that the youngsters have found a game to play."

MacLean's faint smile disappeared. "Youngsters?"

"Dervishton and Falkland are both a good ten years younger than us, and Miss Hurst is—oh, I don't remember her age. She acts enough like a child that I think of her as one."

Diane glanced slyly at Alexander. "Miss Hurst and Miss Ogilvie are very young, indeed. Why, I was just saying that very thing to his grace at breakfast this morning. At thirty, I feel like I'm in a nursery whenever they're about, giggling and carrying on like two schoolgirls."

"Exactly," Georgiana purred. "I'm sure they think of us as positive antidotes."

"Lord MacLean, considering you are nine years older than I am, you must feel especially ancient around them!"

Alexander didn't answer as he watched the game, his brows lowered, his arms now crossed over his chest.

Ah! Georgiana thought. *So that hurts, does it?* She caught Diane's gaze and flicked her fingers toward the terrace door.

Diane scooped up her dog. "Here you go, Muffin. Your Grace, if you will forgive me, I see Mrs. Pruitt. My maid sent my new gown to be ironed, and I wish to make certain it will be ready in time for dinner." Diane disappeared inside with her dog tucked under one arm.

Georgiana forced her hands to relax their grip on the arms of the chair. The wind had lifted and it ruffled MacLean's black hair across his forehead. Finally they were alone, and it brought to mind other times they'd been alone—truly alone. She yearned for those moments, when his touch had marked her as his.

She loved him, yet Alexander didn't seem to notice. Since she'd been rescued from her wretched childhood, she'd been given everything she'd ever wanted, and now she wanted Alexander MacLean to be hers—exclusively, forever.

His gaze was riveted on the tableau on the lawn, his profile in bold relief against the sun-drenched horizon. Georgiana stared greedily, aching for his touch.

A faint smile touched his lips, his gaze warming slightly. Georgiana froze. She'd never seen such an expression on his face. Was it . . . tenderness?

She followed his gaze across the lawn and her heart sank. The Hurst girl had knocked Dervishton's ball into a shrub and she was laughing heartily, the sun caressing her golden hair, the wind playing with her bronze and blue skirts. Dervishton was on his way to retrieve his ball and was holding the cue stick in a mock-threatening manner.

Georgiana's gaze narrowed. "They make a lovely couple, don't they?"

The smile faded from Alexander's face. "Couple?"

"Well, I suppose I shouldn't have used that word; Dervishton is just amusing himself. He's very determined to get under those skirts, and I daresay he'll be successful."

Alexander's gaze turned cool. "Careful, my dear. Your origins are showing."

Her heart skipped a beat. "What do you mean?"

"It's very vulgar of you to make such a statement." His voice was low, soft, almost a purr. "But then you know that, don't you, Georgiana? Roxburge was very careful to teach you *all* of society's rules, wasn't he?"

Georgiana's jaw tightened and she asked in an acid tone, "What's happened to your plan for Hurst, Alexander? Why don't you just ruin her and be done?"

"I explained that. I want to savor this moment."

And her, too? "I think you're falling under her spell."

He turned slowly, his green eyes ablaze. He looked hard and masculine, and her heart thudded against her throat. "I'm not under anyone's spell, including yours."

Georgiana's cheeks grew hot. She should quit—she knew she should, but she couldn't. As if she were outside of her own body, she heard herself say, "When she first arrived, you were determined to have revenge, but something has changed. Last night at dinner, you actually came to her rescue when Diane made a perfectly innocuous comment about her behavior."

"Lady Kinloss's teeth are as sharp as her dog's and you know perfectly well that what she said was not innocuous."

Georgiana couldn't remember the exact comment Diane had made, but she could remember Alexander's sudden blazing look of contempt as he put an abrupt end to Diane's attempt at humor at the Hurst chit's expense. "Alexander, your plans have changed." She leaned forward. *"Admit it."*

"My plans haven't changed."

"You still intend to see to the chit's ruin?"

His dark gaze moved back to the tableau on the lawn. "Eventually, yes. But first . . ." He smiled, a faintly wolfish air to him. "First I have a few tasks to complete."

What did he mean by that? Georgiana wished she dared ask.

His gaze wandered back to the lawn billiards game. "Everything is going well. You'll see soon enough. Caitlyn has proven to be a more worthy opponent than I expected."

His unmistakable admiration raked over Georgiana's sensibilities. *Damn it, the girl is more intelligent than I thought. She's playing him, and he, blinded by her seeming innocence, is falling for it like a fool.* "You're allowing this—this *nobody* to get the best of you. Ruin her and be done with it."

MacLean stiffened, and in the distance a low roil of thunder echoed over the clear, sunny horizon.

The billiards players paused, all of them looking toward the surprising noise except Caitlyn, who turned instead toward the terrace.

Alexander strode toward Georgiana and glared down at her. "I will say this one time only: I will handle this matter as I see fit. When I decide the time has come to ruin Caitlyn Hurst, not even the devil will be able to stop me. But until that time comes, you will leave this affair alone and keep your opinions to yourself. Do you understand?"

Because she had to, Georgiana nodded. With both relief and a sense of aching loss, she watched him turn away from her and go to the edge of the terrace. Georgiana blinked back tears. *By God, if I can't have you, no one will.*

She'd ruin the girl if MacLean wouldn't. It would take so little. *Look at her out there, shamelessly flirting, playing Dervishton against Falkland as if she really were someone.*

Alexander's gaze was locked on the girl now, watching as the wind got the better of her bonnet and sent it tumbling across the green lawn. Instantly every man in the game dropped his cue stick and ran after it. Caitlyn laughed as Falkland, Dervishton, and Caithness jostled one another, fighting for the right to catch the bonnet and return it to its rightful owner.

Miss Ogilvie now came up and slipped an arm about Caitlyn's waist, and the two stood, arm in arm, laughing at the men's display of gallantry.

Georgiana's stomach tightened in disgust. *So the little fool enjoys being the center of attention, does she? We'll see about that!*

Georgiana noted how Alexander's mouth thinned when Dervishton returned triumphant. He presented the bonnet ceremoniously. When Caitlyn placed the hat upon her head, he offered—and was allowed—to tie the bow beneath her chin.

"If you'll pardon me, Georgiana, I'll leave you to enjoy your terrace in peace," Alexander said.

Georgiana found it difficult to swallow. "Perhaps we should take a ride and enjoy the day. If you'd like, I can change into my habit and—"

"No, thank you." He smiled, a cool glint in his eyes.

"I think perhaps I may play some lawn billiards. I haven't done so since I was a child."

He bowed, turned, and strode off the terrace. Moments later, he joined the group on the lawn.

Georgiana had seen more than enough. She tossed aside her blanket and stormed inside, taking out her wrath on the first servant she saw.

The time had come for her to take matters into her own hands. And Caitlyn Hurst didn't stand a chance.

Chapter 15

Do wha' ye say ye will, and the world will be kinder to ye than no'.

OLD WOMAN NORA FROM LOCH LOMOND
TO HER THREE WEE GRANDDAUGHTERS ONE COLD EVENING

Caitlyn went to dinner that night distracted by a number of things—her upcoming challenge, certainly, but also the thought of Alexander MacLean.

He'd surprised her by joining their lawn billiards game. She'd been winning until MacLean showed up and, taking the black cue stick, showed them all how the game was supposed to be played. With deadly precision he passed by her and Sally and spent the remainder of the game repeatedly knocking Dervishton's and Falkland's balls into the shrubbery until both men protested heartily. Their antics had been quite amusing, and Caitlyn didn't know when she'd laughed so hard. She'd seen a side of MacLean she'd never thought to see. While she couldn't really imagine him being playful, he'd gleamed with a dark sense of humor that had even Sally watching him with admiring eyes.

The other members hadn't been so fortunate. By the end of the game, Dervishton had been thrown into a sulk, while Falkland lodged a formal protest with Caithness, who, having had his ball knocked into a stream, had finally offered himself as game official.

Caitlyn's original reason for playing had been to garner information from Dervishton about Lord Dingwall's current situation. She quickly discovered that the young lord had none, though; his family had been out of the countryside for too long to be of any use. Though disappointed, she hadn't allowed that to spoil her enjoyment of the afternoon.

The only thing that had threatened her enjoyment had been the sight of MacLean watching from the terrace, the duchess reclining on a chair beside him. Though Caitlyn could see little of the duchess's expressions, she had the uneasy feeling she was being mocked. Lately, it seemed the duchess couldn't talk without hinting that Caitlyn was inadequate in some way. Worse, the older woman was becoming more and more possessive of MacLean.

Now, finally ready to go down to dinner, Caitlyn paused at the foot of the grand staircase and adjusted her long gloves, glancing in the large mirrors that flanked the foyer to make sure that her white-and-rose silk gown hung just right. The duchess might mock many things, but she couldn't say a word about Caitlyn's wardrobe.

A noise at the top of the step caught Caitlyn's attention, and she turned to find the Marquis of Treymont and his lovely wife coming down the stairs. Her red hair swept into a pile of graceful ringlets on her head, Honoria smiled as she reached the foyer. "Miss Hurst! Good evening."

Caitlyn curtsied. "My lady. My lord."

"I see you caught a bit of sun today," Treymont said.

Caitlyn smiled ruefully. "I'll never be fashionably pale, as I can't seem to stay out of the sunshine."

Honoria grimaced. "I'm the same way, though I burn like a lobster. I just cannot give up my rides."

"You both look beautiful." The marquis's smile glinted, his blue eyes striking against his dark hair.

Caitlyn chuckled. "Very well said, my lord."

"Absolutely brilliant," Honoria agreed, looking at her husband with a loving, laughing gaze. "I'm impressed."

"You should be," he answered promptly. "Miss Hurst, how was lawn billiards? We were going to join you but decided to instead take a ride to the loch in this fine weather."

"You missed quite a match!"

"Did everyone play?"

"Oh, no. Lady Elizabeth had a headache, Lord Dalfour was determined to take a nap, and Lord Roxburge was indisposed—"

"Which means he was sleeping in his favorite chair in the library," Treymont said with a smile.

"Exactly. Lady Kinloss is unimpressed in general, so she stayed away, as did her grace."

"Her grace." Honoria sniffed.

Caitlyn raised her brows.

"Honoria," her husband said in a warning tone.

"I'm sorry, but it's unfair how that woman has treated poor Dingwall!"

"You know Lord Dingwall?" Caitlyn asked.

"He's a distant cousin of my wife's," Treymont said, "which is why she tends to be a bit protective of him, whether he deserves it or not."

Honoria sighed. "He's suffering, poor man."

"I feel for his tragedy, but he didn't need to set the dogs on us." Treymont shook his head. "He's a mean old codger."

"He set the *dogs* on you?"

"Yes, four of the vicious creatures," Honoria said. "I can only recall one time, years ago, when Dingwall was pleasant to us."

"I remember that. I happened to see the duchess riding through town just as we spoke to Dingwall." The marquis grimaced. "I'd just had a dealing with her that had left me rather out of sorts, and I said—"

"Something he shouldn't have." Honoria shot her husband a dry look. "Dingwall brightened right up and even complimented Treymont on his coat. It's the only time he's said a nice word to either of us. It's as if he felt united with us against a common enemy."

Caitlyn could understand. She felt a connection with the marchioness already.

Honoria smiled at Caitlyn. "Why did you wish to know about Dingwall?"

"Idle curiosity. Shall we join the others?"

The three of them entered the dining room.

There, Caitlyn listened with amusement to Sally teasing Caithness about his lost billiards ball and barely noted the roast duck. But her attention was thoroughly caught several dishes later when she was presented with a chocolate trifle set in sweetened crème.

Thick and rich, the trifle soothed her stretched nerves. Smiling to herself, she closed her lips over the spoon and allowed the sweet treat to melt over her tongue. The rich cream sent a shiver of satisfaction through her. She was just lifting the final spoonful to her mouth when she caught Lord Dervishton staring at her. The man's gaze was locked on her mouth, his expression a combination of sensuality and greed.

Caitlyn's cheeks heated and she quickly finished her dessert, looking anywhere but at Dervishton.

In not looking at Dervishton, she found herself looking at MacLean. He met her gaze and quirked his brows, a mocking smile in his eyes as he glanced at Dervishton. She smiled at MacLean in return, and without a word, from opposite ends of the long dining table, they reached agreement that Lord Dervishton was a fool.

Then Georgiana said something in a rather loud voice that required an answer from MacLean, and he reluctantly turned away from Caitlyn. The duchess was looking especially pretty this evening, her red hair swept up into a complicated style decorated with emerald pins that made her bright blue eyes glow. She wore a lovely yellow silk gown with cap sleeves, set with an emerald bow at each shoulder that screamed elegance and grace.

Blast her.

As Caitlyn watched, Georgiana leaned in and placed her hand on MacLean's by his plate. Then, with a deliberate smile, she looked at Caitlyn and murmured something to MacLean.

He quickly glanced Caitlyn's way, his brows snapping down when he found her gaze on him. Embarrassed, Caitlyn returned her gaze to her own plate, but not before Georgiana said something in a low voice that made MacLean flash a wicked grin.

The duchess was mocking her and MacLean was going along with it. Caitlyn hid a scowl, fighting a desire to dump her water goblet all over the duchess's fine gown. But such behavior would cause Caitlyn and her family far more harm than it would the duchess.

Blast it, but life wasn't fair. It would be better if—

Something caught Caitlyn's eye. Mrs. Pruitt stood outside the dining room doors, vigorously dusting a vase on a stand.

Caitlyn frowned. Mrs. Pruitt was a housekeeper with a large staff; such housekeepers did not dust, especially in the hallway outside of a dinner party.

Something was going on. What was the housekeeper up to?

Caitlyn didn't have to wait long. A liveried footman entered the hallway. He looked around, and seeing no one else in sight, he casually walked toward Mrs. Pruitt. When he was level with her, he dropped something on the floor without looking at her, then casually walked past.

Mrs. Pruitt barely waited for the young man to leave before she pounced upon the folded note and stuck it into her pocket. As she turned toward the servants' hall, she caught Caitlyn's gaze.

Mrs. Pruitt looked right, then left, then slipped the folded note from her pocket and waved it meaningfully, mouthing something unintelligible. Caitlyn frowned. Mrs. Pruitt went through the charade again, with more exaggerated motions, which made it even more unintelligible.

Caitlyn shook her head and Mrs. Pruitt sighed, then pointed to the steps. *That* Caitlyn could understand and she nodded. Mrs. Pruitt brightened, then disappeared up the stairs.

Caitlyn was dying to know what was in the note. Did it have to do with Lord Dingwall?

"That's odd" came MacLean's rich voice.

Caitlyn held her breath. Had he seen?

"What's odd?" Georgiana asked.

MacLean looked right at Caitlyn, though he spoke to Georgiana. "I thought I saw something it the hallway."

As Georgiana turned to look, he shrugged and said, "But whatever it was is gone."

Caitlyn had to count to ten to keep from letting the oaf know what she thought of him, especially as he continued to smile as if hugely amused.

She waited until a lull in the conversation, then announced, "I'm afraid I have a headache. I hope you will forgive me if I retire to my room?"

Sally led the cacophony of well wishes, and Dervishton offered to escort her to her door. Caitlyn held him off with the suggestion that not only was her head aching but her stomach, as well.

That killed the light in his eyes and she was able to leave the room alone. The moment she was out of sight, she lifted her skirts and ran up the stairs to her bedchamber.

"Ye aren't goin' to like what we discovered," Muiren said, looking aggrieved.

"Aye," Mrs. Pruitt said, clicking her tongue. " 'Tis no' good news."

"Verrah bad news," Mrs. Sterling added darkly.

Caitlyn had been surprised to find the seamstress waiting in her bedchamber with Muiren and Mrs. Pruitt.

According to Mrs. Pruitt, the older woman would be of great help. Inordinately tall and angular, with broad shoulders and a large, hooked nose, her bristly gray hair pulled back in a severe bun, Mrs. Sterling was an imposing character.

"So what have you discovered?" Caitlyn asked.

Mrs. Sterling said, "If ye arrive like a regular guest and just walk up to the front door, ye'll ne'er get in. His butler is told to toss into the street anyone who knocks on the door. Of course, ye dinna have to worry about that until ye've faced the barbed fences and a field of thistles and—"

"Fences and thistles?" Caitlyn rubbed her forehead, her mind spinning with images of bully butlers and thistle fields. "Goodness, this is going to be difficult."

"Aye," Muiren agreed. "Which is why we've brought ye Mrs. Sterling."

"She can help us," Mrs. Pruitt said.

"She knows a back way into the house?"

Muiren beamed. "Och, no, 'tis better than that: Lord Dingwall's butler is her son."

Mrs. Sterling puffed up. "Aye, miss. Little Angus is old man Dingwall's butler. I'll go with ye an' make sure he lets ye in. He willna turn out his own mother."

"There's more, miss," Mrs. Pruitt said proudly. "Mrs. Sterling knows his lordship's stomach, too. Cook's been working on a basket fer ye to take with ye in the morning."

"That's so nice of her! I'll stop by the kitchens and thank her."

"Och, miss, we're all fer ye," Mrs. Pruitt said, as Mrs. Sterling nodded. "The upstairs maids, the belowstairs washing staff—all of the women in the house are behind ye."

"And Sean, too," Muiren said earnestly, turning pink when Mrs. Pruitt sent her a dark look. "Well, he is! He brought ye a map o' Dingwall's house."

Mrs. Pruitt said in a stiff voice, "Muiren's Sean had his cousin's wife's sister draw up a map of how t' get to Dingwall's house—"

"—*and*," Muiren continued, "a rough sketch of th' house itself, should ye need it."

"That's so nice of him!"

"It is," Mrs. Pruitt said, though she eyed Muiren darkly as she added, "Dinna think that just because we've an emergency on our hands, ye can get away with breaking the house rules by courting a footman."

Muiren looked as if she very much might like to argue, but Mrs. Sterling held up her large hand. "Och, Muiren, dinna fear. I've known Brianna Pruitt fer nigh on forty years now, and she has a soft spot fer a good romance, especially one o' her own."

Mrs. Pruitt turned pink. "I dinna know what you're talkin' about."

"Oh? What about the footman when ye were an undermaid fer the Duke of Carlyle?"

"That wasn't a—"

"And Lord Coldburg's valet? And the groomsman from the—"

"Alyce Fia Sterling! That is quite enou', thank you!" Her face red, Mrs. Pruitt turned back to Caitlyn. "As I was sayin' before all this silliness, we want t' send ye into battle fully girded."

Muiren nodded. "Ye need weapons if ye wish to slay the dragon Dingwall."

Caitlyn had to smile at that. "From what I've heard of him, he would like that name."

"He deserves it, fer he breathes fire at the world, he does," Muiren said.

Mrs. Pruitt reached into her pocket and pulled out the note Caitlyn had seen earlier. "Here ye go, missus—the map t' reach the house."

"That's a great help. I couldn't see the house from the lawn so I wasn't even sure which direction to go."

"You'll find it right enou' now. But there's bad news to go wit' the good: Lord Dingwall owns a mass o' brutal dogs that'll chase whoever he points his bony finger at."

"I've heard of his dogs."

"Och, they're a legend in these parts."

Mrs. Sterling cleared her throat. "But 'tis no' the dogs as are the worst o' it. 'Tis the biting horse."

Caitlyn blinked. "The . . . did you say the 'biting' horse?"

"Aye. Dingwall put a fence about the field in front of his property, then he placed a monstrous mean mare in it. She'll take a morsel as big as yer hand out o' ye. She's an old horse, and mean as they come."

Caitlyn's shoulders slumped. "I thought the most difficult part of this task would be convincing Lord Dingwall to visit the duchess's house. Now I think that might be the easiest part! There's a biting horse, attack dogs, a man who won't allow anyone inside the door—and heaven knows what's after that!"

Mrs. Sterling grinned. "'Twill be an adventure, it will. But ye'll have weapons, a map, and me as yer guide. All ye need is a stout heart."

Warmed by the woman's encouraging smile, Caitlyn felt a surge of hope. "I'm ready when you are!"

Chapter 16

꧁ ꧂

Wish ye, will ye, it's all up to ye.

OLD WOMAN NORA FROM LOCH LOMOND
TO HER THREE WEE GRANDDAUGHTERS ONE COLD EVENING

$\mathcal{C}$aitlyn tucked her hair into her plain bonnet and tied the ribbons under her chin. "So Mrs. Sterling is waitin' for me by the stables?" she asked Muiren.

"Aye, miss."

"Excellent. I'll fetch the basket from the kitchen and we'll be off to Lord Dingwall's. Wish me luck."

"Och, I'll wish ye more than luck miss! Ye're fightin' this war fer the honor o' every woman in the castle."

Caitlyn laughed. "And I'll win it for us, too. This is a surprise attack in every way: Dingwall doesn't know he's about to be invaded, and MacLean thinks I'm stumped." Nothing would delight her more than to shake Lord Imperturbable's façade. She was certain that beneath that controlled exterior beat a heat of— well, not gold, but perhaps an acceptable one of solid iron or brass. Something one could use for a doorstop if one were so inclined.

Muiren eyed Caitlyn up and down. "Miss, do ye think 'tis a good idea to visit his lordship dressed as a commoner? He might mistake ye fer a milkmaid or such."

Caitlyn looked down at the plain gray gown and old brown boots she'd worn to travel to Balloch Castle. "Yes. From what I've heard, Lord Dingwall has a distaste for the duchess and her guests, so I want to look as different from a guest as possible."

Muiren smiled admiringly. "Very clever, miss. I'll come wi' ye to the kitchens to fetch the basket. What an exciting adventure! I wish ye well!"

This would be an adventure all right. Caitlyn only hoped she didn't return home horse-bitten and dog-chased for nothing.

"So this is where you wandered off to."

Alexander glanced up as Dervishton walked down the path toward him. He'd escaped the confines of the house—and Georgiana's tiresomely sharp comments—and had come outside to enjoy a cheroot. He took a last draw on it, then dropped it to the stone path and ground it beneath his heel. "Hello, Dervishton. I take it that you've given up attempting to convince Georgiana of the merits of opera over theater?"

Dervishton chuckled and came farther into the small copse of trees. It was one of many conveniently isolated portions of the expansive gardens that had been installed by the ever-resourceful Georgiana. She had a partiality for the gardens, and their many luxurious gazebos were furnished with benches and pillows; a few even had curtains that could be drawn. Georgiana's garden was the epitome of lascivious convenience.

A servant left the rear of the house and walked past the garden toward the stables. Alexander idly watched as she moved down the path, her figure obscured by a vast cape, the hood pulled high. An approaching stableboy glanced in her direction, stared as his mouth fell open, then, without tearing his gaze from her face, tripped over his own feet and fell over a low hedge.

Alexander smirked. The fool. To be so obvious in his desire for notice. Alexander had no doubt the maid was laughing at him and would never look at him with respect.

"MacLean, I wish to ask you a question."

Alexander spared Dervishton a glance.

"Georgiana has hinted that Miss Hurst is not of a good family."

Damn Georgiana! "She's quite mistaken. Miss Hurst's father is a vicar. She is also connected through marriage to Lord Galloway, who is not to be trifled with."

"But Georgiana all but said that Miss Hurst is . . . available. And if I were to bid high enough—"

"*No.*" The word cracked into air like a storm waiting, banked and ready. The silence afterward was ominous.

So Georgiana wasn't content to allow him to handle his affairs, was she? He'd have words with her about that. Caitlyn Hurst was *his:* his to punish, his to tease, his to torment.

Dervishton's smile was strained. "Look, MacLean, I—"

"Forget it. You aren't at fault." To keep his anger in control, Alexander focused again on the stableboy. The lad was back on his feet now, bowing as if the maid were the queen herself.

Alexander frowned. Perhaps it wasn't a maid. The woman waved at the boy and hurried on, her drab gray skirts swaying gracefully, a strand of golden hair escaping the hood—

Alexander started. "Pardon me, Dervishton. My groom wished me to stop in the stables before lunch."

"Yes, but about Georgiana—"

"You have my full encouragement in that quarter— but *not* in regard to Miss Hurst." Alexander took off down the path.

"But, MacLean, that's not—" Dervishton called after him.

But Alexander didn't answer, the sway of those gray skirts leading him forward. He stepped around the stableboy, who was standing in the middle of the path staring after the maid. The youth sent him a hard glare, turning a bright red when he realized it was Alexander. "My lord, I'm so—"

"Go about your business." Alexander continued on, his attention on the maid. Her bonnet was as plain as her gown, the deep brim and faded flowers reminiscent of some of the flower sellers who hawked their wares in Convent Garden. *So little Miss Hurst is trying to slip away unnoticed. What is she up to now?*

Alexander reached her just as she turned down the path that led away from the garden. "Going somewhere, Hurst?"

She came to a halt, her back stiffening. She slowly turned to face him, her face framed by the wide bonnet, her brown eyes suspicious. She carried a heavy basket, a cloth tucked securely across it.

Alexander grinned. "If you wish to disguise yourself, you will have to hide your posterior. I recognized it even across the garden."

Her lips thinned with annoyance. "I'll remember that next time I'm in disguise."

"May I ask where you're going?"

"No."

He crossed his arms.

Her gaze narrowed. "It's none of your concern."

"Oh, but I think it is." He glanced at the basket in her hands. "What's in there?"

"None of yo—"

He lifted the basket out of her hands and flipped back the linen cover. "Jellies, jams, some freshly baked bread, and—what's in the crock?" He bent forward and sniffed. "Soup?"

She retrieved the basket and flipped the linen cover back into place. "What I am doing is none of your concern. Now, if you will excuse me, I have an errand to run."

"An errand?" His gaze narrowed a moment before it dawned on him. "You're off to win Lord Dingwall's goodwill with a basket full of incitements."

Alexander knew he'd hit the mark when her chin lifted and her expression closed tightly.

A flush of amusement rippled through him. Truly, he'd never wanted anything the way he wanted to beat this woman at her own game.

He smiled when she said in a pert tone, "I am sure that it's of no mind to you. After all, you declared that no matter what I try, Lord Dingwall will have nothing to do with me."

Alexander grinned down at her, his arms crossed over his chest as he rocked back on his heels. "You could simply save your pride, admit that you've lost, and come to my bed now." Even in her plain clothing, there was no disguising her beauty. He was especially fond of the bonnet, which framed her face and made her brown eyes seem even larger.

She regarded him with a determined expression. "I'm going to win this, and *you,* my lord, will be on your knee. Wait and see!"

Alexander shrugged. "You won't succeed. Dingwall hates the duchess."

"Well, if I fail—and I don't believe I will—it won't be for lack of trying."

He rather liked it when she lifted her chin like that. "A few slices of freshly baked bread and some soup won't break a decade's old feud."

"How I go about this is none of your concern. I'll see you this evening, MacLean. *With* Lord Dingwall." She spun on one heel and left, her basket clutched against her.

Alexander waited until she disappeared around the stables before he followed. A loud chorus of female voices raised in greeting made him pause at the edge of the stables and peer around the corner.

Every maid in the house seemed to be standing there, and Caitlyn was welcomed like a hero of a classic Greek myth. *Good God, MacCready was right: she has every female firmly on her side.*

Caitlyn spoke to a tall, large-boned hulk of a woman with iron-gray hair tied back in a bun. She was almost twice the size of Caitlyn, her shoulders as broad as a farmhand's.

They said farewell to the group, then headed toward the low fence that surrounded Lord Dingwall's land. The women watched them until a call from the kitchen door made them hurry away. Alexander followed Caitlyn toward the fence, his long strides quickly overtaking her and her companion.

Caitlyn looked over her shoulder and saw MacLean approaching, his dark hair ruffled by the breeze, his green eyes agleam, his stride purposeful. She couldn't help a small thrill of excitement from racing down her spine as she gestured for Mrs. Sterling to continue. With a glare at MacLean, the older woman huffed on to the fence, well within earshot.

"What do you want now?" Caitlyn asked impatiently.

"I came to give you a word of advice."

Caitlyn hesitated. She wasn't sure if she trusted him, yet she was determined not to miss any important information. "You've been anything but helpful up until now."

"But this time I am quite certain there is no way in hell you'll succeed, so I can afford to be generous. I've heard that Lord Dingwall takes a walk every afternoon around three. If you can't get into the house, that may give you access to him."

"Oh, we'll get into the house. But thank you for your advice, I'll let you know if we needed it."

"There is also the little matter of the horse."

"I already know that it bites."

He grinned, his eyes crinkling in an alarmingly attractive way. "Do you know about *all* of the horses?"

She glanced back at the field, which looked empty. All she could see was a sea of grass that led to a manor house on a small rise.

"I have no desire to see that beautiful skin bruised." He slipped his finger along her cheek, leaving shivery tingles in his wake.

She jerked away. "Thank you for that bit of knowledge. But bite or no bite, you'll never see my bared skin."

From by the fence, Mrs. Sterling gave a supportive, take-that "Humph!"

MacLean's gaze narrowed. "We'll see about that."

Drat the man! Every time he had the chance to muddle her thinking with a kiss or a touch, he took it. Well, she'd show him!

She stalked to the fence, put the basket through the rails onto the ground, and nimbly climbed over. As she waited for Mrs. Sterling to do the same, she glanced under her lashes at MacLean. His brows were raised, a look of surprise—appreciation?—on his face. Well, he *should* be appreciative. She'd been born and raised in the country, and if there was one thing she knew how to do, it was how to scale a fence.

When Mrs. Sterling joined her, Caitlyn picked up her basket and set out for the house. It took almost twenty minutes and a good deal of it was uphill, but she didn't see one sign of the biting horse.

"Of course I didn't," she muttered as she marched behind Mrs. Sterling's broader back, keeping a sharp lookout for snapping dogs. "Just you wait, MacLean. This evening I'll have finished my task, and you haven't even started yours!"

An hour and a half before dinner, Alexander said, "MacCready, gather my army."

The valet, who had just set a stack of fresh hand towels by the basin in the corner of the room, turned to look at Alexander. "Your army, my lord?"

"Yes, you said you'd recruit some helpers. Where are they? Miss Hurst had an entire platoon of women to see her off on her voyage to Lord Dingwall's house."

"Oh, *that* army. Well, my lord, it was not as easy to convince the men to join our cause as I hoped. I was reduced to offering bribes."

"*What?*"

"The men don't dare to be open in their support of you for fear of retaliation from the other side."

"Fools, the lot of them. What can the females do besides overstarch neckcloths?"

"Actually, my lord, the females have done quite a bit more." MacCready opened the wardrobe to reveal a stack of white shirts with iron burns, two waist-coats with every button snipped off, and boots that appeared to have been blackened with coal dust.

"Good God!"

"Precisely, my lord. Not only must I inspect every housekeeping item before it comes into the room, but I must also check for hidden items in your food and drink—"

"Drink?" Alexander glanced at his decanter of port and frowned. "The port is excellent."

"*That* port is excellent because I personally fetched that decanter of port from the library. The brown tea that was sent up as 'port' was not excellent."

Alexander had to admit that Caitlyn had made this little game interesting. He never knew what would happen next. "Have we *no* assistance?"

"I found only two, my lord."

"I'm disappointed in the lack of backbone displayed by the males here. Well, collect our two volunteers and bring them here. Miss Hurst will arrive at dinner empty-handed, and I wish to have my task completed by then. It will take more than one person to capture the bow from that monster Lady Kinloss calls Muffin."

"Yes, my lord. I shall bring them here immediately." MacCready bowed and left.

Alexander finished tying his cravat, wondering how Caitlyn was faring. A faint flicker of worry raised its head. *She's fine. She had that hulking guard of a woman with her. Besides, what's the worst that could happen?*

Well . . . the dogs could attack her, or that damned biting horse. And what if Dingwall really was crazy, not just justifiably angry with Georgiana?

Alexander restlessly went to the window to look at the road. Nothing moved as the sun sank over the lake. No horses were coming or going, and the stables were still.

Damn it! He turned away and crossed to the fireplace, which crackled merrily. He grasped the fire iron to stir the logs, and the handle came loose from the shaft, which clanked noisily onto the marble hearth.

Grumbling, he bent down and picked up the iron shaft, which immediately slid from his fingers. *What in hell—* He looked at his hands. Black grease smeared his palm and fingers.

Teeth clenched, he threw the handle to the floor and stalked to his water basin. With his clean hand, he grabbed the pitcher and tilted it to pour water into the basin, when *Crash!* The pitcher fell to the floor and broke into a thousand pieces, brown liquid spilling everywhere.

The scent of port tickled his nose. *So that's where they dumped it.*

Alexander stood scowling at the handle left in his hand, his shirt and breeches splattered with port, glass and brown liquid all over the floor, and his one hand still covered in grease. With a disgusted snort, he went to drop the handle, only to find that some enterprising female had coated it with a sticky substance.

He had to open his hand flat and shake it until the damn handle dropped to the washstand.

Bloody hell, what a mess. He looked at his hands, then decided that the port that had landed in the washbasin would have to do. He washed his hands in it, glad to see that it was as effective as water.

The door opened and MacCready entered, pausing as he saw the destruction. "Oh, dear. My lord, I'm so sorry this happened! If you'll take off your shirt and waistcoat, I can—"

"No, thank you, MacCready. I'll wear what I have on until dinner. I might get a bit mussed with this dog."

"Very well, my lord. I've brought your squadron for their first inspection." He went to the door and looked down the hall. "This way, please. Come in!"

In shuffled an ancient man and a pockmarked youth with a shock of bright orange hair. So these were the men who weren't afraid of the women in the household. No wonder: they stood no chance of gaining female attention anyway.

MacCready gestured to the older man. "This is Rob McNabb, and this is young Hamrick Hannaday. They're your squadron."

The old man snapped a smart salute, while the younger man simply looked confused.

Alexander picked up a towel and dried his hands. "Good to meet you, gentlemen. I appreciate your assistance with my little task."

Alexander went to the bed and stripped the case from a pillow, then tossed the case to Hamrick. "Hold on to this." Crossing to the fireplace, Alexander used a throw blanket from the settee to wipe the fire iron clean of grease.

Then he retrieved the empty pillowcase from Hamrick and hooked it over the end of the iron and rested the contraption over his shoulder. "Come, my lads. We're off to hunt."

An hour later, Alexander returned to his bedchamber with his two soldiers.

"Good God!" MacCready said. "What happened?"

Alexander nodded to Hamrick, who held up the pillowcase, a mass of writhing, snarling dog clearly outlined inside.

"You got him!"

"Yes," Alexander said grimly. "Finally. I don't know how, but he saw us coming."

"Aye," Hamrick said, giving a huge grin. "He gave us a run fer our money, he did. Round the library and outside—"

"Outside?"

"All the way to the lake." Alexander dropped into a chair by the fireplace.

"That explains the mud."

"I dove for the little bastard and almost had him."

MacCready eyed Old Rob. "What happened to your hand? Or need I ask?"

"Tha' crazed mutt bit me when I tried to feed it a wee bit o' liver!"

"Ah. And how did you finally catch the wild beast?"

"We smeared a cloth with pâté, and when he came sniffing, we all jumped him." Alexander smiled with satisfaction.

"Aye," Old Rob said. "He's a fierce wee beastie. We could have used the help o' more men."

Hamrick nodded, his orange hair flapping about his ears. "I had 'is leg, and Old Rob had his ear. Lord MacLean whipped that pillowcase out and now we have him!"

MacCready didn't look impressed. "I see. And what do you propose to do with him?"

Alexander rubbed his neck. He was sore and dirty and had bruises on every inch of his body. "All we need is its damned bow, but it must be glued on to the mutt. In all the racing and running and wrestling, it didn't budge."

Hamrick held the pillowcase aloft, and Muffin's snarling snout appeared against the side of the bag. "I'll no' put me hand in there to get his bow, no matter wha' coins ye offer."

"Me, neither!" Old Rob moved his bandaged hand and winced. "In fact, if yer lordship has no more use fer me, I think I'll find me way to the kitchen and see if they'll rewrap me hand."

MacCready opened the door and placed a coin in the man's uninjured palm as he left.

Hamrick hurriedly handed the bag of dog to Alexander and went to get his own coin, then MacCready shut the door.

"There will be no food in the kitchen for either of them," he predicted. "They've joined the enemy, and now they'll discover the price."

Alexander grunted, staring at the bag. "Now, how am I to get the bow? Perhaps I should shake the bag and—"

"My lord, please give me the dog."

Alexander willingly handed the bag over. "What to you propose to do? This task is lethally dangerous. That dog's a vicious, cold-blooded, ill-tempered—"

"The bow, my lord."

Alexander blinked. Muffin's pink bow lay in MacCready's hand while the dog was tucked securely under his other arm, panting loudly and looking absurdly pleased with himself.

"How in hell did you do that?"

"My uncle was a rat-terrier farmer. I grew up around them and know a trick or two."

"A rat-terrier *farmer?*"

"A suppose the term should be *breeder,* but I dislike the common sound of that word."

"I see. So you know a trick or two and yet you didn't offer to help?"

"You didn't ask." MacCready opened the door, patted the dog, then placed him on the floor. "Off to your mistress, you little hell-monger. And don't pee upon the carpets on your way, either," the valet ordered. "Don't think I don't know *that* little trick."

Muffin's tail wagged furiously, and with a bark he ran out of the room, his nails clicking on the wooden hallway floor.

MacCready closed the door. "I shall order you a bath, my lord. You still have thirty minutes before dinner."

Alexander sat up frowning. "Did you hear that?"

"Hear wha—"

"A carriage."

MacCready tilted his head to one side. After a second, his eyes widened. "My lord! You don't think—"

Alexander was at the window in a second. Outside, an ancient carriage had just pulled up before Balloch

Castle. As Alexander watched grimly, footmen immediately ran outside to help.

Though he didn't recognize the old man who was assisted out of the carriage, Alexander did recognize Miss Caitlyn Hurst.

"Damn it. She did it. She brought Lord Dingwall to dinner."

Chapter 17

'Tis a pleasure to win—but sometimes 'tis more of a pleasure no' to be the one to lose!

OLD WOMAN NORA FROM LOCH LOMOND
TO HER THREE WEE GRANDDAUGHTERS ONE COLD EVENING

Caitlyn had indeed brought Lord Dingwall, who wore satin knee breeches, yellowed stockings held up with garters, and a puce satin jacket. His clothing would have been the epitome of fashion twenty years ago, but today they appeared like a costume worn on a stage.

But Dingwall's manners were surprisingly urbane, mainly because he was in a sparkling good mood. Caitlyn stood at his side and beamed, looking so excited and happy that it set the tone with the majority of the guests. Dervishton and Falkland made fools of themselves welcoming the old man. It also helped that the Treymonts were distant relatives; they welcomed Dingwall warmly and with a touch of familiarity that set his acceptance even further.

At the table, Alexander sipped his wine and ignored Georgiana. She sat fuming, ill humor rising from her like invisible steam. It had taken some sharp words to extract a promise from her to accept Dingwall's presence. In fact, it had taken many sharp words. Alexander knew she finally agreed only because she was still clinging to the delusion that she had a place in his bed sometime in the near future. She didn't, of course, and he'd been blunt in expressing that fact, but she seemed to think that something might change.

He sent her a glance and found her looking at something with an expression of hate. He followed her gaze, expecting to find her looking at Dingwall, but her fury was directed directly at Caitlyn.

An uneasy feeling settled between his shoulders. Georgiana wasn't evil, but she could be cutting. He'd begun to realize that one of Caitlyn's many faults—besides being painfully impulsive and stubborn as a mule—was that she met the world with her arms and heart wide-open, which made her vulnerable—a fact she'd deny to her last breath. That very trait made her especially vulnerable to the sort of shenanigans Georgiana was capable of.

Alexander worried about the hatred he saw in Georgiana's eyes. Had his own vitriol against Caitlyn's actions caused it? Or was it because Georgiana was facing a younger, more beautiful, and more taking woman? Whatever had sparked the fire, it was raging now.

A burst of laughter from the other end of the table captured Alexander's attention. Dingwall was keeping the far end of the dinner table entertained, in a marked contrast to the sullen silence surrounding Georgiana. As Alexander watched, Dingwall said something that made Caitlyn chuckle and then reply, her eyes sparkling. Lord Dervishton, who'd somehow managed to trick Falkland into switching seats with him, leaned forward eagerly to catch what she was saying.

Alexander's gaze narrowed.

Dervishton continued to press forward when there was no chance for him, and he was beginning to irk Alexander. It was time he explained to Dervishton why his efforts were futile.

A cool hand was placed over his and he looked up to meet Georgiana's gaze, frosty and demanding. In a low voice that shook with fury, she said, "I've addressed no fewer than three remarks to you and you've not answered a one."

"I'm sorry. I was distracted by Lord Dingwall's puce coat."

Her lips thinned. "Oh? Thinking of getting one?"

"No. I'm distracted, not demented."

She flicked a glance at the end of the table and then back to him. "I wonder."

Alexander refused to rise to her bait. "Dingwall has become the life of the party."

"Of course he has," Georgiana said sharply. "He's in the one house he never thought to be invited into. Why on earth did you demand that I allow that man to come here?"

Lady Kinloss tittered nervously, her gaze darting between Alexander and the duchess and back. "Though

Lord MacLean asked if Dingwall could come, it was Miss Hurst who brought him. I find that very odd!"

Georgiana's lips thinned yet more. "I wish I'd never invited her."

"She isn't up to your usual standards. Not at all!"

Alexander had to bite his tongue to keep from saying something cutting, which would only bring more wrath on Caitlyn's unsuspecting head. "Lady Kinloss, I heard that your dog went missing for a time today."

"Oh my! I was so worried! He was gone for almost an hour!"

"Where was he?"

"I don't know, but he lost his bow and he's been acting most strange since he returned."

"How so?"

"Why he licked the housemaid's hand when she poured him a bowl of milk!"

"Astonishing."

"Yes, and she told me that she saw him making up to your valet in the kitchen. Usually Muffin doesn't like men. I find it most peculiar."

"So do I."

Georgiana sniffed. "Muffin may be turning into a lapdog. If he needs lessons, we can ask Dervishton. He had a head start in that area."

Lady Kinloss giggled. "Or Lord Falkland! Dervishton isn't the only one caught in Miss Hurst's net."

Alexander knew Georgiana was watching him closely to see his reaction, so he wisely hid his irritation at their pettiness. He might fault Caitlyn for many things, but not once had he seen her encourage either Falkland or Dervishton. The problem lay more in the direction of what she *didn't* do. She didn't demand they leave her be, nor would she warn them off unless they were drastically out of line.

Lord Dingwall's voice drifted to their end of the table. Alexander winced as the man, all in a tone of jocular fun, made several critical comments about the house and the food. Alexander was certain his intent was to make Georgiana squirm with anger, and she did.

Alexander was relieved when dinner was finally over. The women walked to the grand salon, while the gentlemen retired to the library for a glass of port.

Once Dingwall was out from under the watchful eyes of the ladies, he began to tell raucous stories about his skirmishes with the duchess, no doubt embellishing them to make himself appear wittier. Within minutes, he had Dervishton, Falkland, and Caithness in stitches.

If Georgiana got wind of this, she was bound to be even more furious.

Eventually, the group began to mingle. Roxburge was speaking animatedly to Caithness about the benefits of bathing in various hot springs, while Dervishton, Treymont, and Falkland were exchanging hunting stories and discussing which area of the local countryside was best for fox.

Dingwall downed yet another glass of port, smacked his lips noisily, and belched, then gave a blissful smile. "Pardon."

"Would you like some more?" Alexander asked.

Dingwall's glass was in the air in a trice. "Dinna mind if I do."

Alexander nodded to a footman, who hurried forward to refill the glass.

Dingwall took another appreciative drink and sighed. "Ah, now. That's the best port I've ever had."

"It is excellent. So tell me, Dingwall, what magic did Miss Hurst perform to get you here?"

The old man grinned, his face wreathed in creases. "You know Miss Hurst?"

"Yes."

"You wouldn't be courting her, would you? I've looked at these other jackanapes, and they don't seem man enough to handle a woman like that."

Alexander was growing more intrigued by the second. "Did she threaten you? Does she have some sort of damaging information? Or did she bring a pistol?"

Dingwall gave a short laugh. "She might have. There's no telling what was in that basket of hers. She kept my horse from biting her by throwing apples at its hooves. It was so busy munching them that it couldn't munch her."

Alexander had to admit that was brilliant.

"And to still the dogs, she had a dozen pig ribs that she threw all of the way on the other side of the road. Off the dogs went, leaving the front door unguarded."

"That was good planning." There had been more to Caitlyn's basket than Alexander had realized.

"You don't know the half of it. I was under siege! And by a mere slip of a girl, accompanied by a giant of a woman with hair in places she shouldn't have. The giant had the nerve to tell me she'd steal my butler if I didn't give the wee lass a listen."

"I take it you listened."

The old man slapped his thigh and laughed. "Damn right, I did. I had to. That butler's worth his weight in gold—and if you knew how heavy he was, you'd appreciate just what that means."

"So tell me, what did Miss Hurst say?"

"She dinna beat about the bushes. She came right out and told me she knew I was no good."

"What?"

"That's what I thought, too. Little mouthy slip of a girl! What could she know? But then she looked me right in the eyes and said, 'I know a way you can turn the Duchess of Roxburge's hair turn white this very evening.'"

Alexander had to smile. "How could you resist such a temptation?"

Dingwall chortled. "I couldna! And let me tell you, it's been worth it and more. I've never seen the duchess so angry, even when I stole her poodle!"

Damn, Caitlyn was an unexpectedly tough opponent. She was resourceful, creative, and capable of getting any number of people to dance to her tune. "I've heard about that poodle."

Dingwall finished his port. "Good dog, that. Wouldn't give him back now if I could. Sleeps on the foot of my bed. I changed his name from Graceful to Butch, though." The old man snorted. "It's a good thing I took him; that stupid name would have ruined him."

Dingwall began to reminisce about his past dogs, Alexander pretended to listen, but inside he marveled at how Caitlyn had met her challenge. He was beginning to realize that no matter what task he set her to, she would find a way to make it happen.

A surge of admiration warmed him. By God, she was an unusual woman. He couldn't imagine ever getting bored with her even if he spent his entire life with her.

Then icy cold gripped his throat. *My entire life? What am I thinking? She is beautiful, intelligent, and unique, but she's also far more than a dozen years younger than I am.*

A whispered voice deep inside him asked, *So? There are couples who have that many years between them and more.*

That was true. Such as Georgiana and Roxburge. Alexander turned to look at the duke, who was now asleep in his chair, his chin to his chest, drool dampening his cravat. Alexander thought of the distaste in Georgiana's eyes whenever she spoke of her husband, and his heart tightened with determination. If he ever took a wife, he'd make certain she'd *never* look at him with such disrespect.

Perhaps it was that, more than anything else, that had made his friend Charles think that taking his life was the only possible solution for his predicament. When a man lost his pride, little else was left.

Alexander hardened his heart. Whatever future Caitlyn Hurst had, it was not with him. As soon as he could, he excused himself and made his way to the terrace. The cool night air whipped across the stone flag way, rustling the shrubbery and murmuring through the trees, stirring up the scents of pine and crushed grass. He rammed his hands into his pockets, lifted his head, and pulled deep, cleansing breaths of cold air into his lungs. The feeling of being pressed slowly subsided, and in its place was an odd emptiness, as if he'd left something behind, but didn't know what.

What is wrong with me? Damned silliness. He turned on his heel and reentered the library. Caitlyn Hurst was not for him, and that was the way it would always be.

"Georgiana, you must be careful," Diane said.

"I'm done with that hoyden and her tricks! She brought *Dingwall* into my house, that—"

"Yes, yes," Diane said hastily, glancing across the room where Caitlyn Hurst sat at a pianoforte talking to Miss Ogilvie, the two laughing merrily. "She brought him here, but you *did* say she might."

"I never said a word to that—that—" Georgiana's fingers curled into the palms of her hands, her nails biting into the skin. "Alexander is to blame for this! I didn't want to believe it, but it's true: MacLean wants the girl." The words tasted like ash on her tongue. MacLean belonged to *her*, not some ill-bred country miss.

Diane gave a nervous laugh. "Do you really think MacLean wants her?"

"I'm sure of it. I've seen the way he looks at her."

"He hasn't been pursuing her like Dervishton."

"Dervishton is merely playing. His finances require him to find himself a wealthy wife or, barring that, a wealthy patroness who will pay for his services."

"Really? I had no idea!"

"Why did you think I'd invited him?"

"He seemed interested in you until—" Diane sent Georgiana a hurried gaze. "I mean, he's quite a handsome man, too, though not as handsome as MacLean."

Yes, Georgiana owed Caitlyn for the loss of Dervishton's attentions, as well. Nothing about this house party had played out the way she'd wished.

"What do you intend to do?" Diane asked.

"I shall assist MacLean in his original game and ruin Caitlyn Hurst."

"How? You can't humiliate her in public; she's made friends. The marquis and his wife think she's charming. It would cause talk and leave you looking far worse than she."

Georgiana's stomach clenched at the thought. She'd fought hard to earn her position and keep it. She hadn't allowed anyone close enough to discover her secrets . . . until Alexander MacLean.

But now she'd lost him, and to whom? A naïve vicar's daughter. Georgiana would get rid of Caitlyn Hurst if it was the last thing she did, but not at the cost of her own position. She'd die before she gave that up. "I'll think of something," she told Diane, and she would.

She wasn't the normal society woman, bound by conventionality. Whether he knew it or not, Alexander MacLean was hers and no one else's. He was just lost for a moment, blinded by the tricks of a country bumpkin whose blood was no bluer than Georgiana's.

"Diane, watch the door. The men will return soon, but I need to have a word with our young guest first."

"What are you going to say?"

"Enough. Now watch the door, and let me know when the gentlemen return." With that, Georgiana made her way across the grand salon until she reached the pianoforte. Fortunately, Miss Ogilvie had just left to fetch another glass of sherry and Caitlyn was alone.

Georgiana leaned over the pianoforte. "I daresay you think you've accomplished quite a feat."

Caitlyn looked up from where she'd been idly playing a children's song. "I hardly think playing 'Five Currant Buns' qualifies as a 'feat,' Your Grace. Had I been playing 'See-Saw, Margery Daw,' I would accept your accolade with pleasure."

Georgiana curled her lip. "My, aren't you full of good humor."

A look of caution entered Caitlyn's face. "Your Grace, is . . . is something wrong?"

"No. I was just feeling sorry for you, that's all."

"Why?"

"Because when you leave us here at Balloch Castle, you'll have to return to"—Georgiana waved a hand—"wherever you came from."

Caitlyn's face tightened but she answered pleasantly, "I'm from Wythburn Vicarage."

"It's quite sad, really, that you must go back at all. I know it'll be very difficult for you. But that is the problem with charity, isn't it? Eventually the project must return from whence it came."

"I look forward to going home," Caitlyn returned evenly, though her color was high and her fingers were curled into claws over the pianoforte. "I'm sure I'll find it refreshing—a breath of fresh air after so much *staleness.*"

Georgiana stiffened, fury slicing through her veins and racing to her head. She wanted to throttle the girl, to close her hands around her neck and twist until she screamed. Instead, she said in a steady enough voice, "Stale? Shall I have a footman open a window? I daresay that's another thing you won't have—footmen and such. Why, you'll undoubtedly be scrubbing your own crockery, won't you?"

Caitlyn's eyes flashed, and Georgiana continued, "I allowed you in this house for one reason and one reason only: because Alexander wished to humiliate you."

"I know. He's told me. But I think he may have changed his mind."

It took every ounce of will that Georgiana possessed to force her stiff cheeks to relax into a smile. "You poor child, is that what you really think? That he's changed his mind?"

Uncertainty flashed through the brown eyes. "I think he has, yes."

Georgiana laughed, fed by the girl's uncertainty. "My dear, you *are* naïve, aren't you? Alexander has been playing you for a fool, and he's enjoyed every moment of it. Come the final day, he will discredit you just as he planned. Why, just last night when we were in bed—" She paused and laughed. "I suppose it doesn't matter if you know he and I share a bed on occasion."

"I had heard," the girl said, her chin high, her face suspiciously pale.

"Well, last night he was laughing about Lord Dingwall and how you came to invite him here."

Caitlyn frowned. "He explained that to you?"

So there is *something there!* "Of course he did. He tells me *everything*."

The girl's face flamed red. "*Everything?*"

"Naturally." Georgiana chuckled. "I must say, you've given us quite a bit of amusement."

Caitlyn blindly locked her gaze on the music on the pianoforte. Her hands were curled into fists in her lap, her back ramrod straight, her jaw tight. Every word the duchess uttered seared like a burn.

"Oh, look," the duchess purred. "There he is now. Excuse me, Miss Hurst. I'm wanted elsewhere."

Caitlyn forced her fingers to uncurl, and began to play another simple piece. Could it be true? *Had* Alexander agreed to her tasks merely because he wished to mock her to his lover? Was she being made a fool of?

Anger trembled through her. She'd ask Alexander, though she feared the truth. The only way the duchess could know about the tasks was if Alexander had mentioned them to her.

Not five minutes ago, she'd been ecstatic. Not only had she convinced Dingwall to visit, she'd also had a brainstorm in the carriage and had thought of the perfect task to finally break MacLean. She'd been abuzz with good spirits, but a few minutes with the duchess had left her angry and upset.

Arguing loudly, Dervishton and Falkland made their way to her side. She played a few more ditties and was relieved when Caithness brought Sally over and Caitlyn could beg her to take her place. Sally agreed with alacrity, and soon the room was filled with a perfectly played Italian aria.

Caitlyn looked for Alexander and found him standing to one side of the fireplace, his head bent to catch Georgiana's words, his expression intense.

Caitlyn had to bite her lip to keep from marching up to them and . . . What could she do? A slap would be too kind, a kick too quick, and a verbal punching too tame. For the first time in her life, she wanted to actually *hurt* another person.

The realization cooled her blood. As impulsive as her nature was at times, she'd never condoned violence. Yet she couldn't quell the furor that raced through her veins. Was it because Georgiana had been so snide? Or was it something more? Something about MacLean that made her want *more*?

His head was bent low so he could hear Georgiana and a lock of hair had fallen over his brow. As Caitlyn watched, he looked up and met her gaze.

A deep warmth began in the pit of her stomach and spiraled through her. It was as if, with that one look, he'd touched her, bared skin to bared skin.

Caitlyn's breath came harsh and ragged, her nipples peaked, and a deep ache built from her core. God, she wanted him. Memories of their passion in the library flooded her, sending heated longing through her.

Her desperate need must have shown in her eyes, for MacLean's gaze heated as well and his expression grew hungry. She took a step toward him and his gaze suddenly narrowed, the heat leaving his face in an instant.

She hesitated, and his lids slid down to shield his gaze, a cold, almost haughty expression appeared on his face. He said something and Georgiana looked over her shoulder and laughed.

Caitlyn stiffened with hot embarrassment. She was a mass of confused, uncomfortable feelings and thoughts. She had to bite her lip to halt the tears that threatened. Should she flee and retire to her bedchamber before the tears fell?

But before she could move, MacLean excused himself from Georgiana's side and walked toward Caitlyn.

Good God, he's coming here! What does he want? Perhaps now is the time I should ask him why he broke the rules of our agreement? But . . . do I really want to know?

He bowed impersonally when he reached her.

Something has changed; I can feel it. Her jaw tight, she managed a curtsy. When she straightened, he was regarding her with all the warmth of a marble slab.

"I was surprised you managed to bring Dingwall to dinner."

"I told you I'd do it. Did you get the bow from Muffin?"

"Of course. It's in my room. I'll bring it down to breakfast tomorrow."

Every word was chilled, sharp. Feeling as if a large stone were lodged in her chest, she managed a faint smile. "Very well. Did you . . . have any trouble?"

He shrugged. "Of course not. It's just a little dog, after all."

Blast it! That should have been difficult.

As if he could hear her thoughts, he gave her a cold smile. "I'm fortunate in that my valet seems to be a dog hypnotist of some sort."

"That's an unfair advantage."

"When you had the entire female staff at your beck and call? I hardly think so." He crossed his arms over his chest and looked down at her cooly. "We've one more task, and I have my challenge at the ready. Do you?"

"Yes."

"Proceed, then."

"In the story, the hero donned a costume and slipped into a dinner party to procure a magic harp."

"I'm to find a 'magic harp,' then, which is really . . . ?"

"There will be a real harp in the music ensemble playing for the ball. Lady Kinloss told me about it."

His air of suspicion increased. "That's it?"

"Just be sure you don't trip on your skirts."

He didn't move, his expression arrested. "Skirts?"

"That's part of the task. The hero donned a costume, in this case a woman's gown. You're to come to the costume ball in skirts."

His gaze narrowed. "You would make a fool of me."

"And you didn't hope to do the same by sending me to Lord Dingwall's? You wanted me to return muddied and horse-bitten and—"

"Fine," he said grimly. "Then your last task shall be just as difficult. At one point in your fanciful story, Olwen disrobed and swam in the fountain to distract a group of marauders intent on capturing her beloved. You will do that for me."

"At the party! I would be ruined!"

"I didn't suggest you do so at the party, though that is tempting. No, this last task is for me and me alone. If I'm to take you to mistress, I wish to see you beforehand."

She shivered at the way his gaze scoured her, as if she were already naked. "I . . . I could get caught."

His smile turned wicked. "*You* suggested we choose our tasks from that damned book. Well, I did. You will swim naked for me, or I win."

Her hands fisted, blood pounding through her at his dismissive tone. "Fine! I'll do it!" She would, too. It wouldn't be that bad, as long as no one knew. "I'll do it late at night, after midnight."

He shrugged. "You may do it whenever you wish, but you'll do it. You like to pretend that you're braver than you are, but we'll see, won't we?"

"At least I'm a person of my word, unlike you."

His smile faded. "What are you talking about?"

"We agreed not to tell the other guests about our wager, and you told the duchess!"

"I did not."

"She said you did—and *I* certainly didn't tell her about it."

"Neither did I. I don't know how she came to find out, but it wasn't from me."

Caitlyn glared at him. "Just admit it. I know you two are—" She couldn't get the words from between her lips.

His brows snapped down. "My business is no concern of yours."

Oh! He couldn't even deny it! "Once these tasks are finished, I'll look forward to never seeing you again!"

"Once this wager is done, you'll see a lot of me—for I shall keep you abed for the entire two weeks, except when I dress you in lingerie and have you parade before my friends."

Caitlyn gasped. "You'd do no such thing!"

"Wouldn't I? For two weeks you will belong to me, body and soul." His voice was so low and warm that he almost purred. "And you may be right—perhaps I wouldn't parade you before my friends. In fact, I may not give you permission to rise from my bed at all."

Caitlyn lifted her chin and glared at him, even as she felt a surprising flare of excited anticipation. She *wanted* more of MacLean, but not like this. "When and *if* I decide to take our . . . physicality further, I will do it under my own terms and no one else's."

His jaw tightened, and in the distance, a low rumble of thunder told her she'd scored a hit.

"You're sadly mistaken if you think you're going to have a say in that matter," he snapped, every line of his body stiff with anger. Outside, the shutters banged against the house as an ominous wind rose.

She cast a glance toward the duchess and found the woman watching them, a pleased smile on her face. Caitlyn forced herself to return the smile. The duchess could smirk all she wanted; MacLean wasn't with her now. He was with Caitlyn, his entire attention focused on her even though he was angry. She liked his attention on her and no one else, liked it a bit too much, in fact.

Somehow as the days had passed, she'd changed her mind about what she wanted from MacLean and hadn't even realized it. She no longer wished to prove herself; instead she wanted MacLean's respect and admiration. How could she gain that from him when his final task—to swim naked before him—robbed her of those very things? How could she win the contest if she lost the real prize—his respect?

He bowed, his expression icy. "I'll bring the bow to breakfast in the morning. As to the rest of the contest, we are set. Do you agree?"

"I don't like the task you've set before me."

He gave her a dark smile. "I know." With that, he turned and left.

Blast it, she'd have to find a way to complete his final task in a manner that allowed her to maintain her dignity. But how?

Aware of Georgiana's pointed stare, Caitlyn turned and joined the other guests.

Chapter 18

Sometime in yer life, ye'll have to tell yerself no to something ye may want more than life itself. Tha' is when the women are separated fra' the bairns.

OLD WOMAN NORA FROM LOCH LOMOND
TO HER THREE WEE GRANDDAUGHTERS ONE COLD EVENING

As Caitlyn crossed the salon, Lady Elizabeth approached asking about Lord Dingwall's biting horse. Apparently he'd been telling tales, enthroned on a settee on the far side of the room, and Sally and Honoria were laughing at his description of how Caitlyn had made her way into his house.

Caitlyn managed to answer all of Lady Elizabeth's questions, but it was nearly half an hour before she could escape. She bade Dingwall good-bye, pleading fatigue after her adventures. The old man surprised her with a resounding kiss on the cheek and made her promise to come and see him. She did so with pleasure, and was rewarded with a fond smile.

Then Caitlyn finally made her way out of the room. She had just reached the landing when the sound of feet behind her made her pause. Had Alexander come to explain his cool reception this evening? Or— "Oh. Lord Dervishton."

Dervishton's gaze narrowed. "Were you expecting someone else?"

"No, no. I wasn't expecting anyone. Are you retiring, too?"

"I saw you leave and couldn't allow you to do so without an escort." He took her hand and pressed her fingers to his lips, his eyes bright. "You appeared a bit bereft this evening. I take it that MacLean has finally shown his true colors?"

She stiffened. "I don't wish to discuss anything about MacLean, my lord."

"Of course you don't, but please, just hear me out." He still held her hand, his fingers dry and warm over hers. "Miss Hurst—Caitlyn—if I can be of any service to you, please just say the word. I have a carriage here, and if you'd like, I can whisk you away without the slightest effort."

She frowned. "Lord Dervishton, it's most improper for you to offer such a thing."

He smiled and shrugged. "Who is to say what's proper and what isn't? I saw your face when MacLean rejected you, and I wished to offer you my protection."

"Your . . . protection?"

He placed her hand on his heart, his eyes warm. "Caitlyn, you must have noticed how I feel about you. I am enamored. In fact, I very well may be in love with you."

"Lord Dervishton, please . . ." It was agony hearing words from one man's lips that she desperately wished to hear from another's. The realization made her heart sink even lower. She wanted Alexander MacLean to declare himself to her. She wanted his love, and nothing else. Good God, when had that happened?

Heartened by her silence, Dervishton pressed forward. "Caitlyn, I am not a man of means. In fact, I came to this house party hoping to find a wealthy wife. But then I saw you, and—" He pressed a hot kiss to her fingers once again.

Caitlyn snatched her fingers back. "Lord Dervishton, please! I . . . I deeply appreciate the sentiment, but—"

He kissed her. One moment they were speaking on the landing, and the next he had her against the wall, his arms wrapped about her, holding her until she couldn't breathe.

She fought against him, pressing her hands against his chest, and turning her head to one side to no avail. "Let—me—go!" she said, fighting for air to scream, to seek help, to do something.

He increased his efforts, murmuring against her mouth, "You will be mine. You will—"

A huge crash of thunder shook the house. A shadow blacked out the light, then Caitlyn was freed as suddenly as she'd been captured.

Alexander's face was contorted with fury and another crash of thunder shook the ground, louder and closer than before.

Dervishton, shoved aside, looked as angry as MacLean. "You have no right to interfere!"

MacLean gave him a dismissive glance before he turned to Caitlyn. "Go to your room."

"But I—"

His eyes blazed with an unusual light, the green seeming to swirl. Thunder rumbled across the house, shaking each window. Lightning dazzled her eyes as the wind slammed into the house and rattled every shutter.

At the bottom of the stairs, Georgiana shrilly called for MacLean.

"Damn it, Caitlyn!" she snapped. "You look a mess. Go to your room!"

A *mess*? What sort of man would say such a— Then she caught sight of herself in the mirror on the landing. Her hair had fallen from its pins, her lips were bruised and swollen. If Georgiana or anyone else saw her—

That white-hot gaze landed on her again. "Go! *Now!*"

She picked up her skirts and ran, reaching her room as the storm broke with a howl of fury.

Rain and hail pelted against the window and lightning flashed blue-white in the room, which was dimly lit by a bedside candle and the crackling fire. In the hallway came the sound of a scuffle, a muffled shout, and a noisy crash. The storm's fury intensified, drowning out all other noises, and Caitlyn heard nothing more. She'd thought she knew the power of the curse, but the sheer power of the storm was like no other.

She shivered and went to the bellpull to summon Muiren, but just as her fingers closed around it, her door was rudely opened and MacLean strode in.

She caught her breath. His cravat was ruined, one coat sleeve was torn at the shoulder, and a cut by one eye trickled blood, as did one on his lower lip. His eyes were agleam with masculine confidence, a satisfied smile curving his mouth. He closed the door and gestured toward the empty lock. "Where's the key?"

"Muiren put it in the top drawer of the dressing table. I've never—"

He strode across the room and fetched the key, then dropped it into her hand. "From now on, you will lock that door. Do you understand? Dervishton is not to be trusted."

She nodded, then shivered. "I never expected him to . . ."

"Someone gave him the notion that you're only a half step above a lady bird," MacLean said grimly.

"Ah. Her grace."

MacLean's gaze flickered over her. "Are you hurt?"

"No, you came in the nick of time. But you clearly took a beating."

"Dervishton made a few paltry attempts to retaliate. He did not win the fight."

"Good God. If you look like that and you won, what does *he* look like?"

"A bloody mess." MacLean's smile faded. "You're certain he didn't hurt you?"

She smiled. "Do I look hurt?"

"No. You look . . . delectable." His gaze heated and the air between them grew heavy as if weighted with a million thoughts and feelings, all of them too tangled to unwind into coherent thought.

"Sit down and let me clean those wounds," she ordered in a husky voice, pointing to the chaise by the fire. She whisked over to the pitcher and basin on the washstand and dampened a hand towel. *Keep your wits, Hurst. Just because you're alone with him is no reason to panic.* But it wasn't panic. Something far more dangerous made her blood race and her hands tremble.

She turned from the washstand and pasted a smile on her lips. "I have three brothers, so I'm quite used to dealing with split lips and black eyes."

He crossed his arms. "I'm not in need of a nursemaid."

"Good, because I'm no nursemaid. Once I've washed off the blood and made sure you don't need stitches, I'll turn you over to your valet. *He* can be your nursemaid." She crossed to the door and locked it.

"What are you doing?"

"I don't want someone to burst in on us while I get you cleaned up."

He scowled. "Just give me the towel."

"No. You can't see where it's cut, and I can."

"Very well, damn it!" He went to the chaise and sat with a scowl. "Just hurry up and do it."

Moving to stand between his knees, Caitlyn was achingly aware of him. She placed her hand beneath his chin and lifted his face, his warm, whisker-roughed skin making her fingertips tingle. She dabbed the cut on his lip, wincing when he did so. "That hurts."

His gaze, liquid and dark in the dim light, met hers. "No." His voice was low and deeper than usual.

She gently wiped the blood from his chin, then moved to the cut below his eye. Cleaning the blood off with a few gentle pats, she was relieved to see that the wound was minor. "It's not deep, but your eye will be bruised in the morning."

The warmth that emanated from him drew her closer. She leaned against his leg as she pretended to examine his bruises more closely, in reality admiring the masculine line of his mouth. Why did he have to have such a beautiful mouth, one that begged so to be kissed?

Outside the storm raged, the rain sluicing against the windowpanes. Inside the bedchamber, the fire warming them, the light flicking over MacLean's face, it was as if they were the only people in the entire world.

"Caitlyn," he whispered, his breath harsh.

She dropped the towel on the floor and reached for him, sliding her arms around his neck. "Kiss me."

He pulled her close and their lips met as a rumble of thunder shook the house. There was no gentleness in this kiss, no caution. It was purely hot and urgent.

Caitlyn shivered as Alexander's hands roamed over her body, warming, molding, tempting her to move closer, to be more daring. She slid her hands into his thick, black hair, burying her fingers in the soft waves. She devoured him with her kiss, branded him as hers, urging him with her tongue to be bolder, to take more, to—

He pushed her back, his breath harsh. "Caitlyn, we can't do this. I will have you in my bed when I win the wager and not before."

Blast the damned wager! He was going to be honorable *now*? She couldn't accept that, though his pride seemed to hold him firmly against the notion. Then inspiration struck. "If I lose, I must come to your bed. Correct?"

"Yes." He looked weary.

"Then I see no conflict. This isn't your bed."

His lips twitched. "You are determined in this?"

She slid her hands to his face and lifted his mouth to hers. "Please, MacLean. I've thought of nothing else for the last few weeks. I just want—"

Alexander kissed her. He couldn't have said no now if he tried. Having their legs entwined, her full breasts pressed to his chest, her warm skin beneath his fingers, was driving him *mad*.

He wanted her passionately, desperately, and completely. But she was an innocent. Could he really—

With a muffled oath, she answered his unspoken question when she pressed herself fully against him, hooked a heel over his calf, and kissed him for all she was worth.

In that moment, Alexander was lost. He could fight himself, stifle his own urges, but not hers—never hers. Sweet, impulsive, savoring life, she made him feel more alive than he'd ever felt.

He covered her mouth with his, mastering her even as he was mastered. He slid his hands over her, lifting her skirts and pushing her gown aside as he settled her on his lap, her knees to each side of his hips as he possessively explored every lush curve, every smooth expanse of skin.

He untied her gown and pushed it down over her shoulders to expose her lush breasts. Cupping them in his hands, he marveled at the silken texture of her skin, then bent his mouth to them and teased the nipples to hard peaks.

Caitlyn moaned and writhed against him, clearly hungry for more, savoring the feelings the way she savored her food. He kissed her from her plump lips to the gentle curve of her shoulder, and she pressed against him, asking silently for more, her hips restlessly pressing against his erection.

God she was a handful, and she seemed to know exactly what she wanted. *This is definitely no virgin.* Relief flooded through him and his passion exploded with full force. He unlaced his breeches, releasing his cock, groaning when she tried to help, her fingers brushing against him. Then he pushed aside her chemise and lifted her up until she was poised over him.

Eyes locked, panting heavily, he pressed the tip of his cock against her slick opening.

For a long moment they stared at one another, then she placed her hands on his shoulders and pressed down, over him. With a gasp, he slipped into her tight wetness, keeping his eyes open to absorb the look on her face.

Her face was flushed, her skin glistening, her lips red and swollen from his kisses. Her long, gold hair tumbled about her in silken swirls, her gown opened to reveal her smooth skin and gorgeous breasts. He was so overcome with her that for a moment, he had to stop and fight for control.

She wiggled and pressed down more, and his cock slipped farther inside her, her velvety heat unlike anything he'd ever felt. He grasped her waist tightly, but refused to help her—she had to control this, and she was doing a damned fine job.

Inch by delicious inch, she lowered herself onto him. Her tight wetness almost undid him. His body was drenched with sweat, his muscles screaming as he clenched them to hold off the explosion.

She pushed down more . . . then stopped, wincing in pain.

Shocked, his gaze locked with hers. Was she a—

Hands gripping his shoulders, she thrust herself down completely over his cock. A spasm of pain flickered over her face, followed quickly by blissful pleasure.

Alexander could no longer think. He rocked into her

hard and fast, caressing her breasts, kissing her deeply as he increased the tempo until she was gasping, her skin dewy with exertion and flushed a delicate pink.

She was so beautiful—so *his*.

Suddenly she arched, her legs gripping his hips as she pressed against him, gasping his name and shuddering, tightening unbearably around him, stroking him with her heat and wetness.

And holding her close, he finally surrendered his control, tumbling over the edge of pleasure after her.

"Gor, what a storm we're havin'!" Muiren, who'd been towel-drying Caitlyn's hair after her bath, shivered as lightning lit the room, starkly white before disappearing. "I canno' remember when we've had such lightnin.'"

Caitlyn didn't answer. Her heart was too full, her thoughts too confused. Fortunately Muiren didn't require a response as she was full of news herself.

The fight between Lord Dervishton and Alexander had ended with Lord Dervishton being carried away on a makeshift cot. Since Lord MacLean had disappeared a short time after that, no one was sure how injured he was, but Muiren had caught sight of him going into his room and said she detected little beyond a bruised eye. Caitlyn could have told the maid exactly how little harmed MacLean had been, but she wisely said nothing.

"Which, if ye'd seen Lord Dervishton, would tell ye all ye need to know about Lord MacLean's ability to fight!"

"So one would think," Caitlyn murmured.

"Aye, miss! No one knows what they were fightin' over, though 'tis said Lord MacLean told his man 'twas a lady's honor." Muiren continued to comb Caitlyn's hair before the crackling fire. "Obviously, he meant her grace."

Caitlyn was glad Muiren was so caught up in her tale that she didn't really expect any responses. Caitlyn's mind was too full of Alexander to respond with more than vague answers.

"Och, her grace looked like the cat as swallowed the canary, she was tha' pleased to be fought over," Muiren went on.

Caitlyn was amazed how she'd given in to her passions so completely and without thought. It made her realize that since the first time she'd met Alexander MacLean, they'd been heading toward that exact moment. In a way, it was a wonder it hadn't happened earlier.

What an *incredible* experience. Nothing had prepared her for the way her senses could explode or how long afterward a touch of euphoria would linger. Caitlyn rubbed her arms and shivered.

"Miss, ye're cold!" Muiren fetched a blanket and put it about Caitlyn's shoulders.

Caitlyn managed a smile. "I'm fine. I think my hair is plenty dry now, so I'm going to go to bed."

"Aye, ye're worn-out, aren't ye. No wonder, with th' excitement ye've had today."

You have no idea. But it wasn't just the physical aspect that made her so weary, it was the emotional aspect, as well. Afterward, Alexander had held her for such a long time that she'd thought he'd fallen asleep. Yet the second she'd moved, he'd released her, looking down at her with a dark, unfathomable gaze that had shaken her to the soul. In his eyes she'd seen wonder and dismay, uncertainty and sadness. *What had he meant by that look?* He'd been unaccountably quiet, the air around him heavy with tension. She'd tried to make light of it and had even attempted a joke, but he would have none of it, simply regarding her with a grave look before he'd dressed and left, telling her they'd talk later.

Caitlyn had been bemused by events and she hadn't protested, though she'd felt all of two feet tall when he'd left so quietly. Her heart still ached from the sound of the door closing behind him.

"We're all mighty proud o' ye, miss," Muiren said. "Ye're well on yer way to winning the wager."

"I couldn't have done it without you." Caitlyn settled into the huge bed, gratefully snuggling down between the covers.

"Do ye know the next task ye have to compl—"

A light knock sounded on the door, and Muiren puffed out her cheeks. "Who could tha' be at this hour o' the night?" She hurried to the door and opened it.

The fire flickered wildly, a stream of cold air rattling against the closed windows.

From the bed Caitlyn couldn't see the visitor, and after a few words Muiren closed the door and returned to the bedside, a pleased look on her plump face.

"Who was it?"

"It was Mrs. Sterling's niece, who's the upstairs maid here. She found this earlier in MacLean's bedchamber and brought it to ye." Muiren proudly held out her hand. In the middle of her palm lay Muffin's bow.

"Oh, Muiren, no!"

"No?" Muiren blinked. "But if MacLean canno' produce the bow, surely it means ye've won."

"That would be cheating. He completed his task, and it's only right that he get the credit."

Muiren's face fell. "If ye think so, miss."

"I do. We must put this back in his room as soon as possible."

"But . . ." Muiren bit her lip.

"But what?"

Muiren hesitated, then said in a rush, "If his lordship realized one of the maids took something from him, miss, he might tell her grace and—" The maid made a helpless gesture.

"I hadn't thought of that." Caitlyn considered the options. Finally she nodded. "Just put it on the dressing table and don't worry; I'll take it back to him." Not only would it keep the staff from getting into trouble, but it would give Caitlyn a chance to speak to his high-and-mighty lordship. Their business wasn't finished, not by a long shot.

"Thank ye, miss!" Muiren put the bow on the dressing table, turned down the lamps, made sure Caitlyn was tucked in, then went to the door. "G'night miss!"

After the door closed, Caitlyn lay in the dark, listening to the sound of the raging storm. The wind whistled and moaned, and rain slashed down in waves that made an almost hypnotic sound. Heavy rolls of thunder shook the house from the ground up.

Caitlyn closed her eyes, though her body was as alive as the thunder-filled air. *So that was love-making. How glorious! I finally know what the poets write about, what lovers dream about, and what I've always longed for.* She'd never felt so enthralled, so *alive*. But had MacLean felt the same way?

The question burned through her heart, bright and aching.

A flash of lightning lit the room and she sat up, realizing sleep was not coming. She'd planned to take the bow to MacLean in the morning, but she couldn't wait.

For a moment, she longed for the peace and quiet of the vicarage. Somewhere away from the drama and troubles she'd found here.

But, oh, how she'd miss Alexander. Though she tried to pretend otherwise, it was true. Every day, she'd bounded out of bed and hurried down to breakfast, every inch of her alive at the thought of seeing him, of teasing him, of winning a glinting smile, or even one of his famed annoyed looks. She loved all of his expressions—except the cold one he'd given her tonight in the grand salon.

She pressed her hands over her eyes. *Blast it, was he involved with Georgiana?* Caitlyn couldn't accept the idea. The woman was so hard, so jaded, and had little beyond a cold, impersonal prettiness to recommend her to a passionate and fiercely independent man like Alexander.

Caitlyn knew she shouldn't feel jealous—she had no claim on the man and didn't wish for any. Still, she wished she understood him better. Perhaps . . . perhaps she should just *ask* him how he meant their relationship to progress, and what feelings, if any, he had for the duchess. That's what a bold woman would do, anyway.

Caitlyn threw back the covers, stuffed her feet into her slippers, tugged on a robe, and snatched up the bow.

She silently made her way down the hallway. A faint light showed under MacLean's door, but no noise came from the room. Or was there? Was that a woman's voice she heard? Surely he wasn't with the duchess right *now*!

Her heart thudded sickly and Caitlyn's hand clenched around the bow. She pressed her ear against the door panel, but the noise from the storm obscured all other sound. *Blast it, I want to know if she's in there!* If MacLean thought he could hop from Caitlyn's bed to the duchess's, he had another think coming. She'd just—

The door opened, a large hand closed about her wrist, and she was yanked into MacLean's room, her slippers left in the hallway.

MacLean scowled down at Caitlyn. "What in hell are you doing here?" He'd just been on the verge of going to bed, even though it would be futile since all he could think of was making love to Caitlyn. She had filled his senses in a way no other woman ever had.

That she'd been a virgin had echoed through his mind over and over. For days he'd wondered whether she was, for her manner was so confident, her interest in their physical contact so genuine. Whatever she was, she'd been extremely eager, and had luxuriated in their lovemaking in a way that was spontaneous and incredibly *fascinating*.

Still, she should have admitted that she was a virgin, and if he'd been able to feel past his throbbing cock, he might have been upset. But their lovemaking had been so spectacularly worthwhile that he couldn't dredge up more than mild irritation. But that had been then, and this was now. As soon as the blood returned to other parts of his body, realization of what had happened began to seep in. He'd expected Caitlyn to be upset, or at least a little misty-eyed at the huge change in her circumstances, but she'd merely given him a sleepy, sensual smile that made the blood surge back to his cock.

Too bemused to speak, he'd washed, dressed, and left, unable to do more than promise to speak to her at a later time. He'd arrived in his bedchamber to find a hawk-eyed MacCready, whom Alexander had dismissed as soon as possible. After that, he'd spent the time pacing madly, wondering what in hell he was supposed to do now.

Would she expect him to offer her marriage? If she did, she would be sorely mistaken. He had to end this relationship, had to stop this spiral out of control—with her, this was the way things had always been. Something about her sparked his rebellious soul.

Yet the more he enjoyed being with her, the more determined he was to keep from entangling himself in her life. The trouble was that he didn't just *enjoy* being with her—he desired it, yearned for it, *craved* it. *Was this how Charles felt? Desperate to have her, regardless of the cost?*

Well, he wasn't going to make the same mistake. He could fight this craving. Once the newness of the conquest wore off, his mind would return to rights and he could go on with his life unfettered.

When he'd left Caitlyn and retired to his bedchamber, he'd told MacCready to mix him a bowl of hot buttered rum. Though three glasses of the lethal concoction had warmed him from head to toe, they had done nothing to calm his racing thoughts.

Nothing could calm those except another hour with Caitlyn, sinking into her softness, soaking in her heat. The thought had made his cock harden again, as if it hadn't just been sated. Good God, had any man ever been so enthralled with a woman's touch as he'd become in a few short moments? He'd been with scores of women, and none of them left him burning for more the way she did.

He'd thought about returning to her room, though it would be a mad, crazed thing to do. If they were caught, there would have been only one answer—marriage. When he'd gone to her bedchamber before, he'd been so furious about Dervishton's treatment of her, and worried that she'd been frightened, that he hadn't thought of that. Now, he was perfectly able to think, and discovered a more upsetting fact—he didn't give a damn about the cost of his behavior anymore. Caitlyn Hurst was *worth* taking a chance on, *worth* whatever ill might happen, if he could just sink into her one . . . more . . . time.

He'd been in the process of drinking even more rum punch, trying to stave off the desire to return to Caitlyn's bedchamber, when he'd heard a sound in the hallway.

He'd thought maybe Georgiana had sent one of her servants to listen at his door; he'd never expected to yank a disheveled and pink-faced Caitlyn Hurst into his room, her golden hair about her shoulders, robe falling off one shoulder, her creamy skin on display to his hungry eyes. He devoured the sight of her, his rum-warmed body flaring to life yet again.

His heart pounded in his throat and he had to clear it before he could speak. "What are you doing here?"

She pointed to the floor.

He looked down, the bow resting beside his foot. He frowned. "Where did that come from?"

"One of the maids brought it to me."

"What? She stole it from my chambers?"

"Yes, and I told her it wasn't fair. I didn't want the duchess to punish her, so I brought it—"

Alexander yanked her against him and kissed her. He knew he shouldn't, but he didn't give a damn. He wanted this woman, needed her *now,* and watching her lush lips form word after word was driving him mad with need. He stopped her the only way he knew how, by kissing her senseless. He'd had his fill of her once tonight, but somehow it wasn't enough. Their lovemaking had just made him thirstier, desperate for another taste. The realization scared the hell out of him, even through the fog of heated lust.

But his passion was fanned by the excitement of the storm roaring overhead and the feel of her glorious blond hair, streaming down around her. The soft curls cupped her breast on one side and tumbled over the other so that nothing could be seen but the turgid nipple, covered in the thin silk of her night rail.

He had her all to himself, here in his own room, within his arms. And as his lips touched her, he realized something equally as wonderful—she was just as glad to see him as he was to see her. His soul stirred to life at the realization and they melted together, no words blocking their way, no thoughts holding them apart.

Caitlyn kissed him passionately, her arms encircling his neck, her breasts pressed through her night rail against his bared chest. His heart warmed and he lifted her into his arms and carried her to the settee by the fire.

He placed her against the cushions and lay beside her. The firelight glistened on her hair, her dark eyes were mysterious, her skin creamy and warm. God, she was beautiful.

Beautiful, a voice inside him whispered with the inexorable truth, *but not for you.*

The thought held him in place, his heart sinking.

Her smile slipped and she lifted a hand to his cheek. "Alexander? What's wrong?"

He caught her hand and kissed it, closing his eyes as his lips touched the soft skin. He'd never wanted anything more in his life, and it was agony knowing that she was so close, so willing, and he would have to turn away.

Why did I pull her inside my room? Damn the rum for clouding my judgment.

She stirred, her other hand coming to rest on his cheek. "Alexander," she whispered, "what is it? We've already . . . this isn't anything new. We can—"

He opened his eyes, his heart pounding so hard in his throat that his voice came out as a harsh whisper. "We can't do this."

"Why?"

"Caitlyn, no matter what happens here, I will not marry you." *I'd rather die than watch your passion turn into disgust.*

She looked puzzled. "But I haven't asked you to."

It took a moment for the words to sink in.

A damnably mysterious smile touched her lips. "I thought we could just enjoy each other for the time we do have."

It was so tempting. "And afterward?"

A sad look entered her eyes. "We become past acquaintances. Isn't that the way it usually works?"

It was indeed, but somehow it didn't seem right this time. He opened his mouth to say so when she looked him directly in the eyes and slipped a hand inside his robe. Her warm fingers closed over his erection, bringing his thoughts to an abrupt halt.

He could no longer breathe and he knew in that instant that it didn't matter—it didn't matter if she wished for more or less from him, or if this moment could cause their doom or end their lives in society.

All he could do was take her as she wished to be taken. Overhead the storm crashed and rumbled, as inside the room, Alexander MacLean once again succumbed to Caitlyn Hurst's magic.

Chapter 19

❧

Dinna wait fer love to find ye, me dearies. Go out and find it yerself. Life's too short fer waitin'.

OLD WOMAN NORA FROM LOCH LOMOND

TO HER THREE WEE GRANDDAUGHTERS ONE COLD EVENING

"*G*ood morning, my lord! You are certainly a late sleeper today."

Alexander stirred, wincing as his head informed him of the amount of rum he'd had last night. But the rest of his body told him something else, for he felt relaxed and replete. *Ah, Caitlyn.* Images from the night before arose, hours of teasing and pleasure. Images of Caitlyn writhing beneath him. Caitlyn with her eyes closed in ecstasy as he took her time and again. Caitlyn with her legs wrapped about his hips, her skin glistening with moisture as she gasped his name for the hundredth time. His cock grew hard, and his mind cleared. *Good God, is she still here?*

He sat bolt upright and looked around. MacCready was stirring the fire; a tray sat on a small table by the chaise. Alexander looked at the settee. Though the pillows were mashed, no one would guess what had occurred there. He glanced around the room and saw no evidence of Caitlyn at all.

It was a bit disconcerting. She'd surprised him with her enthusiasm and creativity, which made her absence all the more felt.

He swung his feet off the side of the bed and rubbed his face. Good God, how could he have allowed this to happen? What in hell had he done?

"A bit of a hangover, my lord?" MacCready was looking into the empty rum pot.

"Aye, but it will leave soon enough." Alexander tried to think, but couldn't. All he could do was call himself a fool.

Well, they'd finish their wagers, then leave this damned house party and return to their lives. He'd run the MacLean clan, and she would eventually marry.

His heart unexpectedly ached at the thought. *That could be me. I could* demand *she marry me; she gave herself to me.* But for what purpose? A year or two of happiness and sexual fulfillment, then he'd grow older and the years between them would be more obvious, more of a problem. She would eventually wish she were married to a younger man and would take a lover. And who would blame her?

"MacCready, set out wash water and my clothes. I wish to go down to breakfast as soon as possible."

"Right now? But it's hardly nine o'clock. You never appear before ten."

"Then there will be more bacon for me."

"But, my lord, surely—"

"*Now.*"

MacCready's lips tightened, but he said nothing more as he laid out Alexander's clothes.

Judging from the sounds coming from the breakfast room, more than one person was already there. Maybe Caitlyn? No, she was probably still in her room, recuperating from last night. He was exhausted this morning and she must be, as well. He could only hope she hadn't awoken regretting their impulsive encounters.

Heart heavy, he walked into the breakfast room and came to a complete halt.

Looking delicate and fresh, her hair still damp from a bath, Caitlyn was resplendent in green brocade with rose trim. Alexander wasn't sure of her expression, for he didn't dare look at her for long. She sat between Lady Elizabeth and Lord Falkland, Miss Ogilvie sitting across from them, in deep conversation with the Earl of Caithness.

There was no sign of Dervishton, which was a good thing. Alexander wasn't through with him just yet.

Alexander murmured a greeting to Falkland, but kept his eyes from Caitlyn, giving her time to compose herself. This had to be difficult for her, and he wished he'd caught her by herself so he could reassure her that he would protect them both. He'd discreetly reassure her with a compassionate, calming look for now.

He filled his plate with whatever was closest on the buffet, took the seat opposite hers, and stole his first glance.

To his surprise, she appeared neither pale nor wan, but amazingly calm and healthy, laughing at something Falkland said and eating with the enthusiasm of a sailor who'd been living off hardtack for the last six months.

The sight disconcerted Alexander, and he frowned.

Caitlyn sent him a grin, a decidedly devilish expression in her brown eyes. "Good morning, MacLean. I can see you have quite an appetite today."

"What?"

"Your plate."

He looked down and realized he'd placed about fifteen sausages and nothing else on his plate. "Oh. Yes, well, I wished to keep Falkland there from stealing them all."

"I don't even eat sausage!" Falkland protested. The young lord immediately began to discuss the various meats he did and did not eat, and Alexander wished he hadn't mentioned sausage at all.

The meal passed with interminable slowness, the women talking excitedly about the masquerade that was planned for the evening's amusement. While

Falkland and Caithness agreed with every comment put to them.

He was relieved when Caitlyn finally excused herself to change into a walking gown so she could accompany Miss Ogilvie for a stroll about the lake.

Alexander waited a moment, then excused himself and went after her. He caught her on the stairwell. "Caitlyn!"

She turned to face him, a spontaneous smile curving her mouth. "Yes?"

She is genuinely glad to see me. His heart leaped at the thought and he smiled back at her, savoring the warmth of her welcome.

Then he caught himself. *What in hell am I doing? She's not for me.*

As his smile dimmed, so did hers, a look of uncertainty in her face. "Did you . . . did you wish to speak to me?"

He steeled himself. "Yes. I . . . I . . . I . . ." Good God, why *had* he chased her out here into the hallway? He'd wanted to speak to her, but he didn't have a specific topic. He'd just . . . wanted to see her.

The realization struck him like a hammer. *Am I beginning to actually care for her? That's impossible! I've only known her a few months, and most of those I was simply trying to win my way into her bed.*

He rubbed his neck, suddenly weary. What was he doing?

She smiled as if sensing his uncertainty. "Actually, I'm glad you caught up with me. I want you to know that I think last night was"—her cheeks flushed but she continued resolutely—"it was very nice."

Nice? Hell, it'd been a lot of things, but *nice* wasn't one of them. It had been wonderful, fantastic . . . his balls still hummed from it. It had also made his life unbearably complicated. "I'm sorry about the whole thing."

"Sorry?" she said in an odd voice. "You're *sorry*?"

He had to move away from this dangerous precipice that his heart was perched on. If he didn't, there would be nothing but pain for them both. "Caitlyn, I—"

"There is nothing to be sorry about. I made the decision to enjoy your company, and I did. I certainly don't expect you to apologize or offer marriage or—"

"That's good," he snapped. "Because I don't plan on marrying anyone, ever."

She flushed, her mouth tightening. "No, of course not. Although *some* people might see such intimacy as the sign of more than mere friendship." Her chin was high, her gaze locked with his. "I'm talking about love, MacLean, in case you missed it. But you wouldn't know about that, would you?"

He was a welter of confusing sentiments, but he refused to examine which. "I can't offer you either love *or* marriage, so it's best we keep them off the table."

She gave a brittle laugh. "You're so focused on those blasted wagers."

"Aren't you?"

She shrugged. "I suppose so." Her eyes glistened as if she were on the brink of tears. "Fine, MacLean.

We'll keep this relationship focused on our wagers. That, and nothing more."

"Good."

She turned and ran the rest of the way up the stairs, leaving him alone and feeling oddly bereft. What in hell was wrong with him?

He was definitely in lust, and perhaps deeply in like, for she was an extraordinary woman. But was he in love? Was it too late?

It couldn't be; he wouldn't allow it.

Irritated at himself, he returned to his room and rang for MacCready, deciding to spend the rest of the day on his horse. At least it wouldn't befuddle him and leave him feeling as if, in some indefinable way, he was lacking.

The carriage rumbled up the narrow road, swaying over the uneven surface.

Muiren stuck her head out the carriage window and peered up at the house perched on the cliff overhead. "Who'd have thought Old Woman Nora would live like a queen in such a grand house?"

Caitlyn smiled. "Mam's done well for herself, considering she had nothing at one time."

"Married into money, did she?"

"Yes, although grandfather used to say he was the one who got the bigger prize. She's dreadfully spoiled. Grandfather was crazy about her and could never tell her no."

"She's a strong woman, I'll tell ye that."

"So she is." Caitlyn was glad she'd inherited some of that same strength. But though she could hold her own in most areas, she was woefully weak where Alexander MacLean was concerned.

"Ye think yer mam can help ye with the last challenge?"

"She has to. I'm at a loss as to how to complete it without losing my reputation."

Muiren turned red. "I canno' believe MacLean would ask ye to do such a thing! He's no' much of a gentleman to ask ye to bathe naked in the garden fountain. I dinna care if he stole the idea from a famous myth or no'!"

"He's not a gentleman at all." Which was no surprise, as he'd told her that on their first meeting. What had been a surprise was the discovery that *she* was no lady. She'd always had her suspicions. Her sister Triona was always polite, always proper and gracious. Caitlyn had spent her entire life trying to live up to that standard and failing miserably, but never had she rushed so headlong into such "nonladylike" behavior as with MacLean.

And while she enjoyed their mutual passion immensely, something had changed. Whether with her or him, she didn't know, but it left her feeling bereft and sad. She'd hardly eaten anything since breakfast. Surely Mam would know how to cure such an illness?

The carriage climbed the final steep curve and turned onto a beautifully groomed drive that lead up to a large, square stone manor, the roof covered in deep gray slate tiles, the walls of the darkest gray river rock, the mullioned windows glistening in the sun.

"Yer mam dinna dress as if she lives here."

"I know. It's the bane of her servants' lives, too."

The carriage pulled to a halt just as the front door opened and an elderly woman wrapped in a shapeless, gray pelisse stepped onto the stoop, a large covered basket over her arm. She stopped when she saw the carriage, and her weathered face broke into a grin when Caitlyn leaned out the window and yelled, "Mam!"

Too impatient to wait for the footman, Caitlyn opened the carriage door, hopped out, ran to her grandmother, and was instantly enveloped in a hard hug. As thin as Mam was, she was amazingly strong.

"Och, me girl! What are ye doin' here?"

"I came for some advice."

"Ye did, did ye?" Mam couldn't have looked more pleased. "Ye'd best come in, then."

Caitlyn eyed Mam's basket. "Were you off on an errand?"

"Aye, but it can wait. 'Tis just some jellies and such fer the Roberts and their new babies. She had twins, she did. I suggested she call them Caitriona and Caitlyn like ye and yer sister, but she'd none o' it—probably because they were boys."

Caitlyn laughed. "I daresay that was it."

Muiren, who'd just arrived carrying a basket of her own, smiled at Mam and bobbed a curtsy. "How do ye do?"

Mam eyed the basket with interest. "What's that?"

Muiren flipped back the cover. "Yer granddaughter said we couldna come without some sweets fer ye. There's nut bread and marmalade, scones and fresh-churned butter and—"

"Then why are we waitin' out here! Open the door and someone take this basket to me breakfast room!" Mam turned and headed back into the house, leaving Caitlyn and Muiren to follow.

Muiren was escorted by the housekeeper to the kitchens, while the very proper butler promised Mam that he'd ensure the delicacies in the basket were brought to the breakfast room with all due haste.

Mam then took Caitlyn by the arm and drew her into the small, cozy, well-appointed room and shut the door behind them. "All right, lass, tell me why ye've come to see me in such a dither."

"I'm not in a dither."

Mam lifted her brows.

"Well . . . perhaps a *little* dither." Caitlyn sighed and followed Mam to a small table before the fireplace. As she took her chair, Caitlyn said, "I'm sorry I haven't written as often as I should."

"Och, ye're like me and no' have the time to write a letter. The one ye wrote me when yer sister eloped with Lord Hugh was a muddle to decipher."

"I was upset."

"I could tell. And ye're upset now. What's brought ye to me, lass?"

"I'm in a quandary about Alexander MacLean."

Mam's eyes widened. "Alexander MacLean? I thought ye were enjoyin' yerself at a house party at Balloch Castle?"

"I am, but . . ." Caitlyn fidgeted with her gloves. "Mam, MacLean is at the house party, too."

"Ah! Ye didn't mention that in yer letter."

"No. I should have, but it didn't seem that important at first, and then—" Caitlyn searched for the words. *Then it became too important to mention in such a casual way.*

"Then what?" Mam said impatiently. "Will ye just blurt it out? I'm an old woman and canna take such suspense!"

Caitlyn had to smile. "You'll outlive us all, Mam."

"I hope not. Now tell me what's got ye so upset."

"When MacLean and I knew one another in London, we were . . . I suppose you'd call it flirting."

"I would, would I?"

"Yes."

"So ye flirted whilst in London and then met again by accident at Balloch Castle?"

"It was no accidental meeting. MacLean admitted he was responsible for my being there. He and the duchess used to be—" Caitlyn couldn't get the words past her lips.

Mam nodded. "I'd heard tha', but it ended months ago. He's no' the sort o' man to linger long wit' a woman like her. Or any other woman for tha' matter."

Caitlyn winced. "You know the duchess?"

"Aye, I do," Mam said in a glum voice. "Better than she'd like. She once worked in one o' yer grandpapa's mills."

"Worked in a mill? That can't be the same woman!" Mam lifted her brows.

"Goodness." Caitlyn shook her head. "I would never have believed that."

"Well, ye can, fer 'tis true. She dinna want anyone to know about it, but a few of us are old enou' to remember it very well." Mam tapped her fingers on the table before her and said in a thoughtful voice, "So MacLean used his connection with the duchess to get ye to visit. Did he tell ye why?"

"For revenge. He planned on ruining me for what happened with Triona and Lord Hugh."

"But they're happy as can be! I jus' saw them yesterday, in fact."

"I pointed that out, but he was still angry. Although there was no full-blown scandal, people talked, and since Hugh and Triona had left for Scotland, and I'd been sent back to Wythburn, he was left in London to take the brunt of it."

"Och, so his pride was hurt."

"Exactly. When I arrived at the castle and realized what he'd planned, I made a deal with him. We're to complete three tasks each, and the first one to fail, loses. If I win, he's to forget the incident and plan no more revenge, *and* he has to propose to me in front of every member of the house party. I shall refuse him, of course." At one time, just saying that had made Caitlyn grin. Now, for some reason, she took no satisfaction whatsoever in the thought. In fact, it made her heart ache.

Mam looked impressed. "How came he to agree to that?"

"He set conditions for me if *I* lost."

Mam's brow rose. "Such as?"

Caitlyn's cheeks colored. "I'd rather not say."

"Humph. I see how it is."

Caitlyn wisely held her tongue.

"So, lassie, how can I help ye out of this mess?"

"We've based the tasks on the ancient myth of Olwen, and my final task is . . . difficult. Do you remember when Olwen bathed naked in the fountain to distract the enemies?"

Mam stiffened. "That arse didn't ask *that* o' ye!"

"I'm afraid he did. And I told him he had to wear a gown. In public."

"Ye dinna! After knowin' how much his pride means to him—"

The door opened and the butler came in, bearing a tray of delicacies from Muiren's basket and a pot of gently steaming tea. Mam waited impatiently for the butler to set up the tea, then shooed him off, barely waiting for the door to close before she turned to Caitlyn. "Ye're playin' wit' fire, lass, but I think ye know tha'."

"I do, but . . . Mam, I don't know what it is, but I can't help myself! Whenever he's around, I *want* to goad him and make him react. I can't seem to stop."

Mam sighed. "Ye've got it bad, don't ye, lassie?"

Caitlyn's heart squeezed and a tear welled.

"Och, dinna cry." A frothy lace handkerchief appeared and Mam pressed it into Caitlyn's hand. "We'll find an answer fer ye." Mam poured them some tea and arranged some cakes on two plates, her brow furrowed as she thought. "Tell me about these other wagers, how they played out."

Caitlyn did so, Mam nodding thoughtfully as she listened. Afterward they sat in silence, sipping their tea.

Mam sighed. "What to do, what to do . . . Ye are to swim naked afore him, but if ye're caught, then ye'll be ruined fer certain—and yer family with ye."

"Exactly."

"Hmm. What ye need to do, then, is to control the situation. Control MacLean."

"Control MacLean? How on earth—"

"Och, let me worry about the details; I think I know just what ye need." Mam's gaze sharpened. "Whilst I can help ye with yer wager, I canno' assist ye wit' the true problem here. Ye know what tha' is, don't ye, lass?"

Caitlyn quietly placed her teacup back on its dish. "Yes. I love him." Saying it out loud wasn't as difficult as she'd thought it would be.

Mam nodded. "How does he feel about you?"

"He sees me only as a challenge. I know he doesn't love me."

"Ye're certain of this?"

"I am. I asked him this morning, and he—" Caitlyn tried hard to keep the tears at bay; her throat was so tight she couldn't swallow. She loved him so much, but all he could offer was a brief physical relationship. Sharing their passion had only made matters worse. Every time they were together, in bed or out, her feelings for him deepened. "I can't settle for a half of a relationship, and that's all he has to offer."

Mam's blue eyes darkened in concern. "Och, lassie. Ye look so sad."

She *was* sad. Every bone in her body seemed weighted, her chest ached, and her eyes stung. But she wasn't the sort of woman to give in. She had a few more days before she had to leave Balloch Castle, and she'd make certain those days counted.

She blinked back the tears that threatened, lifted her chin, and looked her grandmother in the eye. "So you have an idea of how I may fulfill my task? I want to leave Balloch Castle as a winner."

Mam grinned and rose to rummage through a small desk in one corner of the room. "Here 'tis. *This* will solve yer problems." She placed something in Caitlyn's hands.

Caitlyn blinked at the tiny vial closed with a whittled cork. "But—"

"Four drops o' this in his drink, and he'll no' be

able to move fer two, perhaps three hours. Ye can have yer swim in the fountain in full view o' him, and he'll no' be able to raise a call and cause yer ruin." Mam chuckled. "He might no' even be able t' blink."

"Is it dangerous?"

"Not wit' four drops. Not even wit' eight. If ye gave him twelve or more, I might worry, but there's no' that much in tha' bottle."

Caitlyn closed her fingers around the vial. "Mam, thank you."

Mam sighed and placed her hand over Caitlyn's. "Lass, I dinna solve yer greatest problem, and ye know it. That one, ye'll have to work out fer yerself." She kissed Caitlyn on the forehead. "But ye're a smart one, ye are, and I know ye'll work yer way through it. Jus' promise me tha' when the time comes, ye'll listen to yer heart. That will tell ye what to do."

"I promise, Mam—but I don't think MacLean and I will have a 'time.' It's just not meant to be."

"We'll see, lass. We'll see." Mam then turned the topic to Caitlyn's sister Triona, and how well she was doing with her new stepdaughters, and about the horses Lord Hugh was raising on his estate.

Caitlyn listened, always interested in how her twin sister was doing. But deep in her heart, another voice was whispering, telling her that her heartache was just getting ready to begin.

Chapter 20

❧

'Tis a fool who tries to think his way t' his own heart.

OLD WOMAN NORA FROM LOCH LOMOND
TO HER THREE WEE GRANDDAUGHTERS ONE COLD EVENING

"My lord, I must ask you to reconsider that costume."

"No."

"People will talk."

"Let them. I like it." Alexander glanced at himself in the mirror. He was wearing knee boots of thick fur wrapped with leather lacing, and a long kilt that came past his knees. A sporran hung from the wide leather belt at his waist, weighing down the kilt to keep the winds from exposing him. A wide swath of the kilt rose across his chest and over one shoulder.

"My lord, at least wear a shirt with your"—Mac-Cready shuddered—"skirts."

"I am going to Georgiana's masquerade as my own ancestor Duncan MacLean. He didn't wear a damned shirt and I'm not going to, either."

"He was a barbarian, my lord."

"Tonight, so am I. Open the door, MacCready."

Sighing his displeasure, the valet did as he was told.

Alexander had spent the entire day riding as hard as he could across the Roxburge lands. The ride had cleared his thoughts but had brought no real answers. *When she loses the wager, as she's bound to do, I'm to take her to be my mistress for two weeks. Should I really risk making things more difficult? But can I resist the opportunity?*

He didn't think he could. The thought of having the lushly curved Caitlyn for two sensual weeks made his body ache. Damn, how he lusted for her!

In the back of his soul came a whisper: *But is that all? Is it just lust? Or are you as weak as Charles?*

He paused by the top step and looked down the hallway. Where was she, anyway? She'd left the house shortly after he had; he'd seen her climb into a carriage just as he'd ridden his horse onto a rise.

He'd watched the carriage bowl down the drive and had been tempted to follow it, but he'd resisted the silly desire.

Instead, he'd ridden hard, trying to burn some of the lust from his veins through hard exercise. When he finally returned to the house, he'd been informed that Caitlyn had not yet returned, and that the other guests had all retired to their rooms to bathe and dress for the masquerade. Georgiana had invited a good number of local guests and was predicting a squeeze, which suited Alexander fine. The bigger the crowd, the easier it would be to whisk Caitlyn away for private speech when he finally won this contest.

He walked down the stairs, the ball already in progress. He passed the Marchioness of Treymont on the bottom step. Dressed in a pale green gown covered with silk flowers, she was probably representing spring, an attractive choice for someone with her white skin and reddish hair. Her gaze locked on his kilt and she faltered on the steps, flushing a deep red before she looked away and hurried past.

Alexander's grin widened. He wanted to shock the masses tonight, to scandalize the whole stuffy lot of them. He was tired of playing polite guest, and this would definitely set the tongues wagging. The thought pleased him, and he swaggered a bit more as he entered the drawing room.

Through a room filled with spring sprites, princesses, and ice fairies, Caitlyn immediately drew his eye. He stopped then, his feet suddenly rooted to the floor. She was dressed in a gown that appeared to be made of silver tissue. The silver would wash out many blondes, but Caitlyn, with her rich, pure gold hair and dark brown eyes, seemed to shine in it, her coloring augmented in some way he couldn't fathom.

Her gown was in the medieval style, the neckline round, the long sleeves falling to a point over her slender fingers. Her hair was down, braided to one side in a style reminiscent of times long gone. No jewel offset the long braid, which was held by a complex-winding black ribbon. He hardened just thinking of how that luxurious braid would look unbound, the silken gold tresses streaming over him and his pillows again.

Alexander had to force the image away—he didn't dare allow himself to react fully in a kilt. Nearby, Lady Elizabeth caught sight of him and his costume. She openly gaped until her companion turned to see what she was reacting to, and the two women stared, not looking away.

Alexander gave them a mocking bow and walked farther into the room, ignoring the immediate spate of shocked murmurs and whispers. He was far too busy admiring Caitlyn.

He wondered who or what she represented. Maid Marion perhaps? Or— Ah! Hanging from her girdle was a series of embroidered disks depicting a silver comb, a small golden boar, and other images from the myth.

He chuckled. She was playing Olwen herself, each charm representing one of the challenges.

She hadn't yet seen him, being deep in conversation with Miss Ogilvie, who was dressed as a milkmaid. Caitlyn's long golden braid swung gently, caressing her hip and making him yearn to grasp it and turn her to him so he could plunder her soft mouth.

He'd always thought he admired women who were more deliberately feminine; women who were conscious of their female wiles and blandished them with ease. Now he was beginning to think that sort of woman was too predictable, too stale.

Caitlyn's straightforward enthusiasm was refreshing. She wasn't shy or retiring and possessed a surprisingly earthy streak that he liked, reveled in, and responded to on a very, very intimate level.

Apparently he wasn't the only one who did, for a quick glance around the room found Lord Dalfour listening with half an ear to Georgiana as his gaze was glued to Caitlyn. Lord Falkland was staring open mouthed, and even Caithness, who'd made no secret that he admired Miss Ogilvie, was eyeing Caitlyn appreciatively. In addition, a half a dozen other men that Alexander didn't recognize were swiftly converging on Caitlyn.

If he didn't hurry, she'd be surrounded. He couldn't wait to wrest the statement from her lips that he most longed to hear: "You win."

Hands closed over his arm as Georgiana suddenly appeared at his side. "Alexander! What a pleasant surprise." Her icy blue eyes raked him from head to toe. "My," she drawled. "You came as a barbarian. How apropos."

"I came as my ancestor Duncan MacLean." His gaze narrowed as he saw that she, too, wore a blue plaid over her shoulder. Alexander frowned. She wore the MacLean plaid that matched his kilt.

"Do you like it?" she purred, smiling.

"No."

After a stunned moment, Georgiana managed a fake laugh. "Alexander, please! It's merely a coincidence. I had no idea what you were wearing."

Hadn't she? No doubt one of the maids had mentioned seeing the plaid in his room earlier. "Where's Roxburge?"

Georgiana nodded to one corner, her expression dismissive. "He is by the punch bowl."

The duke was dressed as a fool, complete with dunce cap and a multicolored cape. Though it was only nine in the evening, he already looked ready for bed and a cup of warmed milk. For the first time, Alexander felt a wave of pity.

"Excuse me, Georgiana, I believe I'll share a glass of punch with your husband."

"With Roxburge? But why?"

Alexander bowed and left. He made his way to the duke's side, where he waited for the right time to remove Caitlyn from the throng of men that now surrounded her.

Finally the call for dinner sounded. As people milled around, looking for their partners, he headed for Caitlyn, where two gentlemen were vehemently arguing over the right to take her down to dinner.

"Ah, Miss Hurst, there you are! Are you ready for dinner?" Alexander asked.

The gentlemen broke off their argument, their eyes widening when they saw Alexander's bulging arms.

Caitlyn hesitated, then placed her hand on his arm, her fingers cool on his bare skin. "Of course. It will be our last dinner together."

"Last? We still have tomorrow, and then the two weeks after that." He smiled down at her as the crowd slowly moved toward the dining room.

No responding smile lit her eyes. "Perhaps."

Alexander's humor fled. Something was different about her tonight, something somber and . . . sad? He tucked her hand tighter in the crook of his arm and pulled her to one side, allowing others to walk on past. "What do you mean by that?"

Her eyes were shimmery, as if she held tears at bay. "Only that you may not be the one to win this wager."

A few final couples walked past, casting them curious glances. As the final couple disappeared through the doors, Alexander led Caitlyn to the blue salon. Inside, he closed the door.

Her chin rose. "People will notice we're missing."

"Not for another ten minutes." He grinned wolfishly. "Admit it, Hurst: I've won. I wore a skirt to the party. Are you truly going to entertain the masses with a naked dip in a fountain?"

Her chin lifted, her mouth thinning. "This contest isn't over. I still have time to make my move."

"Oh? So you're going to do it?" He laughed, disbelieving. "You'd be ruined, which is what you were trying to avoid to begin with."

Her gaze flickered to his face. "Perhaps."

"Caitlyn, you can't mean that . . ." Good God, she looked deadly serious. "Caitlyn, it would be foolish to do such a thing, and you know it."

"I *must* win this wager. I refuse to be your mistress—and I will do whatever I must to make sure that never happens."

His jaw tightened. "Even ruin your name?"

"I've found something that means far more to me than my pride."

"What?"

Her gaze met his, and in that second he knew the answer. She cared for him. Shock and disbelief coursed through him. She didn't just care for him, she *loved* him. He could see it in her expression as plainly as if she'd said it aloud.

No. She can't— I can't allow that. If she cares, then I . . . Alexander looked at her—*really* looked at her. In the soft candlelight she looked even younger, no more than eighteen. The mirror over the fireplace reflected the face of a mature man, one who'd lived too hard, too well, and too fast. Even if she loved him now, what would happen later? *Could I bear to lose her then?*

He knew the answer with every ounce of his soul.

With a heavy, bitter heart, he sneered, "Don't get maudlin on me, Hurst. Our wager was to settle one thing only: the penalty for your deception in London. Tonight you will admit you've lost, and you will stay with me for two weeks as you promised."

It was all he'd have to remember her by, once she left for good, but at least he'd have that. Two short, precious weeks—and then he'd never see her again. His chest felt odd, as if a metal band pressed the air from his lungs, and his eyes were burning from the smoky candles.

Two weeks. It wasn't much, but it was all fate would allow him, and he, desperate soul that he was, would take it.

"Well, Hurst? What do you say?"

He expected her to flare back at him with that fine spirit she possessed. Instead she regarded him sadly for a long moment, then turned and left him, the door clicking quietly behind her.

Much, much later, Caitlyn stood on the terrace bundled in a thick cloak, the cool night breeze making her shiver. It was well past four in the morning, the last of the guests finally gone. Everyone had gone to bed except Alexander. As usual, he'd headed for the study for one last glass of port before he retired.

"Are ye sure about this, miss?" Muiren asked.

"Yes." Caitlyn looked up at the castle windows. Only one or two were still lit, and as she looked, they, too, darkened to black. It was time.

She looked through the library window at Alexander, who poured himself a glass of port, then took a chair by the fireplace.

"He's not facing the right way," Muiren hissed.

"I know. I must get him to turn around. Mam said the drops would work quickly." Caitlyn looked at Muiren. "Are Mrs. Pruitt and the others in place?"

"Aye, Mrs. Pruitt locked all of the other doors and is watching the garden gate. 'Tis the only other way into the garden here, miss. The others are ready as well."

"Very well. I'll be right back."

Caitlyn put her hand on the cold brass knob leading inside, her gaze locked on Alexander. He sat with his back to her, his black hair thick and curling at the neck as he sipped his port. She waited for him to finish the drink. *Please, Mam, be right about the drops.*

She had been careful not to put more than four in the glass.

He placed his empty glass on a table and stood, ready to retire for the night.

She took a deep breath, then turned the knob and walked in.

He turned, his brows quirking down. "Caitlyn! What are you doing here?"

She came farther into the room, the cloak swirling about her. "I came to fulfill my part of our wager."

Alexander frowned. She was cloaked head to foot, but her expression caught his attention the most. She looked so sad, as if the entire world had betrayed her.

His heart constricted. He couldn't stand this another moment. He'd been lying to himself that he could take Caitlyn as a mistress, even for an hour.

He shook his head, his voice thick as he said, "Caitlyn . . . don't."

"Don't what? Don't stand aside and allow you to win?" She smiled sadly. "I'm not."

Alexander didn't give a damn about the wager. He just wished he could erase the sadness from her eyes. Just the sight of it was holding him down and it took an effort to say, "I'll forgo the last wager."

Anger flared in her eyes. "I don't need your pity."

But he didn't pity her. He *loved* her. The words seared through the odd fog that was settling over him. He wanted to tell her that, to explain to her that he loved her so much that he couldn't bear to see her grow tired of him, to watch as her interest waned.

But he couldn't.

She seemed to realize his distress, for she crossed the room toward him, her sweet fragrance wafting about her. She stood in front of him and gently pushed him into the seat behind him.

He must have sat, but he never felt it. His knees and arms were leaden, though he was wide-awake and his senses clear, even acute. He was vaguely aware he should be upset at the lack of response of his limbs, but he was just so glad she was here.

She bent down until her lips were beside his ear. "I am a woman of my word. What I say I will do, I'll do. I wish our time together had been different"—her voice broke, taking his heart along with it—"but we are what we are, and fate doesn't grant us every wish."

He tried to breathe in the sweet scent of her, to savor the soft brush of her hair over his cheek as she stood.

"Watch, Alexander—for this is the last you will ever see of me." She went to the terrace door, opened it, and slipped outside to the garden.

She reached the fountain, and through the open door he watched as four female servants appeared. They unfolded a large sheet, then held it aloft so that it shielded the fountain from the upper windows. They then turned their backs to the fountain, never releasing their hold on the sheet. Caitlyn glided to beside the fountain where a shadowy companion came to assist her as she shed her slippers and, with a shrug, tossed off her cloak.

She was gloriously naked, the silvered moonlight caressing her curves, highlighting the mold of her breasts, the gleam of her shoulders, making her long hair shimmer like moon dust.

He was mesmerized, his gaze locked on her as she slipped into the black water of the fountain, gasping at the coldness. Her nipples instantly peaked as the water cascaded over her breasts, shimmering down her flat stomach and across the gentle swell of her hips. Quiet splashes filled the air as she submerged herself completely. Then, looking his way, she rose from the water like Venus, the water sluicing over her.

Alexander gripped the arms of his chair until his fingers ached.

Her shadow companion brought the cloak and wrapped her in it, helping her put on her slippers. She would be freezing cold now, her body shaking with tremors.

All Alexander could think about were her last words to him: that he'd never see her again. He watched, helpless, as she turned and disappeared from sight, her handmaidens following, leaving the cold air to blow through the terrace door, the desolate fountain splashing tauntingly in the distance.

"A carriage? Right now?" The duchess looked surprised.

Caitlyn, glad she'd found the duchess alone before breakfast, nodded, forcing the words past the tears in her throat. "Yes, please. I . . . I wish to leave immediately. I . . . I just received a letter from home and . . . it's very important I return at once."

A pleased look entered the duchess's blue eyes and she didn't question the improbable story but purred, "Of course. I'll call the carriage at once."

"Thank you."

"You'll wish to pack—"

"Muiren is seeing to it right now."

Georgiana wondered what had happened to cause such a precipitous departure, but decided she didn't really care. Whether the chit had finally had a falling out with MacLean, or if she'd given up her desperate hopes of trapping him into a relationship—it didn't matter. All that mattered was that she'd be gone. Of course, it wouldn't hurt to place a few final nails in the coffin, just so the silly girl understood how things truly were.

Georgiana smiled sweetly. "Poor dear, you look devastated. May I . . . my dear, I know we've not had a chance to speak often during your stay, but would you mind a word of advice from an older, more experienced woman of the world?"

Caitlyn stiffened, but Georgiana ignored her. "I know what's been going on between you and MacLean, and it's perfectly natural that someone like you—so innocent and from the country—should find a sophisticated man like him devastatingly attractive."

"Your Grace, I don't know what you think, but—"

"Hear me out. I'm doing you a favor. MacLean's tastes run the gamut from sophisticate to ingénue. It's normal for a man of his—shall we say 'appetites'?—to wish for variety. That's why I have these little parties. So he can appease his desires."

"You invited me just so he could—"

"And others before you, yes."

The girl's back couldn't be stiffer, her face almost white. Satisfaction rippled through Georgiana. "You might think this odd, seeing as he and I are—" She chuckled. "But we understand and appreciate one another. That's why, when the duke finally dies, Alexander and I will marry."

"He's already told you this?"

"Yes."

Caitlyn's heart ached anew as she made a jerky curtsy. "I'm happy for you, Your Grace. I . . . I think the carriage must have arrived. I'll see myself out."

All too soon, Caitlyn was sitting beside Muiren in the carriage, her trunks strapped to the back as they traveled through the moonlight.

Caitlyn watched the night slide away before her eyes. She couldn't seem to focus on anything, her mind ringing with the duchess's last words and, more compelling, images of Alexander.

She closed her eyes and saw Alexander from earlier this evening, wearing the garb of a clan laird from an era long gone. His broad chest had shockingly been bared revealing hard muscles that were cut and carved, making her mouth water. Wrapped around his narrow hips and tossed over one broad shoulder was a length of plaid. A fur sporran had rested amid the folds about his waist, weighing down the front of the kilt. Fur boots tied on with leather strips emphasized the sheer power of his legs.

Her body tingled all over, and her heart pounded against her throat, as she thought of making love to him again. Though she'd felt frozen just a short time ago, she was now damp from the heat that shivered through her, from memories of MacLean's large hands, of his hard mouth, of the demanding feel of him between her thighs—all of the things she'd shouldn't have enjoyed, yet had.

Her mind flickered back to the duchess and her final, poisonous words. Caitlyn wasn't sure she believed the woman, yet she couldn't deny the pain the words had caused. One part of it was true, for Alexander had told her it was—that the duchess had invited Caitlyn at his request. The thought that he could collude with such a cold, superficial woman gave Caitlyn pain. How could he have a relationship of any kind with such a horrible person?

The entire visit had been nothing but a manipulative sham. Tears seeped from her lids and she fumbled for her handkerchief, glad Muiren was soundly asleep.

Wiping her eyes, she decided she'd been naïve to think she could change Alexander's mind about her, or anything else.

The wagers had been a mistake fom the beginning. A horrible mistake that had pushed them together more and more, when the safest course would have been to stay away from one another. Damn it, was she *always* to suffer from her inability to do what was safe? Was she always to follow the riskier path?

She looked out the window at the disappearing house. MacLean would be able to move soon. Perhaps he would go to the duchess's bedchambers for the rest of the night. The thought pained Caitlyn, but she held it tight. She had to think things like that, to keep herself from lamenting what might have been.

Still, her eyes filled with tears. Why couldn't Alexander be the sort of man to long for a normal marriage?

This evening, when she'd looked across the room and met his hot gaze, she'd felt an answering spark deep down in her soul, an urge to throw caution to the winds and run straight into his arms. To run her hands over his warm skin, to trace his deliciously defined stomach, and press hot, mad kisses over his strong jaw until he shuddered against her.

The problem was, it wouldn't be enough. She wanted all of him, or nothing. And as she looked out into the dark night, her tears began to fall again. For nothing was exactly what she'd gotten.

Chapter 21

Do what ye will, love will always find the way.

OLD WOMAN NORA FROM LOCH LOMOND
TO HER THREE WEE GRANDDAUGHTERS ONE COLD EVENING

Caitlyn leaned her forehead against the cool glass of her bedroom window. Outside, lights from the house reflected off the snow. England was blanketed with the stuff, and it seemed it would never stop.

Her sister Mary knocked on the door, then entered. "I brought you some hot milk. I thought it might help you sleep."

"I'm fine, thanks."

"No, you're not. My room is below yours, and I can hear you pacing most of the night." Mary handed a steaming mug of milk to Caitlyn. "Drink this."

Caitlyn dutifully did as she was told, though she felt like doing anything but.

Mary adjusted her shawl over her night rail and went to a chair by the fire. "Is it ever going to stop snowing? It's done nothing else for two days."

"It's better than the rain we had last week."

Mary made a face. "Rain, snow, I'm tired of it all."

Caitlyn sighed, her breath making a circle of fog on the damp window as she watched the white flakes drift slowly down. "It was pretty, at first."

"It's still pretty, but we don't need more. Father says we'll have to shovel the walks again if this keeps up." Mary shivered. "I wish he and Mother hadn't had to travel in this sort of weather, but who would guess Aunt Lavinia would really succumb to heart palpitations? She's been claiming that for years."

"I'm just glad she's recovering. Mother is very fond of her sister."

"As are we all," Mary agreed.

The cold wind seeped around the glass, and Caitlyn shivered. She pulled the curtain half-closed, then crossed to the fireplace and curled up in a chair across from her sister.

Mary's dark brown gaze rested thoughtfully on Caitlyn. "Have you finished the reticule you were making?"

"No."

"Did you read the book William gave you, about the abducted heiress?"

"No."

Mary nodded as if she wasn't surprised. "I suppose you haven't also done any tatting, embroidery, or—"

"I haven't done anything today," Caitlyn interrupted shortly.

"We're all worried about you."

"Why?"

"Because you don't do anything but mope about the house. You barely even eat."

"I'm perfectly fine. It's just this weather."

Mary lifted her brows. "I think it's because of MacLean."

Caitlyn closed her eyes and wished for the umpteenth time she hadn't confided in her sister, but she'd had to tell *someone*. Of course, she hadn't told her every detail—some were too private, and painful, to say aloud. Still, Mary knew enough, and what she didn't know, she had probably guessed. "Mary, don't."

Mary sighed. "I know, I know. I just—" Her brow lowered. "Caitlyn, be sure you're being completely honest with yourself. You shouldn't feel so low, unless—"

"Unless what?" Caitlyn said in a challenging tone.

Mary hesitated, then said quietly, "Unless you care for him."

Caitlyn's heart swelled so much that her chest ached.

Mary sighed. "I just thought— I'm sorry. I don't mean to pry. I'm sure you'll figure out what you feel as time passes. Perhaps then you'll feel more like talking."

"I'm sure I will. Thank you, Mary." Tears threatened, and Caitlyn hurriedly gulped the milk.

Mary stood and gave Caitlyn a hug. "Very well, then. Sleep well."

The door closed, and with the quiet click of the latch Caitlyn's feelings ripped through her, good and bad alike.

She loved Alexander MacLean deeply and passionately, with her entire being. Through a storm of tears she blindly found her bed, threw herself across it, and wept.

When she could finally weep no more, she rose, washed her face, put on her night rail, and turned off the lamps. Then she climbed back into bed and lay for a long, long time, wishing she could stop thinking, stop feeling.

Eventually she fell asleep, only to wake to the sound of a branch tapping on the glass.

She frowned sleepily. That wasn't a branch. It sounded more like a pebble or small rock.

Click! Click! . . . Click! Click! Click!

She tossed back the blankets and swung her feet over the side of the bed. Had one of her brothers been locked out of the house again? They usually knocked on William's ground-floor window, but perhaps he was sleeping too soundly to hear. She grabbed her robe from the bed pole, then looked for her slippers.

Crack! Glass shattered across the floor as a small rock sailed into the room, the chilled wind rushing behind it.

"For the love of—" Caitlyn yanked her robe tighter, stuffed her feet into her half boots, and ran across the room. Her boots crunched on the broken glass as she threw open the casement and looked outside.

The wind tugged her hair and made the tree by her window sway. Below, the snow was ruffled like the waves in the ocean. And there, standing directly beneath, his black cape billowing about his broad shoulders and booted legs, stood the man of her dreams.

Her heart thudded, her palms grew damp. Was he here to declare himself? Had he realized the emptiness of his life without her?

Alexander turned slightly, and she could see his expression. But he wasn't smiling a loverlike sort of smile, he was . . . scowling!

"Are you wearing shoes?" he demanded.

"Shhh!" She glanced over her shoulder, hoping Mary wouldn't burst through the door.

"I will not shhh!" he retorted, lowering his voice to a shouting whisper. "Are you wearing *shoes*? There has to be glass all over that floor and—"

"*Yes*, I'm wearing shoes," she snapped back.

His expression was so harsh, his voice so unwelcoming, that her excited anticipation deflated.

Whatever he wished of her now, it had nothing to do with love. Disappointment left a bitter taste on her tongue. For one fleeting second, she'd *hoped* yet again. Hoped with all her life, all her being. And with that pure flush of hope, she'd expected a dramatic, loverlike gesture from him. Instead, she got a barking whisper suggesting she was stupid enough to walk on broken glass! *Damn* the man!

But . . . what was she thinking? This wasn't a normal man she was thinking about. This wasn't one of the dozens who had written sonnets to her eyes, or brought her flowers, or sent her pretty presents wrapped in silver paper.

No—this was a man who couldn't pay a compliment without also noticing that your slippers were a bit worn. This was a man who couldn't look a woman in the eye when he should be declaring himself, yet could do nothing else when he seduced the chemise right off her.

Then you had his full attention: his gaze never flickered during those moments, but devoured you whole. Because then, he wasn't vulnerable—you were.

But when the time came to say how he felt, what he felt, and how much he felt, he was as awkward as a youth.

Awkward because . . . he cared more than he'd ever cared before?

The thought crystallized in her heart, lifting it back up again. Was that it, then? Was he simply incapable of expressing himself because he cared *so much*?

"Move to another window." He pointed to the window on the other side of her bed, then walked in that direction.

"No."

He stopped and looked back at her. "What do you mean no?"

"If you have anything to say to me, then do it now."

"Or?"

"Or I'm going back to bed."

She could feel his irritation in the way the wind rattled the creaky house. But some of the harshness had left his face, and his eyes gleamed with a quiver of humor. "Still bossy, aren't you?"

"It's only been a week."

"Eight days, fourteen hours, and thirty-two minutes."

She bit her lip. "You . . . you've been counting the time." Hope rose again.

"Yes, now move to the other window!" he ordered.

Caitlyn's temper snapped. "If you're here merely to fume at me, then save yourself the effort."

"I've ridden nonstop through the most horrid weather, and won't—"

She slammed the casement closed, more glass tinkling to the floor. Then she stomped to the bed, kicked off her shoes, and climbed under the covers with her dressing gown still on. Why had he come all this way just to yell at her? And what had taken him so damned long, too?

The wind picked up, blowing through the broken windowpane. MacLean would freeze if he didn't seek shelter soon. She thought of tossing back the covers and peeking out the window, but forced herself to remain in bed.

If he decided to stand in the freezing wind with nothing but a cloak and caught his death of a cold, what was it to her? She might love him, but it was obvious he didn't love her, so maybe it would be better if he just curled up somewhere and died.

She tried to imagine him in bed and weak, coughing, as his brothers lined up around him. That would irritate him to death, being hovered over like an invalid, even if he was one. It would serve him right, too. Still, a tear fell from her eye at the thought of Alexander being gone.

Blast it, she couldn't even dredge up a good dislike of the man even after he'd broken her—

A noise sounded outside her window, and she sat straight up and stared. A hand wrapped in a muffler stuck through the broken pane, felt around for the latch, found it, and swung open the casement.

Then MacLean was inside her room, his cape swirling about him as he locked the window and closed the shutters over the broken pane.

He turned, tall and forbidding. "You just had to have a room on the third floor, didn't you?" His gaze flickered over her, a greedy expression in his eyes.

She yanked her blankets to her chin, hot and cold at the same time.

Alexander's blood thundered through him. He'd thought he was prepared to see her again, but he hadn't been. Nothing could have prepared him for the sight of her leaning out her window, snow swirling about her, her hair a golden spill over her shoulders, her brown eyes wide and filled with emotions—irritation, wonder, curiosity, concern.

"What do you want?" Her voice, low and vibrant, warmed him far more than the faint fire in the grate.

He frowned. "It's cold in here."

"It wasn't until you broke my window. Was that necessary?"

It was for his temper. "I didn't mean to break the glass. I just wanted you to open it."

"I was on my way. I thought it might be my one of my brothers. Sometimes they sneak out and the doors are locked."

She shivered, and he immediately crossed to the fireplace and added a log, then stirred the flames until they were hotter. Then he walked to the door and stuck a chair under the handle.

"What are you doing?"

"Giving us a little time."

"Good! I want to talk to you."

"I, my love, don't wish to talk to you. Not now, anyway."

She frowned. "What do you mean?"

He strode to her wardrobe and threw it open. "You'll need a good heavy cloak. Here's one." He brought it to the bed.

"MacLean, I am not putting on a cloak."

"Yes, you will." He grinned, and she realized that he looked tired; deep lines were carved down each side of his mouth.

Her heart softened, but she hardened it firmly.

"Hurst, what in hell did you dose me with that left me unable to move for two hours?"

"I don't know. Mam gave it to me. She said it was safe so long as I didn't give you too many drops."

"I owe your grandmother a good talking to; I had a hell of a headache the next morning."

So had she, but from crying. The memory stiffened her resolve. "Well, *you* picked that wretched task, not me."

"I did, and I've been a damn fool a hundred times over." He reached over and yanked off her blankets. "Put on the cloak and let's go."

"Why?"

"Because we're getting married."

Caitlyn's heart quivered. "You want to marry me?"

"As soon as possible."

"Because . . ." She looked up at him, her heart in her eyes.

"Because I need you in my life. I'm not the same without you, Caitlyn. When you're not nearby I'm—" He raked a hand through his damp hair, a bemused expression on his face. "I can't explain it. I'm just not . . . complete."

Hope flashed blindingly, but she shoved it down. "What about Georgiana?"

His brows snapped down. "What about her?"

"She was your mistress."

"Long ago. I haven't touched her in almost a year."

"She said—" Caitlyn couldn't get the words past her lips.

"Damn it, Caitlyn, I don't know what she told you, but the only truth is that I allowed myself to be flattered into her bed, but it didn't last."

Caitlyn's heart eased. "She said some horrible things."

"She's a horrible woman. Once we're married, I promise that we'll never speak to her again. We'll even cut her direct, if you'd like."

Caitlyn liked that a lot. "We can invite Lord Dingwall over often, though. Georgiana would hate that."

Alexander's mouth quirked into a grin. "I've a feeling I won't be so fond of it myself, but if it makes you happy, then I'll do it."

Her heart was warming. Caitlyn met his gaze and asked softly, "Alexander, why did you come for me?"

"Because I *had* to. You—" He struggled to find the words and, finally, with a muffled curse, he dropped to one knee, took her hand, and held it to his heart. "Caitlyn, I've done nothing right since I first met you. I've been out of my mind wanting you, which blinded me to even more important matters."

"Like?" she said breathlessly.

"I love you." His deep voice held the faintest tremble.

Tears sprang to her eyes.

He kissed her fingers. "Caitlyn, I'm not a young man. I'm almost forty. You're twenty-three."

"What does that matter?"

"When I'm fifty, you'll be thirty-three and just as beautiful as you are right now."

"MacLean, is *that* what this whole thing has been about? You think you're too old for me?"

"Not now. But I feared that later, the differences would create a rift between us. That I'd have to watch you grow disinterested and slip away from me."

She smiled softly. "That will never happen."

"If it does, it'll be worth whatever pain it causes, if I can just have some time with you now. I love you, and I'm sorry I didn't admit it to myself until you were gone." He cupped her chin and lifted her face to his. "I love how impulsive you are, how your eyes shine when you laugh. I love how you savor every bite you eat. I even love how you snap at me when you're annoyed. The truth is, I just love you. It's that simple."

Caitlyn's throat was too tight for her to answer. He loved her—he *truly* loved her. She could only—

Knock! Knock! Then Mary's voice came through the door. "Caitlyn, are you all right? I heard something break."

"I'm fine!" Caitlyn called. "I just dropped my mug."

"And . . . I thought I heard a man's voice."

"Ah, no." Cait lyn looked mischievously at Alexander, then grabbed her cloak and yanked it on, whispering, "I must leave her a note and—"

"No, you don't," he whispered back, finding her boots by the bed. "I've already taken care of it. Your parents will return in the morning and they know I've come for you."

"My parents? But how?"

Laughing softly, he pushed her boots onto her feet. "I—"

"Caitlyn?" The knob rattled. "What's wrong with this door?"

"It's closed. Good night, Mary!"

MacLean opened the casement and climbed out onto the closest limb, then reached back for Caitlyn.

She tucked up her skirts and followed him without pause, her heart singing. Carefully, they climbed down the tree. When they reached the bottom, he pulled her into his arms and kissed her thoroughly.

She smiled. "Where are we going?"

"To your grandmother's. She's expecting us." He glinted a smile at her. "Your grandmother came to see me."

Caitlyn gaped.

"She had a lot to say, none of it repeatable since I am a gentleman."

"She has a sharp tongue."

"I doubt you know the half of it. When she was through shredding my character, I told her that whatever she had to say about my behavior toward you, I would not only agree, but admit that I'd acted worse."

"Alexander, I didn't behave, either."

He grasped her gloved hands and pulled her against him. "But *I* put you in the position of having to prove yourself. I had no right to do that. My only excuse is that I was a fool and I couldn't leave you be."

"Alexander, please, don't—"

"Hear me out, Caitlyn. I didn't treat you with the respect you deserve. Your grandmother was right about that. I'm sorry, and I won't ever do such a thing again."

Caitlyn peeped up at him. "Did Mam give you a horrible scold?"

He chuckled, the sound vibrating through his chest. "You have no idea. After she'd calmed down and I'd explained my feelings, she demanded that I fix things. So I have. On the way here, I went to London to visit your parents and—"

"You didn't!"

"I did. Your grandmother gave me their address. Your mother was charming and your father, once he was through being furious with the way I tricked you into our wager—"

"You didn't trick me."

He kissed her nose. "Actually, we tricked one another, but that doesn't matter. What does matter is that because I made a clean breast of the issue and confessed my sins, your parents not only forgave me, but they gave me their blessing."

She blinked up at him. "They said you could steal me out the window?"

He laughed softly. "No, they might be a little shocked at that. I merely told them that I was going to fetch you to your grandmother's so we could make arrangements. They're to follow with your brothers and sister for the wedding in two weeks time."

"Wedding? *Our* wedding?"

He lifted Caitlyn and swung her around, a deep laughter rumbling through him. "Ah, Caitlyn, my love!"

Her heart sang—*sang,* her ears humming along. He loved her! It was all worth it for this one, glorious moment.

MacLean took a suspiciously shaky breath, then his arms tightened about her so much that she had to protest. He silenced her protests with a passionate kiss, one that was everything she wanted.

And she knew that this moment was just the beginning. Before them were new tasks, new challenges, perhaps new troubles. But from now on, they'd solve them together—hand in hand.

Epilogue

Och, the dream o' me life has been to dandle me own great-grandbairns upon me knee!

OLD WOMAN NORA FROM LOCH LOMOND
TO HER THREE WEE GRANDDAUGHTERS ONE COLD EVENING

"He's the spittin' image o' his father." Mam tickled the baby's dimpled chin. "Jus' look at those green eyes!"

Mary, sitting by the fireplace in a rocking chair, hugged the baby tighter. "Little Ronan is so beautiful, Caitlyn."

"So is Alexandra." Triona, sitting across from Mary, held another tiny bundle. She brushed her fingers over the baby's soft cheek, a look of wonder in her eyes. "It's so lovely that you had twins, and they're one of each—a boy and a girl."

From the settee near the window, Caitlyn smiled contentedly and adjusted the blanket Alexander had so carefully tucked about her legs before he'd left to help his brother Hugh with some new foals. "I wouldn't know how adorable my babies are, for I've only been allowed to hold them long enough to feed them."

Mary grinned. "Mother and I are leaving this afternoon, so you'll get your chance then."

Triona touched Alexandra's tiny gold curls. "I asked Hugh if we might stay another day or two. I know you could use the rest."

Caitlyn watched the gentle glow in Triona's gaze as she looked at Caitlyn's new daughter. From across the room Caitlyn exchanged a concerned glance with Mary. Triona and Hugh had been trying to have a baby for years, but to no avail. It was almost heartbreaking to see her holding Alexandra so lovingly.

As if she knew Caitlyn's thoughts, Triona sent her a calm smile. "It's a good thing I have my stepdaughters to cuddle, or I'd feel cheated!"

Triona had inherited the title of "mother" from three girls Hugh had taken in when they'd been abused and neglected by their own mother. The warm light in Triona's eyes made Caitlyn relax. "And they are wonderful girls. I shall call upon them often to help with their cousins."

"They'll love that." Triona's hazel eyes gleamed with love. "When we realized it might not be in our future to have children of our own, Hugh and I decided not to lament what we didn't have, but to celebrate what we *did* have. Our daughters are the centers of our lives and we feel no lack." Triona kissed the baby's nose.

Mam snorted. "I think ye're bein' a mite hasty, sayin' such a thing."

Triona sent Mam an amused glance. "You gave us potions and they didn't help. It's just not meant to be."

"Och, ye'll see. These things take time, they do. Me potions will work yet."

Caitlyn watched as her grandmother and sisters held her new babies, a feeling of deep happiness warming her through and through. She and Alexander had the sort of marriage she'd always dreamed of having—they were partners in every sense of the word. Even now, she couldn't help but smile when she thought of how he'd come to the nursery to make sure she was reclining upon the settee as ordered, and how he'd tucked the blanket about her, saying it was too chilly by the window to be without one.

After five years, he wasn't so hard-hearted and he laughed far more frequently now. Everyone commented on it, even his own brothers when they came to visit.

Things had changed at Wythburn, too. Against Father's wishes, William had joined the navy and went off to sea. When he came to visit, Caitlyn was amazed at how tall, bronzed, and broad-shouldered he'd become. Robert had gone to Cambridge, where he was the lead student as they'd all predicted, his interest settling on ancient cultures. And Michael was finally healthy enough to join the squire's son on a yearlong trip through the ruins of ancient cultures on Italy, Greece, and on into Africa. Father was green with envy over Michael's good fortune, and they all eagerly awaited the letters telling of his adventures.

Though Mother had been worried about Michael's weak lungs, the warmer climates had done what no amount of medicine in damp England could and, if his letters were to be believed, he was now amazingly robust.

Mary rubbed her cheek against Ronan's head. "Why are babies so *adorable*?"

"God made 'em that way so ye'll fergive them fer messing their nappies." Mam ran a gnarled hand over the baby's head. "He's strong, this one. That's a good thing as he'll lead the clan one day."

Mary frowned. "Mam, what about the curse? Is it over? Everyone has completed a deed of great good. Fiona stopped a clan war by marrying Jack; Gregor and Venetia are involved in so many charity ventures that I can't even begin to name them; while Hugh adopted three girls and has given them a lovely home. Dougal rescued Triona when she almost drowned—"

"And he's done more than that," Triona said. "He and Sophia are buying the abandoned MacGulloch house, fixing it, and donating it the church to use as an orphanage. The current orphanage is about to fall down."

Mary nodded. "And Alexander takes care of all of the needy on his land."

"Aye, he does more fer them than most lairds," Mam agreed.

"So has the curse ended?"

"I'm afraid not," Caitlyn said.

All eyes turned her way. "Yesterday, some fool allowed one of his prize bulls to escape and run through town. Someone was almost trampled, but was saved by the smithy in the nick of time. Alexander was furious when he found out."

"So *that's* what caused that little storm," Triona said.

"Yes." Caitlyn sighed. "I hoped the curse would be broken, too, but—"

"Well that's the problem wit' curses," Mam said. "They're rooted in myth, and 'tis possible we have it wrong."

"Wrong?" Mary blinked. "Then . . . the part about the deed of great good is untrue?"

"Perhaps," Mam said. "We won't know until the bairns come of age. The curse doesn't set in until then."

"So it *might* be broken, but won't show up until the next generation. At least that's something." Mary rose and brought Ronan to Caitlyn, and settled the sweet-smelling baby into her arms.

Caitlyn nuzzled his cheek and smiled. "Curse or no curse, these will be happy children. That's all I can do for now."

Mam smiled. "'Tis more than enough, me dear. Love is a powerful thing, far more powerful than a mere curse."

Caitlyn slipped a finger into Ronan's small fist, smiling when he tightened his grip. Aye, curse or no curse, the MacLean family was strong and happy and loving.

A movement out the window caught her eye and she saw Alexander riding across the moor toward the castle, the wind ruffling his thick black hair. Hugh rode on a golden horse behind him, the streak of white in his hair agleam.

If they hadn't vanquished the curse with this generation, they'd do it with the next. The MacLeans' tenacity, intelligence, and capacity for caring knew no bounds. Together, with those who loved them, they could overcome any obstacles that remained.

Caitlyn kissed her son's forehead and smiled into his sleepy green eyes. "I promise that you're destined for a happy, healthy life, my son." For with Alexander by her side, she could do anything.

Fantasy.
Temptation.
Adventure.

Visit PocketAfterDark.com, an all-new website just for Urban Fantasy and Romance Readers!

- Exclusive access to the hottest urban fantasy and romance titles!

- Read and share reviews on the latest books!

- Live chats with your favorite romance authors!

- Vote in online polls!

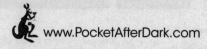

www.PocketAfterDark.com

26119

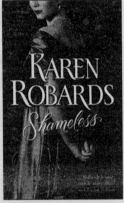

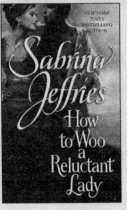

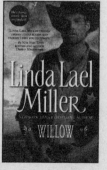

Fall in love

with a bestseller from Pocket Books!

FERN MICHAELS
The Delta Ladies
When one man confronts two women from his past, there's
bound to be a little trouble … and a lot of passion.

JULIE GARWOOD
Heartbreaker
A thrilling excursion into the soaring heights—
and darkest impulses—of the human heart.

LINDA HOWARD, MARIAH STEWART,
JILLIAN HUNTER, GERALYN DAWSON,
AND MIRANDA JARRETT
Under the Boardwalk
Experience the cool breezes and hot passion of
summer loving in this unforgettable new collection!

And look for the thrilling
new Bullet Catchers Trilogy
by Roxanne St. Claire!

First You Run
Then You Hide
Now You Die

Available wherever books are sold
or at www.simonsayslove.com.

19098

Get intimate
WITH A BESTSELLING ROMANCE
from Pocket Books!

Janet Chapman
THE MAN MUST MARRY
She has the money. He has the desire.
Only love can bring them together.

Starr Ambrose
LIE TO ME
One flirtatious fib leads to the sexiest
adventure of her life....

Karen Hawkins
TALK OF THE TOWN
Do blondes have more fun? He'd love to know—
but it takes two to tango.

Hester Browne
THE LITTLE LADY AGENCY
IN THE BIG APPLE
She's a manners coach for men, and
she's working her magic on Manhattan!

Available wherever books are sold or at www.simonsayslove.com

POCKET BOOKS
A Division of Simon & Schuster
A CBS COMPANY

19584